The Middle of Somewhere

What Reviewers Say About Bold Strokes Books

"With its expected unexpected twists, vivid characters and healthy dose of humor, *Blind Curves* is a very fun read that will keep you guessing." – *Bay Windows*

"In a succinct film style narrative, with scenes that move, a character-driven plot, and crisp dialogue worthy of a screenplay … the Richfield and Rivers novels are … an engaging Hollywood mystery … series." – *Midwest Book Review*

Force of Nature "…is filled with nonstop, fast paced action. Tornadoes, raging fire blazes, heroic and daring rescues… Baldwin does a fine job of describing the fast-paced scenes and inspiring the reader to keep on turning the pages." – *L-word.comLiterature*

In the Jude Devine mystery series the "…characters seem fully capable of walking away from the particulars of whodunit and engaging the reader in other aspects of their lives." – *Lambda Book Report*

Mine "…weaves a tale of yearning, love, lust, and conflict resolution … a believable plot, with strong characters in a charming setting." – *JustAboutWrite*

"While these two women struggle with their issues, there is some very, very hot sex. If you enjoy complex characters and passionate sex scenes, you'll love *Wild Abandon*." – *MegaScene*

"*Course of Action* is a romance … populated with a host of captivating and amiable characters. The glimpses into the lifestyles of the rich and beautiful people are rather like guilty pleasures … a most satisfying and entertaining reading experience." – *Midwest Book Review*

The Clinic is "…a spellbinding novel." – *JustAboutWrite*

"*Unexpected Sparks* lived up to its promise and was thoroughly enjoyable … Dartt did a lovely job at building the relationship between Kate and Nikki." – *Lambda Book Report*

"*Sequestered Hearts* … is everything a romance should be. It is teeming with longing, heartbreak, and of course, love. As pure romances go, it is one of the best in print today." – *L-word.comLiterature*

"*The Exile and the Sorcerer* is a mesmerizing read, a tour-de-force packed with adventure, ordeals, complex twists and turns, and the internal introspection of appealing characters." – *Midwest Book Review*

The Spanish Pearl is "…both science fiction and romance in this adventurous tale … A most entertaining read, with a sequel already in the works. Hot, hot, hot!" – *Minnesota Literature*

"A deliciously sexy thriller … *Dark Valentine* is funny, scary, and very realistic. The story is tightly written and keeps the reader gripped to the exciting end." – *JustAbout Write*

"*Punk Like Me* … is different. It is engaging. It is life-affirming. Frankly, it is genius. This is a rare book in that it has a soul; one that is laid bare for all to see." – *JustAboutWrite*

"*Chance* is not a novel about the music industry; it is about a woman discovering herself as she muddles through all the trappings of fame." – *Midwest Book Review*

Sweet Creek "… is sublimely in tune with the times." – *Q-Syndicate*

"*Forever Found* … neatly combines hot sex scenes, humor, engaging characters, and an exciting story." – *MegaScene*

Shield of Justice is a "…well-plotted…lovely romance…I couldn't turn the pages fast enough!" – Ann Bannon, author of *The Beebo Brinker Chronicles*

The 100th Generation is "…filled with ancient myths, Egyptian gods and goddesses, legends, and, most wonderfully, it contains the lesbian equivalent of Indiana Jones living and working in modern Egypt." – *Just About Write*

Sword of the Guardian is "…a terrific adventure, coming of age story, a romance, and tale of courtly intrigue, attempted assassination, and gender confusion … a rollicking fun book and a must-read for those who enjoy courtly light fantasy in a medieval-seeming time." – *Midwest Book Review*

"*Of Drag Kings and the Wheel of Fate*'s lush rush of a romance incorporates reincarnation, a grounded transman and his peppy daughter, and the dark moods of a troubled witch—wonderful homage to Leslie Feinberg's classic gender-bending novel, *Stone Butch Blues*." – *Q-Syndicate*

In *Running with the Wind* "…the discussions of the nature of sex, love, power, and sexuality are insightful and represent a welcome voice from the view of late-20-something characters today." – *Midwest Book Review*

"Rich in character portrayal, *The Devil Inside* is an unusual, unpredictable, and thought-provoking love story that will have the reader questioning the definition of right and wrong long after she finishes the book." – *JustAboutWrite*

Wall of Silence "…is perfectly plotted and has a very real voice and consistently accurate tone, which is not always the case with lesbian mysteries." – *Midwest Book Review*

The Middle of Somewhere

by

Clifford Henderson

2009

THE MIDDLE OF SOMEWHERE

ISBN 10: 1-60282-047-3
ISBN 13: 978-1-60282-047-0

This Trade Paperback Original Is Published By
Bold Strokes Books, Inc.
P.O. Box 249
Valley Falls, NY 12185

First Edition: January 2009

This is a work of fiction. Names, characters, places, and incidents are the product of the author's imagination or are used fictitiously. Any resemblance to actual persons, living or dead, business establishments, events, or locales is entirely coincidental.

Credits
Editors: Cindy Cresap and Stacia Seaman
Production Design: Stacia Seaman
Cover Design By Sheri (graphicartist2020@hotmail.com)

Acknowledgments

As this is my first published novel, it's tempting to thank everyone from the writers that have inspired me to whatever genius invented spell-check. But I'll spare you this. There are, however, a number of key people who deserve mentioning. Len Barot, a plate spinner of such skill and magnitude it's staggering; Cindy Cresap, my astute editor whose notated comments often had me laughing out loud; Stacia Seaman, who kept me from making some serious faux pas; Sheri, for the super cool artwork; and all the other women of Bold Strokes Books, too numerous to mention, but who are responsible for propelling this publishing phenomenon. I'm also eternally grateful to the stalwart crew in my weekly writing group: Phil Slater, Sallie Johnson, and Gino Danna—and to James Simmons, my expert on all things Baptist. And then there's Dixie Cox, my partner of seventeen years, who was not only a great source of Texas trivia, but was also the one who kept saying, "Keep writing!" Without her the world would be a bleak place indeed. And lastly, let me not forget you, the reader. May millions of blessings shower down upon you.

Dedication

For my mom, Jane Henderson, a true language aficionado

CHAPTER ONE

Left to myself, I never would have stopped in that eighty-grit-piece-of-sandpaper town long enough to pick up a soda and a bag of beer nuts. Thanks to Pebbles, my '66 T-Bird, erupting into one of her anxiety attacks, I didn't have that option. With Pebbles, it's all about getting attention—my attention. She'll break a belt or bust a hose just to see if I care.

I'd fallen in love with her for her looks. Her midnight black chassis and chrome detailing I could have resisted, but when I got inside her and felt that mint condition, red, rolled vinyl interior I was a goner. I never even lifted her hood. Too bad I didn't know what I know now, what Ford *really* stands for: Fix Or Repair Daily. As usual, I rushed into love. It's a problem I have, and the one I was running from, or trying to, if Pebbles hadn't been making it so damned difficult.

Before I took off on my Springboard to a New Life Tour—what I was calling my desperate getaway from San Francisco—I had her radiator, alternator, and most of her hoses replaced. I wanted her to know I cared. But as usual, she wanted more. Crossing the New Mexico/Texas border, my high-maintenance honey began testing my love, knocking and squeaking her complaints. I urged her to keep a stiff upper lip until we made it to Oklahoma.

It was my twenty-eighth birthday; I had other things on my mind.

Like the fact that it was a hell-hot afternoon and I was driving through the middle of nowhere pulling a piece-of-shit-travel trailer, a Burro to be precise, my very own little egg on wheels. Pebbles and I had looped down from San Francisco to Tucson to purchase The Egg from my friends, Camille and Sus, who'd abandoned San Francisco a year earlier—under much sweeter circumstances. They'd fallen in love and wanted to experience this newfound love in a warmer, yet still trendy, setting. Anyway, they said they'd sell me the trailer for next to nothing, and, seeing as "next to nothing" was pretty much all I could afford once I'd cashed out everything I owned—the desperate hope being that the heart-wrenching memories of my last failed relationship would be purged alongside my crap—I'd swung down to scoop up the Egg on Wheels. I then stayed with Camille and Sus long enough to be thoroughly nauseated by their coo cooing and nibbling off each other's plates, and set out for the Michigan Womyn's Festival, the lesbian Mecca. The haven we flock to with tents, sleeping bags, small trailers, and RVs—anything to be with the throngs of women that show up. Then for one whole blissful week, we get to hold hands, kiss, lie on the grass together listening to music, all without anyone casting a judgmental eye or accusing us of going to hell—or worse, converting their daughters. Some go in search of love; some for community; some really do show up for the music; and some just want to see what it feels like to be able to walk around with your shirt off. Me? I wanted a new life and figured I could make some connections there.

I'd given myself three weeks' travel time, figuring I'd stop along the way and see some country. I wasn't wild about taking a southern route, but picking up the trailer had made it impossible not to, for at least the first part of the trip. I confess to a profound mistrust of the South, especially Texas. My mistrust is so profound that Camille and Sus had had to dissuade me from taking a route hundreds of miles out of my way to avoid Texas altogether. They told me I was being a paranoid Californian, that not all Texans were gun-toting, gay-hating fundamentalist Yahoos.

So now here we were, Pebbles, the Egg on Wheels, and me rattling along on a stretch of road without another car in sight. The land was flat and hot as a stovetop griddle. Sweat ran from my forehead into my eyes, blurring my vision. My thighs, I was certain, were permanently adhered to the vinyl seat. Ah, the Texas panhandle, what better way to see it than traveling with no air-conditioning in a car that's clunking through her final aria?

I knew I was really desperate when I began using visualizing techniques. Some of my New Age pals had tried to "open me up to the abundance of the universe" by teaching me to magically poof a new reality into existence by altering my expectations. At the time, I'd thought they were nuts. Now, I was praying they weren't.

I visualized a service station with a fully stocked vending machine and sparkling clean floors. I visualized a smiling mechanic in neatly ironed coveralls—and all of his teeth intact.

I passed a junked-out truck trailer with the words:

EVERYDAY SOMEONE KILLS JESUS WITH THEIR SINS!

So much for visualizing, I thought and hunkered down into the steering wheel, determined to make it to the next town. I should have taken the interstate. At least there I could have flagged somebody down—somebody who'd remembered to pay the cell phone bill.

I looked down at Wild Thing, my pet name for the lifeless cell phone on the seat next to me, and remembered the day I left, how I'd shoved everything from my desktop—including my cell phone bill—into a box labeled "Important Shit." Hell, I had so many bridges burning in my wake it was a miracle my butt wasn't on fire.

I wonder what Ruby's doing right now?

I clicked on the radio.

"It was the voice of Jesus," a woman drawled through the speaker on the dashboard. "I heard it plain as day. He woke me from a dead sleep and told me to go to the water tank."

A call-in show about miracles, just what I need. For about the zillionth time I reminded my shoulders they didn't need to climb up my neck.

"I'm afraid of heights," she confessed with her heavy Southern accent, "but somehow I climbed up that ladder. It was hard in my housecoat and slippers. I kept slipping, but He gave me strength. He lifted my legs. And when I got to the top of that ladder, I couldn't believe my eyes! Right there, flopping around in that tank of water was my little Mittens! She's my newest calico, a curious little booger. She'd somehow fallen in, bless her heart. She was just a clawing away at those slippery sides, but couldn't get a hold. She was so panicked, so scared…"

A male talk show host interjected, his tone smooth as a good malt whiskey. "So, listeners, are *you* feeling panicked? Scared? Alone?"

I flipped stations and came across the queen of tough love, Dr. Laura, humiliating some sobbing young woman for letting her boyfriend have "dessert" before committing to "dinner."

I clicked off the radio.

Up ahead was a road sign. It was covered in bullet holes.

WELCOME TO RAUSTON COUNTY
BIRTHPLACE OF CHARLENE WANDRA

I checked my rearview mirror for any discernable difference between where I'd come from and what I was now entering. *Nada.* Just more of the never-ending barbed-wire fence with tumbleweeds piled up against it. I kept on, basically because I had no choice. That and Charlene Wandra, whoever she was. I mean, who could resist?

About the time that Pebbles was adding new clanking and rattling sounds to her repertoire, I got my first sight of a Rauston residence: a run-down house surrounded by a boneyard of used farm machinery and rusted-out cars. As I passed, I spotted an old geezer sprawled out in a rocker on the wraparound porch, sleeping. He was slouched so far down in the chair his skinny butt was about to slide right off. He held his hat over his chest like he was listening to the national anthem. A red sign was propped on a porcelain toilet bowl by the porch. It read:

FOR SALE

Scrawled beneath this, like an angry postscript, were the words:

AS IS!

I considered stopping, but the place gave me the heebie-jeebies, like if I stopped we'd never leave. Pebbles would wither away into one more rusted-out car on his lawn and I'd grow old, die, and be buried out in the backyard under a pile of rotting appliances.

A few miles farther, I passed a run-down shack that also boasted a roadside sign. An empty Hefty bag was wrapped around the leg of the sign.

LUNCH SPECIAL
USED TIRES AND AMMUNITION

Three beat-up pickups were parked in the dirt lot. I was starting to get punchy by this time and began amusing myself with visions of pot-bellied ranchers in those nylon mesh John Deere caps, chowing on used tires. "Boy, the tread on mine is done just right. How's yers?" "Doesn't get better than this! Pass the bullets, wouldja?" Pebbles gave me about three seconds to indulge in this merriment, before ruining it with a huge CLUNK! BANG!

Suddenly I had no power and was coasting down the rural highway. I furiously pumped the accelerator. It revved, but wouldn't take.

I coasted past a residential trailer with a makeshift sign.

BEAUTIFUL NAILS BY K'LYNN.

Next to this was a display of prefab vinyl-top, aluminum-legged carports. All of them were miserably wind-skewed. Another sign was duct-taped to the leg of one.

ASK K'LYNN FOR DETAILS

Should I pull over?

I decided against it. I was still coasting pretty fast. Who knew? Maybe that service station with the smiling mechanic was up ahead. Then my speed began to decrease.

I stubbornly kept on, lurching back and forth in my seat trying to keep up the momentum, all the while cursing myself for not paying my cell phone bill, and for not signing up with AAA, and for being so out of control of my life that I was driving though Texas in the middle of summer in a car that was cute to look at, but a mechanical mess inside. Soon it was clear I either had to pull over or I'd stop in the middle of the highway. Adding the day I bought Pebbles to my list of things to curse, I steered her onto the side strip, pulling up next to a brick sign with black metal letters.

RAUSTON BAPTIST CHURCH

I hit a pothole and Pebbles lurched to a stop, almost causing me to get a case of whiplash. Something popped behind me.

Shoot!

I hit the steering wheel with both hands. *Shoot! Shoot! Shoot! Shoot! Shoot!* Then just sat there.

And sat.

Gazing at the coral and turquoise thunderbird dangling on my rearview mirror and refusing to cry. I'd bought the trinket off an ancient Indian in Tucson whose eyes sparkled like diamonds. He'd promised it would protect me. "Thunderbirds are symbol for Godly Strength," he'd said, but I bought it because it went with my car.

"Godly strength. You hear that?" I said to Pebbles.

The silence that followed was crushing.

I considered going to sleep. The problem was I'd have to wake up.

I considered abandoning Pebbles and the tagalong Egg on Wheels, just sticking out my thumb and see where it got me. I never got the chance to run the pros and cons of this second option, because the life

I was trying to run from caught up with me, popping up in the form of a gut-wrenchingly painful memory of a day even worse than this one. A day I'd thought was just another crappy day at the Copy Shop where I worked.

It was bad enough that I'd been assigned to floor duty. Defenselessly roaming through stressed-out customers with all their copy needs and foul moods is something I wouldn't wish on my most despised enemy. Top this off with the fact that the copiers were malfunctioning with a vengeance and everybody seemed to be in some kind of unnatural hurry. The worst was this way-unmellow hippie chick trying to copy programs for a wedding that was to take place, across town, in half an hour. When she beckoned me across the room, her fervor led me to believe one of the copiers had caught fire.

Why do I let myself care about these people? I angled my way through a floor packed with other needy customers.

The copier, it turned out, had semi-devoured the chick's master copy. From the part that wasn't crunched into the piece-of-shit feeder, I could see it was a pen and ink curly-cue deal with flowers and lots of hearts. Granted, it wasn't not my style, but being somewhat of an artist myself, I knew a drawing that intricate had taken her some time. "Uh…" I said, so she'd know I was really smart.

"This can't be happening!" the chick squealed.

"I'm sure we can fix it…"

I was stalling for time. I had no idea how to fix it. The master was mangled. That's pretty much a done deal in the land of photocopy catastrophes. Looking at her, I had the feeling she was trying to keep from throwing up. She had one hand over her mouth and the other one wrapped around her belly. Using my most soothing tone, I said, "We just need to…um…pull it out—without ripping it."

"My sister's going to kill me!" she said through her fingers.

"Your sister's getting married?" I asked brightly as I tugged at the artwork. That's when I noticed my fingers were sticking to the paper. I spotted an open glue stick on the table. *No wonder! This brain-dead chick didn't even leave time for the glue to dry!* Despite her negligence, I managed to ease her artwork out in one piece. There was a huge crease down the middle of the central love heart.

"Voila!" I said, handing it back to her and sidestepping what we both were thinking: the heart now looked broken. I suppose I should have recognized the broken heart as an omen. I didn't, though. I just went on to my next distraught customer, oblivious.

By the time I got home, all I wanted was a cold beer and one of Ruby's shoulder rubs. I climbed the flight of steps to our flat and unlocked the door. Immediately I sensed something was missing. Typically, I chose to ignore the feeling. What can I say? I have an ostrich for a totem animal. I headed for the fridge. Whatever it was, a cold Beck's would solve it. "Rube? Your copy specialist is home!" I announced, prying open my beer. When she didn't respond, I assumed she was napping. Ruby is one all-star napper.

I headed toward the bedroom with thoughts of waking her, slowly, kiss by kiss, but stopped abruptly. The bamboo-beaded curtain with the hula girl was missing from our bedroom doorway. The curtain had moved in with Ruby. She liked the way the hula girl danced whenever you pushed through the beads, said it reminded her to dance. I loved that about Ruby. She'd dance, with or without music, anywhere, anytime.

I'm not sure how long I stood in the hallway mustering the courage to take the three steps into the bedroom. I do know that when I finally did, my shitty day at the Copy Shop seemed as insignificant as a fingertip paper cut. There, lying on the crisply made-up bed, was our one and only cutting board. We'd picked it up at a garage sale a year earlier when we'd moved in together.

But it wasn't the cutting board that was stabbing at my gut; it was the half of a peach sitting right in the center of it. It was a precise cut. The stone was still in it.

"Eating peaches" was our code word for lovemaking. We could say it anywhere: crowded elevators, grocery lines, libraries. "I'm in the mood for a peach. How about you?" As I stood there, I remembered Ruby whispering it to me that morning. We were snuggled in each other's arms; I'd just punched the snooze alarm. "Want a peach for breakfast?" Ruby'd asked. But I was afraid I'd be late for work. Or afraid I'd never make it to work if I indulged in the kind of breakfast Ruby was suggesting. We had that effect on each other. I was already on Copy Shop Probation due to one too many of our "breakfasts."

Copy Shop Probation: It didn't get much lower than that.

"Babe, I can't be late again," I'd told her.

She'd responded by pressing her naked body up against mine, and whispering, "This job is killing you."

I'd pried myself away and rolled out of bed. "It's paying our rent." Then, to kill the mood completely, I'd sniffed the armpits of yesterday's shirt to see if I could wear it again. "Or were *you* planning on paying the rent this month?"

Why do I always have to resort to sarcasm?

I looked at the made-up bed, bedspread smoothed and pillow plumped. That hurt. It was the first time in our whole relationship Ruby had ever made the bed. Suddenly, I was certain that she'd left a note. I charged through the flat searching countertops, the desk, the fridge, the little pad where we wrote down each other's phone messages. *Nada.* But I was determined there had to be a clue as to why she'd left. She always left a clue.

I began rummaging through drawers, closets, the medicine cabinet, but the only clue I found this time was that she'd removed every piece of herself, her basket of makeup, her shelf of journals, the espresso maker her mom had given her for Christmas, even one of our matching towels.

She's probably at Peter and Kevin's.

Lately, Kevin had become her partner in self-absorption. I pictured the two of them hunched over a line of coke, she complaining about me, and he, about Peter. I picked up the phone, but my finger hesitated over the auto-dial. Did I really want to beg her back? Again? What would I promise this time?

An ugly thought passed through my mind: *Maybe she's not at Peter and Kevin's. Maybe she's at Bette's.*

Slowly, I placed the receiver back down and walked to the bedroom. Before I knew it, I'd hurled my Beck's into the wall. The green glass shattered against our oh-so-trendy exposed brick wall. Amber liquid dripped toward the floor, cutting shiny trails of tears. *I've got to get out of this city. Got to get away from that peach.*

❖

A semi hauling cattle barreled by, jolting me from my cheery memory. My face, damn it, was drenched in tears. I flipped down the sun visor to check out how puffy my eyes were. If I was going to be flagging people down, I didn't want to look like some battered woman. Before I knew it, I was eye to eye with the photo of Ruby that, in a moment of weakness, I'd slipped beneath the clip-on mirror. It was one of the promo pictures for her band; she was blowing a kiss to the camera. An electric fan gave the effect that she was standing outside in a storm; her ratted, bleached hair with the black highlights wafted around her face, her favorite silk blouse with the long draping sleeves hugged so close to her body you could see she wasn't wearing a bra. I considered tossing the photo, but flipped the visor back up instead. *Later,* I promised myself.

Then I looked back at that sign. This time I noticed the addendum:

RAUSTON BAPTIST CHURCH
GO WITH GO !

Behind it sat a yellow brick church with a squatty steeple. Despondent, I pushed open Pebbles's door, peeled my sweaty legs from the vinyl seat, and got out onto the shoulder of the road. And just at the moment when I might have laughed at the irony—broken down flat at the altar of Go !—a mini dust devil swept through, spiriting all possibility of humor away.

CHAPTER TWO

There were a few cars in the parking lot, so I knew there were people inside. *Could services be going on? It is Sunday, but it's close to two thirty.* As far as I knew, church was a morning thing—not that I'd ever been. I pictured myself pushing through the big double doors and devout parishioners craning their heads around to shush me. Or maybe they wouldn't get the chance because I'd turn into a pillar of salt the second the preacher or reverend or pastor or minister or whoever the hell he was raised his pointed finger toward me and shouted, "Lo, we have an unbeliever in our midst!"

I decided to wait out whatever was going on. Sooner or later people were going to have to come back out to their cars. In the meantime, there was the possibility someone helpful might drive by. I turned away from the church and squinted up and down the blistering highway. Its identical horizons offered nothing more that vanishing blacktops undulating from heat. A sweltering spit of a breeze pelted my legs with dust.

The Panhandle of Texas, what a low-down place to be stranded.

So I wouldn't feel like I'd lost complete control of the situation, I walked back to the trunk for my ratchet. That's when I noticed that the trailer hitch had busted. *Perfect!*

I grabbed my ratchet from the trunk, popped the hood, and stared. I knew it was pointless; the only constant with Pebbles is that she's never simple. I probably wouldn't love her so much if she were, but that was a whole mountain of dysfunction I wasn't ready to scale just yet.

Right about that time, two hugely overweight women pushed

through the church doors. Both were gussied up in oversized polyester dresses and toting empty platters as they waddled their way down the path from the church. One wore yellow, the other teal. The yellow one wore her dress cinched in with a white, faux-leather belt where her waist should have been. Her plump feet were squeezed into ivory patent leather, low-heeled pumps with dainty bows perched over her bulging toes; her legs were stuffed into nylon stockings like two sausages. In contrast, the teal one's dress looked like a sheet thrown over a piece of furniture. A sturdy man's watch was pushed halfway up her meaty, freckled forearm, and her shoes were immaculate white lace-up Keds. I blew them off as a female version of Tweedledee and Tweedledum and wanted nothing to do with them.

As they made their way down the cement path, each transferring her enormous weight from one leg to the next, each breathing heavily, they were arguing. Being someone who despises confrontation, I always notice arguing.

"What some people deem appropriate to bring to a potluck, I will never understand," the yellow one said.

The teal one, lumbering a few steps behind, used a hanky to pat her forehead. "You're just grumpy because we were on cleanup again."

"Fish wrapped in seaweed. That is what it was! I would not feed that to my dog!"

"Now, you know you don't have a dog and you never *did* have a dog, so I don't know why it is you always insist upon telling me what you would or would not feed to your damn dog." With this, Teal raised her hanky to the sky and spoke directly to God. "Excuse me, Lord. I know I said I'd stop my cussin' but surely you can assist me with one of your miracles and bestow some sense onto this little sister of mine!"

I turned my back to them and pulled a spark plug, hoping it would appear that I knew what I was doing. Surely, someone more qualified than these tugboats of flab, sweating up yards of polyester, would exit the church to help me.

From behind me, I heard one of them venturing off the cement path. Her feet crushed the chunks of packed, sun-dried mud as she heaved her way toward me. *Please don't talk to me. Please don't talk to me,* thrummed through my brain as I examined the spark plug like it might have something to do with my troubles. The sound of her labored breathing told me she'd come to a stop right behind me, and, strange as it sounds, I could hear her ticking. It was a soft tick, like a clock, but it was definitely a ticking.

"Looks like you're in a mess of trouble," she grumbled.

You think?

I took a deep breath, hoping to keep the anger out of my voice. *Ladies and Gentlemen, which will it be? Yellow or Teal?*

I turned around.

Teal.

She was peering past me into the engine, a bead of sweat streaking its way down her temple. A ridiculous bow was clipped jauntily into her short, graying hair like an afterthought, as if she kept it by the door to throw on for special occasions. "What's more," she continued, "You're wasting your time with that spark plug. You broke a U-joint. Your drive shaft is dug into the ground. I saw it from up by the church."

I palmed the spark plug and leaned back on Pebbles. "My drive shaft?" I know next to nothing about mechanics and assumed when she said "dug into the ground" she was using a metaphor.

She lifted a disapproving eyebrow, reminding me of one of those great-horned owls I'd seen on the nature channel. I crossed my arms trying to hide the fact that I wasn't wearing a bra. Not that I have much in the way of tits, but sweat had plastered my lightweight cotton tee to my nipples.

"Are all them holes for real?" she finally said.

At first I didn't know what she was talking about, then realized she was focused on my pierced eyebrow. My ears were covered in piercings as well, but it was the eyebrow that seemed to be bothering her. Involuntarily, my hand rose touch it. "Uh. Yeah."

"What, you got started and couldn't stop?"

"Somcthing like that."

I shifted my attention to Yellow. Her pumps were poised on the cement just shy of the dirt. I noted how she now held both platters stacked one on top of the other. She met my gaze and pinched out a little smile. Her eyes were filled with such compassion—pity, really—that it made me feel like a malnourished, one-legged orphan. "You need to be somewhere soon?" she asked. "If so, you might need to make a phone call."

"I was hoping I could get to a garage." I returned her smile.

Teal grunted dismissively, turned her back to me, and began walking to the cement path. “It’s Sunday. Old Luke closes down on Sunday.”

Furrows appeared in Yellow’s pale forehead. “We are not just going to leave her here.”

“Who said we were?” Teal grunted as she stepped her spotless Ked onto the cement.

Yellow shifted the platters to her ample hip. “Well, where are you going?”

“I’m going to get Pastor to bring his tractor over. We’ll have him tow her to our place.”

“Uh, that’s not really necessary,” I blurted.

My remark hit Teal’s back like a thrown rock. She stopped walking and spoke without turning around. “You got somewhere else to go?”

Yellow clicked her acrylic fingernails against the bottom of a platter.

I stammered, “Is there…a…uh…campground? Or a Motel Six or something?” Then, trying to appear nonchalant, I took a swig from my bottle of water. It tasted like hot bathwater.

Teal pivoted slowly on the cement and fixed her owl eyes directly onto mine. “Honey, I don’t know where the heck you’re from, or where the heck you’re going, and frankly I don’t care, but what I *can* tell you is where you are. Rauston, Texas. Only reason anyone ever stops over here is if they got family, and if they got family, they got no need for motels or hotels or what have you. As for camping, not even a fool would think of it. Between the scorpions, fire ants, and dust storms you’d be begging for mercy in no time. So batten down your hatches or whatever it is you need to do to get ready to be towed, cuz you’re going to spend the night at our place. That, or we can leave you here by the side of the road. You do have plenty of water, don’t you?”

In point of fact, I didn’t. I’d planned to fill up when I stopped for the night. I guess she saw this in my face, because she commenced hauling her way to the church, muttering, “Lord, have mercy, this life and one more.”

This left me and Yellow standing there, she on the cement path that went from the church to the adjacent parking lot, and me on the blacktop. There was nothing but fifteen feet of red dirt between us. We smiled awkwardly. Then she sucked in a little air as if she was about to speak, but a truck rumbled by, pulling a small backhoe on a trailer. She looked at me apologetically as if the interruption was her fault.

Once it was past, she said, "You'll have to excuse my big sister. I swear she's as stubborn as a wart. Daddy always said that she came out of Mama that way, one part sweet and ninety-nine parts stubborn! He was stubborn too. That's where she gets it." She shifted the platters to her other hip. I could tell the weight of them was getting to her. "But where are my manners? My name is Rose. Rose Wilbourne. But you can call me Piggin. Everybody else does. Welcome to Rauston."

I fiddled with the cap of my water bottle. *Surely I misheard her. Surely she said Peggy, not Piggin. But then that doesn't make sense. Peg's not a natural nickname for Rose.* I looked up from my water bottle and smiled. *Why do I even care? It's not like we're at the beginning of a meaningful relationship or anything.* I knew the next appropriate gesture would be for me to introduce myself, but it was like someone had put the DVD on pause.

She stood there, her pumps angling slightly outward, an expectant smile on her face, and those heavy platters gaping empty on her hip while I stood there, frozen, gazing into those eager little eyes of hers. As I fixed my eyes on a hint of tension perched between her perfect eyebrows causing shallow rifts in her otherwise smooth Mary Kay skin, a crazy idea thrummed through my mind. *If I say my name, I'll no longer be a watcher of this movie, I'll be sucked into it.*

I have no idea how long the two of us stood there staring into one another's eyes. I do know it was long enough to feel uncomfortable. I saw it in her stance. I could almost feel her toes curling inside those tight little pumps of hers.

As for my body, I could barely feel it. I'd gone completely numb. The only parts I felt were my vocal cords, and they were stretching tighter and tighter by the second. I didn't realize I wasn't breathing until, to my horror, my lungs grasped for air and out of my mouth erupted a sob-like hiccough.

Just one.

Because my vocal cords clamped down doubly hard to make sure another would not follow. But alas, the damage was done. With just that single surge of sound, the movie started back up. And, sure enough, I'd been sucked into it—without even saying my name.

"Oh, sweetheart," she began, "here I am talking your ear off and you're in the middle of a real bad day. You know, I think there's probably still some food left inside. We should get you something to eat. I know that always makes me feel better. Irma Sellers brought some coconut cream pie that could turn any bad situation better. I just bet I could find you a piece."

Ignoring her, I took another swig of bathwater.

CHAPTER THREE

Teal lumbered back down the cement path toward us. "He's on his way. Let's just pray he doesn't decide to educate us in mechanics. Lord knows the man can preach, but when it comes to anything practical, well let's just say, he couldn't pour water from a boot."

The one I was calling Peggy, laughed. "Don't mind Heifer. Even the sweet scent of honeysuckle has been rubbing her wrong today."

This time my mind didn't fix what my ears had heard. *Heifer? Did she really just call her sister Heifer?* I glanced at Teal to see if she'd taken offense. Her hand, making an awning above her eyes, threw a shadow across her face, so it was impossible to read her expression. "I'm just speaking the truth," she said. "Lord knows I am! The man needs to learn what he's good at and what he's not."

The church door pushed open revealing a tall, chiseled-face man with slicked-back chestnut hair and sideburns. He strode toward us smiling, a silver belt buckle that read JESUS accenting his pelvis. The sleeves of his button-down were rolled up. "I hear we got ourselves an opportunity to spread a little of the Lord's love with a stranger. Broke down right at our doorstep, I do declare!"

Anxiety crept up my spine. He seemed way too happy about my misfortune. Convert! Convert! Convert! might as well have been flipping 'round and 'round his eyeballs like dollar signs on a winning slot machine.

"Just a little car trouble," I said, consciously broadening my stance. I'm not a tall woman, so I've learned to make myself appear more formidable. Or at least that's what I hoped.

He extended his smooth, long-fingered hand toward me. "I'm Pastor Williams."

"Eadie," I said, meeting his outstretched hand with a solid grip of my own. "Sorry to put you out."

He seemed startled by my grip and placed his other hand on my shoulder as if to one-up me. "Now, now. Nobody should ever start out a conversation with 'Sorry'!"

I'm surprised I even heard what he said. He had me trapped, and I hate feeling trapped. I ordered my knee not to jerk up and ram his nuts. Fortunately, for him—and me—he let loose.

"Right nice little vehicle you got here. What is it? Sixty-six? Sixty-five?"

"Sixty-six."

He moved with such blatant disregard to the heat that it made me wonder if being one of Jesus's promo guys had scored him some kind of immunity to physical discomfort. "Shhhenandoah Valley!" he uttered as if it were a cuss word. "She is real pretty, I do mean to tell you."

"Too bad looks aren't everything," I said, making a point not to look at Piggin. I didn't want her squawking about how I'd nearly lost it. I sure didn't need any of these Yahoos feeling sorry for me.

"So what do you think, Pastor?" Teal asked, "Could you give her a pull to our place? I figure we could set her up by the old house. Have to make two trips, though. Her trailer busted off."

Pastor Williams was clearly not a man to be rushed. "Well, I thought we might look under that hood first. See if it's not something simple." He stepped over to Pebbles and peered into her engine.

"Front U-joint's busted," Teal said, putting her large hands on her hips. "I told you that."

"Well, now, Grace, you never know," he said.

Grace? This heap of impatience is named Grace?

She rolled her eyes for my benefit, said, "Pastor, I wish you'd call me Heifer like everybody else."

He looked up from the engine. "Now, Grace, I don't believe for one second that Jesus would call the two of you Piggin and Heifer."

Piggin? Heifer? You've got be kidding me! I flicked my attention over to Piggin. She was smiling and shaking her head. This was clearly an ongoing battle between the pastor and her sister…Heifer. "You two are just going to have to agree to disagree." Piggin spoke as if talking to preschoolers.

Her name is Piggin...

Grace snorted.

And hers is Heifer...

I reached into the car for my cell phone. *Okay, Jesus, if you're really out there, show me a miracle! Fire this puppy up.* Not that I knew who I'd call, but I was feeling desperate. I needed a lifeline to the real world. I hit the Talk button. *Still dead.*

So much for Jesus.

Pastor Williams looked at the engine. "Maybe we should check your fluids."

Stay the hell away from by fluids, mister.

"It'll be a waste of all our time," Heifer said. "Can see it plain as day from the church. Her drive shaft is rammed into the ground."

Pastor Williams put his hands up in the air. "All righty, Grace. I just thought we might consider all the possibilities."

Piggin walked over to an Olds Ninety-eight to rid herself of the cumbersome platters.

Rammed into the ground? I dropped to my knees and peered under Pebbles.

Her guts are spilling out!

"Whhoooeee! What a mess!" Pastor Williams said, having kneeled right next to me. "Look at that! Right into the ground." He looked at me. "That must have been one abrupt stop you made, missy."

"Lordy Lordy," Piggin said breathing heavily from the short walk to her car. "It is hotter'n a fry baby in you know where."

Pastor Williams got to his feet. "We're gonna have to get this over to Old Luke."

Piggin's hands pressed down on the front of her skirt, Marilyn Monroe style, the effect being entirely different without air gusting up from a grate below. She spoke carefully, as if she didn't want the pastor to think she was trying to tell him what to do. "That's why we thought you could pull her trailer over to our place."

"You'll have to make two trips, the car to Old Luke's and the trailer to our place. She busted the jack," Heifer added. She did not speak carefully, just to the point.

The pastor let Pebbles's hood slam shut. "Y'all's place is a bit far, don'cha think? Might as well just set her up at my place. I'm sure the missus could use a little company."

If I'd had anything to eat that day I'm sure I would have thrown it up on the spot. I was picturing me and the missus sipping tea while the pastor entertained us with after-dinner selections from the Bible. "I really don't want to be any trouble."

"Now don't you worry, Miss Eadie. We'd love the company." Again, his hand on my shoulder. "My wife's been feeling a bit poorly as of late, and I think having another female around might just be the ticket." His hand squeezed my shoulder. "Now don't you go anywhere. I'll be right back with my John Deere."

Once he'd driven off—yellow, eighties Cadillac with a white vinyl top—Heifer shook her head in disgust. "Feeling a bit poorly, is she? Suppose that's why she never comes to church."

"Don't be hateful, Heifer."

"That woman has been feelin' poorly since the day she moved to Rauston. She's allergic to small-town living is what it is. Thinks she's too good for the rest of us."

As the two of them continued to bicker, I went to the trunk to pack a bag of essentials. I'm not sure what I thought I was going to do—Walk? Curl up next to a tumbleweed?—but there was no way I was going to celebrate my twenty-eighth birthday with the belt-buckle Jesus and his depressed wife. "I really do appreciate all your help," I stammered, "but really there's no need…"

Heifer looked up from their bickering and put her hands on her hips. Her dress was drenched in sweat. "This is just plain unacceptable. Last thing this girl here needs is to get stuck listening to Sylvia Williams whine about her migraines and how she never used to get 'em back in Amarilla. I swear it's like listening to a tortured mule."

"Heifer, you're scaring her."

"I mean to. I want her to know if she's got any tricks up her sleeve, now's the time to pull 'em. I wouldn't wish Sylvia Williams on the devil himself."

I found myself starting to warm up to Heifer. "Why can't I just spend the night here? I've got the Burro. I'd just need to get my water tank filled up."

Piggin shook her head. "Pastor Williams wouldn't have it. He'd be afraid the Methodists would swoop you up."

We stood for a few more seconds, each of us lost in thought. Then Heifer snapped her fingers. "Piggin, take her home."

Piggin cocked a pencil thin eyebrow. "What are you cooking up, Heifer?"

"I'm gonna call on Old Luke's conscience."

"But it's Sunday! He'll be down at the co-op in the middle of a game of Chicken Foot!"

Heifer started back toward the church. "Just scram! I got to go stop the Pastor."

"What are you up to?" Piggin yelled after her.

She wasn't the only one who wanted to know.

"Irma's still in the church, isn't she?"

"Her car's still here."

"Good. She can let me into the office. I'll ring him and say we don't need him after all. I'll tell him that Old Luke just happened to be passing by."

"With his tow truck? On a Sunday?"

"I'll tell him it's a miracle! You know how that man loves to believe in a miracle," she said before disappearing into the church.

"Well, there's no use arguing with her once she's got her mind made up," Piggin said, sighing. "You hungry? I made some biscuits this morning that are light as air."

CHAPTER FOUR

Piggin carried on a running commentary as we cruised through the blink of a town. She told me who owned what and whether they were Baptists, Methodists or, "heaven forbid," Church of God. "All that speaking in tongues just doesn't sound like the Jesus I know."

Some I listened to, some I didn't. I adjusted the vents of her Olds Ninety-eight so they shot directly at me, slouched in the seat, and soaked up all that cool, cool air. Outside, everything looked wilted. Not a shade tree in sight, just mesquite and dirt. On the floor of her car were old church programs, candy wrappers, and Big Gulp cups. The whole interior was in need of a good Armor-Alling too. Being a neatnick myself, it surprised me how her mess relaxed me. At least I had one virtue up on her.

We passed a storefront window that had RAUSTON AMUSEMENT ARCADE painted directly on the glass while the sign from the previous business was sported on the plaster above: a big Rx floating in the middle of a bunch of dancing pastel capsules and pills.

Ruby would have loved it.

Ruby...

Ruby and her partner in crime, Kevin, were sprawled out on the divan—not the couch, mind you, the divan. Kevin's boyfriend, Peter, would never have anything as gauche as a couch in his home. His apartment was done up in early-sixties swinger décor. Vintage. Between us, on a kidney-shaped white Formica coffee table, sat a large beveled mirror with flamingos etched into its edges. Centered on the mirror was a rolled-up dollar bill lying on its own reflection. I watched

Ruby thump a small Ziploc of coke to get the white powder to collect in the corner.

"Oh, Eadie, It's too early to go. It's not even midnight!"

I pulled the Visine out of my pocket, doused my eyes, and threw it to her. "Come on, sweetie. I've got to work in the morning."

The Visine landed on the couch by her leg. She readjusted her position, knocking it to the floor. Our brains were pickled in martinis. Kevin had just bought a new retro martini set and we'd been called over to celebrate. I knew when we were invited that it was just an excuse for the two of them to indulge in nose candy.

I squinted my eyes, trying to focus on the Ruby I loved. The one who hadn't yet been broken by the harshness of the music industry, the one whose lyrics and voice were so full of raw truth that audience members were certain she was singing *their* heartbreak, *their* passion. On stage, Ruby didn't channel the muse; she was the muse. And her band, Last Nerve, was her life. I hated the record label that had promised her so much, then delivered so little. It broke her, and I blamed them.

I stood and walked toward the door. "I have the early shift tomorrow."

The baggie was still between her fingers. A bad sign. "Who needs to make copies in the morning?"

"Ruby, I know this is hard for you to believe, but some people arrive at their jobs, fresh copies already in their hands, by nine a.m."

Kevin looked up from the crossword puzzle he'd been pretending to work on and said to her, "Do you want to spend the night, pumpkin?"

I felt like punching a hole in the wall; I crossed my arms instead.

Ruby wrinkled her nose flirtatiously. "I would if I didn't think you'd forget me the moment that big brute of yours comes home."

Lucky for you, Kevin, you're a flaming queen. Otherwise, I'd rip out your jugular.

Pasty white Kevin tossed the paper to the floor and rolled himself into an upright position. "Where is he, anyway? He said he'd come right home."

Ruby, baggie still in hand, was having fun ignoring me. It was one of our sick little games. "See what I mean?" she whined to Kevin, "You've already forgotten all about me! You play such the little wife for him."

Kevin looked at me in mock sympathy. "Oh dear," he said, "Not even midnight and your girlfriend's already turning back into the fag hag she really is."

Ruby kicked him with her perfectly manicured foot. She didn't like him giving me attention. I watched as she went in for the kill. "Evil Stepsister seems to be feeling a tad defensive, don't you think, Eadie? I think he's wondering why his Prince Charming isn't home yet. Where could he be, I wonder? Where, oh where, could he be?"

I downed the last of my martini. "Come on, Ruby, you two are starting to get ugly."

In a huff, she threw the coke on the table, got up from the divan, and wound her incredible mass of ratted hair into a knot. Then she leaned over, not only to remove Kevin's crossword pencil from his mouth, but also to flaunt her cleavage, not at me, but at Kevin. She never let him forget that she was the one with the real tits. "Don't worry, Kevi, I'm sure he'll come home to you in the end," she said, pushing his pencil through her bun to hold it in place. She slung her leopard print purse over her shoulder. "Isn't that how the fairy tales always work out? *Happy endings and all that shit?"*

"That lot is the future site of our new church," Piggin said, startling me out of my memory.

I glanced out the window. Right in the middle of a vacant lot was a sign with a fund-raising thermometer stuck in the ground. Beneath the thermometer were the words: SHORT ON FUNDS? GIVE A PRAYER!

"That's one of the things that Pastor Williams has really got us fired up about, a new church. He's got the deacons—heck, all of us!—working on fund-raising. Thinks we'll attract more members if we have a nicer building. Really, he's right. Our current church has all kinds of problems, the latest being the plumbing. Last Sunday the toilets completely backed up and those that had to go had to drive to K'Lynn's. You probably saw her nail salon on the way into town."

I imagined parishioners standing under those skewed carports waiting to enter the tiny nail salon and hoped K'Lynn had at least made a few sales.

"Whatever you do, don't bring up the new church to Heifer. She's dead set against it and she'll talk your ear off about it. She'll tell you how we don't need a new church, how we just got to fix up the old one, and how raising the money for a new church is going to take money away from our Helping Hands program. She and Pastor Williams are on opposite sides of this coin, I can tell you."

She laughed. "But here I am burning a hole in your ear about all this church business. Goodness gracious! What do you care about all this?"

I slouched further down in my seat. *My thoughts exactly.*

We drove through a residential section, then pulled onto an unmarked road. Every half mile or so, we'd pass a trailer or small brick or wooden house surrounded by some kind of fence. From what I could gather, the more well-to-do lived in the brick houses. (Picket fences and lots of yard art.) The less fortunate got the wooden houses and trailers. (Chain link fences and even more yard art.)

One particularly less fortunate family was sitting out on the twisted porch of a dwelling, half trailer and half wooden add-on. They'd hauled a swamp cooler outside and had it plugged into an orange extension cord. They were sprawled around it on a beat-up couch and several worn desk chairs, drinking from plastic tumblers the size of paint cans.

"Those are the Milsaps," Piggin said. "I swear they are the unluckiest bunch of sad sacks a person could meet. Why, just last week, Maxine Milsap said she'd bought her first lottery ticket. Then, the next day when she saw the winning numbers, she was certain they were the ones on her ticket, because she's got one of those photographic memories you read about. Anyhow, the ticket somehow wound up in the laundry, and she'd used extra bleach that day, as one of the kids had come down with lice. Well, that ticket just up and disintegrated. She tried to tell Jameson down at the market what had happened, and he said if it was up to him he'd believe her, because he'd seen her photographic memory in action one time when she'd disputed a grocery receipt. I guess she reeled off the items just perfect, price and all. But the folks at the lottery, he said, wouldn't see it that way. They needed proof and they could care less about her photographic memory.

"Anyhow, that kind of thing happens all the time to those Milsaps. Shoot! The oldest boy got himself in a motorcycle wreck just last year. Ripped his leg right off. Has to do his business in one of those plastic bags now. It's a real shame too. Made his money bull riding at the rodeos before the accident. I don't suppose he'll find himself a girl now, not in his condition."

Fifteen minutes later, we were pulling into a circle driveway and up to one of two trailers.

"Home sweet home. This one's mine, the other belongs to Heifer. I sure hope she's got that car business worked out with the pastor. He's not going to like it if he brings his tractor 'round to the church and there's nothing to tow. Lord, that man loves towing things with his tractor." She cut the engine. "Sweet Jesus, I have to use the little girl's room! It's those raw red onions that Minnie Bell puts in her potato salad. It sure tastes good, but it makes me have to pee something awful."

With a sense of resignation, she opened the car door. The hot air stormed in. I leaned back in my seat as she heaved herself out of the car.

I dropped my head to my chest. *What the hell am I doing here?*

"You come on in when you're ready. I expect you're kinda shook up from your car breaking down and all, but there's nothing to be done about it today, so you might as well see where it is the Good Lord plopped you down. It's not much, but we call it home." She opened the back door and pulled out the platters. "Heifer'll most likely have Old Luke pull your trailer over by the house there." I looked in the direction she was indicating. There was no house, just some blackened lumber and the remains of a brick fireplace.

"Now, I really gotta use the girls' room. Like I said, come on in when you're ready. I'll make us up a nice glass of iced tea. You do drink iced tea, don't you?"

"Yeah."

She closed the car door, taking a moment to pop open the trunk first, then made her way toward the trailer. Before climbing the three steps up to her porch, she turned to check on me.

I was still sitting in the closed-up car.

I smiled.

She smiled.

I could tell she thought I was thick. I thought so too. Who, in their right mind, would sit in a car on a boiling hot day, with all the windows rolled up and the air-conditioning off? Weren't there stories of dogs dying under these circumstances?

She shook her head and disappeared into her trailer.

I remained where I was.

I'd been traveling alone for two days, barely even speaking to the folks at the quick stops. Now, here I was, in the company of another person, and I felt more alone than ever. "Shit," I said to the pine tree air freshener hanging from the dashboard. "Shit. Shit. Shit. Shit!"

I sat a while longer.

And then some more.

I didn't actually open the car door until I was certain I'd consumed the last swallow of oxygen. Air swooped in to fill the vacuum. I peeled myself off the seat and unloaded the few bags I'd managed to throw together before leaving my Egg on Wheels by the side of the road—just in case the Old Luke thing didn't work out. Unsure whether I should bring my stuff into Piggin's trailer, I stood there for a few seconds, in a daze, then tossed my stuff on the hood of the car. I needed to look around, get my bearings.

It felt good to be outside, even if the soles of my dime-store flops were softening from the heat, allowing burrs and other small sharp things to puncture through. The quiet was working wonders on my nerves.

A lizard skittered across the driveway.

Of the two trailers, Piggin's appeared to be the older. It also appeared to be the more unkempt. Bags of bottles sat on the wooden porch. A floorboard car carpet hung on the railing. It was severely faded, making me wonder how long it had been out there. A Mexican blanket drooped askew on her porch swing.

Heifer's trailer was much neater. In fact, it was so neat it looked uninhabited. The curtains hung with military precision. And there was no porch, just a large awning over the door.

Once upon a time, Eadie T. Pratt was taken in by two old maids living in side-by-side trailers in a town the size of a tick. Priceless.

I walked over to the pile of blackened wood to the right of the trailers. Some was still standing, creating a spooky sort of skeletal sculpture, like the bones of some desert creature that had fallen over one day and died. Twenty or so cement piles, and pipes that looked like old plumbing, were also scattered around. And then of course the toppled brick fireplace covered in weeds.

A jackrabbit bolted from behind a woodpile. He tore off toward nowhere, then abruptly stopped and looked back at me. I held his stare, afraid if I moved he'd take off. The shadow of a buzzard or hawk circled the area. The bunny's eyes and mine remained locked, which, considering the threat that loomed above him, I thought was pretty brave. My mouth began to dry out. I thought of the iced tea that Piggin had offered.

"What?" I asked the bunny. "What do you want?"

The bunny twitched his nose.

"So this is your place, is it?"

Another twitch.

"Well, chances are you're going to be sharing it with me tonight. That is, if this Old Luke guy comes through." Figuring he couldn't understand me, I asked, "Want to know a secret?"

As he didn't say no, I continued. "Today's my birthday. I'm twenty-eight. What do you think of that?"

He seemed unimpressed.

"What, you're not going to sing?"

His muscles tensed as if he might make a run for it.

"All right. I'll leave you alone. Besides, her place is probably air-conditioned; I don't suppose you can offer me that."

I broke his gaze and took in the wavering horizon. A line from the *Ancient Mariner* passed through me, something I'd been forced to memorize in high school. *Water, water everywhere. Nor any drop to drink.* Except this was land. So much land a person could drown in it.

CHAPTER FIVE

Despite my protests, Piggin was certain I must be starved on account of my "ordeal." I took a sip from the giant plastic tumbler of iced tea she had waiting for me. I sat at her kitchen table trying my hardest to look appreciative as she whipped us up what she referred to as "a snack," but looked to me like a four-course meal. I was tempted to tell her that my whole bleeping life was an ordeal and so far I'd made it through just fine on coffee and hummus on toast.

I hate eating with people I don't know; it's so intimate.

From my vantage point, planted in front of the swamp cooler, her trailer appeared cluttered, but homey. Piled by the door was a stack of *Country Living* magazines and just from looking around, I could tell she took their tips to heart. Decorative borders sporting sprays of wheat tied up with curly ribbon trimmed the walls, tchotchkes were sprinkled everywhere: on free-hanging wicker shelves, above the kitchen cabinets, on the windowsills. The table was chrome with a red Formica top, right out of the fifties. Potholders hanging from sunflower magnets stuck to thc hood of her stove said things like, "Too many cooks spoil the broth!" "Mi casa, Su casa."

Why bother talking if you can have your potholders say it for you?

Piggin pulled a Pyrex casserole from the refrigerator and peeled back the Saran Wrap. It was then that I noticed her fingernails. I couldn't believe I hadn't spotted them earlier. They extended well beyond her fingertips, a good 3/4 inch at least, and each one had its own little rainbow sprayed across it.

"I know I'd be hungry," she said, popping the casserole into one of two microwaves. "Stress makes me hungry. Always has. 'Course by the look of me, you'd think I was stressed out all the time." She laughed at her joke, smacking those plump, fingernailed digits onto her thighs. It was a strange laugh, shallow and stuck in her throat, like it didn't want to travel down to her heart. I considered joining in, but wasn't sure how it would be received. It's one thing to laugh at your own weight problem, but someone else's? I reminded myself she wasn't bothered by people calling her Piggin. Still I didn't laugh; it seemed tacky. I smiled one of those awkward smiles that feel more like stretching your lips than displaying emotion.

She returned to the refrigerator and began rummaging through it again, giving me an excellent vantage point for viewing her ample buttocks. "Truth is, I like to cook," she said, taking out a Tupperware container and sniffing its contents. "And if you like to cook, you might as well eat; that's what I say. No use letting everyone else have all the fun! You like green rice?"

"Sure," I said, figuring that whatever the hell it was it was probably good for me being as it was green. "But you know, you don't have to go to all this trouble. I'd be happy with a piece of toast."

She dumped a green cottage-cheesy mixture into a bowl. "These are just leftovers, sweetheart. It's no trouble at all. Besides, when Heifer turns up with Old Luke, it'd be rude not to offer him something. Here, we're yanking him from his game of Chicken Foot. I tell you, that man is as skinny as a blade of grass, but he loves to eat. Now there's a case of someone loves to eat, but *can't* cook. I do believe if it weren't for the church he'd live on pork rinds and jerky. I swear, he's always got a pocket full of jerky! 'Course he gets the good stuff offa Big Earl Stokley's farm. Big Earl makes up the best darn jerky. Says it's 'cuz his steers feed on four leaf clover. 'Course that's a bunch of bull and everybody knows it. His steers are eating the same buffalo grass everybody else's are, but he sure does make some good jerky." She pulled another bowl from the refrigerator; this one held something orange.

I considered offering my help, but as it involved more than spreading things on toast, I was out of my league. That and I wouldn't be able to continue drying out my sweat-drenched armpits in front of her swamp cooler. "Could I ask you a question?"

She looked up from the bowl, a concerned expression on her face. "What's that, sweetheart?"

Now I'd done it. I'd meant for this to be along the lines of the other conversational patter we'd been having, but with her gazing right at me, her head cocked in a most caring manner, I was reduced to stammering. "I was just wondering, I mean, I'd noticed you and Hei…your sister… have nicknames and I was just wondering…"

She laughed that strange shallow laugh again. "Those nicknames kinda threw you, did they? You're not the first. I've been called Piggin so long I just don't give it much thought anymore. Our daddy's the one started it. I don't think he meant any harm by it, but I know some folks think it's mean-spirited. Pastor Williams for one. We keep trying to tell him folks around here won't know who the heck he's talking about if he calls us Rose and Grace, but he just won't listen."

I nodded, then picked up one of her little rooster napkin rings and began scrutinizing it. *How could anyone not be hurt by being called Piggin?*

She went back to sprinkling brown sugar on the orange stuff.

"We don't do marshmallows on our sweet potatoes," she said. "I hope you don't mind. We're both kind of partial to salty."

"Sounds good," I said, relieved to be on safer ground. I really didn't want to get into some big heart-to-heart. I don't trust my heart anymore; it has a brutal sense of humor.

She checked the casserole in the first microwave and put the orange stuff and the green stuff in the second one. "Pretty much everyone around here has a nickname. It's kind of a small-town thing I guess, or maybe it's a Texas thing, I don't know. But our family's a perfect example, well, except my mama, God rest her soul. Her name was just so pretty no one ever wanted to call her anything else. Dahlia. Dahlia Meeks. That's before she married my daddy, that is. Then of course she became Dahlia Wilbourne, but folks always referred to her as Fred Meeks's girl. Everybody always loved Old Pappy Meeks. He was a good man, he truly was. Broke his heart to see his only daughter wind up with a man like J.D., which is what everybody called my daddy on account of his love of Jack Daniel's. His real name was Louis. Went by that when he first rolled into this town with his pocket full of cash, spending it up like he was some kind of rich man. They say my mama just hung her dreams onto him like laundry onto a line. But that line was like a—oh, what do you call those things I saw on TV?—a holo-something or other. You know, an illusion. It could no more support her dreams than a bunch of air—hot air. 'Course, she'd never say so. She came from that kind of mentality 'if life gives you lemons, make lemonade.' Have you heard that one?"

"Uh, yeah. I think I saw it on a poster in my dentist's office or something. It had a picture of a couple of dressed-up kittens at a lemonade booth."

"How cute!" She poured a brown gelatinous substance into a pitcher and added it to the other stuff in microwave number two. I took a sip of the iced tea and willed myself to be thankful.

"Well, that was my mama all over. Never complained. Five kids and old J.D. drinking up our land payments, but she wouldn't complain. No siree! Course, when Baby Boy, he's the youngest, accidentally burned the house down, she just kinda gave up. That's when the church stepped in…" She lifted her right palm to the ceiling—"Thank you, sweet Jesus!"—then resumed her food preparations. "…and helped us buy the trailer. They passed the plate and came up with a down payment. What choice did they have? Us five kids and mama without a place to lay our heads and there's old J.D. down at the bar searching for his lost dreams at the bottom of a whiskey bottle. Shoot! Pappy Meeks musta been turning in his grave. I tell you this trailer wasn't on the land more than two days before Mama took to the bedroom with a bottle of vanilla. That was pretty much it for her. Sent us girls into town whenever she'd run out. Heifer says my back room still smells like vanilla. I don't smell it, though. Guess I've grown too used to it. Funny how that works sometimes…"

For a brief moment anguish contorted her face. I tried to think of something to say to change the subject, but just like that she snapped out if it and pulled a Ziploc of biscuits from a counter-top breadbox stenciled with the Eiffel Tower.

"Here I am veering off the track again! Good thing Heifer's not here. She gets so mad at me when I veer off the track. I swear it's my hormones. Sometimes I don't even remember there was a track to begin with. Heifer'll tell you I've always been this way, but I don't think it used to be so bad. Do you remember what I was talking about, sweetheart?"

I took a stab. "Nicknames?"

A microwave dinged and I felt as if I'd answered the million-dollar question.

"Oh, that's right," she said as she placed the biscuits on a plate. "Like I said, we all got 'em. We call John, our brother, Tiny, and he's bigger than a house. Then there's Sweet Ginger. Well, I don't suppose that's really a nickname…her name *is* Ginger, but nobody ever calls her that. It's always Sweet Ginger this and Sweet Ginger that. Oh, she was an angel…'Course, these days her halo's gone a little crooked. But no matter. She'll always be our Sweet Ginger. And then there's Jesse. Why, we've called him Baby Boy since the moment he turned up in that bassinet. Now he's forty-eight years old, but we still call him Baby Boy. His wife calls him Jesse, and that's as it should be, but she's the only one." She looked up. "Do you like butter beans?"

Right about that time, I heard the sound of a truck pulling into the driveway. Relieved to have a reason to remove myself from the food preparation, I bolted from my chair. Maybe, by some miracle, Old Luke and Heifer had come to tell me that Pebbles was up and running and I could ditch this scene.

When I opened the door, Heifer was just backing herself out of the passenger seat of a big pickup. A tall, skinny geezer I assumed was Old Luke had already made it around to the front of the truck. The way his overalls drooped off his bony shoulders, the guy looked like a human hanger. His hands were in his pockets, his attention on his boots. They were your basic Sears work boots, but brand-new.

I went out to meet them.

The Burro was already sitting on the other side of Heifer's trailer by the "old house." I was more than a little taken aback by how at home it looked surrounded by all the cockleburs. I spotted my bunny pal sniffing a tire. Pebbles was nowhere in sight.

Piggin came out onto the porch. "Looks like you got yourself some new boots, Luke."

"Yes, ma'am. I figured it was time."

"Well, they look real nice."

"Thank you. Not as comfortable as the old pair." He scratched his head. I got the feeling talking wasn't one of his strong points.

Heifer, now fully planted on the ground, groused, "Your car's at his place. He'll look at it first thing in the morning." Then she began marching toward me—well, not so much toward me as toward Piggin's trailer—giving me the impression that I was just something in her way. "Good Lord, Piggin, I hope you've got some cold tea made up. This heat's about to give me a coronary!"

I moved over to make way for her. She took hold of the railing and began heaving her way up the steps.

Feeling more than a bit dismissed, I focused on Old Luke. What was the proper protocol in this situation? "Um, should I pay you for the tow now or should we settle up tomorrow?"

Heifer, one foot already in the kitchen, yelled over her shoulder, "Good Lord, girl. It's Sunday! No one does business on Sunday except Dairy Queen and the gas station." The door banged shut behind her, then banged a second time when Piggin followed her in.

The afternoon grew suddenly and uncomfortably quiet. I looked at Old Luke. He shrugged and fiddled with his hat, then barked, "Come on, Sparkplug."

A giant hound sat up in the bed of truck.

"We're going to be here a spell. Might as well find some shade."

The dog leapt from the truck.

Piggin poked her head out the door and placed out a bowl of water for Sparkplug before retreating back inside.

I looked at Old Luke. "How hard's it going to be?"

"Finding a drive shaft is going to be tough. Could take some time. Then again, maybe not."

I let this information sink to the bottom of my belly. "I really appreciate the help."

He kicked at the dry ground creating a tiny explosion of dust, then drove his hands further into his pockets, which forced his shoulders to slump even more. "These sisters have been good to me. Be thankful it was them that found you."

CHAPTER SIX

Ham, mashed potatoes, sweet potatoes, green rice, biscuits, gravy, creamed corn, black-eyed peas, and beans they kept calling Reba's butter beans sat at the center of the table while Old Luke, me, Piggin, and Heifer sat around it.

"Shall we?" Piggin asked.

Taking this to mean we were supposed to start serving ourselves, I scooped up a dollop of mashed potatoes and plopped it onto my plate.

Heifer cleared her throat, meaningfully.

I glanced up from my lone mound of potatoes.

Heifer nodded toward Piggin, whose head was tilted down toward her clasped hands.

Whoops! The serving spoon leapt back into the bowl, making a most inelegant clunking sound. I chose to ignore it, as did everyone else, and folded my hands.

"Dear Lord," Piggin began. "You have given us so much. And we are grateful, Lord, to be able to share it with someone in need…"

I wondered if Piggin was referring to me or Old Luke. I snuck a peek at him. His head was bowed and his eyes were shut.

Sighing, I refocused on my badly behaved pile of potatoes and thought back to the last meal I'd had with Ruby—or tried to have.

"I'm not hungry," she said, pushing the bag of Burger King's finest off the magazine-covered coffee table.

I cursed myself for not spending the few extra bucks on take-out from Chevy's or Applebees. I hate to appear cheap, even if I am. "You need to eat."

"How about a martini? See if we can get you to quit nagging."

I wanted to yank her to the mirror to show her how much weight she'd lost since Last Nerve split up. But we'd already had that fight. "Just try a few bites."

She picked up the remote and flicked on the TV, not so much to watch it, *but to shut me up.*

"…and another thing, Lord, Les and Darla Wilkenson have been having a little trouble on the home front…"

Heifer cleared her throat.

"…seems that Les is back at the bottle…"

Heifer cleared her throat again.

Annoyed, Piggin looked up from her prayer. "Well, it's true! I talked to Darla just yesterday at the bank."

"Save a few prayers for tonight, Piggin. We're all hungry."

Piggin sighed dramatically. "In Jesus's name, Amen."

I mumbled something that I hoped sounded like "amen" and waited for Piggin or Heifer, or Old Luke for that matter, to begin filling their plates. I wasn't going to make that mistake again.

"Start us off, Old Luke!" Piggin said as if she were refereeing an athletic event.

Old Luke reached for the black-eyed peas. "I sure do thank you for this."

Piggin forked up a slice of ham. "Don't be silly. We took you from your domino game. Least we can do is feed you." She passed the platter to me. "Besides, it's always a pleasure to see you. Pastor Williams was just asking about you this morning."

"Piggin, leave the poor man be. And pass me the butter."

"I was just making conversation, Heifer."

"You were not. You were trying to get Old Luke to come to church. Church is just not built into some folks' constitutions. I don't know why it is you refuse to understand that."

I passed the ham to Old Luke, hoping for a moment of eye contact. I wanted him to know that he wasn't the only one who didn't have church built into his constitution, but his attention stayed on the food, robbing us of what could have been some excellent bonding.

Piggin passed me the biscuits. "I simply want him to know he's welcome if he should ever want to come."

Heifer passed Reba's butter beans. "I expect he knows that, Piggin, seeing as you tell him that every time he comes out for a visit. I'm surprised he's still willing to make the drive out here."

Either Piggin couldn't think of a response, or she made a point not to have one. From her self-righteous expression, I suspected it was the latter. And as neither Old Luke nor I had much to add to the conversation, their bickering was replaced by the sounds of serving spoons scraping earthenware.

Once my plate was piled with food, all I had to do was make up my mind where to start. I decided on a buttered biscuit drenched in gravy. I picked up my fork, hacked off a wedge of the steaming biscuit, swirled it in a pool of gravy, and shoved the gravy-soaked biscuit into my mouth as if the world owed me. The flavor took me completely by surprise. The light flakiness of the biscuit combined with the heavy, perfectly seasoned gravy was the happy childhood I never had. To my embarrassment, I actually moaned as the biscuit melted on my tongue.

Amused, Heifer looked up from her plate. "Piggin, I believe the girl likes your biscuits."

Piggin coyly dabbed her mouth with a paper napkin. "You should taste them when they're fresh out of the oven."

"That gravy…" I said, unable to come up with words to describe it.

"Our mama's recipe. Now try some of Heifer's black-eyed peas. Folks at the church just go crazy over Heifer's black-eyed peas."

I scooped a spoonful of the rich, saucy peas into my mouth, and taste buds, long dormant, began to sing. As the meal progressed, each lusciousness eclipsed the last. For a while I even forgot about Ruby, and my broken-down car, and my lack of funds, and the fact that I was hinging my entire future on some cosmic connection to be made at a women's music festival in a state I'd never been to.

It wasn't until Old Luke placed his final piece of ham on a biscuit, making it into a little sandwich, and Piggin served herself up the last few bites of green rice, and Heifer began licking melted butter off her fingertips, that it occurred to me we'd passed through the entire meal without uttering a single word. It was fine by me. I dreaded the inevitable questions that would be asked.

"Shall I make us a pot of coffee?" Piggin asked, getting up from the table with her plate.

"Well, now, Miss Piggin, I sure wouldn't mind a cup," Old Luke responded.

"How about you, Eadie?"

"Sounds great."

"Oh good. I've been dying to try out this hazelnut coffee. Heifer won't have any part of it."

"I just don't see the point of mucking up a good cup of coffee."

"It's a dessert coffee, Heifer. Something new. Surely it wouldn't kill you to give it a try."

"Doesn't sound like you're going to give me much of a choice."

"You can choose to go without."

"Or walk over to my trailer and make a cup of Folgers. I bet Old Luke would like a real cup himself, wouldn't you now?"

Careful not to take sides, Old Luke chuckled. "Never bite the hand that feeds."

Piggin pulled a bag of coffee from the freezer. "Thank you, Luke. At least *someone* around here has some manners. Besides, I bet Eadie's used to all these fancy coffees. Aren't you?"

Not too big on flavored coffees myself, I said, "Whatever you make will be fine."

Heifer shook her head. "Well, folks, looks like we're in for a strong cup of perfume."

Piggin laughed. "One part sweet, ninety-nine parts stubborn! That's my sister!"

Heifer rolled her eyes for Luke's and my benefit, then, smacked the table. "So what's the latest gossip down at the co-op, Luke?"

Old Luke began folding his napkin back into a square. "Rumor has it the fellers from World Mart have found themselves someone willing to sell."

By Piggin and Heifer's response, you would've thought he'd just told them they were in the direct line of a tornado.

Piggin turned from her coffee fixing. "What?"

Heifer sat forward in her chair. "Who?"

Old Luke began fiddling with a butter knife. "Don't know. All I heard is they come in to see Jameson. Told him they're in negotiations now. Says he's either going to have to move over or join the wave."

Heifer flopped back in her chair and crossed her arms. "The wave! What kind of talk is that?"

"Who'd sell to them?" Piggin asked.

Heifer shook her head. "They're just bluffing. Nobody wants them here."

Old Luke, still playing with his knife, shrugged. "Only reportin' what I hear."

Just as I was beginning to enjoy my new role as audience to their small-town melodrama, Piggin looked in my direction, smiled apologetically, and included me. "You'll have to excuse us, Eadie. This is quite the hot topic in town. World Mart has been trying to move in for the last year, but so far the residents have been keeping them out by refusing to sell property. They can't very well move in if they don't have the land."

Disgusted, Heifer grumbled, "Now it looks like we got a weak link."

Old Luke stood. "Well, Miss Piggin, Miss Heifer, s'pose I should be moving along."

Piggin looked up from pouring the coffee. "You're not staying?"

"I hope you'll excuse me, but the more I think on it, the more I think maybe it's the coffee's been keepin' me up at night."

Piggin stopped pouring. "Well, I sure wouldn't want to keep you up."

He smiled. "I appreciate that, ma'am." He took his felt hat from the peg by the door and, holding it next to his chest, turned toward me. "You come by tomorrow morning and we'll take a look at that engine."

"Will do," I said, wondering how the hell I was going to get there.

"You keep your ear to the ground, Luke," Heifer shouted as he headed out the door.

Neither sister spoke for a few seconds. Then Heifer abruptly got up from the table. "I told you he wouldn't drink that perfume."

Chapter Seven

I tried to decline the peach cobbler that Piggin set before me. It wasn't my association with peaches that bothered me. Cooked peaches weren't the same as Ruby's and my peaches; they didn't have the fuzz, the delicate seam, and, most importantly, they didn't explode when you bit into them. I declined because I couldn't imagine putting one more thing into my mouth. I was stuffed.

Piggin wouldn't hear of it. "Fruit is good for you, sweetheart. You ought to a least take a bite." She said this while scooping my serving onto a dessert plate.

Five minutes later, all that remained was a scraped-clean plate. Spotting a crumb under its rim, I pressed my finger on it, then brought it to my lips. The flaky pastry dissolved on my tongue.

My plan was to sit around long enough to be polite, then withdraw to the Egg for what I considered a well-deserved nap—that is, if I didn't die in a puddle of sweat and self-pity first. I halfheartedly listened while Piggin and Heifer hashed around the World Mart business, absently nodding when it seemed appropriate. Like when Piggin informed me that Jameson, who currently owned the market where everyone shopped, was the son of the man who'd opened the grocery back when she and Heifer were kids.

Nod.

And how he would no doubt be put out of business by this huge chain.

Nod again.

"His daddy was good to our mama when times were rough."

Smile and nod.

I looked forward to the following day, when all that would be left of this backfired birthday would be what I could see in my rearview mirror. *Although I am eating well...*

Piggin heaved herself up from the table. "I think I'm going to lie down for a spell. This day has plumb worn me out."

I slid my feet back into my flops. *Naptime!*

"I guess that leaves the kid and me here to do dishes," Heifer replied.

I cleared my throat. "Uh, yeah. I was just going to offer."

Heifer reached across the table for a toothpick. "Oh you were? Well, then, I guess that makes me supervisor."

I missed Piggin the moment she waddled down her wood-paneled hallway. Maybe it was the way Heifer's arms were folded across her pendulous breasts, her eyes trained on me like I was some annoying gnat.

I pushed my chair away from the table and stood. "So, looks like you've got a dishwasher."

"I don't, Piggin does. Still gotta rinse real good though, otherwise the food'll stick."

"Thanks for the tip." I began to clear the table, wondering if the whole chore would be filled with these managerial gems. I turned on the water and waited for it to get warm.

"Seems funny to take off on a long trip if you know you got car problems."

Here come the questions. I began to rinse the glasses, wishing like hell my back wasn't to her. "Uh, yeah..." I accidentally bumped a coffee mug into the counter. "Shi...!"

She ignored my faux pas. "You must have some real important business somewhere."

"Well, actually," I said, trying to sound cheery, "I'm on a bit of an adventure."

She laughed so loud she snorted. "I get it. You had to make a quick getaway!"

Feeling a sudden urge to defend myself, I turned to face her. She wasn't looking at me, though. She was scratching her thick thumbnail against what appeared to be a bit of dried-up food stuck to the oilcloth. *What did I think I was going to say anyway?* I went back to loading dishes, supremely aware of the rip under the pocket of my cut-offs. In the morning when I'd pulled them on, I'd thought it was cute how my Jockeys peeked through. Now, I wished I'd chosen a pair with a little more coverage. The whole situation reminded me of being called on to go to the blackboard in grammar school.

I took refuge in a favorite memory.

Standing on the sidewalk in the Tenderloin, one of the seedier sections of San Francisco known for its strip joints, hookers, and drug dealers. My clothes and hair covered in sheetrock dust. I'd just been dropped off by the guys I worked with. On Fridays, they'd often end the day at this strip club, which left me two choices: go with them and get a ride home afterward or walk to the nearest bus stop and scrounge for the fare. It was demeaning enough to be the only woman on the job site, but having to put up with their antics at the strip club was unbearable. "Yo, Eadie! This one your type?" Me being a lesbian was real funny to these guys. Real funny. Which is why today I was busing it.

As I walked to the closest bus stop, I passed a newer club—one I was pretty sure didn't include women taking their clothes off. On the door was posted a Xeroxed flyer that said Happy Hour with Ruby Dakota and the Last Nerve. I decided to check it out. If I timed it right, maybe I could still get a ride home with the boys. And a beer sure sounded good. I ran my fingers through my hair to dislodge some of the sticky white dust and tried, with not much success, to brush off my clothes.

The place was a dive with character. There were Daliesque murals painted on all the walls with random items—Barbie dolls, kitchen utensils, old computer components—epoxied to them making for a 3-D effect. The band was between sets. I ordered a beer from a bartender with a tattooed head and sat down at the bar. The place was roughly half full, mostly punks, sprinkled with a few Tenderloin types drawn by cheap drinks.

"Let me guess, you were scattering your dead mother's ashes out by the sea and the wind came up."

I twisted around on my bar stool. A very attractive female dressed in a tight wifebeater T-shirt and ripped-up jeans was standing next to me. She had lots of silver jewelry and bleached blond hair with black highlights. Very cool. I looked down at my dusty clothes and laughed. "It's a bit more mundane, I'm afraid."

"No," she said, playfully sarcastic, and signaled the bartender for a refill. "You don't look like the mundane type."

"Sorry to disappoint," I said. "Underneath this exotic exterior resides a Jimmy Stewart personality."

She leaned in and asked, "Are you loyal?"

Taken aback by her bluntness, I blurted the truth. "To my detriment."

She smiled and locked her gorgeous green eyes in on mine. "That's good, because I wouldn't let you take me out if you weren't. I demand loyalty."

Swallowing my beer suddenly became difficult.

Just then a scrawny guy in a retro plaid polyester jacket stepped up onto the small stage. "And now, let's welcome back Ruby Dakota and the Last Nerve!"

"Gotta go," she said. "Stick around, though. I'm a real Jimmy Stewart fan." With that, she ran up to the stage and grabbed the mike.

Needless to say, I missed my ride.

Heifer cleared her throat and spat into a napkin. "Those don't go in the dishwasher. Gotta be washed by hand."

I removed the antler-handled steak knives from the silverware basket in the bottom rack. "No problem." Then, to keep it light, said, "These are interesting."

"My daddy would be glad you thought so. They're one of the few things he ever came home with after a night of cards."

"I'm sorry."

"Why? Wasn't you losing our grocery money."

"I just meant I'm sorry your dad was…"

Heifer folded her arms and leaned back in her chair. "What? What was he?"

It gave me the feeling I was in one of those interrogation rooms in a film noir, she being the big burly cop and me, the good-for-nothing criminal. "I don't know. I'm sorry I even said—"

"There you go again! Sorry!" she spat. "Nothing I hate worse than people saying sorry when they don't mean it. Had more empty sorrys in this short lifetime than there are useless knickknacks in this here trailer." She reached above the table to a shelf crowded with salt and pepper shakers, picked up a ceramic cowgirl and cowboy, and spoke in a hushed tone to keep Piggin from hearing. "You gotta ask yourself what's the point of having all these if you're not gonna use 'em? Course Piggin don't see it like that. It's a *collection*, she tells me, and there's nothing wrong with a few *collections*. Look around here. You call this a few?"

I scanned the room, and sure enough, what had appeared to be just a lot of clutter transformed itself into a series of meticulously displayed collections. Heifer pointed to a grouping of tiny spoons with the names of states on their handles. "Looking at these you'd think she'd been somewhere, which couldn't be further from the truth. She's afraid to travel. Gets folks at the church to bring 'em to her. These are made for people who've been places, I tell her, to remind them of their trips. Or how about those?" she said, pointing to a dusty frame protecting a bunch of antique-looking valentines. "And those are just the tip of the iceberg. Her closet is filled with boxes of love letters, all written to people she's never heard of. Got folks scouring their attics, thrift stores and such. Says they make her cry. Why do you want to do that, I ask her. Didn't get enough of it when we were kids?"

Unsure how to respond, I asked, "Does she have any of her own letters in the collection?"

"S'far as I know she only ever got that one, and it was from a boy so sweet he could stick his pinky in your coffee and that'd be all the sugar you'd need. Then...well...let's just say circumstances scared him off. That and old J.D. Never could stand any of the boys taking his Rosie's attention, that's what he called her when his friends were over. She wouldn't be Piggin anymore. She'd be Rosie—his Rosie. He'd yell, 'Rosie! Come on out and sing for the fellers!' Had a voice as pretty as an angel, she did. 'That's my little nightingale, boys. My own little nightingale,' he'd say."

I began to get a sick feeling in the pit of my stomach, and it had nothing to do with indigestion. What was she evading by using the word "circumstances"? What had happened to Piggin?

Heifer began to rotate the cowboy pepper shaker on the table. "She can still sing up a storm. Does every Sunday, but now her voice just makes folks nervous. The longing in it scares 'em." She sighed and placed the cowboy and cowgirl set back on the shelf. "I suppose none of us likes being reminded of what *could* be."

I nodded. Was she actually trying to have a conversation with me, or was she just killing time? Before I had too much time to think about it, she lugged herself up to standing. "You about done over there, kiddo?"

"Yeah," I said, "I just gotta wipe down the counter," and proceeded to do so.

As I dried my hands on the dishtowel, she stated matter-of-factly, "You'll need a plug-in for your rig."

I folded the towel and threaded it through the refrigerator handle. "Well, it would make it easier, but I could manage…"

"You can plug into my trailer. There's an extension cord in the shed. There's a fan out there too. Got a bit of a rattle, but it'll move the air around."

Chapter Eight

I lay on my back, in the dark, in a bed that just hours before had been my dining area. The place was about fifteen feet stem to stern and eight feet wide, and stank of coffee and patchouli, reminding me of the good times Camille and Sus had no doubt experienced. Hoping to quell my sudden wave of claustrophobia, I reached above my head and flicked on the overhead reading light. While the light helped to eliminate the creepiness factor, it didn't change the fact that the fiberglass Egg was the first residence I'd ever lived in where I could be in the bedroom, dining room, sitting area, and kitchen all at once. The screen door, loose on its hinges, rattled with the blustery wind. It was a hot, dry wind, which had come up at sundown. Each unsettling gust rocked The Egg.

When I'd abandoned Pebbles I left my watch strapped to her stick shift; now there was no way to know what time it was. I just knew it was dark and I wanted to be sleepy. Suddenly, my screen door, caught by a huge gust, flew open and slammed against the side of the fiberglass shell. *So much for the locking screen door feature,* I thought while rolling out of bed and searching for something with which to secure the door. A flimsy twist tie was the best I could come up with. I hoped it would hold for the night. The place would be beastly hot with the main door shut. I wired the screen door and flopped back onto my bed. The wind teased the door's aluminum edge, causing it to whine.

"Shit! Shit, shit, shit, shit!"

And the damn door was the least of my problems. How was I going to pay for getting Pebbles fixed? I had a little extra cash, but not much, and Ruby—damn her!—had maxed out my only credit card.

Well, in truth, we both had. She had a relentless hankering for the finer things in life, and I had a relentless hankering for her.

"We could die tomorrow," Ruby said, playing with my earlobe. The two of us were lying naked in bed after a particularly fulfilling morning lovemaking. "Call in sick."

I scooted myself into a sitting position. "For a week? Tell them, 'Yeah, I'm pretty sure I'll feel better in a week.'"

She picked up my hand and began sucking my fingers, one by one. "A road trip would be good for us…" she said between thumb and index finger.

That's how I lost the drywall job.

"Shit!" I had the urge to kick a hole through the fiberglass wall, but depression and practicality squelched it.

Still flat on my back in The Egg, I reached over to the kitchen counter and grabbed the Womyn's Music Festival printout. ABSOLUTELY NO REFUNDS was branded in the small type at the bottom of the page. Surely I'd still be able to get there on time, even if I had to give up the sightseeing part of the trip. I just needed to figure out where I was going to get the money. As I put the brochure back, I caught a whiff of my armpit.

It was time to try out my shower. I'd been avoiding this, as I was sure it wouldn't work or its pitiful water pressure would feel more like drool than a shower. Reluctantly, I peeled off my T-shirt and shorts. They were covered in a fine red dust, as was the rest of me. I tossed them in my laundry bag—a plastic 7-Eleven bag to be exact—and squeezed into the cramped shower stall, just inches from my toilet seat. To my relief, water did come out of the spout. The trick was getting the drizzle the right temperature; the thing had a hair trigger. To avoid alternately scalding and freezing, I had to flatten against the walls. After a bit of negotiating, I did finally manage to have a showerlike experience, washed my hair and everything. It felt good. The highlight of my day, actually.

I put on my SILENCE=DEATH T-shirt and decided to use it exclusively for bed. I sure couldn't wear it out and about in downtown Rauston. Then I got my journal and art supplies out of the kitchen cabinet. My journal is ninety percent pictures. Any words that wheedle their way in do so in the form of accents to my pen and ink and watercolor images. As I flipped through, looking for the next free page, I came across the drawing I'd done the night I'd first kissed Ruby. Pinwheels and confetti. The day she left me, I'd painted our bed with the cutting board and peach just as she'd left it. Above the bed, however, I'd painted a thunderhead spitting rain, the bottom of the bed losing all its definition as it melted into a puddle.

I'm a tad overdramatic in my portrayals, but the point of drawing them is to make me feel better. I've been doing it since I was a kid. When you have parents that can't see beyond their own pity-party soap operas, you've got to find someone who will listen. In my case that someone turned out to be an eight by ten blank book with a black cover given to me by a grade school art teacher who said I showed promise.

I picked up my number two pencil and began drawing a monstrous egg. Inside I sketched myself opening a huge present with lots of curly ribbons. I drew the wrapping paper peeling back and the top pried off. From it, squeezed caricatures of Piggin and Heifer: tiny fat bodies with giant heads. I gave Piggin's face an enormous smile with tears shooting from her eyes like a sprinkler. On her head was a hat like a cupcake. Heifer was trickier. I didn't have a read on her yet. I sketched her with one eyebrow cocked and looking out of the picture as if to say, "Mind your own business!" For the hell of it, I turned the bow she wore to church into a miniature cowboy hat.

Once it's sketched, I begin phase two: water coloring. I'd do the final pen and ink the next day when the paint was dry. I like to come back to my pieces the next day. It brings a perspective.

The wind, blasting through the screened skylight window, lifted the page of my journal, causing the border of car parts and dollar bills I was working on to streak. Frustrated, I put my brush into the jar and reached for a tissue to blot it. Then I heard the strange wail.

Coyotes.

The last time I'd heard them I'd been sitting at a campfire at Girl Scout camp. The counselor, taking the opportunity to educate us, began telling us about the trickster nature of the coyote in Native American culture. Annie Jerome, next to me, was so scared she'd reached out to hold my hand. Feeling brash, I'd put my arm around her to comfort her. I'd thought it was a good cover and that no one would know how I felt inside. No one would know I was pretending to be her boyfriend. The next morning, however, the counselor pulled me aside and gave me a vague talk about "being appropriate."

I picked up my pencil and sketched a few coyotes around the edges of the egg. I titled the entry COYOTE BIRTHDAY.

CHAPTER NINE

Early the next morning Piggin and Heifer gave me a ride to Old Luke's garage on their way to the local bank where they both worked. We made plans to meet up for dinner. "Give a call if you need a ride home. I can take my lunch break whenever," Piggin said before driving off. I smiled and waved, inwardly flinching at her use of the word "home."

Old Luke's place looked more like a convalescent home for vehicles than it did a garage. Weed-covered, junked-out cars and farm machinery surrounded the half-acre property, while closer to the garage waited an array of vehicles that still had a chance—or so I assumed. I passed a tractor with a horseshoe welded to its steering wheel and a Chevy pickup with no hood and sauntered toward the outbuilding that served as his garage. The door gaped open and I saw Pebbles in one of the two bays, but no sign of Old Luke.

To the left of the garage sat his house, or dwelling I suppose I should call it: an ancient Revcon RV. By the junk stacked around it, I got the feeling its wild and carefree traveling days were well behind it. A sign tacked to the door read BEWARE OF DOG. Sparkplug was sacked out in a shady spot beneath a tire. He slapped his tail once, just to let me know *he* knew I was there, then went back to snoozing.

It occurred to me that Old Luke might be sleeping too.

I hate waking people.

I stepped inside the dimly lit garage, prepared to wait, and was hit by the smell of gasoline and cigarettes. Clearly, his shade-tree operation was beyond state inspections. "Hello? Anybody home?" I said tentatively.

A scraping sound came from under a Toyota four-door pulled into the other bay. Old Luke's new boots were scrabbling to pull him out from beneath the jacked-up car.

"Punctured gas tank," he griped, coming into a crouched sitting position on what looked more like a wide skateboard than a dolly.

I tried to mask my pre-caffeine grouchiness with a chipper smile. It hadn't occurred to me when I'd turned down Piggin's offer of breakfasting together that his garage would be out in the middle of nowhere. I'd assumed he'd be on the strip and I'd be able to pick up coffee and a bagel while I waited. "Uh, hi. Hope I'm not too early."

"Nope. Just about to get to yours." He gestured toward a coffee pot and a selection of stained mugs. "Help yourself."

There is a God, I thought as I made my way over to the grimy coffee shrine. I chose a mug adorned with two chubby cherubs that were gazing into the distance while strumming on lutes. *Come on, you two, pull some heavenly strings for me, would you?*

While Luke reorganized his ratchets, I wiped out the mug with my T-shirt. A family-size can of Coffee-Mate and a box of sugar bumped elbows with a jar of bolts and O-rings. Also on the greasy countertop lay a tarnished soupspoon, its shallow center discolored by a coffee ring. I gave it the once-over with my T-shirt as well. "I sure appreciate you doing this."

He pointed with his thumb. "Couch is around the side."

Feeling dismissed, I made my way around the outside of the garage.

The couch turned out to be a propped-up car seat with a big wooden cable spool serving as end table for empty beer bottles and a can brimming with hand-rolled cigarette butts. I sat. *Not even 9:00 and my pits are already soaked in sweat.*

I took a sip of what tasted like yesterday's coffee and watched the grasshoppers popping around in the weeds. *Please let this not be as sucky as it seems.*

Old Luke sauntered around the side of the garage with a metal folding chair and his own cup of coffee, Sparkplug lumbering ten paces behind.

I guess I wasn't being dismissed; he was issuing an invitation.

Old Luke placed his coffee on the spool end table next to mine, parked his skinny butt on the chair, and pulled out a bag of Drum tobacco and a pack of rolling papers. "You smoke?"

"No," I said. "Thanks, though." It occurred to me he might not have been offering me one, so I amended my statement. "I mean for my car…fixing it…or trying to…"

He rolled his smoke one-handed, licked the edge, and bit off the tip.

Sparkplug redug a hole that looked like a favorite spot and lay down in it.

I tried to look at ease. "That's a good dog."

"Been with me near fourteen years."

"That's longer than any relationship I've ever managed," I said only halfway joking.

He cracked a one-sided smile and lit up his smoke.

I took another swig of coffee. At least it was strong.

Gesturing toward the top of a utility pole, he said, "This one sings to us every morning and evening."

A bird was perched on the pole, chest glowing yellow in the morning sun. I was amazed I hadn't noticed it; the thing was singing its little heart out.

As we sat listening, I felt like an intruder on Old Luke's and Sparkplug's morning routine. I reflected on my own morning routine of the last month: lying in bed and wondering who Ruby was with. Old Luke's routine was definitely healthier, cigarette and all.

"You know what kind of bird it is?" I asked.

Old Luke pinched out his smoke. "Meadowlark. One of God's finest creations." Tossing his cigarette butt onto the overflowing can, he stood, sighing. "S'pose I should take a look at that car of yours."

I followed his lead and stood too.

"You planning on helping?"

"Well, I just thought…" But I don't know what I was thinking. Probably something along the lines of how the hell am I going to pay for this? Not exactly the most comfortable place to begin a business transaction.

Fortunately, he didn't wait for me to explain myself. "There's a box of doughnuts by the cash box," he said over his shoulder. "Help yourself."

I followed him in, poured myself another cup of coffee, and nabbed one of those powdered sugar jobbies, something I hadn't had since I was a kid. Breakfast in hand, I walked back around to the couch. *Make it easy on him, Pebbles. For once, make it easy.*

My appreciation of the doughnut was eclipsed by self-flagellations.

Bite. Chew. Why hadn't I gotten the car thoroughly checked out before I left? Swallow. And why had I left with such scanty funds? Bite. Chew. I was always in such a rush to leave. Swallow. Couldn't I ever be satisfied with my life? I barely tasted the doughnut. It left its mark, though. Sugar plastered all over my chin, hands, and the front of my T-shirt. I decided to locate a hose and wash up.

As I made the corner of the garage, the pastor's Cadillac cruised into the driveway. I tried to slip out of sight, but it was too late. He'd spotted me and was waving out the window. He had somebody with him too. I smiled and went about the business of searching out a hose. My plan was to appear confidently absorbed in what I was doing so he wouldn't feel the need to socialize—or worse, try to save my pitiful soul. I kept him, and his friend, in my peripheral vision, just to play it safe.

His friend turned out to be a kid, twelve or so, who appeared to have Down syndrome, that big lower lip and small beady eyes. From where I stood it looked as if his T-shirt had Dolly Parton on it.

I was so busy trying not to look like I was gawking I nearly tripped over the outdoor faucet. It was a knee-high pipe jobbie sticking out of the ground by Old Luke's Revcon. I turned my focus away from the pastor and onto what I was doing before I did something stupid, like spray water all over the place. Wouldn't that be a classic Eadie move? I bent down to turn it on. The handle wouldn't budge—even when I used both hands. I squatted, giving it everything I had. Still nothing.

"Need some help?"

It was the pastor. He'd snuck up on me, and in my surprise, I'd tipped backward. My ass was now firmly planted on his ostrich-skin boot.

"Didn't mean to startle you," he said chuckling.

I slid off his boot, declining his offer of help up, and grumbled, "I'm fine," then stood, albeit somewhat ungracefully, on my own.

"Well, let me make it up to you by helping with this little thingy here."

Before I could say, "No. And put a lid on the patronizing tone, asshole," he nudged past me to the stubborn faucet. To my sheer delight, he couldn't turn the water on either. He put his whole back into it, his fancy boots digging into the dirt. He tried a second time. And a third. Attempting to mask his annoyance, he straightened up and wiped his hands on his crisp Levi's. "Dern thing is rusted out."

Old Luke and the Down syndrome kid joined us, robbing me of the opportunity to say something snotty. Old Luke tipped his beat-up straw hat, a la Roy Rogers. "Pastor Williams," he said.

The kid stood behind him, hands in his pockets. And I was right; it was Dolly Parton on his T-shirt. LOVE, DOLLY was scrawled underneath the picture with a bunch of XXXs and OOOs.

Pastor Williams, determined to recover from his ineffectiveness with the faucet, smiled his toothy grin. "Seems you got yourself a rusted-out faucet, Old Luke."

Old Luke cocked his head. "Hmmm. Worked this morning." He reached down and, with seemingly no effort at all, turned the knob. Water splashed onto the dry dirt, making the first spots on his new work boots.

"Old Luke sure is strong!" the Down syndrome kid said.

Pastor clapped the kid's shoulder a little too enthusiastically. "He sure is, Buddy Bud. He sure is."

Turning it back off, gently this time, Old Luke muttered, "Needs a new washer, so I gotta crank it down tight." He glanced at me as he said this and I felt my heart swell. I was getting to like this old bird.

As I knelt to wash up, Pastor Williams pulled Old Luke aside.

"Told Reenie Peterson I'd pick up her car, seeing as I'm headed that ways anyway. She's in need of some more counsel, don'cha know. I'll get her to drive me back."

"Fine by me," Old Luke said. "The keys are in it."

Pastor Williams leaned in and spoke in a confidential tone. "Thing is, I promised Jameson I'd let Buddy Bud help sweep the church." He glanced over at Buddy Bud, who was blissfully unaware that he was being talked about, having focused in on trying to catch a grasshopper. "You're a real fine sweeper, aren't you, Buddy Bud?"

Buddy Bud looked up from his prey and wagged his head up and down. "I sure am! I'm a real good sweeper!" Then he went back to the grasshopper.

The pastor laughed.

I turned off the tap and shook my hands dry. *What's this guy trying to manipulate Old Luke into doing?*

The pastor spoke to Buddy Bud again. "But sweeping's not going to happen today, is it, Buddy Bud?"

"Nope. No sweeping," Buddy Bud said, pouncing on a grasshopper and missing.

"See now, Buddy Bud remembered how last time I went to counsel Reenie, you had some important work for him to do here…"

I hated the way this guy was using Buddy Bud. Why not just ask Old Luke to look after him? Why try to make it sound like it's Buddy Bud's idea?

Old Luke removed his straw hat and scratched his head. "S'pose I could find something for him to do. Figure you'll be back in an hour or so?"

"The usual."

I cringed. *What a slimeball! Getting his rocks off down the road by taking advantage of a guy who'd never say no.*

The pastor bent down and smiled at Buddy Bud. "If you do a good enough job, I just bet we can find you an ice-cream cone somewhere today."

My eye-rolling was lost on the grasshoppers.

After Pastor Williams drove off in Reenie Peterson's Toyota, Old Luke poured out the contents of three big jars, each filled with a different kind of hardware, onto one drip pan and handed it to the kid. "Think you could sort these for me, Buddy Bud?"

Buddy Bud took the pan of assorted hardware and three empty jars. "I'm a good sorter!" The way he walked around the side of the garage, holding the pan out front like it was a science project, gave me the feeling he was pretty familiar with the place.

"That was nice of you," I said to Old Luke.

He picked up his dolly. "Had a kid brother like Buddy Bud."

I ambled around the side of the garage, leaving Old Luke to his work, and found Buddy Bud sitting on the ground amidst grasshoppers and cigarette butts, sorting. I introduced myself.

"Eadie rhymes with needy," he said.

Ouch! That hurts. "It also rhymes with greedy!" I said, grabbing a nut from his tray.

He laughed. "Hey!"

And so the two of us got down to sorting, me acting as a kind of coach.

"Where does that one go, Buddy Bud?"

"In *this* jar!"

"How come?"

"It's got a point!"

"Do you know what it's called?"

"It's a screw!"

"How about this one?"

"It's round!"

I snagged him a doughnut too. When I handed it to him, I got the feeling the sugary doughnuts weren't new to him, that he and Old Luke had shared a doughnut or two in the past.

"Does that taste pretty good?"

"Like sunshine."

I smiled, impressed by his colorful description. "You want to play a game?"

He wiped his sugared fingers on Dolly Parton's face. "I sure do, greedy, needy, meaty Eadie."

I positioned the three jars about four feet from the drip tray and began tossing the hardware into them like shooting hoops. "Two points."

Buddy Bud clapped his hands. "Me too! Me too!"

It took him awhile, but once he got the hang of it, he was pretty good. "Two points!" he'd yell and clap. "Two points!" He was having so much fun he didn't even stop when we heard Reenie Peterson drop the pastor off. Of course, I tried to sneak a peek, curious about this wanton woman. Unfortunately, due to the light, I couldn't see much, just a slender arm reaching out from something sleeveless.

"Don't you think you ought to go?" I asked.

"Nope. He'll come get me," he said tossing a nut. "Two points!"

If it was okay by him, it was okay by me. I wasn't his babysitter. I tossed a screw. "Robbed! She bounces off the rim!"

A few minutes later, Old Luke rounded the garage. "Hate to ruin your fun, but I've checked out your car."

My stomach tightened. "No problem. We're just about finished."

Buddy Bud tossed a washer into the jar. "Two points!"

"Like we thought, the drive shaft is shot and your rear shocks are shot."

I tried to keep my face neutral, but there were two questions that were busting to get out. How much? And how long?

"I've put a couple a calls out for a sixty-six drive shaft."

"And?"

He shook his head. "Don't look good."

The doughnut and coffee began to sour in my stomach. "So what are you saying? My car's basically done for?"

"Well, there are a few places I could still try. They'd have to ship it, though."

"How much is this going to cost me?" I asked making a real effort to maintain eye contact.

"Depends on if we find you a drive shaft or if I gotta build you one."

"You can do that?"

"I could. Got a lathe in the back. Could pull a drive shaft off one a the junkers."

Dollar signs floated in front of my eyes. "Could you give me a ballpark?"

He looked at his boots and fiddled with the brim of his hat. "I'd say anywheres from six hundred to eight hundred bucks."

The heat of the day pressed in around me. I had exactly four hundred eleven dollars and seventy-five cents until my next, and last, paycheck was automatically deposited into my account. And even once that happened, it'd be cutting it close—too close. Then, somewhere, in the back of my hearing, boots crushed against the hard dirt. I focused on Buddy Bud. He was eyeballing a grasshopper that had landed on his drip pan. He made a grab for it. "Two points!" he said holding his sweaty fist in the air.

"Um, would you need it all up front?" I blinked to keep a bead of sweat from running into my eye. "I mean…I can get it, it's just that…"

From behind me, I heard Pastor Williams say, "I think the church may be of some help here. You go ahead and do what you can do, Old Luke, and I'll see what I can do."

I spun around. What was it with this guy? Why did he always show up when things were screwing up for me? "Uh, that's all right! I can—"

He cut me off and spoke in that patronizing tone of his. "We have a program for this kind of situation, Eadie, and Rose and Grace are on the committee that oversees it. I'm sure they wouldn't be opposed to helping you out." He looked back at Luke and executed a small nod and smile, like parents use when dealing with unruly children. "Go ahead and order that part or whatever it is you gotta do."

I wanted to yell, "I can take care of myself!" but obviously, that wasn't the case. I bit back my pride. "Um…Thank you…"

Buddy Bud, releasing the grasshopper from his fist, yelled, "Ice cream time!" Remarkably, the grasshopper was unharmed.

The pastor laughed. "Can't much argue with that."

I ran my fingers through my hair, trying to make sense of what had just come down. *The church is going to pay for my car repairs? Why would they do that?* Something wasn't adding up. I glanced at Pastor Williams, who'd squatted down to finish the sorting. With quick, catlike movements, he managed to make Buddy Bud's accomplishments of the last hour seem like nothing. I glanced over at Old Luke. He was scratching the back of his head as if he too was trying to figure out the pastor's offer.

The hardware sorted, Pastor Williams got to his feet and asked pleasantly, "You need a ride, Eadie?"

Although it seemed hypocritical to accept, not one, but two favors from a guy who I was positive preached fire and brimstone for homosexuals, I accepted.

What choice did I have?

CHAPTER TEN

After Pastor Williams and Buddy Bud dropped me off at my trailer, I finished my journal entry from the night before, snacked on some stale popcorn, wrapped duct tape around a dangerously frayed electrical cord on the fan Heifer had loaned me, and still had half a day to kill before my six o'clock dinner date with Piggin and Heifer. I decided, for lack of anything better, to nose around the old burned-out house.

Another thrilling chapter in the exciting life of Eadie T. Pratt.

Stepping inside its periphery was like stepping back in time. Tucked beneath weeds, embedded in the dirt, wedged under dry rotted boards, were antique nails, bottlecaps, colorful chips of glass, the blade of a steak knife, and other random reminders of human existence. I remembered Piggin saying something about the house burning. It had to do with her brother, but what were the details? An accident? Or could it have been intentional? Either way, the two of them living next door to the burned-down remains of their childhood home was depressing. Why hadn't anyone cleaned it up?

Semi-unconsciously, I began collecting the hodgepodge of debris and placing it at the base of an old brick hearth. With each item, I speculated about its function in their lives. I began by making a circle of blue and green chips of glass. *Old medicinal bottles? A matching set of tumblers?* An old corroded spoon was lying face down in the dirt. *I wonder who used this last?* I placed the spoon inside the circle, making a spoke. Halfway through the circle I started thinking about my own life instead of theirs. How could I get my car fixed without feeling indebted to the pastor?

Who can I call? A gnarled stick that made me think of a magician's wand created another spoke. *I'll ask to borrow Piggin or Heifer's phone.* I picked up a rusted file. *Needy Eadie.* Another stick and a row of pebbles became two more spokes of the wheel. *Peter and Kevin would probably loan me the money.* Unable to find what I needed for a final spoke, I pulled a short pencil from my pocket. *But I'd have to admit I've stalled out on the way to the Womyn's Music Festival, or "Land of Labia" as they insist on calling it.* An undulating line of small round things: bottle tops, washers, buttons. One of the buttons was shaped like a daisy, like it had come off a little girl's dress. *Of course, they'll tell Ruby.* I found another chip of blue glass. *What if she answers the phone?* A knot of thin wire.

I could call Mom… I shaped the wire into a circle. *Maybe for once that new boyfriend of hers won't answer the phone and tell me what a fuckup I am.* I wrapped the wire around the periphery. *Sure, Eadie.* Using, small evenly spaced stones, I weighted the wire down. *Dad?* I stepped back from my creation. *Does his ashram even have a phone?*

My bunny acquaintance from the day before hopped out from beneath his pile of boards.

"What do you think?" I asked him.

He wrinkled his nose.

"So true. It does look like a mandala." Not that I knew shit about mandalas. Just that they were round and supposed to be powerful. I added my pocket change into the design. *Maybe I'll get lucky and it will multiply…*

It made me a tad uneasy when I realized the mandala mixed my story with Piggin and Heifer's. I tossed a pebble and inadvertently scared my bunny friend, sending him scampering off. I was sad to see him go. It's not often one gets along so well with the neighbors.

Massaging my lower back, tender from bending and days of driving, I decided on some exercise. An outlying stand of cottonwoods seemed a good destination. I stopped by my trailer for provisions and started to walk what from the onset looked like a quarter mile, but partway into the miserably hot trek started to seem more like two. The breezeless air was suffocating, the sun relentless. I cursed myself for not changing into sneaks. Small rocks and other ouchy things flipped up the back of my Tevas and lodged beneath the soles of my feet. I rationed my eight-ounce bottle of water.

Once I'd reached the cottonwoods, I was rewarded by a small spring—more of a burble really, but enough to support the several trees and the various shrubs that hugged it. A handful of small tawny birds fluttered from tree to tree, chattering, no doubt, about my arrival. A yellow butterfly flitted among some thistles.

I dipped my bandana into the small pool of clear water and squeezed it over my head. An involuntarily shiver shot up my spine as the cool threads trickled down my dusty face and neck. It felt good: the trees, the water, the birds, all of it. *Potable?* I decided not to risk it. All I needed was to get sick.

A protruding tree root made for a perfect seat; I could lean back on its trunk while dipping my sore feet into the water. I pulled the joint I'd brought with me from my pocket. *And now, folks, it's time for a little inspiration.* Already light-headed from the sun, it didn't take much, just a few tokes, which was good. I was almost out of weed.

My muscles relaxed. My mind went warm and fuzzy. I stretched my arms up and a couple of vertebrae popped into place. Across the spring, a lizard napped on a rock. I leaned back, closed my eyes, and listened to the burbling of the spring, the twitterings of the small band of birds…

❖

I woke disoriented and pushed myself up into a sitting position, my head thick with compressed dreams, all forgotten. *Where am I?* Woozily, I took in the spring, the trees. Long shadows sliced the earth. The birds were gone. *Shit! How long have I been sleeping?*

My neck was kinked. I rolled it from side to side, massaging the nape. *I couldn't have slept through dinner…could I?*

I briskly made my way back to the trailers. The sun, low in the sky, burned into my retinas. My tongue felt woolly. Squinting, I took my last swig of water and tried to make out if Piggin's car was in the driveway. The light made it difficult, turning the Wilbourne homestead into one big lumpy silhouette.

When I finally made it back, sure enough, Piggin's car was right where she'd parked it the other day. I glanced at Heifer's trailer. The lights were out. *They must already be eating.* I continued on to Piggin's, berating myself for having slept so long. Her front door was open.

Through the screen door I could hear them talking. I started toward the steps. Then I heard what Piggin was saying.

"Well, if she does come back, I think we should help her. I mean, I don't suppose I agree with how she chooses to present herself. That hair for one thing, it's just an unruly mop of curls in need of a good styling. And all those pierces, especially the one in her eyebrow. What would make such an attractive girl want to do that to herself? Certainly no man is going to be interested in her looking that way."

Does she think I split? I took a few steps backward around the side of the propane tank.

"She's coming back, Piggin. Her trailer's still here." Heifer sounded irritated.

"Then where is she? She said she'd eat with us."

I cringed. Piggin sounded hurt.

Heifer sighed. "I'm sure there's a logical explanation."

"Pastor said he dropped her off around noon."

"I'm more worried about what *he's* up to than I am about her." I heard what sounded like tin foil being ripped from the box. "Why is he all of a sudden so interested in our Helping Hands Program? Since he's gotten here, he hasn't been one bit supportive of Helping Hands and now all of a sudden he's signing up a girl who doesn't even go to our church."

"Heifer, just because Eadie doesn't attend Rauston Baptist doesn't mean she's not deserving." Piggin pushed through the screen door onto the porch.

I hunched down behind the propane tank, praying she wouldn't see me. Oblivious, she shook out her dish towel and walked back inside letting the door bang closed behind her.

Heifer persisted, "I'm just saying, I don't trust his motives."

"That is downright hateful of you, Heifer! I don't know why you insist on carrying this grudge about the church hiring him. I know he wasn't your first choice…"

"Or second!"

"Well, the Elders didn't see it that way—and still don't't! And frankly, neither do I. He's got big plans for Rauston Baptist."

"That's exactly what I *am* worried about!"

The sounds of cabinets opening and closing, water running, and the squeaking of the trailer on its cinder blocks followed. *Should I interrupt? Act as if I've just showed up and not heard any of this?* I took a tentative step forward. A twig snapped under the weight of my foot. The trailer grew quiet. I crouched down.

Heifer began again, this time in a much quieter tone. "Doesn't he ever remind you, just a little bit, of J.D.?"

Something crashed to the floor. Piggin screeched, "Now look what you went and made me do! There's milk everywhere!"

They continued to argue above the sounds of water filling a bucket and a broom sweeping up broken glass.

Heifer spoke with shortened breath, as if her labors were strenuous. "Didn't mean to upset you."

"Why can't you let bygones be bygones? Why do you always have to dredge up the awful in folks? Daddy had his problems. He drank too much and he wasn't always as Christian as he could have been. I know that! But he was not a bad man! He wasn't! And neither is Pastor Williams. He's devoted his life to Jesus. What more do you want, Heifer?"

Broken glass slid from dustpan to trash can.

"I'm sorry I said a word," Heifer mumbled.

"You are not! You're just plain hateful sometimes!"

Feeling like the ultimate eavesdropping sleaze, I began to wend my way back to my trailer. I'd make my excuses later. I thought back on Heifer's words, "J.D. never could stand any of the boys taking his Rosie's attention." An uneasy feeling grew in my stomach.

I'd just made it back to the path when the door flung open. I jumped. I could hear one of them coming out onto the porch. Not wanting to be caught walking away, I pivoted on the ball of my foot and began walking toward whichever sister it was, as if I were just now showing up for dinner. Heifer was draping a wet throw rug over the railing. Unsure if she'd seen me, I said, "Hey," and raised my hand up. Belatedly, I realized I should have sounded remorseful for having missed dinner.

"Well, look who it is."

"Uh, sorry I missed—"

"Meet me over at my place. I'll be there in a minute."

From inside I heard Piggin ask, "Is that Eadie?"

Heifer went back into the trailer and the two of them talked some more, but I didn't stick around to listen. I'd heard enough as it was.

❖

Horizontal swatches of fuchsia and orange slanted across the turquoise sky. In the distant east, a flat-topped thunderhead tossed angry forks of lightning. A meadowlark, like the one I'd seen at Old Luke's, sat on a utility pole singing a song so glorious, so uncompromising, you'd think the sun couldn't set without her.

Sitting on Heifer's stoop, I had a hard time appreciating any of it. I focused on the bats, swooping for bugs like kamikaze pilots, but pulling out at the last second. I tossed a pebble up in the air to see if I could fake out their radar. It worked. I tried it again. It worked again. Apparently, they were no smarter than humans.

Piggin's screen door banged shut. I watched Heifer undertake the arduous process of hauling her weight down the three steps. She used the handrail like a cripple. *God, I hope I never get that fat.* Once on flat ground her stride became purposeful, right in my direction.

"Here," she said thrusting a tinfoiled plate at me, "Piggin wrapped up your dinner."

I took it from her, said, "Thanks," and stepped aside to let her past. "You know if I'm getting in the way…"

"How can you get in the way when you're not here?"

"Look, I'm sorry about that. I fell asleep by the spring. You know, by the cottonwoods…"

This stopped her. "You been out to the spring?"

I nodded.

"Lord, I haven't been out there in years. Used to be J.D.'s favorite drinking spot. Mama'd send us out there looking for him." She opened the door and a cool blast of air escaped. "You had Piggin worried somethin' awful."

"I'm sorry. Maybe I should go apologize."

"Save it for later."

I stood on her stoop unsure what to do next.

"Well, don't let all the cool air out, girl. Come on in."

She flicked on the light and stood just inside the door. "Don't that feel good? Piggin likes to go without air-conditioning in the evenings. Says it's better for her skin." She flicked on the light. "But I can't stand going without my air conditioner."

Heifer's trailer had none of the cutesy dressings of Piggin's. Instead, it had a practical quality, like a job-site trailer, except immaculate. The colors were the muted golds and browns of the seventies. One wall even had that tacky crackle-mirror effect. The curtains were drawn, blotting out the sunset.

She indicated one of two wooden kitchen chairs. "Sit."

I did.

She opened a kitchen drawer and pulled out a fork and knife. "Water or Coke?"

I placed my plate on the table. "Water would be great." In truth, I wanted to drink water from my own fridge in my own trailer while I ate at my own table, but I'd already screwed up this dinner thing once. "I guess I got dehydrated. I think that's why I fell asleep. It sure gets hot here. I can't believe how long I slept."

Heifer seemed to be somewhere else, so I shut up and watched her fill my glass from the tap. She placed the water by my plate. "Don't get much company here. Mostly we hang out at Piggin's."

I was struck by her use of the term "hang out." It didn't seem natural for her, and I had the impression she was using it on my account, trying to sound cool. She sat down opposite me, gesturing with her Coke can. "Well, dive in. You missed them at their best."

I peeled back the tinfoil. A cloud of savory steam wafted up: Chicken and dumplings and a side of green beans with crunchy fried onions on top. Suddenly, I was starving. "This smells great."

As I pigged out on fluffy, gravy-coated pillows, she went on to describe the Helping Hands Program, how she and Piggin had started it, how a portion of the tithes went to a fund that could be drawn on by church members in need, but in return they had to work off the money. There was a list of projects, she said, that other church members needed help on.

"So how do I fit in?" I asked piercing another dumpling. "I'm not a church member. And no offense, but I don't plan on joining."

She stood to get me a napkin. "Didn't suppose you would. All you kids are the same, think you don't need it."

It seemed the wrong time to bring up the patriarchal overthrow of the early goddess religions, so I shifted gears. "I just don't see how…"

She stood for a moment, paper napkin in hand, looking through me. "Pastor's got something up his sleeve."

"Excuse me?" This was the last thing I expected her to say. I'd thought we were talking about me.

She handed me the napkin. "How he's got it figured is, since you're our guest, you're entitled. Makes sense, I suppose, in a way. Piggin and I have never made use of the program and we've put an awful lot into it." The counter, as she leaned back on it, cut into her flesh. "But it's going to rile some folks."

"I don't want to cause any conflict," I said, wiping a blob of gravy off my shirt.

She drummed the side of her Coke can, lost in thought. "I suppose we just go along. See what he's up to."

This was getting interesting. "So, you want to use me as bait?"

"You'll need to go to church, of course. People need to see you. We go three times a week."

A fried onion got caught in my throat. *Three?*

Shuffling over to a stack of papers on the kitchen cabinet, she said, "I've got a copy of the list around here somewheres. Been fixin' to retype it." She donned a pair of Dean Edell's and began flipping through the pile, stopping on a pink Xeroxed sheet. "Here we go." She adjusted her cheaters. "You any good with kids? They're needing some help at Sunday School."

I shook my head. The idea of leading a bunch of snivelers in singing hymns suddenly made walking to the Michigan Music Festival seem like a real option.

"You could read Betty Simon her romance novels. She's eighty-seven, blind as a bat, but she loves her romance novels."

Now this was more up my alley. I could get my car fixed by reading about "throbbing members" and "quickening pulses." What a gas.

"Says 'Must be willing to do bathroom duty.'"

I cringed. "Next?"

"Jameson, down at the market, wants some painting done."

"That could be a bingo. Is that the place Old Luke was talking about? The one that was being forced to join World Mart's 'wave'?"

She looked over her reading glasses at me. "You ever done that kind of work?"

"Sure. I've done wall repair too. That is if he needs it. I was low man, or woman, in a drywalling enterprise."

"You seem kind of small for it."

"Hey," I said, making a muscle. "I can hold my own with the best of them."

Amused, she put the list by the phone. "I'll talk to the committee, and to Jameson. He's a good man. Got a boy, though, Buddy Bud, he's a little slow."

"I met him at Old Luke's."

Again she scrutinized me over her reading glasses; this time, however, she didn't say anything.

"I liked him," I said. "He's a good kid. And for being a little slow, he's pretty smart."

She nodded. "He is that. He'll use it too. Got me to give him three helpings of dessert once."

I laughed.

"What was he doing at Old Luke's?"

"The Pastor dropped him off before going to visit some woman."

"Reenie Peterson?"

"I think so."

She shook her head, then, went to get herself another Coke. "Poor Reenie. Gotten a real case of sad since high school."

"Maybe she should have tried leaving Rauston." My words came out snottier than I'd intended.

She popped the top of her soda can. "Oh, she did, but she was an only child, so when her mama died, the whole property went to her. Just now moved back. Brought a gem of a husband with her too. Roy's his name. You'll hear about him at church. He's a gift from God, that man is. Works in investments and has got us hooked up with one that's really paying off. It's going to help fund the new church."

It was such a relief to have moved on to a topic that didn't involve me that I asked, "So why do you think she's so unhappy?"

She shrugged. "Piggin'll tell you it's 'cuz she couldn't have kids, that she can't quite get right with God about it. Piggin's got a real sense about these things. S'pose that's why Reenie's been spending so much time with the pastor. She's trying to understand God's plan."

That, or the pastor's giving her a little something old Roy couldn't.

She picked my empty plate up off the table and brought it to the sink.

I stood to leave.

She turned, leveling me with her gaze. "If it was me stranded by the side of the road, what would you have done?"

Suddenly, I couldn't pry my eyes from a list of numbers she had taped by her phone. They were all in neat columns with names written by them. "Um, I would have done the same."

She let out a snort-laugh and crossed her arms. "You would."

I forced myself to look at her. "Uh, yeah." The expression on her face made me want to defend myself. *The city's different. People don't help each other in the same way.* But my excuses were lies. I would've passed her by, because all I would've seen was a fat piece of trailer trash. Yet here she was going out of her way for me. She and her sister were doing more for me than my so-called friends would have.

Busted, I slumped back down in my chair. "I don't know. That's the real answer. I don't know what I would have done."

She cocked her head and put her hands on her hips. "You good for this? I don't want to get this whole thing rolling if you're just going to skip out."

Like a kid in the principal's office, full of good intentions, but short on discipline, I nodded. "I'm good for it."

❖

Later that evening, back in The Egg, I was drawing in my journal. The image I was working on was a road with an abrupt left turn. There was a soft rapping on the door. I didn't need to get up. My table was about two feet from the door. "Hey, Piggin, what's up?"

She was dressed in the same muumuu and house shoes she wore earlier, and held a flashlight and a small plate. "I hope I didn't wake you," she said, switching off the flashlight.

"No, no. I was just in here drawing."

"You an artist?"

"More of a scribbler."

She shifted from one foot to the other as if something were bothering her.

"You want to come in? I have a little couch in here."

"That's all right." She peeked in. "Looks real cute, though." She thrust the plate toward me. The rhinestones on her fingernails flashed in the light of my trailer. "I brought you some brownies. I keep 'em in the freezer, so they might still be a little cold."

I took the plate. "Thanks," I said and figured that would be the end of it, but she didn't leave.

"Just wanted to let you know we're real happy to have you here." Due to the dark, it was difficult to see her expression, but I had the feeling she'd been crying.

I waited. Why had she come? We stood at the door like teenagers on a first date, waiting for someone to make the first move. She finally gave in.

"I've asked the Milsaps to return our ranch truck for a spell. That way you can have some wheels," she said offhandedly.

"You're kidding. That would be awesome."

"Well, it's something."

"I can't figure out why you guys are being so nice."

She looked pleased. "We're real proud of Helping Hands."

"You sure you don't want to come in?" I could tell she had something on her mind besides the truck and Helping Hands.

"No, I need to get to bed." She flicked on her flashlight and turned to leave, but stopped before taking a step. "You'll find nothing but love here." She said this with her back to me.

Unsure how to respond, I said, "I get that," and nodded my head like she could see me.

"Well, good." Her tone had an air of finality, as if she'd gotten something big off her chest. "You have a nice night, now. Don't let those bedbugs bite."

As I watched her waddle away, haloed in light, I wondered, *What went on in this family?*

CHAPTER ELEVEN

Piggin and Heifer were off at work, so once again, I had the place to myself, which made me a tad uneasy. It would have been one thing if I'd been a good Texas Christian who'd fallen on bad times, or a family member, but they didn't know me from Adam. They were leaving themselves wide open. Piggin had even left her trailer unlocked so I could make myself lunch. Didn't she know there were evil people out in the world ready to pounce on this kind of kindness? "Crash Milsap'll be coming by this morning with the truck," she'd said before leaving. "If he's thirsty, there's Cokes in the fridge."

I cursed myself for being too ethical to consider burglary, and resigned myself to wait for him.

I hate waiting. I'm way too nervous.

I distracted myself by doing more poking around their weed-infested acreage. That is, until my shin cracked into an iron stake. A lone horseshoe sat next to it. This gave me a mission, which was exactly what I needed to keep my mind off waiting: Find the other stake. The density of the weeds made the search difficult, grasshoppers leaping this way and that, but once I found the stake, I also found the other three horseshoes. From the looks of the spread, I deduced the last game had been interrupted years ago and no one had touched them since. I cleared the path from stake to stake, yanking weeds and raking the dirt with an old broken-toothed rake. *If only the crap in my brain and heart could be scraped up this easily.* Of course that was a laugh. It would take a squad of bulldozers to move the kind of disillusionment weighing me down.

Once the area was reasonably cleaned up, I began tossing shoes.

By eleven thirty my horseshoe game had greatly improved, but there was still no sign of the Milsap kid.

What if he doesn't show? I'll be stuck here all day.

I tossed some more.

By twelve there was still no sign of him and I really started getting antsy. There were things I needed to do: grocery shop, check in with Old Luke. I considered calling Piggin and asking her for the Milsaps' number, but felt I was already being nuisance enough. I did a few yoga stretches, avoiding a sun salutation—it was doing a fine job without me—while using the tail of my T-shirt to mop the sweat from my face.

At twelve fifteen an ancient Ford pick-up screamed into the driveway, fishtailing to a stop. I raised my hand over my eyes, trying to get a bead on the kid getting out of the truck through the sizable cloud of dust he'd stirred up. About sixteen, torn-up T-shirt, Levi's 501s with split knees, boots, and ball cap. He looked like he had something to prove, and that always makes me nervous.

I swaggered over, trying to project that I could hold my own. "You Crash?" He was a good foot taller than me.

He slouched and squinted his eyes. "Yup."

I could see him trying to figure me out. Clearly, I wasn't the two-stepping kind of filly he was used to. I thrust my hand out. "Eadie."

"I know." He reached out a callused hand with grease under the fingernails.

I prepared for a monster grip, but it never came. Just your basic how-do-you-do handshake.

Once we'd gotten that out of the way, he did that gross thing that teenage boys do. He crossed his arms, tucking each hand under an armpit. I hoped this wasn't one of his regular moves, as I'd just touched one of those hands.

"It sure is nice of you to bring the truck over."

"Had to take it to the dump first. It was filled with tires."

"You in the tire business?"

"Naw. Pa was fixing to make bed liners for trucks out of 'em. That was about two years ago. Got everybody to bring him used tires."

"Sounds like a good idea. Recycling's always a good thing."

He gave me this look like I'd just said, "Yes, I eat used tires with ketchup," then bent down, picked up a pebble, and hurled it at the road; a gnarled ponytail hung from beneath his ball cap. "'Bout three months ago Ma got fed up with his tires all over the place and asked to borrow Piggin and Heifer's truck so we could load 'em up. When Pa seen what we did, he wouldn't let us toss 'em. Them tires been sitting in the truck ever since."

"He's not going to be pissed you junked them?"

He shrugged, studiously keeping his eyes off me, picked up another pebble, and hurled it. "Guess we'll find out."

We entered an uncomfortable silence. At least it was for me. He was looking out at the road as if it held great meaning, and I was looking at him—the side of his head, actually, where his cap tucked behind his ear. *Great, a showdown. Who's going to speak first?*

Determined not to be the one to break, I also picked up a pebble and flung it toward the blacktop. The boldness of the act felt good, and it occurred to me this wasn't a bad way to deal with awkward situations at all. Just throw rocks, for God's sake! I picked up another, this time adding the descending whistle of a bomb dropping from a plane. When the pebble hit the blacktop I vocalized an explosion.

After my fifth pebble detonation, Crash broke. "You're crazy!"

I halted my Attack of the Exploding Rocks and did Groucho Marx eyebrows at him. "More fun than being normal. You want a soda before I drive you back?" I've no idea what prompted this act of hospitality on my part, but it surprised both of us.

"Um, I guess."

We made our way toward Piggin's trailer, he, stopping to remove his cap and shake his head as if trying to dump his thoughts onto the ground. Sixteen is such an awkward age.

"You okay?" I asked.

He flipped his head up and secured his cap back in place. "You're sure not who I was figuring on!"

This thing he had for talking about me like he knew all about me was starting to annoy. "How so?"

"Let's just say we don't get too many punk rockers around here."

"Punk rocker, huh?" I generally preferred to think of myself as an Urban Renaissance Dyke.

He shrugged. "Ain't that what you are?"

I decided it was pointless to try to educate him. With any luck, I'd never see him again anyway. I slipped inside Piggin's to get the Cokes. He made no move to follow. When I returned, he was sitting on the deck with his back against the railing and his cap tipped down hiding all of his face but his mouth. I had the impression he was trying to look studly. I handed him his Coke, and since he hadn't snagged the porch swing, I did.

"So how did you get your name?" I asked, sounding more schoolteacher-y than I would have wished.

I watched his mouth form the words. "Used to break stuff as a kid, I guess." The way he emphasized the words "as a kid" made it sound like this was decades ago.

I waited for him to elaborate, maybe offer a specific or two, but he was too busy trying to appear manly, rhythmically tapping his finger on his can as if listening to music. I racked my brain for other topics that might get him talking. The best I could come up with was, "You like living here?"

He shrugged and took a sip of his soda.

I took one of mine.

He sipped.

I sipped.

God, this is tiresome!

Then, as if he were picking up a previous conversation, he asked, "Did it hurt?"

I answered him in my most nonchalant who-gives-a-shit voice. "What's that?"

He indicated my eyebrow.

Of course! The wicked eyebrow ring. "At first, yeah. Not now, though."

He crushed his can, one-handed, and dropped it by his leg, then crossed his arms over his chest and did the armpit thing again. "My pa would kill me if I did that. He's already pissed enough that I won't cut my hair. Says he's gonna cut my hair off some night when I'm sleeping."

I couldn't help but smile. My mom had made similar threats to me, only hers had involved dragging me to the beauty parlor in my sleep. "That's what so great about turning eighteen. You can move out and do what you want."

He thought over my answer. "Only way my turning eighteen will change anything is if I leave Rauston. Folks around here, they're just…" He didn't finish his sentence, but I knew what he meant. Rauston didn't seem like the kind of place that was too big on following the beat of your own drum.

He peeked up from under the brim of his cap and said, “I think it’s cool.”

That’s when it dawned on me that the kid was trying to impress me. Me! An unhealthy role model if ever there was one. The realization almost made me spit out my soda. “So what do you say we blow this joint and get you back home?”

“Cool.”

As we walked to the truck, I was amused by how my insight into his motives had shifted my perception. Mr. Bad-ass had turned into goofy puppy. I swear, the kid trailed so close behind me he nearly gave my sneaker a flat tire.

“You got any tattoos?” he asked.

I showed him the wing of my dragon. To do this I had to pull up my T-shirt sleeve. “This is why I haven’t gone sleeveless since I entered Texas.” I said letting the sleeve drop. He blushed, I suppose because he was imagining where the rest of the tattoo went.

“I’m gonna get me one some day too. Just haven’t figured out what yet.” Then he showed me how to check the gas gauge. It involved using a coat hanger. “Other’n that, she works pretty good. ’Course there’s no air conditioner. And this one window, here, takes two hands.”

I got in and adjusted the seat so I could reach the pedals. “You got some long legs, my friend.”

He smiled shyly. “I guess.”

It was hard not to like him, considering if I’d grown up in Rauston, I’d probably be just like him, a kid dying for bohemia. Hell, if I’d grown up in Rauston, I’d have run away with the circus, stowed away on a UPS truck, anything that would have offered me a broader scope. Still, I didn’t much care for being a role model. Way too much pressure.

Using the choke took a little practice, but once I got the truck started, she had quite a rumble. I pulled out onto the blacktop.

Driving a truck in Rauston, I realized, was going to have its advantages. Not only was it high enough to take the back roads, but also I’d be incognito, blending in with all the other old trucks.

That, and I’d be big. And big, in Texas, is a good thing.

Crash directed me to a dirt-road shortcut. When I glanced over at him, his finger drumming on the side of the truck to that music only he could hear, I thought to myself if this kid had grown up in San Francisco he'd probably be sporting dreads and tie-dye. Then I had a bolt of inspiration.

"Crash, you know where I can get some pot?"

His fingers stopped drumming, as if his private music source had been suddenly switched off. I began to panic. *Shit! Did I misjudge him?* Visions of some redneck sheriff handcuffing me and dragging me off to the county jail came to mind.

Thankfully, his fingers started up again. "How much you want?"

As I pulled off the irrigation road and back onto the highway, we talked through the specifics. He told me he'd drop it by sometime tomorrow. I asked him to try to make it in the middle of the day so Piggin and Heifer wouldn't be around. He thought this was a good idea too.

We came up on the dilapidated half-trailer, half add-on with the swamp cooler set up on the porch that I'd passed with Piggin the first day here. He asked me not to pull into the driveway and seemed uneasy. I understood immediately. I was the same way as a kid. I never knew how drunk my mom would be, or how inappropriate my dad.

I pulled onto the berm by their mailbox. "The Milsaps" had been painted onto the curved aluminum without much planning. The P and the S cascaded down the side of the box in order to fit.

I put the truck in neutral and pulled my wallet from a satchel.

Crash picked a scab on his knuckle as I peeled off the fifty bucks for my pot. I could tell he wanted to say something.

I handed him three tens and a twenty.

He stuffed the money in his pocket. "So you're going to be doing Helping Hands."

"Yeah," I said cautiously. "How did you know?"

He pushed the button on the glove box causing it to spring open. "It's supposed to be anonymous, 'cept everybody always knows who's gettin' it." He slammed it shut. "My dad works for Helping Hands sometimes too."

"Oh yeah?"

He returned to his scab, this time sucking the knuckle. "Not everybody's happy about someone outside of Rauston Baptist getting the money."

Unconsciously, I pushed in the truck's clutch. "How do they…"

But he opened the truck door and hopped out. "Don't worry," he said leaning on the open door. "I'll stand up for you. Just watch out for my dad." He slammed the truck door shut and made his way across the berm toward his house, turning to wave good-bye when he reached the dirt front yard. The wave was actually more of a "go on now, don't get me in trouble."

In lieu of a wave, I shot him a peace sign, then revved the engine.

It was time to check out this Jameson's Market. I needed to see what the hell I was getting myself into.

CHAPTER TWELVE

Jameson's Market was right off a Norman Rockwell canvas: hardwood floors, molded tin ceiling, shelves trimmed in polished aluminum that were neatly stocked and marked clearly. Handwritten notices said, ADD A KICK TO YOUR POTATO SALAD WITH PICKLE JUICE! AND SAY GOOD-BYE TO UNWANTED CALORIES!!! HAVE A MELON SLICE FOR DESSERT! The three checkout stands were free of conveyer belts—not a bar code or club card scanner in sight—and the two cashiers chatted with the customers as they cheerfully typed in prices they either knew by heart or found on little orange stickers stuck to each item. One cashier looked like Barbara Bush, the other like a young Patty Duke, flippy hairdo and all.

I was next up in Patty Duke's line.

A kid in Barbara Bush's line tugged on his mother's sleeve and asked if she'd seen my ears and eyebrow. "They're tagged! Just like the sheep in 4-H!"

I smiled and did one of those forced isn't-he-so-cute chuckles, but Mom refused to make eye contact.

As the small market didn't carry hummus or baba ganoush, two of my usual staples, I'd stocked up on peanut butter, a bunch of bananas, a too-soft loaf of wheat bread, canned coffee, half-and-half, raisins, some unknown brand of yogurt, a few apples, a box of tampons, dishwashing liquid and a sponge, chips and salsa, a family size bag of M&Ms, and a roll of T.P. I put my hand basket down. Our line had come to a halt. Patty Duke was discussing a Jell-O recipe with an octogenarian couple. The two of them were purchasing a tub of Cool Whip, and I got the feeling Jameson's was a daily excursion for them, that they'd find excuses to come, a box of instant chocolate pudding, a can of tuna, just so they could visit with friends. I pictured their cabinets overrun with items they didn't need.

In the other line folks were talking about some fair they'd all been to or knew about. They were also studiously ignoring me.

"I was surprised Irma Cook didn't enter her apple butter this year," the mom of the snotty kid said.

"Now, you know her arthritis has been acting up on her something awful. I think it was just too much for the poor dear," Barbara Bush replied.

A matronly thirtysomething piped in, "I do believe I'd have put mine in if I'd known she wasn't entering. I might have actually placed, for a change."

They all laughed.

I shoved my basket forward with my foot, assuring myself they weren't actually speaking in some kind of code. I'd come in hoping to get a look at Jameson, but a big-eared stock clerk had told me he was out to lunch.

In an effort to fit in, I picked up an Enquirer and began flipping through the pages. Some cruel photographer had snapped way too many pictures of famous actresses' cellulite.

A commotion by the door pulled my attention from Julia Roberts's bikinied butt. Buddy Bud had his hands to his head and a horrified look on his face. Around his feet were a few dozen boxes of Diamond Blue Tip Matches, which moments before had been neatly displayed on a shelf by the entrance. An extraordinarily tall man stood next to him. He looked tired. *Jameson?*

"Pick them up, son," he said.

"I will, Dad!"

It was Jameson all right.

Buddy Bud dropped to his knees and began scooping the matchboxes up, crushing them to his chest.

"Careful." Jameson sighed.

"Well, look who's back," Barbara Bush chimed. "How was lunch?"

"Grrrrreat!" Buddy Bud responded, glancing up from his pile of matchboxes. "Tuna melt and potato chips!" As he replaced the boxes on the shelf, I noticed he still wore some of his lunch dribbled down the front of his Angelina Jolie Tomb Raider T-shirt.

The old woman in front of me picked up her Cool Whip and, followed by her doddering husband, made her way toward Jameson and Buddy Bud.

Jameson, easily a foot taller that anyone else in the vicinity, bent forward and took her palsied hand. "How are you, Effie? Snookie? You find what you need today?" Patience hung on his shoulders like weary wings.

"Is that the owner?" I asked Patty Duke.

She eyed me suspiciously. "We're not currently hiring, if that's what you're asking." She punched in the price of my Skippy.

Before I could tell her where to shove her attitude, Buddy Bud spotted me.

"Two points!" he yelled.

I smiled and waved. "Hey, Buddy Bud! How's it going?"

"Going good, Eadie! Going good! I had a tuna melt samwich and potato chips!" He took his father's hand and began to yank him in my direction. Jameson let himself be dragged along, tossing an apology to Effie and Snookie over his shoulder.

"Dad! Dad! 'Member I told you about my new friend Eadie? The one who's really nice? The one who gave me a doughnut and showed me about two points? This is her!"

I could have kissed his oversized forehead. Just like that, he'd transformed me into an insider. On the other side of the counter, Patty Duke's face twisted into a smile so forced it came out more like a grimace. She was obviously unable to put the freak in front of her and the concept of "really nice" into the same thought.

I reached my hand out to Jameson. "Hi, Mr. Jameson. I probably should have called before I came…"

"Oh, yes," he said, a charmingly crooked smile lighting up his face. "You're going to be helping me with some painting. Somehow I hadn't put two and two together, that you're the same person that Buddy Bud talked about." His words made it sound as if I'd already been hired, which was a tad unsettling.

"That's okay. No reason for you to. I had some shopping to do, so I figured I'd just come check things out."

Patty Duke, who'd finished totaling my groceries, said in a fake-happy voice, "That'll be thirty-one seventy-five."

"Thirty-one seventy-five!" Buddy Bud repeated.

Jameson put his hand on Buddy Bud's shoulder, "Give her the employee discount, Kitty."

Patty Duke, against what was obviously her better judgment, made sure to stare a few daggers at me before punching in the discount. "Twenty-eight fifty-eight."

I wish I could say I was a better person and didn't revel in her loss of face, but it couldn't have tasted better. I pulled out my wallet and handed her two twenties.

"While you're here," Jameson began, "why don't you come upstairs and I'll show you what we've got going on?" He turned to Patty Duke. "Kitty, would you mind putting her perishables in the refrigerator? I think Hazel can handle the customers."

She made a point not to look at me. "Of course, Mr. Jameson."

I followed Jameson and Buddy Bud to the back of the store and up a creaking wooden staircase, leading to the private sanctum of the market. It was a cluttered office on a mezzanine; a window next to his desk looked down onto the entire market.

Jameson walked over to a coffeemaker. "Can I offer you some coffee, Miss…?"

"Eadie T. Pratt. But please, just call me Eadie."

"Would you like some coffee, Eadie?"

"Sure. That would be nice."

"Cream? Sugar?"

Before I had a chance to answer, the phone rang.

He signaled me to serve myself and answered it. "Jameson speaking."

I fixed myself a cup of what smelled like excellent French or Italian roast and poured real half-and-half into it. My taste buds couldn't wait.

Jameson hunched over his desk, elbows resting on the desktop calendar, phone in one hand, the other hand on his forehead. I sat down and sipped on the gloriously dark, oily brew and tried to appear as if I wasn't listening in. It was easy at first, as he wasn't saying anything besides, "I see…I see…Sure…"

Buddy Bud tightened the laces on his shoes.

Then the conversation got meatier.

"That's quite an offer. Certainly something to think over…Yes, I can see how it would help with 'the transition,' as you call it…No, I couldn't possibly make that kind of decision on such quick notice. To be honest with you, sir, I'm in the middle of a meeting…All right…" He took out a pencil and scrawled out a number. "I'll get back to you…I'm not sure I'll have an answer for you by then, but I'll give it some thought…Thank you…Thank you…" He hung up the phone, but continued to stare at it as if it were a traitor.

I glanced over at Buddy Bud, whose antennae were tuned into his father's change of mood as well.

Jameson tapped the side of his face with the pencil as he spoke. "Well, isn't that the darndest thing? World Mart just offered me a job. A management position."

"Is that those bad men, Dad? The ones trying to 'change the face of Rauston'?"

Jameson sighed. "They're not bad, Buddy. Just businessmen."

Satisfied that no one was threatening him or his father, Buddy Bud went back to fiddling with an untied shoelace. "Hazel says they're 'rotten to the core'!"

Jameson looked at me apologetically, then walked over to help his son tie his shoe. "She's just worried, Buddy. Sometimes folks say things they don't mean when they're worried."

"Like when you yelled at me on the ladder?"

"That's right, Buddy. Like when you were on the ladder."

Shoe double-knotted, Buddy Bud stood. "I got to go to the baffroom."

"Okay, Buddy. But after the bathroom, I've got a job for you."

"Okay, Dad!"

Once Buddy Bud had left the office, Jameson began to fix himself a cup of coffee. "Sorry about that. I don't mean to waste your time."

"It's all right. I haven't really made too many commitments yet."

He laughed. "That sounds nice." He returned to his desk, coffee in hand.

Maybe it was the fact that he kind of looked like Abe Lincoln—without the beard; or how patient he was with Buddy Bud; or that he was one of the first people I'd met since coming to Rauston who didn't appear to be personally insulted by my style. Whatever it was, I found myself growing a soft spot for Jameson.

He showed me the shelves he wanted painted. They were the ones next to his desk surrounding the window overlooking the store.

"I've been meaning to do this since Buddy Bud's mama died four years ago."

"I'm sorry," I said.

"Thank you." He looked, for a moment, as if he was going to say more about the loss of his wife, then moved on to the logistics of painting the shelves. He asked me if I'd be willing to work with Buddy Bud. He'd wanted it to be a father/son project, but between running the market and keeping things going at home, he never seemed to find the time. "I think he could be good at painting. He's very meticulous. If someone would just take the time to teach him…"

I told him I'd be happy to work with Buddy Bud, and we arranged for me to arrive the next day at nine a.m.

The worry lines on his forehead relaxed briefly. "I'll try not to get in your way too much."

"More like, we'll try not to get in yours," I joked. I couldn't believe how this was working out. Painting his shelves would be cake. *Michigan Womyn's Festival, here I come!*

He leaned as far back in his office chair as it would let him, his long legs allowing his feet to stay firmly planted on the floor, his coffee cup supported against his belly. "I'm doing this for Buddy Bud."

I nodded that I understood, although I wasn't sure I did.

"Times are changing, and I'm not sure places like this will survive."

Wait. I thought we were talking about Buddy Bud and painting.

He continued. "…I guess it was bound to happen, hard as we tried to keep them out…"

Okay. We've moved on to World Mart.

I pictured the two octogenarians who had been in line in front of me negotiating a self-serve register at a giant retailer, her palsied hands turning the item round and round as she searched out the bar code while he tried to figure out which buttons on the scanner to push.

Buddy Bud burst into the room. "Dad! Dad! When I went downstairs to the baffroom…"

With one last sigh, Jameson shrugged off his melancholy and slipped into dad mode. "Buddy Bud, you know how we've talked about knocking."

"I know, but—"

"Catch your breath."

"But—"

"Catch your breath, son."

Buddy Bud transferred his weight to the outside edges of his feet, crossed his arms, and zipped his lips horizontally.

Jameson glanced at me, his expression one of mild embarrassment that I'd seen him in such a vulnerable state. "Buddy's working on not being quite so wound up," he said before returning his focus to Buddy Bud. "You okay, Bud?"

Buddy Bud nodded.

"Would you like to hear some good news?"

Buddy Bud nodded again.

"You're going to be doing a project with Eadie."

Buddy Bud pressed his arms to his sides and lifted his eyebrows. "Cool!" He then abandoned this stance and rushed me, nearly knocking me off my chair with his hug.

Jameson smiled. "So much for containment."

"I love Eadie!" Buddy Bud crooned, his arms locked around me. "I love her, love her, love her, love her!"

I chuckled self-consciously. Outward expressions of affection have never been my strong point. Fortunately, Jameson bailed me out.

"Buddy Bud, what was it you came in here to tell me?"

Buddy Bud released me from his vise grip. "Mrs. Franklin is upset that we're all out of that nice tea-rose soap that she likes and wants to know if you're going to order more."

Jameson downed the last of his coffee and stood. "I'll go down and talk to her."

As the three of us trooped down the narrow stairway, Jameson in the lead, me next, and Buddy Bud conga-lining in the rear, Jameson said, "Might not be such a bad thing to have someone else to do the ordering."

I didn't believe him for a second.

Chapter Thirteen

Before preparing my first in-trailer dinner, a good old peanut butter and banana sandwich with a side of chips and salsa followed by a sliced apple and some M&Ms, I popped over to Piggin's to give her an update on my working for Jameson and thank her for letting me use the truck. I considered stopping by Heifer's first, but, as usual, her place looked uninhabited. I found her at Piggin's. The two of them were sitting at the table with a tiny, lively woman with big, big hair. It was teased out six inches beyond her skull and sculpted into a do that would give Tammy Faye a run for her money.

"Don't tell me, this must be Eadie," she said when I poked my head in the door. "I've heard all about you."

What have they told her? I thought as I smiled my biggest smile. *That I'm Rauston Baptist's Helping Hands Recipient of the Month?*

"Eadie, this is Reenie Peters," Piggin said.

"Hi, Reenie." I tried to keep my thoughts from showing on my face. *Her and Pastor Williams doing the nasty is too hilarious. Him in those boots and her with that hair!* "I'm just going to stay a minute."

"Doesn't mean you can't sit down," Reenie said, patting the outer edge of her hair as if talking might muss it. Her nails were painted with those extra-white tips. "I was just about to leave an hour ago, wasn't I, ladies?"

Piggin and Heifer both laughed. All three were drinking Piggin's sweet tea, and it looked like they had quite a caffeine buzz going.

"How you liking Mayberry, Eadie?"

"Before you sit, get yourself a glass from the shelf," Piggin said.

I grabbed a tumbler and pulled up a small chrome stepstool by Reenie.

"Reenie's the one donating the land for the new church," Piggin said.

Perhaps it was the size of her hair that had kept me from noting the size of her breasts right off. They were mammoth. Her comparatively slender waist was defined by a silver concho belt that pulled in her pink and white seersucker western-style dress, accentuating her breasts to their fullest. A discreet flash of silver betrayed the pins holding back the straps of what I imagined was a white Playtex Cross Your Heart bra.

"Mama, God rest her soul, loved that little church. It's her you should be thanking. I swear, ever since she died and left me the ranch she's been nudging me to do something for Rauston Baptist. Besides, I want to see Mama again. Lord knows I don't want her up there waitin' for eternity. She'd never forgive me."

Piggin laughed out loud while Heifer simply smiled and shook her head in amusement. The two of them obviously got a kick out of Reenie, and I could see why. The woman had sparkle.

"Lady Frank, Reenie's mama, died last year," Piggin explained. "That's when Reenie moved back home."

"Used to live in Houston," Heifer added from her spot by the droning swamp cooler.

"Brought her wonderful husband with her too. He's been such a blessing for Rauston!"

Reenie laughed. "I swear, Eadie, you ever seen a town so small?"

I admitted I hadn't, and took a swig of the sweet tea.

"I was telling Pastor Williams just the other day, nothing has changed since I left. 'Cept of course the Dairy Queen. It's quite an improvement from…"

"Shakey's Burgers!" the three of them chimed.

I listened politely while they recounted good times, and not so good times, at Shakey's. Then, because I couldn't rein in my bratty self, I said. "I was at Old Luke's when Pastor Williams picked up your car." I was hoping for a flash of guilt to validate my suspicions.

Suddenly, the laughing stopped and the room went silent. Reenie adjusted herself in her chair, swiping her hands along her thighs presumably to straighten her dress, although it looked just fine to me.

"It's all right. She doesn't know," she said finally. "But you might as well. Everybody else in town does." She turned toward me and opened her arms as if to present herself. "This beautiful body of mine, try as it might, has never been able to hang on to a child. I've lost two husbands over this bum womb, gone into who knows how many depressions, and still can't seem to come to peace with the fact." She smiled with her lips tightly sealed and, once again, straightened the skirt of her dress. "Pastor Williams has been an angel, though, coming up to see me every week." She directed this next bit to Piggin and Heifer. "Says I should look at what I have to be grateful for. And I suppose he's right. I got my health, a beautiful house, and"—she put a hand, sporting a rock the size of Kansas, over her heart—"Roy. Oh, that man does love me."

And he's obviously got money.

Right then Reenie's purse began chiming the tune, "The Yellow Rose of Texas."

"Speaking of," she said pulling out her cell phone and flipping it open, "Hi, hon."

"Roy's in investments. Got himself a real good job," Heifer whispered.

Reenie plugged her free ear with her finger. "I'm on my way." She rolled her eyes for our benefit. "Piggin and Heifer's. And Eadie's with us…" She smiled at me apologetically. "Uh-huh. That's her."

She wagged her head from side to side indicating she wished he'd hurry up, then pulled the phone down from her mouth. "He says to say hello to you three beautiful ladies. And, Piggin, he says he still can't get his mind off your fried chicken from Sunday's potluck."

Piggin, clearly delighted, said, "Tell him that this Sunday I'm bringing my catfish."

Roy's lip-smacking response was so loud we could all hear it.

Piggin and Heifer exchanged satisfied smiles, while Reenie closed out her conversation.

Reenie clicked her phone shut. "I should go. I promised him meatloaf. Lord knows, that man loves a good home-cooked meal." She laughed. "And you better stop raising that bar, Piggin," she said standing. "Oh, and by the way, ladies, he promises to sign those papers authorizing the land over to the church, so I can pass them on to the Elders." She zipped up her bag. "He's such a knucklehead! Got himself so caught up with Jubilee Trust Fund he's become a birdbrain about everything else. This morning I put them smack next to his coffee and he walked out without signing them. I swear, this 'being incorporated' has just been a pain in the neck. He insisted on it when we got married, said it would help with taxes—and I'm sure he's right, he is the financial genius—but it's just seem to make things more complicated." She rolled her eyes again. "Men!" Then she kissed everyone on the cheek, including me, and was out the door.

Now, I was confused. She seemed devoted to her husband. Still… something about her and the pastor didn't sit right. It was hard to imagine him effectively counseling anybody, especially about something as sensitive as miscarriages. If she hadn't been past her childbearing years, I'd have wondered if he weren't trying to give her a shot of his own holy water. If so, they sure had everybody snowed—or Piggin and Heifer at any rate. The way the sisters continued to yak about Reenie and "her wonderful husband" after she left, you'd have thought the Petersons each already had one foot in heaven.

"This Jubilee Trust Fund he's got the church involved in is such a miracle," Piggin said getting up from the table. "Between that and her donating the land, we're finally going to get our new building."

"Old one's got plumbing problems," Heifer said. "Has for years."

"You staying for dinner, Eadie?" Piggin asked.

I stood. "No. I got some groceries today and thought I might just stay in tonight—try out my table. Thanks, though. You guys have been amazing. And I love that truck!"

Heifer nodded. "I learned to drive on that truck."

"If you change your mind, we'd be happy to have you," Piggin said. "I'm making chicken fried steak."

As I walked my glass over to the sink, I caught them up on my job with Jameson. "Looks pretty easy, so I'm hoping to be out of your hair in about a week."

A dryer buzzer went off in Piggin's laundry closet and she got up to go take care of it. "You are not in our hair!"

Heifer tapped the top of her tea glass with her finger. "Saw you cleaned up the horseshoe pit."

"Uh, yeah. I hope you don't mind…"

She traced the rim of the glass with her thumb. "Used to play all the time."

Before stepping out the door, I turned. "You know, I bought enough peanut butter and bananas for three."

She laughed and yelled to Piggin, who was in the hall unloading the dryer. "The kid's offering to cook! Peanut butter and bananas!"

"On bread," I amended. "I'd even toast it."

Piggin pulled out a dress the size of a circus tent. "Can we take a rain check?"

CHAPTER FOURTEEN

A series of gunshot knocks assaulted my door, startling me awake. *What the fuck? Where am I?* I opened my eyes. Nothing but black. My heart raced as consciousness pried its way into my dream state. *Trailer. Rauston.*

More loud rapping. *Shit! The Milsap kid narced on me!* I clicked on my bedside light and thrust myself up from the warm mattress. My eyes recoiled from the harsh light. I shut them. "Hang on!" I croaked.

"Well, don't take all day about it!"

The voice was Heifer's. She didn't sound happy. I yanked on a T-shirt and pair of shorts. "Hang on," I repeated, visions of a Texas jail cell flashing through my mind. I pushed open my trailer door. Heifer stood there in her housecoat and sneakers.

"Put on your shoes," she said. "Sweet Ginger's gotten herself into trouble again."

I searched the contents of my brain, *Sweet Ginger...Sweet Ginger...* I remembered Piggin rattling off her family's nicknames. *Sweet Ginger, little sister.*

"Just a sec," I said before letting the screen door swing shut between us. I pulled on my sneaks without socks, relief flooding my adrenaline-saturated body. *No guilt. It's not me in trouble.* I pushed through the door. *But what does she need me for?*

The vastness of the star-studded sky stopped me dead. Three hundred and sixty degrees of forever is hard to take in all at once. "Wow," I said.

Heifer let go of her urgency and followed my gaze. I could feel she was seeing a sky she'd long taken for granted. "It's something, isn't it?" she said in a voice absent of her previous irritation.

As we stood there, two tiny specks gaping into the face of infinity, I realized that I did have something to offer back to the Wilbourne sisters: new eyes. "You don't get skies like this in a city," I said.

"Sometimes I think that's what God created the Panhandle for: to showcase His celestial masterpiece."

I let the word "His" roll off my back. I'd never seen the whole Milky Way before, and I didn't want semantics to ruin the moment.

Our silence was punctuated by a soft ticking sound. It was the same ticking I'd heard the day I'd met Heifer. Pulling my attention from the sky, I sneaked a quick look at her wrist to see if she was wearing a watch. She wasn't.

Heifer cleared her throat. "Piggin must have taken her raisins. I knocked on her door 'til my knuckles hurt."

"Raisins?"

"Soaks 'em in whiskey. Good for the arthritis. Once in a while she takes too many, though. Stick of dynamite can't roust her then."

I chose to take this as an apology for waking me. "That's all right. So what are we doing?"

"Rescuing Sweet Ginger from one of her good-for-nothing boyfriends."

"And I'm needed because…?"

"Could take two to load her into the car. Come on, get in, might as well be burning rubber while we talk."

I offered to drive, but Heifer said she'd done it so many times before she could drive it in her sleep. "She and her honey-of-the-night must have closed down the Crowbar."

As we bumped down the rutted dirt driveway and onto the country road, Heifer brought me up to speed. Their little sister, Sweet Ginger, waitressed at a biker bar called the Crowbar. Apparently she was "fond of the goods," and Heifer wasn't just talking about alcohol. "Once she's drunk enough, they all look like her Prince Charming. Or what do I know? Maybe she sees them for the frogs they are and thinks she's the princess who can switch 'em over. Only it usually involves a lot more than a kiss." She sighed. I gathered that these middle-of-the-night, shit-faced cell phone calls weren't all that unusual. Her Harley beaus—

in lieu of communicating their deep inner feelings about not feeling nurtured by the relationship—would occasionally dump her along the road somewhere, stranded.

"She's got three or four she bounces between," Heifer said. "I can't tell any of 'em apart. They all need haircuts and better hygiene techniques, that's for sure. One of them—think they call him Dawg—is missing some teeth on the bottom. Then there's the Vietnam vet, gets real violent sometimes. But none of them—and I do mean none—are worth the labor pains their poor mothers suffered for having them."

"Seems kind of harsh to dump her on the side of the road."

"You don't know Sweet Ginger. When she's been drinking, I've had half a mind to dump her out myself."

We came to the railroad crossing where she said she'd meet us, but there was no sign of her.

"Well, shoot! We're going to have to go looking."

We drove about five miles per hour down the deserted road with me scanning the right while Heifer scanned the left. The headlights illuminated broken bottles, fast food wrappings, and cups that littered the berm. I even spotted what I thought was an armadillo starting its precarious journey across the highway. *Good luck to you, buddy.*

"One time she was passed out by a tumbleweed, so look real close."

Just when I was starting to wonder if this was all a waste of time, I saw someone walking up ahead. "I think I see her."

"Thank you, Sweet Jesus," Heifer said, pressing the accelerator.

We pulled up next to a voluptuous bottle blond in tight jeans and a low cut, empire waist blouse. She ignored us and continued walking, her four-inch heels grinding the asphalt with each determined step.

Bringing the Olds Ninety-eight to a crawl, Heifer leaned toward me and yelled out the open window. "Where you headed, Sweet Ginger?"

Sweet Ginger pressed forward, not even turning to look at us. "I'm gonna kill that sorry-ass dinky dick, and don't you try and stop me, Heifer." Her heel hit an uneven spot, twisting her ankle, but it wasn't enough to stop her momentum.

"You'll be walking to sunrise, honey. Now get in the car and let me take you home."

"I'm not going home!" Her heels continued their rhythmic crunching across the asphalt.

"Then why'd you call?"

Sweet Ginger stopped abruptly and pivoted toward the car. "I don't know," she said accusingly, the smeared mascara marking her face like war paint. "Suppose I was feeling like a victim, but now I've seen the light and I'm mad as hell!"

Heifer stopped the car. "Now why don't you let me make you a strong cup of coffee and we can talk all about it. If you still want to kick his you-know-what after that, you can take my car."

I recognized the technique, had used it on Ruby many times myself. Bribe them with something you have no intention of giving. It's easy with a drunk—they don't remember.

Sure enough, Sweet Ginger took the bait. "I can use your car?"

"You bet. Just come back to the house for a cup of coffee first."

It wasn't until then that Sweet Ginger even realized someone was with Heifer. "Who the hell are you?" She seemed more befuddled by my presence than annoyed.

I tried to think of a drunk-friendly response to her question, something simple not involving too much explanation, while I opened the car door. My intention was to give her the front seat. There was no way I wanted her to scoot in next to me, and she didn't seem sober enough to open the back door by herself. Somehow my action threw off her balance, landing her in the dirt. "Shit!" she yelled. I jumped out of the car and thrust out my hand to help her up.

"I'm sorry! I didn't mean to—"

"Jesus Fucking Christ! Don't move so fast!" She took my hand and hoisted herself up. "God damn it, now I'm gonna have a dirty ass." She twisted around like a dog chasing its tail as she tried to wipe her butt free of dirt.

"Just get in the car!" Heifer yelled.

Satisfied that she'd gotten herself cleaned up, Sweet Ginger looked back at me. "Who *are* you?"

"I'm Eadie. I'm staying out behind Heifer's trailer."

"You're Eadie? Piggin didn't tell me you were a dyke!"

I realized I had, in my haste, grabbed my SILENCE = DEATH T-shirt. Obviously, she knew what it meant. "Uh…" I looked over at Heifer to see if she'd heard. She was faced forward, making it impossible to tell.

Sweet Ginger reached for the handle of the back door, but couldn't manage it. "Let me in the goddamned car, Heifer!"

"It's unlocked!" Heifer yelled back.

Once I helped her open it, she spilled into the car with an unladylike "hmph."

As we drove back, Sweet Ginger just couldn't keep her mouth shut. "Jesus, Heifer. I never thought I'd see the day you'd have a dyke staying at your place. What do your Baptist buddies have to say about it? Or do they even know you're associating with a heathen?"

The car got shatteringly quiet. I tried to think of something to say. And Heifer, who knows what she was thinking? A cold wall had grown between us. Once again, I heard the darn ticking noise, only this time it seemed louder, faster. *What the hell is that?* I slumped down in my seat. *I should have told Heifer I was gay. Piggin too. I should have been out in the open from the top. That way, if they'd wanted to kick me out, they could have. Now the whole church is involved and it's gotten way too complicated.* I willed Sweet Ginger to keep her trap shut, but of course she didn't. She was a drunk.

"Aren't you afraid associating with a sinner is going to send you to hell, Heifer?" She grabbed the back of my seat and lurched forward. "Everlasting burning and all that crap?"

Would you just shut up already?

"Or is it exciting for you, Heifer? Is it getting you off?" Mercifully, after this caustic remark, Sweet Ginger fell back into her seat and passed out, boom, just like that.

Heifer and I traveled the rest of the way in stony silence.

CHAPTER FIFTEEN

I hid out in my trailer until Piggin and Heifer left for work. By now, Heifer would have told Piggin that I was a lesbian, and on their arrival home, I was certain they'd evict me. I planned on saving them the trouble. I'd be gone. I just had to choose my exit strategy.

What little night was left after Heifer's and my midnight mission had been filled with fitful sleep, my ruthless mind blaring like a TV with no Off button. *Why didn't I tell Piggin and Heifer I was gay?* I rolled onto my side and tried conjuring a relaxing scene: a burbling stream with little fishies swimming round and round. *Would it have even made a difference? I'm in the goddamned Bible Belt; the only place for a lesbian here is in Hell.* I flipped onto my back: crystal blue sky dotted with white fluffy clouds. *But I'm already in hell. Rauston, Texas: Land of oppressive family values and ignorant minds.* I rolled onto my other side…

By daybreak, not only did I have a crick in my neck, but I'd already come up with several exit strategies.

Coffee, journal, and joint in hand, I made my way over to the ruins of the old Wilbourne house. I needed that big horizon to come to a decision. I sat on the stumpy cement pile by the previous day's mandala and proceeded to light up. If nothing else, I could take the Wilbourne sisters' truck to Amarillo and hop a bus. All I'd have to do is leave them a note with the location, stop by Old Luke's to tell him I'd be back for Pebbles when I had the cash, and swing by Crash's to pick up my weed…

Or I could call Peter and Kevin, get them to wire me some money, Ruby be damned.

As for Jameson, even if he wouldn't care that I was gay, others would. Pastor Williams would find a way to revoke the Helping Hands money; that was for sure. I could picture him and a posse of shotgun-toting Raustonions towing me to the county limits shouting, "Don't never come back! You hear that? Your kind of pre-vert ain't welcome here!"

I took another hit, trying to wipe the tacky spaghetti Western from my mind.

A righteous anger burbled up. Why am I feeling shame? I am a dyke, for Christ's sake. So what? I like being a dyke and am proud of being a dyke—or I was 'til I came to this stupid town. I took another hit. Being a dyke is way better than being small-minded! Still, the feeling that I'd betrayed Piggin and Heifer haunted me. How could I have thought they'd accept me?

"That smells good."

Startled, I jerked around.

It was the Wicked Witch of the Southwest, Sweet Ginger. Her stilettos and tight jeans clashed with the morning hour as she tottered her way over the uneven landscape, stepping around pebbles and weeds as if they were land mines, never once spilling a drop of her coffee. "God, it's bright out here. I can't remember the last time I was up this early."

I pinched out the joint and put it in my pocket, trying to contain my anger. "You scared me."

She seemed not to care and sat down across from me on the old hearth. "What kind of voodoo is this?" she asked gesturing with her foot at the mandala. The toenails peeking through her open-toed shoes revealed chipped scarlet polish.

I crossed my arms, then, feeling that it made me appear defensive, uncrossed them. "It was something to do."

She tapped a Virginia Slim from an almost empty pack and flicked her lighter, totally clueless of the predicament she'd put me in. To my perverse enjoyment, her lighter didn't fire. I didn't offer her mine. I was having too much fun watching her suffer.

"Piece of shit!" she said, shaking the lighter and flicking it over and over again. When it finally did light, she sucked the cigarette like she hadn't had one in days. On her exhale, she nodded toward the mandala and said, "That's my baby spoon."

I reached down to retrieve it. *Fine with me if she wants it back.*

"Don't!" she said. "It looks good there."

I shrugged and left it, squelching the urge to kick the crap out of the whole mandala.

She did a few short tugs at her ratted hair, trying to revive its shape. "I must look like shit."

I chose not to respond, seeing as I wanted to choke her to death. *If she'd just kept her mouth shut last night...*

"You must be Eadie."

I nodded. "We met last night."

"Did we?" She took another long drag. "Guess I forgot. I apologize for any tactless things I might have said while in my inebriated state." She overarticulated these words, giving them a slightly sarcastic tone. I could tell she wanted me to say something to let her off the hook. *Just like Ruby...*

She flicked her ashes into the mandala. "Heifer won't let me smoke in the trailer. Says I stink it up." She messed with her hair again.

My silence was getting to her, and I was glad. Maybe she did have a conscience in there somewhere.

She glanced at the burned-out remains of the house, crossed her legs, then recrossed them. "Shit! You're sitting on what used to be my bedroom."

This took me by surprise. *I thought my cool stoic attitude was making her uncomfortable. Not the house! Or lack of one...*

"It was damned tiny, but it did have a door. I swear to God, that door saved my life more than once."

I expected her to elaborate.

She tapped the side of her mug and stared off into the horizon. A hundred-mile gaze, I've heard it called.

Apparently, she wasn't going to share her simmering hell with me, so I was stuck with my own. I picked up my journal and began sketching. It was hard to do with her sitting there, but I was feeling stubborn. *I was here first.* I began with a tiny stick figure running off the edge of the page. One of her outstretched arms had already reached the void. Behind the character, I drew a bunch of flying arrows. I'd just started with the various people riding the arrows, goading them on with whips and reins, when Sweet Ginger spoke.

"You going to smoke the rest of that joint, or what?"

I looked up from my journal. Sweet Ginger had finished her cigarette and was back from whatever past horror she'd visited.

Oh, what the hell. What better for a couple of losers to do? I pulled it from my pocket and held it out to her. "Fire it up."

She took the few steps over and crouched, rather ungracefully, by where I was sitting. This was not a proud woman. "Not exactly hair of the dog, but it'll do," she said, using my cement pile to lean against. She put the joint between lips that sported an outside ring of last night's lipstick. Again, her lighter gave her trouble, forcing her to shake it until it lit. Then, with the competence of a longtime stoner, she took a deep toke and spoke in that tight holding-in-the-hit voice. "The worst thing about waking up here is my sisters don't keep anything stronger than vanilla. I'm surprised they even keep *that,* considering Mama's past." She exhaled a huge puff of smoke and passed me the joint. "Drank herself stupid on vanilla. Have you smelled it in Piggin's trailer?"

"I've only been in the kitchen," I said taking a mondo toke myself. The way she was bogarting, I figured I'd better get some while I still could.

"Next time, check out the back room. You can't miss it."

My lungs filled to capacity, I handed the joint back, willing myself not to cough.

"I used to think it was real special when Mama'd let me lay back there with her. She had the room full of little pillows and shit. And there was this lamp, it had this beaded shade on it, I loved it. Of course, Piggin has it now, in her bedroom." She laughed to herself. "What a surprise! Piggin's whole fucking trailer is a shrine to Mama." She took another long toke and I wondered if she was at the end of her trip down memory lane. But she continued.

"Mama was always good to me. If I was crying, or J.D. was being an asshole, she'd invite me into her room and let me sip on her vanilla. "'Have a little sip of sweetness, honey. Just a little sip of Mama's sweetness.' None of the other kids got that. Just me. I was her Sweet Ginger."

Between the pot and her story, I was finding it hard to hold on to my grudge. She had a grittiness that I related to, appreciated. That's one of the things about smoking a joint with a person; it dissolves the walls. Still, I needed to speak my mind. "You said some pretty tactless things last night."

"What was it this time?" She grimaced and handed back the spent roach.

"You called me a dyke in front of your sister."

"Heifer?"

"Yeah."

She frowned. "So? You are one, aren't you?"

I put the roach back in my pocket. "It's not cool to out people. You should let them do it for themselves." In that moment I was struck with how many times I'd had to come out in my life. It wasn't the one-time thing most people assumed. "I'm not sure I'll be welcome here now."

She nodded and stood, using the cement pile to help her up, then tapped another Virginia Slim out of the pack. "Heifer won't kick you out."

"How do you know?"

"She keeps bailing me out, doesn't she?"

"You're family."

"The black sheep. Shit! Those two have disinherited me so many times I've lost count." She sat back on the brick hearth. "I'll tell you what you gotta do. Act like nothing happened. It's a survival technique that one masters here in Rauston—unmitigated denial."

I lifted my eyebrows, surprised by her articulateness.

She must have read my face because she said, "See, you're just like everyone else. You think just because I'm a slutty drunk, I don't read. I hate that."

I held up my hands. "Sorry."

"I betcha I've read more self-help books than all this puny town put together. Not that they've helped much, but then I'm pretty fucked up. I watch Dr. Phil too. Now that's a man to shave your legs for." She curled her lips around her cig and pulled her lighter from her pocket. "So how freaked was Heifer?"

"She didn't say a word to me the whole ride home."

"Oh, honey, that's a good sign. That means she's stuffing it down into that toxic-waste-area of her soul. She'll eat an extra portion of dessert or something to cover it up."

I laughed, then felt guilty for it. I didn't want to start dissing on Heifer.

"You gotta understand, sweetheart…" she said, struggling with her lighter again. I tossed her mine. She caught it, lit her smoke, and almost pocketed my lighter in that unconscious way that smokers do.

I extended my hand.

"Oops," she said tossing it back. She leaned forward with her elbows on her knees and faced me dead-on. "You need a little filling in if you're going to survive what's left of this fucked-up family."

A vulture circled overhead.

"Hold your horses!" she yelled to the bird. "Doc says my liver's still got a few years left!"

I laughed and pulled my knee up, wrapping my arms around it. I was somewhere between dying to know what she was about to say and not wanting to know at all. What were her motives? If she was anything like Ruby, which I was getting the feeling she was, there were always motives.

"All right," she said and took a deep breath. "Heifer would kill me if she knew I was about to tell you this, but I swear, it's for her good as much as yours. She's so stuffed up with secrets even she doesn't know what's true anymore. Now…" She looked over her shoulder as if someone could have snuck up on us unawares, which, considering how stoned I was, wasn't all that hard to imagine. "She'd never admit this—maybe doesn't even remember it for all I don't know—but she has been in love before. Back when she was, let's just say, eighteen or around there. Her name was Lilah."

Suddenly, I wasn't comfortably stoned anymore. I was higher than a kite! And a bit paranoid. And really self-conscious. *Should I appear shocked? Amused? Am I making the proper facial expressions?* I rubbed my eyes and refocused on Sweet Ginger. She was still talking. I could see her lips moving, but my mind was squawking so loud I couldn't make sense of her words.

"…everyone could see the two were inseparable, but chose to believe they were best friends. It's that Rauston survival technique I was telling you about…"

"Unmitigated denial," I said, trying to sound like I wasn't flipping out. *Heifer's a lesbian? How can she live here? Go to church? She must be freaking out about eternally burning in hell.* I watched Sweet Ginger flick an ant off her jeans.

"...I mean, I was only ten or so, but I remember the way the two of them went everywhere together, to dances, fairs, what have you. They were always arm in arm—you know the way girls do. They'd even dance together, but everybody thought it was just so cute." She gestured quotation marks around the word cute. "I'm surprised old J.D. never figured out his daughter was queer, being the sleaze-minded guy that he was, but I guess so long as it kept the boys away, he didn't give a shit."

I nodded and smiled. *Why are you smiling? It's not funny!*

"Even I didn't fully understand 'til this one night when I'd fallen asleep on Pal's bed out on the porch." She gestured somewhere behind me. "Pal was our black Lab. I loved that damned dog. Me and Pal were like this." She held up crossed fingers. "The long and short of it is, I woke up to laughter. It was dark. Heifer and Lilah were sitting on the porch swing. They'd no doubt been to some church function. Those two went to everything. Sang in the choir, did Bible studies, you know.

"I could tell they didn't know I was there, so I kept real quiet. It was fun listening to my older sister and her friend talk big girl stuff. People they knew, who was dating who. But after a bit it got real quiet. I peeked out to see why and they were just staring at each other. Then my sister leaned over and kissed Lilah—on the lips. I couldn't believe what I was seeing. Then I got it. Two girls could be in love just like a boy and girl.

"By now, it was real clear my hiding wasn't a game anymore. What they were doing was a secret. But I couldn't take my eyes off that kiss. I watched my sister slide her hand over Lilah's cotton blouse—not underneath, on top. Now that I think of it, it was real polite the way she held Lilah's breast. I tell you, no man I've ever dated has treated my body with that kind of respect! I'd probably marry him if he did.

"But Lilah pushed Heifer away. Sudden like. 'Don't,' she said. I remember that loud and clear. 'Don't.' I can't remember much more, just Lilah walking down that driveway. And the look on Heifer's face. A silent scream is what it was. A silent scream of pain."

Sweet Ginger's cigarette had burned down to her fingers. She flicked the fragile ash and took a final drag. "Next thing you know

Lilah shocks everyone by up and marrying some loser that'd been after her since freshman year. Some surprise, huh? Moved to Amarillo with him. I think he sells cars or something."

"Wow. She never knew you saw?"

"Nope. 'Course who knows what I've said to her since." She looked directly at me. "I didn't say anything about it last night, did I?"

I cleared my throat. "You did say something about her getting off on me being a dyke."

She winced. "Ouch. I really do have to quit drinking so much."

I tried to imagine Heifer—or was she Grace then?—so passionate, so daring…

Sweet Ginger shook her head. "I've always kind of blamed Lilah for Heifer's heart attack."

"Heart attack?"

She laughed. "You telling me Piggin hasn't told you the famous heart attack story? Shit! She loves to warn people not to excite Heifer—as if that were possible."

"She didn't say anything to me."

"Well, Heifer had a heart attack right after Lilah got married. You think that's a coincidence? What kind of person has a heart attack that young?"

I shrugged. I was starting to feel less light-headed, but the cottonmouth was definitely starting to kick in. I ran my tongue around my gummy teeth.

"You haven't heard her ticking?"

"Um…yeah…?"

She nodded. "Porcelain heart valve. It really gets going when she's upset."

I thought about Sweet Ginger's taunting the night before. It must have been so painful for her.

I watched Sweet Ginger lean down and place her crapped-out lighter inside the mandala. "Needs something to balance it out," she said, then looked up. "Hey, could I get you to give me a ride to my car? If I get back early enough I can give that good-for-nothing dinky dick a piece of my mind. The jerk owes me back my tip money."

I remembered my commitment at Jameson's Market. "Shit! What time is it?"

She shrugged. "You got somewhere to go?"

CHAPTER SIXTEEN

When Sweet Ginger asked me for a ride, I'd assumed the Crowbar was near the spot where Heifer and I had picked her up the night before. Had I known it was thirty miles away in a different county, I would have said no.

"I figured you knew," she said as we barreled down the highway. "Rauston's dry. No bars, no liquor stores, no honky-tonking period. Our location is real convenient for all those churchgoing Raustoners. They can drink and screw around and nobody's gonna know."

"What about God?" I asked.

"What about Him?" she asked back.

Around the time I was supposed to be walking through the front door of Jameson's, I was pulling up behind a lone Dodge Neon in the dirt parking lot of the Crowbar. The word SLUT was traced in the dust on the back window. "Thanks," Sweet Ginger said hopping out of the truck. "I hope this didn't blow your deal at the market."

"So do I."

The Crowbar, just the other side of Rauston's county line, was the perfect example of an establishment for marginalized people. In other words, a dive. Just like the gay bars I'm used to frequenting. That it was daylight and the run-down shack was out there all by itself with no trees or other buildings didn't help to mask its tawdry exterior. The windows were covered in black-painted plywood. Nine or ten empty liquor boxes were stacked around the side, as well as a couple of rusted-out and gutted Harleys.

I didn't feel right just leaving her there, so I waited for her car to start, which took a couple of baby backfires to accomplish, then I peeled out. I had my pal, Buddy Bud, waiting on me. As I rumbled back toward Rauston, I recalled his exuberant hug the day before and how, this morning, I'd been a breath away from bailing on him. *What kind of self-centered jerk am I?* I flicked on the radio to a station blaring a low-budget commercial for some hardware store. Lame as it was, it beat listening to the crap my brain was pumping out.

I was a half hour late when I pulled into Jameson's. I jumped out of the truck and charged into the grocery store preparing to spout one of the millions of excuse/apologies I came up with on the excruciatingly long drive.

Buddy Bud was right inside the door sitting with the Duraflames, his head resting heavily in his hands.

"Hey, Buddy Bud!"

He looked up at me with sad eyes. "Where *were* you?"

"I had to give someone a ride. Sorry."

"Kitty said you weren't coming. She says some people you just can't trust."

Kitty, ringing up a woman's full cart of groceries, glanced smugly over her shoulder. "What a surprise," she crooned. "You decided to show up after all."

I squatted by Buddy Bud, my back to Kitty. "Don't worry, Bud, I won't be late again. This was a one-time thing."

He looked at me skeptically, squinting his eyes so I'd know he was mad, then thrust his hand out for me to shake. "Promise?"

I had the sudden urge to lecture him on the unreliable nature of promises, to warn him that people were basically jerks and broke promises without second thoughts. Sighing, I took his hand and said, "Promise."

Buddy Bud jumped to his innocent sneakered feet and yelled, "Well, come oooon, Eadie! We got work to do!"

No matter what, I told myself, *I can't let this kid down.*

As we passed by Kitty's register, hand in hand, I chirped, "Morning, Kitty!" and tossed her my most charming smile. When she pointedly didn't look up, I added, "Have a nice day!" and offered my smile to the matronly woman she was waiting on. To Kitty's obvious annoyance, the woman smiled back.

Buddy Bud had lots he wanted to show me on our way to the back stairs. "Look, Eadie! They have a pirate on the front of the cereal!" Down the aisle a ways, he held up a can of sardines. "Hey, Eadie, have you ever tried one of these? They're my favorite!" He also had to stop to do one of his other jobs at the market. "Uh-oh, Eadie! This can got turned around backward. It's my job to fix it. That's how I make m'lowance." We'd come upon a whole shelf of upside-down soup cans, and it occurred to me that the stock clerk probably did it on purpose. For all I knew, the customers were in on the trick too.

As we came to the end of the canned food aisle, we nearly bumped into a totally cool-looking woman, about my age, flipping through a clipboard. Startled, she looked up, then smiled a dazzling smile when she saw it was Buddy Bud. "Hey, Buster, watch where you're going!"

She doesn't have a Texas accent...

Buddy Bud began happily twisting his fingers into various knots while shifting his weight from one foot to the other. "No! *You* watch out, lady!"

Her laugh was unapologetic. Her energy light, and seemingly free of emotional baggage. I liked her immediately. Especially her interaction with Buddy Bud. I felt she genuinely liked him.

And her attention to detail was meticulous. She was dressed in a fifties style, black and white polka-dotted skirt, lime green cat's-eye glasses and short flame-red pigtails sticking out the side of her head. My guess was she was riffing off Jane of the legendary Dick and Jane series, or maybe a character from a Donna Reed episode, but the original crispness of the vintage clothing, broken down from years of wear, was now soft, supple, and hung on her most attractively.

Plus she had a sweet spray of freckles across her nose. I love freckles.

Our eye contact outlasted the usual cursory glance and was alarming in its immediacy and authenticity. I even thought I felt the atmosphere around us change. It began swirling, spiral-like from her to me; her to me; her, me.

"I see your friend made it after all," she said, her gorgeous green-eyed gaze finally releasing mine and returning to Buddy Bud.

Please tell me she doesn't think I'm the kind of person who flakes on retarded kids.

"Yup! This is Eadie!" Buddy Bud chirped. "She and I are going to be working on a project."

"I know you are," she said. "You told me all about it, remember?"

"Oh yeah…"

"Hi," I said.

"Hey there," she said. "I'm Cadence, one of Buddy Bud's other pals."

I was struck by her use of the word other, as if she were trying to tell me that even if I flaked on Buddy Bud, he had other people in his life who wouldn't.

Or am I being paranoid?

"Cadence and I have a secret handshake!" Buddy Bud beamed. "Wanna see?"

She put her hands on her hips, mocking annoyance. "Hey! How's it going to stay a secret if you tell everybody?"

Buddy Bud giggled. "Sorry, Charlie."

She bent down so she could be face-to-face with Buddy Bud. "You wanna let Eadie in on the secret?"

Okay, so I'm paranoid…

"A-OK, Roger Rabbit!"

It wasn't that she was astoundingly beautiful. She wasn't. She was all elbows and knees, her eyelashes so blond they almost disappeared. I could even imagine a person calling her plain—if it weren't for that marvelous sparkle. She handed me her clipboard so she and Buddy Bud could perform their secret two-handed pinky shake.

"Nobody knows this but me and Cadence," Buddy Bud said to me earnestly.

"And now Eadie," Cadence said.

He frowned. "Oh yeah…" Then smiled. "But that's okay. I like Eadie. Don't you?"

I willed the blush back down my neck and handed Cadence her clipboard. "Thanks for the demo."

She glanced at my flushed neck, then smiled. "No problem. Any friend of Buddy's is a friend of mine."

Buddy Bud tugged on her sleeve.

"Hey, you want to help me 'n Eadie paint?"

She put a freckled hand on Buddy Bud's shoulder. "Sounds fun, but I've got a job to do too. I told your dad I'd get this computer system up and running by the end of the week."

He sighed, "Okaaay."

Buddy Bud and I watched her walk off. "I think she's beeeautiful," he crooned.

Me too, I thought. *Meeee too.*

CHAPTER SEVENTEEN

Buddy Bud turned out to be a first-class helper. He helped me clear the shelves, helped me load the stuff in boxes, helped me stack them by the door. When it came to vacuuming dust off the shelves, however, he started to get anxious. I turned off the vacuum. "What's up, Buddy Bud?" He pointed to a spider in the corner, then showed me another. Lo and behold, the thing was a condominium of spiders. I assured him there was no need to be afraid, that the vacuum would suck them up, then flicked it back on.

"Stop!" he screamed, "You're killing them!"

I flicked it off.

Buddy Bud pulled an empty pickle jar from a bottom drawer in his dad's desk. He called it his spider catcher.

Half an hour later, when Jameson entered the office, we were still in rescue mode. I shot to my feet. "Prepping's taking a little longer than I expected," I blurted. How could I explain saving spiders?

Jameson laughed. "Relax. I'm well aware of his eccentricities." He leaned his lanky frame into the door casing and watched Buddy Bud gingerly cup a daddy longlegs in his hands, the look in his eyes somewhere between gut-wrenching love and exasperation. "I appreciate your patience, Eadie. I just hope it lasts."

We waited for Buddy Bud to drop the daddy longlegs into the jar, then Jameson walked over to him and knelt. He put his hand on his shoulder. "Bud, I need you to listen to Eadie. You understand me?"

"But, Dad, we can't kill the spiders. They might have babies."

"Buddy…"

Buddy Bud placed the lid slightly askew on top of the jar. "See? I'm giving them air."

Sighing, Jameson hoisted himself up. "Ever since his mama died he's been worried about babies being left behind."

"She didn't die, Dad. She's visiting Jesus," Buddy Bud said, going after another spider.

Jameson smiled apologetically.

I smiled back. What did Buddy Bud imagine when he saw his mother with Jesus? Were they floating around together in a Christmas card? Jesus with his sad eyes and outstretched palms, she with wings and harp? Or were his visions more pedestrian? The two of them sitting at a chrome diner eating everlasting tuna sandwiches. I made a note to ask him sometime.

Jameson pulled a piece of paper from a folder on his desk. Apparently, he wasn't checking up on us, as I'd assumed. "I'll let you get back to your work," he said, glancing at the paper, then made to leave, but stopped just short of the door. "Thank you, Eadie. You've no idea how much this means."

His homegrown sincerity took me so off guard I stepped backward onto the vacuum hose. "Um, it's no problem, really." It's not easy appearing suave when you're almost toppling over.

❖

By about three o'clock all the spiders were collected, we'd drop-clothed the area, TSPed the shelves, and Buddy Bud was starting to get tired. We decided to call it quits. I left him stretched out on the floor listening to a ball game on the radio, eyelids drooping. I was actually glad to stop. It would give me time to swing by Crash's before checking in with Old Luke. I have to admit I was starting to have second thoughts about placing my trust—and money—in Crash. What recourse would I have if he kept the money for himself?

The truck had no air-conditioning, so I drove with both windows cranked down. I flipped through the full spectrum of radio stations before settling on country western. It beat Rush Limbaugh and the myriad of Christian stations. Hot as it was, I began to enjoy the ride. I was a female Jack Kerouac. Sure, I was broken down in a small town, but this was an adventure. Plus, now I had Cadence to think about. She was way too cool to be living in a town like this. What was she doing here?

Before I knew it, I was zooming past the Milsap place.

I slammed on the brakes, glad there was no one else on the road, and threw the truck into reverse. As I backed down the highway and into their driveway, I considered which door to use, the one on the trailer or the one on the shabby wood-slat add-on?

I chose the trailer door and knocked.

What will I say if someone besides Crash answers the door? I decided to use the truck's gas gauge as an excuse. He'd already told me it didn't work and had showed me how to test the level using the coat hanger wire he kept in the truck bed, but nobody else knew that. Or if they did, they'd just think I was stupid. People are always willing to believe women are stupid, especially if it involves anything mechanical.

The door cracked open and Crash's head peeked out. He looked alarmed to see me. "What are you doing here?"

Someone else is in the room with him. I adopted a casual tone. "Could you show me how to check the gas gauge?"

"I already showed you."

"Well, I need you to show me again."

He shot a look over his shoulder into the trailer. Canned laughter from a TV blared inside. He turned back toward me. "All right. Just for a second."

Walking to the truck, he was so nervous I began to worry that my fears of him absconding with my money might be right. "I was hoping to pick up my weed," I whispered.

He shot another look over his shoulder. "Already dropped it by. It's in your trailer."

This I knew was a lie. "It was locked, Crash."

"You think I'm lying?"

"I'm just saying…"

He put his hands in his pockets and looked at me dead-on. "Have you even looked?"

"No. I'm just now getting back from Jameson's."

"Then don't accuse me, okay? You sound like my dad."

I softened my tone. "I'm not accusing you. I just can't figure out how you got in."

"I picked the lock, okay?"

"You broke into my trailer?"

"You told me you didn't want to get in trouble with Piggin and Heifer." He scratched the back of his head. "Anyway, it's under your pillow. I wrote you a note with an arrow on it."

The idea of him breaking into my trailer was unsettling, let alone messing with my favorite pillow.

He crossed his arms around his torso like he was in a straitjacket. "Just so's you know, that lock ain't worth locking. My grandma coulda picked it. And anyway, I didn't steal nothin'."

I stared at the dirt, trying to collect my thoughts. "I'm just not sure what to say, Crash. Breaking into a person's trailer—a friend's trailer—is pretty uncool."

My use of the word "friend" came as a total shock to me. Was I playing this kid? Or was I so desperate I was befriending adolescent rednecks?

Crash's face grew long, like a puppy who'd been caught making lunch out of a favorite pair of shoes. "Sorry. It was the only time I could get out and then you weren't there. I didn't know what else to do. I knew you'd want it…"

He had a point. "All right," I sighed. "But next time—if there is a next time, which there probably won't be—just leave it under a tire or something."

He nodded, "Okay," then glanced at the trailer. "Can you go now?"

"Why are you so antsy? If anybody wonders why I'm here, just tell them I needed help with the gas gauge."

He tugged on his ear. "It's not that. I don't want Dad…"

Right then, a man I assumed was Crash's dad pushed through the trailer door. "Well, who do we have here?"

To look at him it was hard not to think Popeye. He had the long muscled, tattooed arms and short bowing legs. And his neck was ropy like a turtle's; his eyes beady and muskrat-like. He wore no shirt and had a cigarette tucked behind his ear. For all his brawn, though, he wasn't much taller than me.

"Uh, hey, Dad," Crash said, then proceeded to introduce us. "Eadie, this is my dad, uh, Silas. Dad, this is Eadie. She's the one staying over at the Wilbournes'."

"I see the truck. Think I can't figure that out myself?"

Crash shrugged, and in his simple gesture I could see him tuck himself away. Although he towered over his dad, it was clear the man terrified him. *No wonder the kid's so quick to go on the defensive. His dad is a Grade-A jerk.*

I smiled, a technique I love to use with jerks. "Hi, Mr. Milsap. Thanks so much for letting me use this truck." Acting beholden to him would make him feel important, I reasoned. Feeling important is usually all any jerk really wants. Of course, the truck was Piggin and Heifer's, so my having it really had nothing to do with him whatsoever. *Time to see how smart a jerk he is.* I added a touch of hand wringing to really nail the helpless effect. "Crash showed me how to use this coat hanger to check the gas the other day, but I just needed him to show me again."

Silas Milsap crossed his arms and looked me up and down. "Uh-huh," he grunted.

Was he smarter than I'd anticipated? I smiled again, more pitifully this time, but once again, my facial efforts bounced off his cantankerousness like a bullet hitting a Kevlar vest.

I turned back to Crash. "Well, then, thanks for the demo. I should be fine from now on." I pulled the truck keys from my pocket. Sorry as I felt for Crash, his dad was not my problem.

Or so I thought.

"Hang on, missy," he spat. "I got something to say to you."

Crash, whose back was to his father, closed his eyes and dropped his head.

"Son, go get them peaches your mama bought today. Eadie, here, needs to take 'em to the Wilbournes. A little present from the Milsap family."

Crash protested, "Mom bought them for pie."

"Well, I guess she's just gonna to have to go to Jameson's and buy some more, now ain't she?"

Crash didn't move.

"Go on, son! I didn't raise you to disrespect me in front of company!"

Crash looked at me as if to say, Now you get why I didn't want you here? before dashing back to the house.

Silas grumbled, "Boy is thick as molasses and lazy to boot." Then he fixed his cruel, dark, vicious, attack dog eyes on mine while pulling a grimy matchstick from his pocket. Rolling the matchstick between his callused thumb and forefinger, he strolled to within three feet of me. A bead of sweat etched a razor-sharp thread down the small of my back. He spoke quietly, fiercely. "Listen here, missy. You may be able to fool those sisters. Hell, you may be able to fool the whole damn Baptist congregation, but don't think you can fool me. I know what you're up to. I know your schemes. 'Cuz I can see right through you. You and me are the same. We're made the same."

His matchstick rolling grew more aggressive, causing the snake on his right arm to undulate. Biceps flexing, releasing, flexing, releasing.

I became absurdly conscious of my own tattoo, glad it was beneath my shirt. *You and I are not the same.* Adopting a stance I'd learned in a self-defense class, I spread my weight evenly beneath my feet, held hands at my side ready for whatever might come at me.

He continued. "You and I, see, we're smart. We know how to use other people to get what we need. Problem is, sometimes we might just want the same thing, only there's only enough for one. You get my meaning?"

I felt like I was in a showdown—this town's not big enough for both of us—only I didn't have a six-shooter on my hip. I kept my eyes trained on his. There was no way I was going to let him see I was about to wet my pants.

He spat a stringy lugie onto the dirt. "So, if I was you. I'd be real careful."

Searching my brain for a kick-ass response, something that wouldn't provoke, but would let him know he couldn't push me around, my hands began to tingle.

Then, thankfully, Crash pushed through the door and began jogging toward us. "Got the peaches."

Relief flooded my body.

Silas glanced at his son, then struck and lit the matchstick off the inside of his front tooth. He pulled the cigarette out from behind his ear, put it in his mouth, and drew. "It's been real nice to meet you, Eadie. Hope you enjoy your stay in Rauston." With that, he blew smoke in my face and walked back to the house.

I willed my knees not to buckle.

"He's such an asshole," Crash whispered when he was sure his dad was out of earshot.

Willing my tear ducts dry, I choked, "It's okay," and got into the truck.

Crash held the peaches up. "Don't forget these."

"Let your Mom make her pie," I mumbled.

He continued to hold them out to me. "He'll give me a whupping if he sees I didn't give 'em to you."

As I pulled out of the driveway, I had the desire to hurl the peaches onto the highway. *Fuck him and his stupid snake tattoo!* My mind punched and kicked at his accusations as the truck rattled down the patched asphalt. *We are not alike! I didn't ask for that money. The church offered it. And I'm working for it.* I tried focusing on my day with Buddy Bud, how I was teaching him a useful skill, but Silas Milsap's toxic words oozed across my horizon. I cranked up the radio in an effort to block out the memory that his ugly indictment had dug up from my past.

Waking up from a nap, which Ruby and I had begun together in the extra bedroom of Mom's plush Los Angeles condo, I was disappointed to find her gone. My head was groggy and the light coming through slits in the miniblinds had changed from glaring to muted. *I must have been sleeping for hours.*

Mom's boyfriend du jour, Brad the hulk, had gone on a business trip, and Mommie Dearest, unable to stand herself undiluted, sent me two plane tickets with a note. "Isn't it time I met this girlfriend of yours?" For some stupid reason, I'd acquiesced. Probably because I still held on to the sentimental bullshit that mothers and daughters should be close. We'd been there three days and already I was aching to leave. Our flight out wasn't until the following day.

Each day of our visit, seconds after the noon hour, Mom had proclaimed, "It's five o'clock somewhere in the world!" and mixed herself a vodka gimlet. Ruby, thinking this was witty, had joined her. I'd then spent the rest of the day pretending my mother and Ruby didn't have an awful lot in common. Forcing myself to believe this delusion generally resulted in a splitting headache.

I padded down the white-carpeted stairs past the glass-topped table featuring a sculpted stone nude, male of course, and spotted Ruby on the deck with my mother. They were tucked into spa robes indicating they'd hot-tubbed together and were now on to their vodka gimlets. I stood out of sight behind the screen door.

"You've got to take care with Eadie," my mother was saying. "She has a tendency to cling." She took a sip from her drink and added, "I had to be forceful with her as a child."

Ruby looked up from painting her toenails and laughed. "I think she's sweet..." then dipped the brush back into the crimson polish, adding, "but I can see the potential. Since the band's taken off, she's been kinda PO'd I haven't been around more. Did I tell you we have a major record label checking us out?"

My mother gazed wistfully over the Westwood rooftops. "I can see you're going to be good for her. So passionate about your work." She then emitted one of her martyred sighs, the ones that used to make me feel guilty for being born. "Sometimes I think I should have stuck with my acting, She would have learned to share me." She clinked the ice around in her drink, her signal that it was getting low, my signal, as a child, that I should fill it for her. "Promise me you'll stick with your singing, that you won't fall into the trap I did."

Unsure I wanted to hear how my girlfriend was going to respond to this succulent bait, I shoved the screen door open. "Here I am, little Miss Needy."

Ruby jerked around, knocking her drink to the floor. "Shit! Eadie, you scared me!"

I couldn't keep the anger from seeping through my words. "Oh, I'm sorry! You were so far away I got scared. I mean, you know how I like to cling."

Ruby stood, her naked feet surrounded by broken glass and ice cubes. She glanced at my mother, probably hoping Mom would bail her out.

How little she knew my mother.

Mom placed an ice cube in her mouth.

Ruby turned back to me. "That's not what I was saying, Eadie. I just meant—"

"I think what you said was pretty clear. Now that you've entered the limelight, I'm getting heavy on your coattails."

Ruby shut her eyes and flung her arms down to her sides. Her toenails, six crimson and four naked, lined up neatly in a row. "Eadie,

I can't move! Could you at least get a broom? Or something to clean this up with?"

I glared at my mother. "Does this make you happy, Mom? To have my girlfriend confirm your little fantasy that if it weren't for me you'd be a famous actress?"

Mom began chewing her ice cube, a habit of hers I've always hated.

Ruby moaned. "Eadie, please get me a broom…"

"Oh," I said, "*You* need help from little Little Miss Needy?"

"*I* didn't call you that!"

"No. I called myself that, didn't I? Get your stuff. I'm calling a cab."

Before I charged out, my mother crossed her arms, feigning a sigh to heaven.

But in my mother's world, there is no heaven. *Just the condo directly above her.*

The truck hit a pothole, jarring me back to the fact that I was driving. *Focus, Eadie. Focus!* Some unknown country western singer was massacring Patsy Cline's famous "I Fall to Pieces," and I remembered Ruby telling me, "Never sing someone else's song, unless you can do it better." I switched the radio off.

Up ahead there was a man on his knees in the middle of the road. It looked like he was wearing a black cape. As I approached, I realized it wasn't a man, but five or six vultures feasting on some ill-fated animal's carcass. I slowed down, almost to a crawl. They begrudgingly opened their ungainly, black-fingered wings and lifted off the ground, not far, though, their red, featherless faces peering down at me, annoyed. I passed the flattened animal—somebody's dog—and a wave of sadness swept over me. Some kid or rancher had lost a friend.

Parched, I cursed myself for not picking up a soda at the market.

For the next few miles, I tried not to think of the peaches sitting on the seat to my right. I hadn't eaten a peach since the day Ruby left. *A good reason to eat one now,* my inner troll cooed. *It's just fruit! What are you so afraid of?*

I reached my hand into the plastic bag and pulled out the first peach I touched. It was soft, but not too soft. *Perfect.* I held it to my nose, rubbing its fuzzy skin against my lips. The smell was exquisite, like the pungent aftermath of a summer shower.

My teeth cut through the delicate skin into the soft juicy center. The sugary pulp exploded across my tongue, bringing with it a surge of tears so strong I couldn't swallow—could barely see the road. Suddenly there was an SUV on my tail. I tried slowing so he'd pass, but the driver was so brain-dead he just rode my ass that much closer, leaving me no choice but to pull over.

The SUV barreled by, sporting a "Support Our Troops" sticker. I turned off my engine and gave way to sobbing, forcing myself, in between wrenching sobs, to swallow the fleshy sweetness of the peach. *Fruit,* I told myself as my trembling hands returned the peach to my lips, my tongue. *Just fucking fruit!* I could feel warm tears etching lines down my cheeks, past my nose to my chin, mixing with snot and sticky peach juice.

My lungs ached with each grab for air. My eyes stung. The tears weren't about Ruby, either. Not really. I'd been storing these tears for decades, abandoned in the crooks of my arms when there'd been no one to return my hugs, stuck to the souls of my feet when I'd been unable to stand my ground.

Once I reached the peach pit, I was still sniveling but was through the worst of it. I got out of the truck, my legs all wobbly. I needed to blow my nose on something and didn't want to use my shirt. The only thing I could find was an oil rag in the bed of the truck. I used it anyway, then noticed a windmill, water tank brimming, just beyond the fence. I angled my way through the barbed wire and splashed cool water on my face, around the back of my neck, and under my arms. It felt so good, fresh, like I was washing away all the stupid choices I'd ever made.

By the time I returned to the truck, I felt lighter than I had in months—years, maybe. "Thanks, Silas," I muttered as I turned the key in the ignition, "you cocksucking case of jock fungus." A pickup towing a cattle trailer rattled by. I pulled out behind it.

When I turned into Old Luke's driveway, I didn't immediately see him, just Sparkplug lying prone in the shade of a tractor. I got out of the truck. Sparkplug slapped his tail once against the cracked earth, creating a puff of dust. I couldn't resist. "Hey, Sparkplug! Hot enough for ya?" Another slap of the tail.

To my relief, the garage was a few degrees cooler. Luke was under an old Plymouth Duster. I recognized his boots—the new ones. "Luke?"

A voice bellowed out through the open hood of the car. "Yeah?"

"It's Eadie. I was just checking up on my T-bird. Any news?"

"Looks like I'm gonna have to build it myself."

"So, uh, it'll be closer to eight hundred then, huh?"

"We'll see how it goes."

I took this bit of info in and was surprised to find that it didn't totally depress me. I mean, it didn't thrill me, but it was like, okay, why make the situation worse by hating it? "Any idea how long?"

"Depends on how easy it is to pull from the other car."

"Okay then, I'll just check back in."

"Sounds good."

I turned to leave, but something I needed to do snagged my brain. "Hey, Luke?"

"Yeayup?"

"You mind if I hang for a bit?"

"Nope. Make yerself at home."

I left the garage and walked over to Pebbles. She was no longer in the bay, but out with the junkers and covered in a fine red dust. I took a moment to brush off the debris that had collected under her wipers, then opened the door and retrieved the photo of Ruby tucked in the visor. Photo in hand, I tramped into the barren landscape, my back to Old Luke's. Foxtails stuck in my socks, grasshoppers shot from the ground around my calves, a small snake slithered into the weeds, but I trudged on, the hot sun beating down on my head. It was the first time I understood why people in Texas wore boots and broad-brimmed hats. It wasn't all for show, as I'd always assumed. It made good sense.

My fantasy had been to find some poignant place to rip Ruby to shreds and scatter her to the wind. But after the windmill, I no longer wanted to destroy her. Instead, I kissed her once and placed her under a rock. "Bye, Ruby," I said. "I hope you get your shit together." A slight breeze came up. The rock held her in place. "And just to let you know, it wasn't you that made me unhappy, it was me. Always me. I've got a lot to figure out. I never think I'm good enough for the people I fall in love with."

I walked back to the garage, marveling at my new sense of inner peace. Even the grasshoppers didn't annoy me. I noticed Old Luke walking around to his couch. He was looking up at his meadowlark singing away on the wire. Sparkplug was at his heels. "Can I join you?" I asked when I got to within speaking distance.

Old Luke nodded, so I made my way to the old rusted chair and sat. I couldn't shake the feeling that I owed him an explanation. From his perspective, it must have looked like I'd walked out there, talked to a rock, and came back.

"I hope you don't mind, but I'm leaving a piece of my history out there. A photo, actually. I'm trying to believe that if I let the old stuff go, new will come."

"Boyfriend?" he asked.

His assumption made me feel invisible. And I didn't want to be. Not after what I'd just been through. "Actually, it was my girlfriend. I'm a lesbian." I looked at Old Luke for his reaction.

He didn't give me much, just a slight curving upward of the right side of his mouth. "I'll be. Can't say I've ever met one of those before."

"Well, now you have."

He shook his head. "Don't that beat all."

That said, we sat and listened to the meadowlark's inspired song. I was glad I'd told him the truth. *To hell with the consequences*. After a few minutes had passed, I asked, "You like peaches?"

"Sure do," he said.

I retrieved the peaches from the truck and brought them over. He took one. So did I. And this one tasted like a plain old peach. "Good, huh?"

"Sure is."

"They're a gift from the Milsaps. You know them?"

"Yup."

"So you know Silas, then."

"Yup."

"I had kind of a run-in with him today."

Old Luke considered this. "He seems to have run-ins with lots of folks."

I took another bite of peach, wishing Old Luke were more of a talker. "Really?" I asked, hoping to goad him on. What he said was not what I expected.

"The man's got a hole in his soul."

I chuckled nervously. "Don't we all? I mean, some bigger than others, of course..." My sentence petered out for lack of a clear thought.

Again, he considered my words. "Could be. Just some folks know they do and some folks don't. Them that don't, it makes 'em hard to get along with. Can make 'em dangerous—mean."

"How about those who know they do?" I was worried about my own soul. I'd never thought about it being punctured, but now that he'd put the thought in my head... "What do they do?"

He took off his hat and scratched his head. "Far as I can figure, each man gotta work that out for hisself." As an afterthought he added, "Or herself, I s'pose."

I pulled my feet up onto the edge of the chair and looked at Sparkplug. "You dogs have to deal with this heavy kind of stuff?"

Old Luke smiled. "Sparkplug's got enough to deal with in this lifetime. He's got me." Then Old Luke did something he'd never done: he looked me right in the eyes. "You watch out for Silas, ya' hear?"

I nodded, trying not to come off as creeped out as I felt. But I needn't have worried, because Old Luke broke eye contact almost immediately and stood. "Break's over, Sparkplug."

I watched the two of them shuffle back to the garage, feeling very alone. Just me, the meadowlark, a bunch of grasshoppers, and the hole in my soul.

Chapter Eighteen

It was Friday evening and I was driving back from another day of working with Buddy Bud. The job was coming along nicely, slower than if I'd been doing it by myself, but definitely more entertaining. Buddy Bud's shenanigans were good for me. They kept my mind off my problems. Unfortunately, when we finished, they were right where I'd left them.

I'd barely seen Piggin and Heifer since Heifer's and my rescue mission on Wednesday night. They claimed to be busy with church stuff, something about a revival, which was fine by me. Despite Sweet Ginger's reassurances, I was still sure they were going to ask me to leave. Just because Heifer'd once had a homosexual love interest didn't mean she was all groovy with lesbians. In fact, in my experience, people who vehemently repressed their homosexuality were usually the most condemning.

Flicking on my blinker, I prayed they'd be home already, tucked into their trailers with their shoes off. *Maybe I can avoid eviction one more day*. My ostrich totem never quits. I glanced in my rearview mirror. *Shit!* Piggin's Olds Ninety-eight was barreling down the highway behind me. Preparing myself for the worst, I pulled into the driveway.

Piggin was the first of the sisters out of the car. "What a coinkidink!" she said cheerfully. "I hope this means you'll join us for dinner!"

This was *not* what I expected. *Maybe Heifer told her everything and it's all cool.* I glanced over at Heifer. She was pulling herself out of the car, making a point not to look in my direction. *Nope. She still hasn't told her.* Under the circumstances, I thought it wise to decline Piggin's dinner offer.

But Piggin started up again.

"We picked up catfish and hush puppies over at Red's. He fries the best catfish in Texas. Gets the crisp just right. And Heifer's got some leftover potatoes from our Wednesday Bible meeting. Isn't that right, Heifer?" Heifer, now blatantly ignoring both of us, lumbered toward her trailer, her blouse clinging to her wide, rounded back, revealing a bra that pinched in her flesh. Patches of perspiration bloomed under her armpits. Piggin placed a Styrofoam take-out carton on the roof of the car and gave me a look I took to mean, "We should wait until Heifer is out of earshot to continue our conversation." And so this is what we did, Piggin fiddling with the Styrofoam container, which had popped open, and me, just waiting. When Heifer finally shut her trailer door, Piggin said, "She's in one of her moods where she could argue with a fence post. Don't you take her to heart."

I leaned against the warm truck chassis and crossed my arms. "Maybe she's just tired."

Piggin squeezed the bridge of her nose for a couple of seconds. It was an awkward move and made me think she was about to cry. I almost asked if she was okay, but she instantly recovered, thrusting out her hands and wiggling her fingers and making me wonder if that flash of sadness had even happened.

Each nail sported a tiny Texas flag. "What do you think?" Her smile was so forced it looked cartoonish. "I had them done on my lunch break. I saw another gal with the same thing, only hers were American. Cute, huh?"

I nodded, trying to read her mood. "They're amazing. So... intricate."

She retrieved her Styrofoam container from the roof of the car. "You know, with your art skill you'd probably make an excellent nail technician. And let me tell you, they make good money. K'Lynn just bought one of those above-ground swimming pools for her family."

I had to clear my throat to keep from laughing. "I don't know if I have the people skills for it, Piggin." I pulled my satchel from the truck, ready to end the conversation and part ways.

"I don't know what you're talking about, Eadie. I think you're just as sweet as ice cream." Knitting her brow, she scrutinized my physique, like she might if she were a rancher at a cattle auction and I was up for sale. Her expression made it clear I wasn't Grade A. "Have you ever thought about getting a makeover? That can do wonders for a girl's self-esteem. I just read an article about it in a magazine. This girl, she was just so depressed, had been to the doctor and everything. Then she just happened to win this makeover in a raffle or something, and poof! Depression gone. It was a whole new her!"

"Thanks," I said, "I'll give it some thought," and once again made to leave.

"Sweet Jesus! Look at me keeping you out here! Why, it's hotter than two goats in a pepper patch. Let's go inside where it's cool and I'll get dinner going."

"You know, there's some stuff I really want to take care of..."

"That's fine. Come on back when you're done. It's T.G.I.F., for heaven's sake. We girls need to have a good time. Let our hair down. In fact I think I'll make us up my famous cherry/lime coolers."

There was no refusing her.

I popped over to my place, took a hit of pot, brushed my teeth, and headed back over. I found Piggin was on the phone and there was no sign of Heifer. Piggin nodded for me to sit down and continued her conversation. "I'm tellin' you I *know* they got their payoff. I deposited it for them today. Roy Peterson was down there snapping pictures..."

She listened to her friend's response while handing me a turquoise plastic tumbler. It was filled with an iced drink and sported a round slice of lime on its brim. I took a sip of what I assumed was cherry/lime cooler. The sugary syrup from the drink coated my tongue like fresh paint.

Piggin gestured a yapping mouth with her hand. "Yup, twenty percent goes back to the church...I know, and all Ira's medical bills too..." She rolled her eyes for my benefit. "I know, I know...Believe me, I want to. We could use the money. I just got to convince that skeptical sister of mine...Don't I know! She's as stubborn as a warped door!" Then, as if stopping another onslaught of jabbering, she said, "Oh, dear! Eadie's just walked in. I'm going to have to go. All right... I'll call you...Okay...Will do...Bye, now." She hung the receiver onto the cradle of the wall phone and exhaled dramatically. "I swear! This Jubilee Trust Fund has really got people wound up. It's all anyone could talk about at the bank today. And now they're calling me at home."

I hoisted my glass of liquid candy into the air. "T.G.I.F.!"

"And none too soon!" She laughed, picking up her glass. "Oh, and

I completely forgot to thank you for the other night. I heard Heifer had you out on a Sweet Ginger run."

"Glad to help out."

Piggin pulled a Tupperware container from the freezer. "You like gumbo?"

"Never tried it."

"Then you're in for a real treat," she said, plopping an icy block into a pan, then brought the conversation back to Sweet Ginger. "If we didn't get so scared for her out on those roads at night, alone, dressing the way she does, I swear we'd leave her there. Teach her a lesson. But if something bad ever happened…"

"I know the dilemma well," I said. "It's a hard one to figure out."

"Someone in your family?"

I considered confiding that I'd been babysitting my alcoholic mother since I was ten, had subsequently fallen in love with another alkie, followed by two drug addicts, and then Ruby, who was a mixture of all of these, but I wanted it to be an early night. Besides, I was sick of the story—sick of defining myself by it. "Just a friend," I said.

Piggin pulled a pot from a low cabinet. The width of her derriere was astounding. "Once Mama got…sick…Heifer and I pretty much had to bring up Sweet Ginger and Baby Boy. They were so much younger than us."

"Wasn't there another kid?"

"You're thinking of Tiny, but he was born *before* the vasectomy, like me and Heifer. And he didn't have to take care of things the way we did on account of he was a boy, don'cha know."

"I don't mean to pry," I said, fully intending to, "but before the vasectomy?"

"After Heifer, me, and Tiny, Daddy decided no more kids. I think he was mostly worried about the financial. Anyhoo, he got himself the operation to where he'd, as they say, be shooting blanks, but those tubes or whatever grew back together. And boy howdy, when Sweet Ginger was born did he have an awful fit! Said she wasn't his." The next words Piggin spoke so quietly, I barely heard her. "Poor mama endured quite a lot on account of that."

"Did he ever find out the truth?"

"Oh, yes. Doctor finally straightened him out. That's why we got Baby Boy. Daddy decided the failed operation was God's will—not that he was a churchgoing man. Whenever he got drunk you couldn't shut him up about how 'some men are so fertile you just can't hold 'em back.'" She sprinkled salt into the pot. "I think that what's wrong with Sweet Ginger, her heart got broke the day she was born." Then some pepper. "Took a whole year for J.D. to even hold her. She was just a baby, for heaven's sake! But to this day, she's trying to win her daddy's love, that's what I think. That's what all her boyfriends are about."

I nodded. *Born with a hole in her soul.*

Piggin peered into the oven. "You didn't happen to talk to Heifer on your way over?"

My stomach lurched. "Nope."

"This fish is going to dry out if she doesn't hurry up." She turned toward me. "Would you mind knocking on her door and see what's keeping her?"

When I got to Heifer's, I knocked tentatively, then waited. There was no answer. Figuring she might not have heard, I knocked again, louder this time. Still, there was no response. I checked for her car, to see if maybe she'd run an errand, but it was parked in its usual spot. I hated to knock again, sure she knew it was me and just didn't want to answer. Then it occurred to me that something bad might have happened. Maybe she'd fallen, or worse. I put my ear to the door, listened, and cracked the door open. "Heifer?" The brief sound of a muffled garbage disposal slipped out. I took a step inside. "Heifer?" Again, the garbage disposal followed by quiet. Once fully in her kitchen, I realized the garbage disposal sound wasn't coming from the sink, but from the back of the trailer. *So, what is it?* The microwave on the counter dinged.

I crept down the carpeted hall, stopping when I reached the guest bedroom. Heifer was on the newly stripped bed, belly up, a pile of rumpled sheets next to her on the floor. Her mouth was agape, snoring.

I felt immediately guilty. *She wouldn't want me to see her like this.* But what choice did I have? I tiptoed in. *Why am I the one doing this? Piggin should be the one waking her.* I lightly touched her arm. "Heifer?" The microwave dinged again. "Heifer?" She swallowed a snore and gummed at the air, but didn't wake. *This is ridiculous. I should just go back to Piggin's and say I couldn't wake her.* But I tried one more time, this time shaking her gently. "Heifer?"

She startled awake and looked around, disoriented. "Whatchoo doing here?"

"Um. Piggin sent me. She wants to get going on dinner."

She righted herself, blinked a couple of times, and dragged herself off the bed. "Don't know why I bother to change the sheets. Sweet Ginger's only one ever sleeps here." I followed her into the kitchen where she pulled from the microwave a bowl of mashed potatoes, stuck her finger in it, put it back in and pushed a few buttons. "Check it when it dings, will you?" she muttered, shuffling back down the hall.

Is she going to say anything about the other night?

By the time she reemerged, she'd changed from her work clothes into a Dallas Cowboys T-shirt and a pair of workout pants sporting a white stripe up each leg. "I suppose Piggin's in a tizzy," she said adjusting the waistband.

"She's worried about the fish getting dry."

She pulled a dishtowel from a drawer. "She's been driving me crazy all day."

"Heifer, I'm sorry about the other night. If you want me to leave…"

She wrapped the towel around the bowl and grumbled, "Leave? Why would I want you to leave?" I could tell she was trying to sound unruffled, but the ticking of her heart told me otherwise.

"I don't know…I guess I just thought…"

She turned toward me. "Eadie, you are welcome here. Now, whether or not the Good Lord will want you at His Pearly Gates, well, that's between you and Him. But I don't want Him throwing me out because I didn't shelter a wayfaring stranger."

I was tempted to ask her what the Good Lord was going to make of her incident with Lilah, but kept my mouth shut.

She strode to the door. "Take the potatoes, would you?" I pulled them from the microwave using the towel for a hot pad. "As I see it," she said holding the door for me, "what you do in private is your business. Just don't be bringing it around here. Piggin is very delicate and we wouldn't want to upset her."

"Okay," I said, plodding at her heels with the potatoes. "I'll try not to say anything. But I really don't want to have to lie—if I'm asked, that is. I mean, that seems sinful in its own way, doesn't it? I mean, wouldn't the Lord rather I tell the truth?"

"You're going to have to ask Him about that," she said, breathless from the short walk. "And seeing as you'll be coming with us to church on Sunday, I suppose that's as good a time as any."

It was right then that my foot caught on a root, sending potatoes hurling to the ground.

CHAPTER NINETEEN

Saturday afternoon. I was lying on my bed, wilted, while my heat-deranged brain was doing a warped imitation of the Warning-Will-Robinson robot from Lost in Space: Must find air-conditioning. Must find air-conditioning. I picked up my spray bottle of water and gave myself another squirt while lining myself up with the fan's feeble stream of hot air—my cool-off strategy for the last few hours.

Piggin and Heifer were tucked away inside their respective trailers, air conditioners humming, doing who knew what? No doubt their best to pretend the bizarreness of the previous night's dinner had never happened. I pictured Piggin, TV on, madly flipping through magazines while inhaling a giant iced cherry/lime cooler. As for Heifer, I hadn't a clue. Sleeping? Staring at the wall? Watching football? Whatever it was, it was air-conditioned, which beat the hell out of what I was doing—sitting here rehashing the whole thing in my suffocatingly hot trailer.

I'd avoided them all day. As they had me.

I rolled off the bed and crawled to my doorstep, then sat with my head in the shade of the trailer while hanging my legs outside. I couldn't get the disaster dinner to quit its incessant roller-coastering around my brain—and I'm not talking potatoes splattered all over the ground, either. That spaz attack was just the beginning. It got worse. Mostly having to do with the topics, which, much like the ill-fated potatoes, never made it to the table. Like when Piggin kept bringing up "this certain charming young man at our church," as she kept calling him, who'd just come back from Texas A&M and would probably love to have someone his own age to talk to, or go to a movie with. I kept glaring at Heifer, Why can't I tell her I'm a lesbian? and she kept glaring back, Because you can't, that's why. So I had to sit there enduring Piggin's attempts at matchmaking, one after another, after another…

Then there was the moment I coughed cherry/lime cooler out my nose.

But the worst of it came shortly after we finished off the catfish. Piggin was heating oil in the fry baby to try out this new recipe she'd gotten off the food channel for fried ice cream while Heifer was telling her she should consider helping out with the Sunday School. "You'd be great with kids," she said. Piggin snickered. "I haven't heard them making any announcements, have you?" And Heifer said, "You never know." And Piggin said, "Well, *I* know. If they wanted me, they'd ask. That's how it works." And then Heifer repeated to me how good Piggin was with kids. And I said something stupid like, "I don't understand wanting children. It looks like so much work, and half the time they wind up hating you anyway." As I was saying this, Piggin was dropping the first dollop of breaded ice cream into the sizzling hot oil and suddenly began screaming, "My eye! My eye!" and ran to the bathroom with her hand covering her eye. Heifer followed right behind her, yelling, "What happened? What happened?" I got up to go after them, but the phone began to ring and Heifer spat, "Answer it!"

It was Sweet Ginger—Sweet fucked-up Ginger—and she was asking, "How's it going? How's Piggin?" Only at first I didn't understand her because she was slurring her words and there was loud music in the background and Piggin and Heifer were still making a ruckus in the bathroom. But she asked again and this time I understood her, well, her words at least. Her meaning still escaped me. How could she know that Piggin had just splashed hot oil in her eye? I never got the chance to ask her about it, though, because she began blabbing something about it being the birthday of Piggin's kid, the one she'd given up for adoption.

"What?" I said, sure I'd misheard her. I was really regretting having taken a hit of pot before I came over.

"Piggin's big romance. Her *only* fricking romance," Sweet Ginger slurred. "She really loved that boy. And damned if he didn't love her back, the only way that men know how. Daddy wouldn't let her keep the baby. Sent her off. I'll never forget the day she came back…that look in her eye…so sad…so fucking sad…" With a bit more prodding, she went on to tell me how Piggin celebrates the baby's birthday every year and that Heifer always comes over, and, even though they never talk about it, they both know it's the big day. And how she, Sweet Ginger, when she's not too fucked up, always calls, and even though she doesn't talk about the baby either, Piggin knows that's why she's calling. "The invisible baby…" she slurred.

The next thing I knew, Heifer was walking toward me, telling me to go take care of Piggin in the bathroom. She snatched the phone and turned her back to keep her conversation with Sweet Ginger private. I wanted to say, Don't worry, Sweet Ginger already told me all. But she looked so stressed, I kept my mouth shut.

I found Piggin sitting on the toilet, calmer now, with a washcloth over one eye. "It wasn't my eye after all," she said, sniffling. When she pulled back the damp washcloth I saw she had a tear-shaped blister underneath her eye. I asked her if she had any Neosporin and she said she did. So I dabbed a little on and pretended I didn't know about her baby.

And now it was today. And I was hot and wanted to go home, but I had no home. This was it. This little piece-of-shit trailer, sitting next to two bigger piece-of-shit trailers out in the middle of bum-fuck nowhere with a couple of loony-tune sisters.

I noticed a lizard doing lizard push-ups by my toe. He was clearly unaware that it was attached to something as big as me. I kept still. *How did I wind up here? And when am I going to get to leave?* The way Rauston had sucked me in was creepy. *Maybe I'm just like the lizard and standing in front of some giant foot I don't have the brains to see. If so, is it benevolent? Or just toying with me until it stomps down and crushes me?* Right then, while pondering the existence of God, I remembered: *church tomorrow.* I threw my head into my hands. *Shit. Not only do I not want to go, I've got nothing to wear.*

Unable to stand my pitiful self any longer, I stood, sending the lizard scampering off in a tizzy. *I've got to get out. I'm driving myself crazy.* I decided on Jameson's—like I was brimming with options—and gave myself a final spritz of water. I'll brush out some of the trickier edging. Stuff too hard for Buddy Bud to paint.

Jameson had said I could take the day off as he and Buddy were off to a father/son picnic and softball game. But why did I need a day off? I didn't have a life! I was just watching everybody else's.

Then again, the market was air-conditioned.

❖

When I pushed through the doors of Jameson's and felt the cool air surround my body, I almost dropped to my knees in gratitude. Kitty, at her register, was filling out some kind of paperwork. "Hey, Kitty."

Without bothering to look up, she mumbled, "You just missed Jameson. He and Buddy Bud—"

"—are at the picnic. I know."

She shrugged and went back to her paperwork.

I headed for the office. Once there, I dialed Jameson's cell and asked him if it was okay for me to get a leg up on some of the work. It sounded like he was driving.

"Whatever you think's best, Eadie," the tinny voice coming through the line said. "Oh, and that bag of expired and damaged groceries by the door is for you, if you want…Hang on, Buddy Bud wants to say something to you."

"Hi, Eadie!"

"Hey, Buddy Bud."

"Dad bought me my own baseball glove!"

"That's pretty cool. You'll have to show it to me Monday."

"Is Monday tomorrow?"

"No, tomorrow is Sunday."

His voice began to break up. "Maybe Dad'll…" crackle crackle "…to…" crackle "You're…" crackle crackle "…church, right?"

"I'm having trouble hearing you…"

More crackling.

"Buddy Bud?"

Nothing.

I hung up the phone, annoyed that our conversation didn't get to properly close out. *Just like everything else in my sorry excuse for a life.* Sighing, I checked out the bag of groceries. Peanut butter with a ripped label, a box of outdated English muffins, a perfectly good bag of Chips Ahoy!, and two dented cans of baked beans.

Nice.

I changed into my paint clothes, warmed up half a pot of old coffee, and drank a cup while munching on cookies. My feet propped on the desk, I let the effects of the caffeine and sugar have their way with me. It felt good to have a place I was supposed to be. Good to have a purpose. Finished with my snack, I pried open a can of primer, chose my brush, and got to work.

I was edging out the inner back corners of the bookshelf when someone entered the office. Startled, I cracked my head against the shelf.

"Sorry!" a woman's voice said.

I sat back on my haunches and found Cadence standing in the doorway. Once again, her outfit was choice: pedal pushers and a vintage bowling shirt with *Trixy* embroidered over the pocket. She wore her hair in a high, fifties-style ponytail, showcasing her signature lime green cat's-eye glasses. There was a Cat in the Hat Band-Aid on her knee.

I balanced my paintbrush on the edge of the can. "No problem. When I paint I get lost in my own world." I followed this deep statement with this weird chuckle-snort that made me wish my head was still crammed in the bookshelf. Fortunately, she seemed too preoccupied by a shoebox she was holding to give my geekiness much thought.

"Whatcha got?" I asked.

Kneeling by me, she opened the box. A scruffy-looking brown bird in a nest of coffee filters and wadded Kleenex was looking a bit worse for the wear.

"You'd make a good mama bird."

"I don't know about that," she said with a sad little chuckle. "He won't fly. I think he's had some kind of fight or accident. I was hoping maybe Buddy Bud would take him on. He's a real champion when it comes to critters in need."

She was so close I could smell her hair: lavender with a hint of happily ever after. A loose strand curled against her neck. "He won't be in today. He's at a softball game with his dad."

She stood and placed the box on the desk. "Oh, that's right." She bit her lower lip as she considered what her next step should be, then addressed me in a matter-of-fact tone. "You know anything about birds?"

I stood too. "Not really. I just found out what a meadowlark is."

She jauntily dug her hands into her hips, accenting her slender waist. "Well, I can see you're going to be no help. He's a sparrow."

No tiptoeing around eggshells with this woman. I got the feeling if I even came close to a shell, she'd let me know. After my stint with Ruby, she of the deadly eggshell mote, I found this insanely attractive. Besides, I got the distinct impression Cadence was flirting with me.

I cleared my throat and said in an authoritative voice, "Bird identification is out of my area of expertise, I'm afraid."

She lifted one side of her mouth, her eyes full of concern for the bird.

I could have kicked myself. She was clearly upset and here I was making light of the situation.

"I've tried feeding him water with an eyedropper, but he won't take it," she said.

I looked in the box again. The bird was breathing rapidly and missing some tail feathers. "I'm sure he'll be all right." *Way to go, Eadie. Impress her with your vast veterinary knowledge.*

She puckered her lips, then looked at me dead on. "So, you here all day?"

"Uh, at least a couple more hours." I shoved my hands in my pockets. "Why?"

"I've got Jameson's new computer in my car—well, not new, but new to him. It shouldn't take more than a half hour to plug it in and install some software. I could come back."

"If you can work around me," I said, "I can around you."

"Cool." She propped the punctured cardboard top back on the box. "I need it quiet, though."

And boy, did she mean what she said. Once she'd hauled the computer up the stairs and into the room—she refused any help—all talking ceased. It was just her mouse-jockeying at the computer and me edging out the shelves.

Half an hour came and went. She gnawed on her lower lip, her pencil, a knuckle, then, out of nowhere, she'd begin happily humming, zipping her mouse around the pad like a racecar. Listening to her was so intimate, so tender, it made my heart go mush.

I found myself wanting to impress her.

Having cut a perfectly clean edge of primer between the wall and the built-in bookshelf—without masking tape, thank you very much—I glanced over my shoulder to see if she'd noticed and discovered her looking right at me. I nearly died. What kind of gomer needs approval for painting a straight line? She lifted her eyebrows and nodded her head slightly as if to say "Well done." Flustered, I turned around and proceeded to stick my paintbrush in my coffee cup. *Shit! Tell me she didn't see that!* Against my better judgment, I checked. She was focused on her computer, but biting back a grin. *Damn!* Rather than draw more attention to my blunder, I switched brushes and spent the next half hour willing myself not to look at her.

Keyboard keys clicked, a CD was repeatedly inserted and ejected, she emitted a long, drawn-out sigh followed by grumbling something vaguely profane, she got up to check on the bird, sat back down, clicked the mouse some more, hummed more. I had to pee during all this, but I couldn't stand the idea of her finishing up and leaving while I was gone.

I applied more primer.

She sighed again, then pushed back her office chair.

Is she finished? Under the guise of straightening my drop cloth, I casually snuck a peek. She was pointing a pencil at the computer screen as if challenging it to a duel or casting a spell. She must have felt me watching because she glanced over, crossed her eyes, and stuck her tongue out the side of her mouth.

Damn, I liked her.

Was it too much to wish she was a lesbian? But if she was, what was she doing in Rauston? *Then again, what am I doing in Rauston?* Sticking my brush into the gluey primer, I reminded myself of my notoriously faulty gaydar.

Teeth floating, I finally got up to go to the bathroom. Cadence looked up, a quizzical expression on her face. "Gotta go to the girl's room," I said casually, as if I weren't in horrendous pain. She nodded and I sauntered coolly out of the room. Once out of her sight, I flew down the stairs, taking two at a time. *Why am I letting this chick get to me? She's probably a happily married woman with 2.5 children and cable TV.*

When I returned, she was back at skating the mouse around the pad. "Still at it?" I asked, hoping the ban on speaking was over. She shushed me without ever looking away from the monitor. Deflated, I moseyed over to the shelves. Not that I let my disappointment show. No way. I was super-cool. I was a woman with a job, a woman with tools.

I'd just about completed all of the really difficult edging when she leaned back in her chair and clapped her hands together. "Bingo! I just needed to zap the old PRAM."

I tried to appear only mildly interested. "Right on."

"It's always the easy things that trip me up."

Easy for you to say. I hadn't the slightest idea what a PRAM was.

"Sorry about shutting you up," she said. "I get so distracted by humans. They're so much more interesting than computers."

I scraped the excess paint off my brush. *At least she thinks I'm more interesting than a computer.* "Seems like you know what you're doing."

"Mostly it's just persistence." She took off her glasses, rubbed her eyes, put her glasses back on again, then turned her attention to me. Again, I was struck with the forthright nature of her eye contact, only this time I got the feeling she was sizing me up in some way.

I went back to what I was doing, wishing like hell I'd worn a cuter pair of shorts.

"You got plans tonight?" she finally asked.

Is she asking me out? Commanding my face to appear neutral, I brushed the drips from the side of the can. "Not exactly plans. I haven't been in Rauston long enough to make plans." I lifted my eyes to meet hers. "To be honest, I was going to spend the evening figuring out what to wear to church tomorrow…" I was hoping to draw her out with this statement. Would she think it odd I didn't travel with several church outfits? Or would she sympathize with my predicament?

"Wow. Sounds thrilling."

Obviously, I'd need to risk a bit more information. "I packed pretty quickly when I left San Francisco. Didn't think to pack church clothes…"

She sat back in her chair. "You're from San Francisco? That's wild. I'm from Santa Cruz. Well, originally Bakersfield, but I got out of there as fast as I could."

That was a promising little nugget. Santa Cruz was like San Francisco's little sister: way hippy and way gay. "You're kidding me. What are you doing here?"

She laughed. "I keep asking myself the same question."

I waited for her to elaborate, and for a moment it looked like she might. She crossed her arms, then uncrossed them. "Actually, it's a long story. Or not long, really. Kind of short. But big. Very big."

I waited.

She bent down to pick a paperclip off the floor. "You're dying to know, aren't you?"

"Let's just say my curiosity is piqued."

She smiled her disarming smile. "Well, it's going to have to stay that way, because I want to keep this experience to myself for a while." With that, she stood, walked over to the bird, and began fussing with it.

This chick just gets more and more interesting. "I didn't mean to pry."

"You didn't. It was a perfectly normal question. It's just…well… if you'd asked me two days ago…"

I held up my hands. "It's fine. I don't need to know." But how could I not be curious? *Running from an abusive husband? Witness protection program?*

Kitty stuck her head in the door. "I'm going to be closing the store in about twenty minutes. Then I've just got to balance out my register and I'm locking up."

Granted, I have an active imagination and tend to be a bit on the paranoid side, but I swear Kitty relished breaking up my conversation with Cadence.

"No problem," I said. "I can be cleaned up in no time."

"Me too," Cadence said.

When Kitty was safely out the door, Cadence turned to me and whispered, "Does she ever give you the evil eyeball?"

I laughed. "Oh my God, does she. Like she thinks I'm Satan's personal coach." It was such a relief to find a kindred spirit—even if she was running from the law, or a sordid past, or who knew what? I didn't care. She was from the Bay Area!

She began putting disks in their respective sleeves. "Yesterday, I actually got her to smile at me. But it's taken months. I think she's in love with Jameson. She's always bringing him little baked goodies and casseroles."

I began picking up too, readying my paint-laden brushes for the fridge by wrapping them in Saran Wrap. "How long have you been here?"

"I was exaggerating when I said months. I've been here a month and a half, renting a small house out at Minnie Bell's of the famous 'Minnie Bell's Award-Winning Chow-chow.'" She put on an advertiser's voice. "You'll find it in the condiment aisle downstairs."

I tapped the paint lid on the can. "I'll have to try it."

As we continued to chat about trivialities, people we'd both met in Rauston, and the grim ramifications of World Mart moving in, I couldn't help thinking if it weren't for Kitty showing up and giving us a common enemy, we'd never have broken out of our mutually cautious scrutiny. It reminded me of those end-of-flight conversations. The kind where you've been on a six-hour flight making a point not to talk to the person you're squeezed in next to because you don't want to wind up having to gab with them the whole way. Then, as you begin the descent, one of you says something innocuous like, "So, are you done traveling or just beginning?" and suddenly the two of you are blabbing about this and that and you find out you have common interests, maybe even know someone in common, and then you're wishing you had more time to talk, only you don't, because you'd been so busy elbowing out your boundaries.

Although she'd finished her cleanup, I could tell she didn't want to leave. "So you really think it's going to take you all evening to figure out what you're wearing to church?" she asked, putting the top back on the bird's box.

"Considering I may have to piece it together with pillowcases and safety pins, yeah."

She squinched up her nose in that way one does when they've had too much wasabi. It was adorable; her nose had the sweetest little dimple on the tip—and there was that exquisite galaxy of freckles dancing across its bridge. "If I offered to help, would you come celebrate something with me?"

My heart leapt into a little jig. "Uh, sure. I guess. What are we celebrating?"

"Yesterday was my birthday. And I didn't do anything besides the obligatory and somewhat painful phone call with Mom and Dad. So I was thinking if you wanted to come out to my place, I could give my birthday a second try."

"That's wild."

"What?"

"My birthday was Sunday. Only I didn't even do the obligatory, and in my case, *very* painful phone calls with Mom and Dad."

"You're kidding."

"About which part? The birthday or the phone calls?"

"Either. Both."

"Nope. Both true."

She cocked her head. "Then we absolutely must celebrate."

I cocked mine. "Absolutely must."

"The porch, a glass of wine. We can watch the rain come in."

"Rain?"

"That's what they're predicting. Thunder and lightning and everything."

I weighed sitting on the porch with a gorgeous woman, a glass of wine in my hand, watching a thundershower pass through against being stuck in my claustrophobic trailer, rain pelting against its fiberglass wall, worrying about my ever-growing assortment of things to worry about. I mimed a toast. "To mirth-making."

She lifted her air-wineglass to meet mine. "To mirth-making."

We arranged to meet in the parking lot after I finished cleanup and she did a bit of shopping. I'd then follow her to her place. And just when I thought things couldn't get any better, she said, "Oh, and if I'm not out there when you get there, mine's the classic VW bug convertible."

Chapter Twenty

I hustled down the stairs from Jameson's office, my heart pounding. *I have a date! Cadence asked me on a date!* The more reasonable part of my brain interjected: *You can't know this is a date. For all you know, she has a boyfriend back in Santa Cruz.*

If there's one thing I hate about being a lesbian, it's the ambiguity. If I were a guy and she'd asked me back to her place to drink wine and watch the rain come in, I wouldn't have had any doubts about her intentions.

Most likely she'll want to get drunk and harp on men.

Straight women love to complain about men. They spend hours on the phone doing it, forward each other cute little male-bashing e-mails, write to Dear Abby with letters that start with "I have the most wonderful husband in the world, but…", go to book clubs and never discuss the book, just eat chocolate and rail on men. It drives me nuts! Everyone calls me a man-hater because I'm a lesbian, but I like men. Dare I say, some of my best friends are men. I just wouldn't want to sleep with one. Or share a bathroom.

Cadence is from Santa Cruz. She has to at least have been exposed to lesbians.

I reached the bottom step and was about to make the turn into the public part of the market when I heard the coarse, anger-soaked voice of Silas Milsap. It was coming from the dairy section, which shared a common wall with the stairs. *Not him again!* I stopped in my tracks. One step more and I'd be in full view. I retreated up a few steps and sat down, taking refuge behind the EMPLOYEES ONLY! sign that hung on his side of the wall. He spoke quietly, his tone seething. "It don't seem fair. Her getting the money. She ain't even from the church."

My chest felt tight. Why couldn't he shut his trap about that Helping Hands money? Was he trying to turn the whole town against me?

The voice that responded was also one I recognized. *Pastor Williams.* He too spoke in a hushed voice. "Sometimes the scale of justice is bigger than one might be able to comprehend, Silas."

"What's that supposed to mean?" Silas asked accusingly.

I wondered the same thing.

The pastor continued, "When I made my decision to offer money to that poor unfortunate traveler, I had a multitude of things to consider."

I had the urge to whip around the doorway and tell him where he could shove his "multitudes," but felt I was on the verge of hearing something juicy. Silas spoke next.

"I just don't get what's so important it means taking food from my family's mouths."

"Silas," the pastor's voice dripped condescension, "seems to me you're getting mighty used to receiving assistance from Helping Hands."

I pictured Silas shifting his stance, because when he spoke next his tone had softened considerably. "I'm not meaning to sound ungrateful, Pastor. And I'd understand if you felt someone from the church was more in need. But this girl, she looks like she's never walked through the doors of a church in her whole entire life."

Damn right. And proud of it. Then I remembered promising Piggin and Heifer I'd go to church the following day. I leaned into the wall. *Holy Shit. What is my life coming to?*

"Silas, you don't need to worry about this. You got bigger opportunities now. This Jubilee Trust Fund will make it so you never need Helping Hands again. No one in the church will. All you got to do is look at how my life has changed since I was blessed." He paused. "Now, have you just about got your gift together?"

"My sister in Arkansas says she's gonna sent me a check. And I got a brother in Louisiana, just got outta jail. I'm going ask him too, but I'm not sure he'll have it."

"That's good, Silas. Keep working on it—for the sake of your family. It's time you moved on from Helping Hands. It's time you got yourself a real blessing."

A squeaky shopping cart interrupted their exchange.

"Afternoon, Mrs. Sellars!" the pastor chimed in a syrupy voice.

"Why, hello, Pastor. Silas. Hot enough for you?" Mrs. Sellars wheezed as if she needed an oxygen tank.

Pastor Williams chuckled. "If you don't like this heat, Mrs. Sellars, I suggest you keep coming to church. You-know-where is a whole lot hotter than this!"

Mrs. Sellars's laugh was hijacked by a hacking cough. "Oh, dear me…dear me…" she managed through her coughing. "Pastor, you do have a way." More coughing. "I just hope you don't get me laughing tomorrow. I'd hate to start up coughing in the middle of your sermon."

"I'll do my best, but you know how I am," he boasted.

"Yes, I do," she clucked. "Yes, I do, I'll see you tomorrow!"

As soon as her shopping cart squeaked on, Pastor Williams picked back up with Silas. "You're going to have to trust me, Silas. I got the whole church to think about. And there's the new building too. Now, you need some money to get you through the week?"

"Pastor, I don't want…"

"I won't take no. Here, take this. Get something nice for Maxine to cook up for dinner." I imagined Pastor William's clean, manicured hands passing a few crisp twenties into the nicotine-stained, callused hands of Silas Milsap. "You're a good man, Silas."

"Thank you, Pastor. I'm sorry I—"

"No need to apologize. You were just trying to take care of your family. Isn't that right?"

"Um, yes, sir."

I had to admit, Pastor Williams was good, really good. In less than five minutes, he'd manipulated Silas's red-hot outrage into nothing more than a demeaned mumble. *But what is he up to? What are his multitudes of reasons for giving me, a total stranger, the Helping Hands money?* Silas and I were in agreement here. *It doesn't make sense. Is he trying to bribe Piggin and Heifer?* My mind shot back to Piggin telling me how Heifer was dead-set against the new church; how she thought it was taking away from the Helping Hands program. I picked up my bag of groceries. *Why do I even care? I'm gonna get my car fixed and blow this town.*

I peeked around the doorway to make sure the coast was clear, then snuck to the restroom where I changed out of my paint clothes back into my shorts and tee and washed up. I was horrified to see a streak of paint just below my left nostril. Had it been there the whole time I'd been talking to Cadence?

Once reasonably cleaned up, I cruised down the dairy aisle, taking a moment to stow my Saran-Wrapped brushes in the back of the fridge where no one would see them, and made for the door. I hadn't seen either Silas or the pastor and figured they were long gone.

"Whatcha got in the bag?" Kitty asked suspiciously.

Much as I wanted to tell her to mind her own business, the last thing I wanted was to cause a scene. "Outdated groceries. Jameson left them for me."

She eyed me for a few seconds longer, then murmured something that sounded like, "Have a nice day," but could just as easily been, "I know you're gay."

When I pushed out the doors into the parking lot, the first thing to hit me was a wall of impenetrable heat. The second was Pastor Williams chatting with a cowboy in a pick-up. He had his hand on the roof of the cab and was laughing. "All right, then. You be good now. And stay dry," he said, thumping the roof of the truck. Behind him, rain loomed on the horizon. *At least it might cool off.* I walked to my truck, quietly chanting, *Don't see me. Don't see me. Don't see me.*

Out of the corner of my eye, I saw the cowboy pull out of the lot, then spotted Cadence's car at the far end by the road. *But where is she?* I shifted the bag of groceries to my hip and pulled my keys from my pocket, trying to maintain my air of invisibility.

"Izat Miss Eadie I see?"

I looked up, feigning surprise. Pastor Williams's hand was raised in a motionless wave a la a politician. "Yup! Just finishing up some work for Jameson."

He strode over, ostrich boots gleaming against the searing blacktop. "Ran into him at the ball game. He tells me you're working out good. Says Buddy Bud has taken a real shine to you."

"I like him too. He's a good kid." I dropped the groceries in the scorching hot truck, my back to him.

"Everything working out okay at the Wilbournes'?" he asked.

"Working out just fine." I was now standing between the open truck door and the chassis. He was on the other side of the door, his hand gripping the upper edge, essentially trapping me next to the truck.

"So Helping Hands is all right with you then?"

"So far so good. I mean, my car's not fixed yet, but the parts are coming."

His choice to stand so close made me uneasy. Plus, I was damned hot. I put my hand over my eyes to block the sun.

"Rose and Grace pretty much started the Helping Hands program. Did you know that?"

"No. Thanks for telling me."

"Yeah, that Grace! She and I don't always seen eye to eye on matters of the church. Sometimes I believe she feels Rauston Baptist is more of a social service program than a place of worship."

I nodded. *Sounds good to me.*

"But she was dead on with the Helping Hands project. Dead on!"

Now I knew he was full of shit. He'd basically implied to Silas that the Jubilee Trust Fund was going to make the Helping Hands program obsolete.

I retreated inside the truck, immediately regretting my choice. It was about thirty degrees hotter inside. My thighs were literally melting into the vinyl. "It's a good program," I said, reaching over to roll the window down. His fingers hung on the door, making it impossible to close—unless I slammed them in it. He must have felt my sentiment, because he slipped his hand off, allowing me to shut the door.

Just then, Cadence stepped out of the store and waved. I waved back and shoved the key into the ignition. He turned to see who I was waving at, then leaned on the window. "So, we going to see you in church tomorrow?"

He had me all right, just like he had Silas and who knows how many other parishioners? Silas he'd bought with money from his own pocket. Me, he'd bought with money from the church.

"I'll be there," I squeezed through a tight jaw.

"Good!" He gave the roof of the truck two of his trademark thumps. "Oh, and tell Grace that I'm starting to come around to her way of thinking. I'm starting to see the light."

I am not your damned errand girl, I thought. *Tell her yourself.* With that, I started the engine and put it into gear.

CHAPTER TWENTY-ONE

It was amazing how quickly the storm moved in. By the time I pulled into Cadence's place twenty minutes later, the temperature had cooled dramatically and the sky was a deep charcoal full of thunderheads. Cadence leapt out of her VW and headed for a laundry line, next to the house, full of flapping sheets and towels. One sheet had wrapped itself completely around the line, giving it the appearance of a cocoon. "This will just take a minute," she yelled. "Chardonnay is in the fridge. Door's open."

Her house, a small beige deal with shiplap wood siding—and needing a paint job—had a cozy front porch with two rockers. Anchored between the huge tumultuous sky and miles of flat, dusty earth, the house reminded me of the stubby mesquite trees, their stubborn roots digging into the land, daring the wind to blow them away. A wind chime hanging from a porch rafter tinkled wildly. Somewhere, something was unhinged or unhooked and hammered repeatedly against the house. *Loose shutter? Screen door?* I spotted another house in the distance. It was much larger and, unlike Cadence's, surrounded by old trees. No doubt her place was built for a hired hand. Maybe one of those 1920s Sears and Roebucks house kits. Where else would they have gotten the wood? All the trees I'd seen in Rauston were imports, obviously planted to buffer the well-to-do from the harsher elements.

The porch floorboards creaked warmly as I headed for the door. Inside, I found a sparsely furnitured room, which seemed to serve as living room, dining room, and office all at once. There were no curtains on the windows and an old wood-burning stove in the corner. The kind you see cowboys making their coffee on in the movies. In its current incarnation, the stove was home to a bouquet of sunflowers.

I made my way to the kitchen. Wooden cabinets with black wagon-wheel drawer handles and an ancient-looking, deep-enameled sink lined one wall. On another wall was a Kenmore stove and a brand-new refrigerator wedged into an alcove that had obviously been made for a smaller fridge. It was all very utilitarian and gave me the feeling that Cadence wasn't planning on staying long. The only real decoration was a photo on the refrigerator door of a somewhat dour middle-aged couple. If I had to guess, I'd say he—rumpled suit and wire-rim glasses—was a high school principal, and she—pressed dress with a scarf neatly knotted around her neck—was a mortgage broker or real estate agent. *Her parents?*

The door creaked open then banged shut. "Wineglasses are in the cabinet by the sink," Cadence said, scuttling through the house with an armful of laundry. "We're going to get a real storm." A flash of lightning followed by a rumbling thunder shook the house.

We reconvened on the porch just as the rain began to pelt down. "Oh good, you found the bottle opener," she said, sliding into a rocker. More thunder and lightning, this time much closer. "I can't get enough of this thunder and lightning. I wish we got it in California."

I wound the corkscrew into the cork and pulled down its arms, popping the cork. "We get it once in a while." I poured us each a glass of wine.

"Yeah, but not like this."

I made a toast to thunder and our birthdays and we clinked glasses. "Cool place you got."

Our feet were now resting on the rail, mine in my work sneaks and hers bare. I noticed her toes were in perfect size order, making her feet look square, like little pianos waiting to be played. There was an etched silver toe ring on the second toe of her right foot.

As we sipped wine, she told me the story of how she'd found her place, her luck at meeting Minnie Bell at the post office and by chance mentioning to Minnie Bell that she was good with computers. "Turns out she needed my services. She and some of her friends are hoping to incorporate and wanted to know more about the Internet." She went on to tell me about Minnie Bell's associates and their products: Grandma Betty's Award-Winning Jalapeno-Cheese Corn Muffins, Tiny's

Beef Jerky: A chew you'll come back to!, and Sal's Truly Incredible Fudge. "It's amazing to find people who know basically nothing about computers. Just yesterday, I was showing Minnie Bell how to use Quicken."

Interesting. I don't usually associate cute toes with computer geeks.

"At home, I maintain Web sites for several companies and a few nonprofits, mostly in Santa Cruz and San Jose. Since I've been here, I've been telecommuting. That's how I can afford this little junket."

This is new. I'm attracted to a woman who has her shit together.

The more she talked, the more I began to wonder if she wasn't a little nervous to have me there. Then again, there was that secret reason for being in Rauston… *Maybe she's not as together as she wants me to believe.* "So you're trading your services for rent?" I asked, eager to keep her talking. It would keep me from having to recount the lame set of circumstances that had dumped me in Rauston.

"Exactly. And the timing couldn't have been better. Because of this Jubilee Trust Fund, she and her friends are about to come into a lot of money and they're going to use it to market all their products under one label, Taste of Texas. I've been working on a logo for them. They're hoping to branch out. That's why everybody's so upset about World Mart. They love Jameson. Did you know there are people who drive all the way from Amarillo just to buy local?"

I was having trouble focusing on her words. She'd begun playing footsie with herself, the foot with the toe ring kneading the one without. It was sexy as hell. I don't think she meant it to be. In fact, I got the feeling the action was completely unconscious on her part.

The sky lit up, followed by a deafening clap of thunder.

A shiver ran up my spine. "Kind of puts everything into perspective."

"Don't you love it?"

"I sure do," I said as I refilled our glasses. But I wasn't just talking about thunder. "So what's this Trust Fund thing anyway? I keep hearing about it."

She picked up her glass and rested its rim against her lower lip. *No lipstick.*

She sipped.

"Have you met Roy Peterson?" she asked.

"Nope. I met Reenie, though."

She nodded. "Reenie's great. Anyway, Roy's her husband. He's an investment broker of some kind. He's got this thing called divinely inspired investing, which, as far as I can make out, involves a pool of money from Christian-based profit-making corporations all over the world. Also some other Christian institutions I'm not quite sure about. In a nutshell, folks who can scrape together three thousand dollars invest with him—only they call it 'gifting.' And they make huge profits they call 'blessings.' Then they tithe some back to the church, twenty percent I think, for the construction of the new building. So they get 'blessed,' the church gets 'blessed,' and everybody's happy."

"What kind of huge profits?"

"Ten times over."

I lifted my eyebrows. "Thirty thou? Excuse me for being skeptical, but…"

"I know," she said, looking at her glass. "I was too. But it's paying off. People are getting checks."

"Really?"

"Really."

I imagined what I could do with thirty thousand dollars. "Shit. Maybe it's time for me to get baptized."

She laughed. "Watch what you ask for." Then she reminded me of my need for a church outfit.

I dropped my head in my hands and groaned.

"If you don't mind me asking, why exactly are you going if it tortures you so much? I mean, just because Piggin and Heifer want you to go doesn't mean you have to."

I weighed the pros and cons of telling her the truth. Tell her I'm the Helping Hands Recipient of the Month and she'll think I'm a loser. Don't tell her and she'll find out anyway, because everybody knows everything in this blinkity-blink town. And then she'd think—no, she'd know—I was trying to pull one over on her. I opted for loser and told her the complete uncut version. About loving Ruby, then hating her; about my plans to go to the Michigan Womyn's Festival and using my pitiful savings to buy the Burro; about breaking down outside of Rauston Baptist's GO WITH GO ! sign, and being swept up by Piggin and Heifer; about Pastor Williams all but forcing me to take the Helping Hands money; about Silas Milsap's threatening words.

"Wow," she said. "So heavy."

I scanned her face for judgment. There didn't appear to be any. I took a sip of wine. "So, are you surprised I'm a lesbian?"

"No. I pretty much figured you were."

"How come?"

She shrugged. "The confidence with which you wield a paintbrush?"

I laughed. "Right."

This is usually the moment where a person either tells you that they're gay too or makes it very clear they're not. Cadence did neither, which left me feeling like a trapeze artist flying through the air with no one to catch me. "Okay, then," I said.

"Okay back at you." She pulled a speck of something from her wineglass and flicked it over the fence.

My feet still planted on the rail, I pushed back in the rocker as far as it would go. The rain had stopped, but the eaves were still dripping. Everything looked fresh, new. A distant thunder rolled. "Now that I've told you what got me here, don't you think it's only right you should reciprocate?"

She looked into my eyes and spoke with mock sincerity. "My car."

I pulled my feet from the rail, setting the rocker to rocking. "That's *so* not fair."

Visibly flushed from the wine, she sighed, giving me the feeling she was deciding how much to tell me. "I came looking for somebody."

"And…?"

"And I might have changed my mind."

"That's cryptic."

"Maybe. But it's all you're going to get right now." She gulped down the remains of her wine and grabbed me by the hand. "Now let's go get your church outfit together."

Resigned, I followed her inside. She *was* dragging me into her bedroom. What wasn't to like about that?

I should have known better. I've always hated clothes shopping, and this version of it was especially painful. She brought out one frou-frou thing after the next. "No dresses," I'd say.

She'd frown and disappear back inside the closet. "Do you want to fit in, or not?"

The contents of her closet made me rethink my initial assumption that she hadn't planned to stay long in Rauston. It was busting with clothes, most of them vintage and many ethnic. A kimono was crammed between a poodle skirt and what looked like a bridesmaid dress; a suede jacket hung next to a gold lamé dress. "What's with all the clothes?" I asked as she pulled out a sailor suit, scrutinized it, then returned it to the closet.

"I collect them. I've been scouring the thrift stores from here to Amarillo. Oh, you have to see this." She spun around holding a gaudy strapless multi-patterned satin gown. "My most recent acquisition!"

"There is no way…"

"Not for you, you goofball." She held it against herself. "But somebody hand-sewed this. Do you know how many hours that would take? Check out these covered buttons, this lace detailing. And, get this, it has a car wash hemline." She wriggled it on over her clothes. "I mean, is this to die for or what?"

I had to admit it looked great on her, even over the bowling shirt and pedal pushers. "All it needs is one of those pointy princess hats with the veil."

She clapped her hands together delightedly. "I have just the one at home."

I refilled my glass of wine. "Why am I not surprised?"

She held out her glass. "Me too."

Gown still over her clothes, she went back to searching. "I design costumes for a little theater in Santa Cruz. It's the perfect vocation for me. I love to dress people. Too bad it doesn't pay." She stepped out of the closet holding a hideous matching floral polyester top and slacks. "How about this?"

"Please." Her sense of appropriate Rauston church wear was *so* tongue in cheek it left me no alternative but to ask, "Have you ever even been to church?"

"Are you kidding? I was brought up a good Bakersfield Baptist."

"No way."

"Oh, yes. If Mom and Dad had their way, I still would be. It freaks them out no end that their only child is going to burn eternally in hell. It's sad, really."

"I guess I should feel fortunate that all my parents worry about is me screwing up *this* lifetime."

She held up a pair of lime green polyester slacks with a side zipper. "You'd fit right in wearing these."

"Not on your life."

Although I wasn't digging her Rauston fashion choices, her enthusiasm was infectious, and half a bottle of wine later, I actually found myself getting into the spirit of things. Coming across a gray cotton kilt she had folded in a box, I said, "I could do this."

She dropped a baby blue tube top to the floor. "I thought you didn't want to wear a dress."

"This is not a dress. This is a kilt."

She lifted an eyebrow skeptically. "I see."

"What?"

She took the kilt from me and measured it against my waist. "Nothing. It'll look good on you. You have nice legs."

The slight pressure of her hands against my center made my knees go slightly wobbly, and, try as I might, I couldn't attribute the sensation to the wine. "Should I try it on?"

She pulled a short-sleeved white silk blouse from the closet. "How about with this?"

"Perfect." Then it occurred to me if we were going to go any further with this, I was going to have to undress in front of her. Right then, her cell phone rang.

"Hang on," she said, retreating to the kitchen. "It could be Jameson. I told him I'd be around if he had any problems with his new computer."

Feeling an odd mix of disappointment and relief, I sat on her bed. *Get a grip, Eadie. You barely know this girl.* I took a deep breath, assessing my intoxication level. *Nothing's spinning. Could be worse.* I also went over in my head if I'd done or said anything out of line. *So far so good.*

I scanned her room. It was small with a single window, ancient-looking floral wallpaper, one oak twin bed, a nightstand, and a chest of drawers. All of it looked like it had come with the place. On her nightstand were a diary, a candle, and a small pile of books. It was tempting to peek at the diary, but that's one thing I would never do. Instead, I decided to get a bead on her from her books: Annie Proulx, Ian McEwan, Barbara Kingsolver, P.D. James, and Bill Bryson. *An intelligent reader.* I lay back on the bed, feet still on the floor—so I wouldn't start to spin—and flipped through the P.D. James, the only book I hadn't read.

Tidbits of her conversation floated into the room. "It's unlikely that you broke it…I doubt it…It's just freezing up for some reason… Possibly overloaded…Have you tried rebooting?…Rebooting…"

After about ten minutes of this, I got up from the bed and tried on the kilt. It fit perfectly. I went to show her. She was sitting at her computer with the phone in one hand and a madly jockeying mouse in the other, the angle of her legs making the most of her car wash hemline. She lifted her eyebrows, then mouthed the word "perfect." I nodded, hoping for more I guess, but she was obviously talking Jameson through a computer freak-out of epic proportion. Then, when I went to change back into my shorts, the wine began to turn on me, making me question my motives. *Eadie, what the hell are you doing? Stop yourself. Now.*

There's nothing worse than falling for a straight woman, especially the kind that likes the attention and keeps dangling the possibility of romance, but never actually follows through. Or the kind that just wants to see what it would be like, but has no intention of involving her heart. Been there, done that, and have no intention of doing it again.

I wandered back into the living room. She put her hand over the phone and whispered, "I'm so sorry. He's totally…"

"It's fine," I said, heading for the door. "Thanks for the clothes. I'll get them back ASAP."

She stood. "You're leaving?"

I nodded.

"Here." She grabbed a scrap of paper and thrust it toward me. "Give me your phone number. I want to hear how it goes tomorrow."

"I'll call you."

"Promise?"

I felt myself flush. *Damn it!* "Sure thing," I said. Then, referring to her gown, added, "Princess."

Then she squinched up her nose in that totally adorable way and said. "Sorry. I never would have picked up if—"

I put my hand up to stop her. "It's fine. Really." As I walked through the door, kilt and blouse in hand, I vowed to pay my cell phone bill. First thing Monday morning.

CHAPTER TWENTY-TWO

I'd completely forgotten how skirts make you feel like you're walking around in your underwear. As I pushed through the church doors, I willed myself not to tug at the kilt's hem.

The plan was for me to meet Piggin and Heifer in the foyer before services. Looking over the room of gussied-up people, I realized I hadn't thought about what I'd do if I couldn't find them. *Could they still be in Sunday School?* An activity I'd foolishly believed, until that morning, was only for kids.

I walked over to a table covered in church literature and pretended to be interested. I could feel people eyeing me suspiciously. *Haven't they ever seen an eyebrow ring before?* I picked up a brochure about youth programs. *Or maybe it's the kilt?* Placed the brochure back down and picked up a calendar of upcoming events. *Do they know I'm a Helping Hands recipient?* An ancient Southern belle in a lavender dress, leaning on a lace-wrapped walker, smiled at me confusedly, as if she wasn't quite sure if she knew me or not. *Great, the only one smiling at me has Alzheimer's.* I smiled back.

At least I hadn't had to attend Sunday School. Piggin had been eager for me to do so, mostly because she wanted me to meet that "charming young man" she couldn't stop talking about. The vision of me in a Bible study group with others my age was beyond frightening. I pictured me, in my dorky kilt, surrounded by a group of well-groomed young Christians discussing the finer points of the Bible over apple juice and doughnuts, a doe-eyed missy in a pastel poofy-sleeved dress asking, "So, Eadie, would you like to comment on Corinthians verse blah-ti-blah-ti-blah?" I'd have to thank Heifer for coming to my defense. "You don't want to overload the girl," she'd said to Piggin. "Her coming to services is plenty. She can meet us at church later."

I placed the events calendar back on the table, making sure it didn't screw up the carefully fanned display. *Should I go in without them? Or just leave?* I was about to jump on the "or leave" option when Piggin's shrill voice floated above the general murmurings of the crowd. "There she is!" She waved at me from a group of women by the entrance. Heifer was there too but looked less a part of the group, as if she'd simply planted herself there because Piggin had. I walked over, relieved to have someone to attach myself to. Piggin introduced me around and everyone was forced to say "nice to meet you" before we headed into the hall.

Official greeters handed us each a Xeroxed program on 20lb. goldenrod, a customer favorite at the Copy Shop. A crease bisecting the front page indicated that the church copier was in need of servicing. As we were walking down the center aisle, Piggin said, "Coupla years ago we moved our services to ten thirty. They used to start at eleven, but folks who go out to lunch after services complained that the Methodists got all the good tables at Red's Diner." She glanced over at Heifer. "'Course, we don't go out."

Heifer ignored what was obviously a barb.

"Whatever's fine by me," I said, hoping like hell they wouldn't make an exception today and expect me to go out with them. I was eager to minimize my time in the kilt.

About midway to the front of the small church, we reached what Piggin referred to as "our pew." "You two sit. I'm going to say a few words to Boots," she said.

Heifer waited for me to slide in first, which I did, assuming she'd slide in next to me and leave the aisle for Piggin, but she settled herself into the aisle seat, leaving a gaping space between us. "I always take the aisle," she said. "That way I can stretch out my leg if it starts cramping." It was hard not to feel like she was distancing herself from me. I gazed at my boney knees and unshaved legs, wishing I'd opted for the rayon slacks—even if they were mint green. They would have looked better with my Tevas.

I glanced down at Heifer's shoes and felt a bit better about my own. She was wearing those same spotless white lace-up Keds.

"Nice shoes," I said, hoping to instigate a bit of conversation.

"Got bunions," she said. "Only shoes I can find that don't pinch 'em."

Unable to come up with an appropriate response, I began looking around the church. It was lined with stained-glassed windows depicting what I assumed were biblical scenes: lots of halos, men with staffs, random lamb and whatnot. The walls were covered in a dingy, linen-textured ivory wallpaper, while a dark wood trimmed out the windows, doors, and exposed rafters of the high ceiling. Four ceiling fans slowly whirred. In front of the hall was a two-tiered altar. An ornate dark wood podium dominated the first raised level. Giant bouquets of silk lilies sat to the right and left of it. There was also a table with a white sheet concealing something lumpy. On the next level was what looked to me like a theater set. It was a pastoral scene featuring a pool of water, simply painted, but offering an interesting perspective: the top of the pool was bisected horizontally, giving us a partial view of its depths. Brass organ pipes spired above. The organ itself was to the right of the podium. The organist, a blue hair with glasses, flipped through pages of music while Pastor Williams spoke to her. She nodded repeatedly. Behind them, a small motley choir watched over the congregation like a flock of blackbirds.

I scanned the parishioners and recognized Reenie Peterson in the front row. Kitty sat with her hubby a few rows behind, or at least I assumed he was her hubby by the possessive crook of his arm around her. I also spotted Jameson. Buddy Bud was kneeling next to him facing backward so he could see everyone coming in. He waved enthusiastically when he saw me and began to get up. Something Jameson said stopped him—at least momentarily—until Buddy Bud began protesting. He grew more and more agitated. It wasn't until Jameson turned around and also waved at me that Buddy Bud calmed down. Jameson smiled at me apologetically and shook his head, as if saying, "Sorry to put you through this." But that show of affection meant more to me than he could imagine. It made me feel as if I belonged. Quite a feat considering I was a lesbian surrounded by Baptists. I pecked over at Heifer, hoping for—what? A look of approval? An amused smile? She offered neither, her attention on Piggin and Boot's conversation, her stubby fingers gripped around her Bible.

I appeared to be the only one in the room without a personal Bible—and I'm not talking your basic conservative black jobbies either. From where I was sitting I could see a white Bible with gold embossing, a red leather Bible with a built-in fringy bookmark, an oversized Bible with big, easy-to-read lettering, and a kid's Bible with "My First Bible" printed on the cover. The woman to my left had hers tucked into a sturdy nylon cover, backpack material, which held pencil and reading glasses as well.

If they all bring their Bibles from home, what're these? I wondered, pulling a worn burgundy book from a built-in shelf on the back of the pew in front of me. A circular fan on an oversized Popsicle stick fell out from behind it, clattering to the floor. The woman with the sensible Bible cover glanced over at me. I mouthed "Whoops" and reached down to pick it up. Once it was in my hand, I was horrified to find myself nose to nose with a praying pastel Jesus.

Great. Not here five minutes and I've already tossed Jesus to the floor. I flipped the fan over. "Courtesy of Watson Family Funeral Parlor." It was the kind of thing I would have loved had I picked it up in a kitschy store in the Castro.

But this wasn't the Castro.

Not even close.

I placed the fan back in the shelf and concentrated on the burgundy book. BAPTIST HYMNAL was printed on the front. I flipped to a random page and found myself being sucked in by some lyrics that preyed on my insecurities, my vulnerability, and promised me Jesus's undying love. I closed it, forcefully. *Oh no you don't. You're not going to suck me in that way.*

The organ began to play and everyone who wasn't already sitting scuttled to a seat, including Piggin. "Hey, sweetheart," she whispered to me. "You okay? You look like you've seen a ghost."

I put the hymnal back. "Fine. I'm fine."

The organ music subsided and a stocky middle-aged man with a flattop stepped up to the podium. Pastor Williams and two other men sat in chairs next to the podium, hands folded, while the guy with the flattop invited us all to sign what he called the "pew pad." Basically, it was an attendance sheet that got passed down our row. *If you have too many absences without a doctor's note, do you get sent to the pastor's office?* Then he called "Meet and Greet Time." This was particularly painful in that it involved leaving our seats and introducing ourselves to the people around us. Now the people who'd so studiously snubbed me in the foyer had to be nice to me. I mostly let them come to me, except for the little kid I recognized from Jameson's, the one who'd thought my eyebrow ring looked like the tag on his 4-H sheep. After introducing myself, I couldn't resist emitting a soft "baaaaah." He eyes twinkled with delight.

Once we were back in our seats we moved to "Church Life," i.e. Flattop reading announcements from four-by-five cards. They included a rescheduling of a revival planning committee meeting, a "Build Your Own Taco Night" being put on by one of the youth groups, and a bunch of people to pray for: for their health, for their loss, for their new business, for their ailing child. Once finished, he placed his four-by-five cards down on the podium and slowly scanned the room. "But the good news, the really, really good news is"—he paused for effect—"Charlene Wandra is on board to sing at next week's revival!"

A rumble of excitement passed through the room. Behind me, the woman with the lacy walker asked, "What? What did he say? I couldn't hear him." "Charlene Wandra's going to sing at the revival!" "What?" "Charlene Wandra!" I tried to remember why I knew the name, then flashed on the sign I'd seen the day I rolled into town.

WELCOME TO RAUSTON COUNTY
BIRTHPLACE OF CHARLENE WANDRA

"Who's Charlene Wandra?" I whispered to Piggin.

"Only the most inspirational singer that ever lived!" she whispered back. "She stopped singing professionally some years back, so this is truly an honor. And it means we're going to pack the house at next weekend's revival!"

The guy with the flattop put his hands up to quiet everyone. "I know you're all excited, but we have one more announcement to make and I'd like to ask Roy Peterson up here to make it."

I expected Roy to be one of the guys sitting with Pastor Williams, but instead he rose from one of the pews and jauntily hopped onto the raised platform. Although average in height and weight, hair color and dress, there was nothing average about Roy Peterson. He was a knockout. His short chestnut hair, combed back, had an appealing unruliness to it, as did his whole persona. His white button-down shirt, similar to many of the men's shirts, seemed somehow more casual, his light trousers more relaxed. In a word, Roy Peterson had star quality.

When he smiled his dashing smile, I swear I could hear a large portion of the female church members sigh.

"Now I know we all are anxious to get on with our service for today, so I'm fixin' to keep this short. By now, I'm sure y'all are sick of hearing me talk about the Jubilee Trust Fund…"

From the murmurings in the room, I got the feeling no one was sick of him talking about it.

"But I just want to say, the blessings are starting to come in…"

A man in the choir said, "Amen!" And there were more murmurs from the crowd.

"…and the church fund is growing. And it's my thought that we make this revival one to remember by getting as many folks as possible involved. So I'm setting up a scholarship account to help those who need the benefits of the Jubilee Fund, but don't have the means. If there's someone you want to gift into the program, or make a partial gift, talk to me after services." He crooked up his mouth in a boyish smile, and said, "'A feast is made for laughter, and wine maketh merry, but money answereth all things.' And I'm *not* makin' that up, y'all. That's Ecclesiastes chapter ten, verse nineteen. Check it out for yourself. Now God bless!"

I felt bad for the fellow who stepped up to the podium in Roy's wake. He had the same brown hair, same white shirt, but was so dull I couldn't get myself to listen to the prayer he was slogging through. It featured the word "abundance," I remember that. And I remember us all saying, "Amen." The next guy led us in a couple of songs and had the annoying habit of lifting his eyebrows when he reached for a high note. Everyone seemed to be having a ball. Especially Piggin, who seemed to know all the lyrics by heart. As for me, I couldn't decide what was worse: to stand there not singing, or to lamely sing a song I didn't know—and didn't feel. I went back and forth between the two, finally settling on a compromise, mouthing the words. Piggin was singing with such flowery gusto, I figured no one would know the difference.

Then Dull Guy got up again and we prayed again, then Eyebrows led us in another song, and just when I thought this routine would never end, they pulled the white sheet from the table to reveal trays of tiny juice cups and mini oyster crackers and began passing them around. I was bummed when Piggin told me I couldn't have any. "You have to be baptized," she whispered. It was tempting to palm a cracker to try later—I mean, what would happen?—but I resisted and passed the plate on.

I have to admit, compared to his two compadres, Pastor Williams was a breath of fresh air. His eyebrows stayed in place and he knew how to work an audience. The gist of his sermon was to open your heart to God's blessings. "How many of us," he bellowed, "don't feel worthy in the face of God's glory? Don't feel worthy knowing He gave us His only begotten son to die for our sins? But God did not put you here to suffer! Did not put you here that you might shrink away from his vast love! And I'm talking prosperity here, folks. It's not sinful to have a nice house for your family. It's not sinful to have a nice car. He's not asking you to live in poverty!" A twitter of nervous laughter rippled through the crowd and I could tell he'd hit a nerve. He knew it, too, and continued, the organ subtly bolstering his words: "What kind of God would ask you to devote your life to Him only to make you suffer? Certainly not the God I know. Is that the God you know?" More nervous laughter. "Christ has so much love to give you, His well is so deep, and all He asks is that you devote your life to Him. That you live your life for Him! You say yes to this, my friends, and He will shower you—Do you hear that? Shower you—with abundance! Just look at what's happening with our little church. We've worked so hard, our membership has grown so big, and look at what He's giving us! A new church!"

He went on, quoting from the Bible here and there, telling a story about avenues of warehouses in heaven, each stacked to the ceiling with crates full of unclaimed blessings. To me, though, it all began to sound the same.

> "Him. He. He. Hymn. His. Him. He. He. His. He. He. He.
> Him. His. His. He. Him. He. He. He. He. His. His. His. He.
> He. Him. Him. Him. Hymn. He. He. He. He. Him. His. His.
> Him. Him. Him. He. He. He. He. He. He."

I entertained myself by fantasizing about Her, Cadence. Her lips. Her cute nose… I will admit, however, that the concept of devoting one's life to something bigger, to this web of divine love, if you will, snuck past my lesbian fantasies. Especially when I considered the blessing deficit I was currently experiencing. Could it be that I was bringing emotional and physical poverty on myself? That I was somehow too caught up in living a selfish life? Maybe all I needed to do was quit focusing on wanting money and a girlfriend and a place to live and job I liked and parents that accepted me, and focus instead on loving God—and I'm not talking the Him He Hymn His God, but a God that was a bit more, shall we say, equal opportunity—maybe these things would just come to me…

I tuned in to Pastor Williams just in time to hear him invite us to devote our lives to Christ. He gave us all a final meaningful look and turned the congregation over to Eyebrows, who called out a page number in the hymnal. As I mouthed the words, I was struck by the sweep of belonging that passed through the room. Granted, I didn't feel it, but everyone else seemed to. Then one of the guys who'd been passing out the sacred snacks walked back to get this teenage chick—who had a mouth full of braces and a really spiffy Farrah Fawcett hairdo—and escorted her to the front of the church and through a door to the left of the altar. *Virgin sacrifice?* But between verses, Piggin clued me in by whispering, "Baptism."

While I pretended to sing, I peeked up from my hymnal to see Pastor Williams disappear behind the same door. Eyebrows instructed us to turn to another hymn. We sang all eight verses of this one. I gathered it was to give time for the pastor and the girl to change clothes. By the time we saw them again they were walking toward one another in what I'd previously thought was a painting, but now realized was a real pool of water. From what I could make out, he was wearing waders and she a hospital gown. The girl looked frightened, but purposeful, as if she were walking up to the sorcerer's castle in a fairy tale. As she accepted Jesus Christ as her personal savior, I was struck with a weird mix of pity and envy. Hell, I could use a savior too. Just not the one Pastor Williams was serving up. "In the name of the Father, the Son, and the Holy Spirit, I now baptize you," he said before placing a hanky over her mouth and tipping her backward, submerging her into the pool of water. A chorus of "Amen!" burst from the crowd. The girl, Farrah Fawcett do now dripping wet and stuck to her face, blinked a few times, then smiled triumphantly, her braces shining like Christmas tinsel.

The rest of the service was pretty anticlimactic. When the woman with the sensible Bible passed me the donation plate, I almost didn't give. I figured fair was fair. You don't share your snacks with me? I don't share my money with you. But then I wound up throwing in fifty cents. For the entertainment. They had me stand up with the rest of the possible recruits, or "guests" as they called us—at which point the kilt stuck to the back of my thighs, giving the lucky people behind me a great shot of the damn thing stuck in the crack of my butt.

Then, after one more closing prayer, we walked down the crowded aisle toward the exit where Pastor Williams shook each of our hands, providing him one last time to look into our eyes meaningfully. Figuring that was it, that I was now free to go back to my trailer, change clothes and pop by Cadence's to show her I'd survived, I prepared to leave. I should have known better.

"Now comes the fun part!" Piggin said.

My heart skipped a beat. "Fun part?"

"Fellowship Hall for coffee and snacks!"

I glanced over at Heifer. She just smiled.

Chapter Twenty-three

The Fellowship Hall session was an exercise in how many ways I could deal with the question: "And what church do you attend back in California, Eadie?" I couldn't seem to admit to those wide-eyed, pastel-wearing Christians that I was a heathen. The PUT YOURSELF IN JESUS' HANDS mural that dominated the stuffy, low-ceilinged room might have had something to do with it. The painted Jesus had the kind of creepy eyes that follow you around the room. Or maybe it was the freshness that exuded from the newly baptized girl who stood, hair still dripping wet, surrounded by family and friends. Whatever it was, it had me flustered and unable to simply say, "I don't go to church, thank you very much."

My various truth-avoiding strategies consisted of: acting as if the question hadn't been asked and commenting on the delicious fried whatever-they-weres, implying vaguely that I was in between churches, coughing up a swallow of tea and excusing myself to the bathroom, and telling them I was brought up Presbyterian—which is partly true. My grandmother was a Presbyterian, but it never took with my mom. Each of my rambling non-answers invoked the same heartbreaking expression on the asker's face, as if my not having a simple answer to this question was the saddest thing in the world. Except, of course, when I did the coughing-up tea routine.

Having pried myself from a group of elderly women, I glanced around for Buddy Bud, but he was nowhere to be seen. *He and Jameson must have left right after services.*

I walked over to a trash can at the end of the buffet table to toss my empty cup. A couple of kids, in an impromptu game of tag, charged between me and the trash can. Startled, I jumped back.

"You must be Eadie," the guy I cracked in to said.

I whirled around and found myself face-to-face with Roy Peterson. "Uh, yeah. That would be me. Hope I didn't cause you any irreparable damage."

"Nope. Seems I still got all my parts," he said, playfully patting himself down.

Reenie came up and took her husband's arm. "Oh good. I was hoping you two would meet." Remarkably, her hair and tits looked even bigger than the day I'd met her.

"Hey, Reenie. Nice to see you again."

"Likewise." She sounded genuinely happy to see me.

Roy ran his fingers through his already perfectly tousled hair. "Now if you don't mind me asking, Eadie, did today blow your mind, or what?"

"Uh…I'm not sure what you mean."

He laughed. "I'm just saying you don't get this kind of Mayberry action in San Francisco, least not how I remember it. This must seem like Podunksville to you."

"It is different, I'll give you that," I said cautiously.

"Different! Can you imagine these folks in downtown Frisco with all the pretty boys and crazies? Shoowee! They'd blow a gasket!"

Reenie punched his arm playfully and peeked around the room. "Roy! Quiet! They'll hear you."

He grinned at me conspiratorially. "Eadie knows what I'm talking about, don't you, Eadie? This place is off-the-charts boonies."

It bothered me that he was trying to claim San Francisco as his. *That's my city you're talking about, Buster.* I flashed on my flat in the Mission District, on the tiny community garden at the end of my block, on the Women's Building with its eclectic array of classes and programs, the funky coffee houses, the killer burrito place. The fog.

"Rauston's all right. I've met some nice people here."

"I'm not saying anything about being nice or not, I'm just saying it's about twenty years behind the times. Maybe thirty."

Reenie shook her head. "As you can see, Roy's still getting used to it here too. He didn't grow up in Rauston the way I did…"

"And I'm not going to be buried here either, you can be sure of that, darlin'."

Their bickering had the lighthearted quality of new love. "Seems like you've won the church over," I said, "at least from what I saw today."

Reenie jumped in, "Well, he's giving so much—and not only to Mama's church, but to the people in it."

"Honey," he said modestly, "it's my job. I make money when they make money."

She tugged on his sleeve and said to me, "This man is so good. I swear, I don't know what I did to deserve him." She turned to him, as if reminded of something. "I was just over there talking to Frannie Dee Jenkins. She is so thankful to your program..."

"Not my program, sweetie. It's the Jubilee Trust Fund."

"Whatever. Will you listen to me? They're going to be able to get their girl her own dialysis machine." She looked at me. "These poor people have been driving to Amarillo three times a week since her kidney problems started two years ago."

"Will you stop?" Roy said. "My head's gonna get so big I won't be able to fit out that door and then I'm gonna have to spend the night here." He looked at her playfully and touched the tip of her nose. "Now you wouldn't want to have to sleep alone tonight, would you?"

Reenie blushed. "Okay, mister, I just think people should know."

I cleared my throat. "You're giving them the land, right, Reenie? I mean, it sounds like you're doing your share too."

She pulled her eyes away from him. "If I could get Mr. Man here to sign the papers."

He pressed the heels of his hands into his temples. "Shoot! I forgot again, didn't I?"

"And he calls *me* an airhead. Honestly, sometimes I think it would be easier if he didn't work from home. Then he'd have a secretary looking out after him and I wouldn't have to."

"I don't know," he said flirtatiously, "I kinda like you being my secretary..."

Just beyond them, I noticed Heifer at the buffet table picking up used paper plates. It seemed as good a pretext as any to excuse myself. "Okay, you two. I think I'm going to help Heifer with cleanup."

"Had a bit too much Mayberry and ready to go home?" Roy joked.

I laughed and left them to each other. *Is it me, or is Roy a total asshole?*

Heifer was combining several plates of leftover cookies onto one, pausing only to pop the broken chunks into her mouth. Only the perfect ones made it to the plate: Oreos on one side and Nutter Butters on the other. "We can put these out again after tonight's services."

"Tonight's?"

"Don't worry. You're not expected." She handed me several paper plates to toss. "Did Crash Milsap find you?"

"No. Did he say what he wanted?" Crash looking for me could not be good. The only thing we had in common was pot.

"Nope." She popped a particularly large chunk of cookie in her mouth. Actually, it was more like a whole cookie with a broken edge.

As I walked to the trash can at the end of the long table, I scanned the room for Crash. *No sign. He must have left.* Relieved, I turned back to continue helping Heifer with cleanup.

From the far end of the table, I could see that something was terribly wrong with Heifer. The muscles in her face were frozen while her eyes screamed in fear. *She's choking!*

I bolted toward her intending to perform the Heimlich maneuver, but nearly ran into a woman standing not three feet away from Heifer. The woman was facing her too. *Can't she see Heifer's choking? Why isn't she helping her?* I was almost going to scream at the woman to Fucking Do Something or Get the Hell Out of the Way! when I heard her say to Heifer. "Oh dear me. Look how I've come up on you right when you've put something in your mouth."

Instantly, I realized the woman was right; Heifer wasn't choking, she was simply unable to chew. Her mouth had seized up on her. That cookie with the chipped edge was sitting in her mouth—whole—making her face look like a puffer fish. If it hadn't been for her eyes looking so desperate, so full of shame, it would have been funny.

Heifer, seemingly unable to eat while facing this woman, turned away to finish chewing and swallow.

The woman also pivoted slightly to give Heifer privacy.

I bent down to pick up a used napkin. *Why's Heifer acting so weird around the woman?*

"Grace?" the woman said, "Are you all right?"

That's when I knew who it was.

"You do recognize me, don't you, Grace? Lilah, your old friend. I know I must look so different."

Heifer's love. She's come back.

Heifer turned around, her face battling emotions I could only imagine: the disgrace of knowing what she was, of what she'd turned into.

I could hear her heart.

Tick…Tick…Tick…

"I'm so happy you didn't leave after services," Lilah continued. "I missed the Meet and Greet because my sister needed help with her oxygen tank."

I waited for Heifer to say something. Lilah waited too.

Tick…Tick…Tick…

"She said I should say hello…"

Tick…Tick…Tick…

It was so painful I almost walked away, embarrassed for them both, but then my dyke code of honor kicked in and I stepped around Lilah. "Heifer, you feeling any better?" I asked nonchalantly before turning around and feigning surprise at seeing Lilah. "Oh, I'm sorry. Am I interrupting something? I was just checking in on Heifer because she mentioned to me she was feeling light-headed—dizzy. We were talking about taking off, weren't we, Heifer?"

Heifer looked at me like I was out of my mind, but I persevered, holding out my hand to Lilah. "Hey. I'm Eadie Pratt, Heifer's newest friend. Actually it's more like she's my angel. Last week my car broke down here—I was pulling a trailer—and Heifer let me put my trailer on her land until I get my car fixed. Can you believe it? She didn't even know me and she totally helped me out."

I gushed on this way for a while, sneaking an occasional peek at Heifer to see how she was doing. I even managed to signal to her that she had some Oreo cookie crumbs on her blouse, which she clumsily wiped off, but I didn't stop jabbering until Heifer landed back in her body. Then I hit the ball back in Lilah's court. "So, I'm sorry, what did you say your name was again?"

Lilah, obviously taken aback by my flurry of blabbering and gesticulating, introduced herself. "I'm Lilah. I guess you could say I'm one of Heifer's *oldest* friends."

"Nice to meet you." I turned back toward Heifer. "So you feeling better?"

She nodded. "Fine. I'm just fine. No need to make a fuss."

"Are you sure?" Lilah asked. "You do look a little pale."

Heifer glanced around the room. "Piggin's here somewhere. I'm sure she'd love to say hello."

I could have beaned Heifer. *How about telling Lilah she looks good or that you're happy to see her? She obviously came to see you, not Piggin.*

"I'd love to see Rose," Lilah said, fiddling with a dainty gold chain she wore around her neck. Her fingernails were cut short and had a light pink polish on them. A ring on her finger was twisted to the side, the opal digging into her pinky. It wasn't a wedding ring.

Say something real, you two. Take a risk.

Heifer began fiddling with an Oreo on the plate like it was a TV dial. "We're both on the revival committee."

"Oh, are you having a revival sometime soon?"

"Next weekend."

Now that we've graduated to real, let's try something interesting.

Piggin came up from behind Heifer. "Well, shut my mouth! Lilah, what a surprise. What brings you here?"

Lilah reached out her hand. "Rose. It's so good to see you."

Heifer seemed both relieved and annoyed as Piggin took over the conversation, telling Lilah how young she still looked, asking her about her husband, her kids.

"You haven't heard, then," Lilah said, once again fiddling with the gold chain around her neck. "Rude left me."

Piggin pursed her lips and shook her head. "I am so sorry to hear it. He seemed like such a good man."

Heifer continued to focus on the table, but I could tell she was listening, intently.

I busied myself clearing paper cups. I didn't want it to be too obvious that I was eavesdropping.

"It was quite a shock," Lilah said. "For all of us. My oldest daughter is beside herself. The woman he left me for isn't much older than she is."

Piggin put her hand on Lilah's shoulder. "What an upset that must have been. I'm surprised your sister didn't tell us."

Lilah glanced at Heifer. "I'm thinking about moving back to Rauston. I could be closer to her. She needs so much medical care these days…"

Heifer froze.

What do you know? Heifer's still in love.

I knew it for sure when Piggin said, "You must come by for a visit. I swear Heifer hasn't been the same since you left. You two were always such good friends."

If Heifer could have, she'd have climbed under the table. Or spontaneously combusted. "Piggin…" she pleaded.

Lilah studiously examined the floor.

"I'm just speaking the truth, Heifer. And you know it." If Piggin hadn't been so completely clueless, I would have kicked her in the shin. As it was, she kept heaping more and more salt in the wound. "You've never had another friend like Lilah. Never!"

It occurred to me that Heifer probably would have felt better if she *had* choked. At least she wouldn't have had to endure this.

"So, Heifer, you ready to hit the road?" I asked.

"But we're on cleanup," Piggin protested.

I spoke these next words with great deliberateness. "Yeah, but Heifer isn't feeling too well and I said I'd give her a lift home. Isn't there someone else who can do it?"

Piggin looked skeptical. "I suppose…"

Lilah took Heifer's hand. "I'm so sorry. Here you are not feeling well and I've been talking your head off. You should go home with Eadie. We'll have time to catch up. I'm going to start coming down on the weekends."

"Next weekend's the revival," Heifer said. "I'll probably be real busy."

"Oh, don't be silly," Piggin said. "She can come for lunch Saturday. I mean, we girls have to eat, don't we?"

CHAPTER TWENTY-FOUR

On the ride back from church, I thought I'd give Heifer a chance to talk if she wanted to. Granted, it wasn't the most intimate of settings, both windows of the rattling truck cranked wide open forcing us to shout, but it bothered me to see her so shaken.

"Your friend seemed nice," I shouted.

Heifer gazed out the window, the bow clipped in her thinning hair threatening to blow free. I wondered if she'd heard me and tried again.

"You two were good friends?"

A bug splatted into the windshield. I watched as its carcass, propelled by the wind, slowly inched its way across the glass. I decided to try another subject.

"That Jubilee Trust thing is pretty amazing."

"Yup."

At least I know she can hear me.

"So, have you and Piggin done it? Invested?"

She mumbled something back.

"What?"

"Not yet. We're waiting for the revival," she shouted.

"How come?"

"You're going to have to ask Piggin. It was her idea."

I flicked on the radio and we rode the rest of the way listening to songs of heartbreak and deceit. When we pulled into the driveway, a Harley was parked in my usual spot. I pulled to the left of it.

"Got one of her boyfriends with her," Heifer grumbled.

I couldn't make sense of her statement until Sweet Ginger

stepped out of Piggin's trailer. She wore tight jeans with stiletto-heeled motorcycle boots and a low-cut hot pink sleeveless blouse.

"It's about time y'all got back."

I got out of the truck. "Hey, Sweet Ginger."

She teetered down the steps trying to keep her heels from catching in the weathered wood. "Eadie, I barely recognized you in that skirt."

"It's a kilt, actually."

Heifer glared at her younger sister. "Whatcha here for, Sweet Ginger?"

"Well, hello to you too, big sis!"

"Piggin know you were coming?"

"No. And for your information, Buzzard and I were just stopping by to see if I left my wallet here the other day."

"Buzzard, huh?"

"Yes, Buzzard." She put her hands on her hips. "So, have you seen my wallet?"

"Nope."

"Must be at Eadie's, then."

I was beginning to understand Heifer's uncertainty. *Sweet Ginger didn't set foot inside my trailer. How could she have left her wallet there?* "Not at my place," I said.

"It could have fallen behind the cushion," she said, "when we were having coffee in there. Can I just come and check?"

I glanced at Heifer. She wasn't buying it, but what could I do? "Uh, sure…"

"Don't you leave him alone in there," Heifer said wagging her finger in the direction of Piggin's trailer.

Sweet Ginger sighed dramatically. "For Christ's sake, Heifer. He's not going to steal anything."

Heifer didn't budge, her eyes boring into Sweet Ginger.

Sweet Ginger glanced over at me in a last-ditch alliance-building maneuver, which I didn't provide, then she yelled over her shoulder, "Buzzard!"

A thing I can only describe as The Hulk came out onto the deck. His hairy arms and neck bulged from a wifebeater T-shirt and black leather vest. He blinked several times as if adjusting to the sun. There was no way I wanted this guy in my trailer either, and I gave Sweet Ginger a firm look to inform her of this.

"Jesus Christ," she muttered under her breath, then shouted to him, "Wait by the bike! I'll be right there."

"What's going on?" I asked as I strode toward my trailer, Sweet Ginger at my heels.

"Wait 'til we're inside."

Inside, Sweet Ginger plopped on my couch. I stayed standing. Whatever game she was playing was way uncool and I wanted her to know it. "So?"

She fumbled around in her purse, finally coming up with a pack of cigarettes. "I was hoping I could buy a joint off you. We're on a day trip to Palo Duro and I forgot my stash."

"No smoking in the trailer."

She groaned and shoved them back inside. "My sisters must be rubbing off on you."

I eyed her long enough to decide she was telling the truth, then reached for my pot. "You are so going to get me evicted."

"They're not going to evict you. Piggin adores you. She told me so herself."

"Watch by the door, would you? Make sure no one's coming." She stepped over to the door; I began to break up the bud for rolling. "So Piggin told you she likes me?"

"Oh God. You're like a dream come true. Her own little Mary Kay project. She's determined to get you hooked up with one of the good Christian boys. It's her way of saving you." She grinned. "By the way, you do look really good in a skirt."

"You want this joint or don't you?"

She laughed.

The fact that she was enjoying herself at my expense bugged me. "So, this Buzzard, is he the one that dumped you the other night?"

"Buzzard? Shit no! He's like my baby brother."

"So you're not bonking him?"

"I didn't say that. I've got to keep him loyal somehow." She sighed. "But it's only five minutes out of my day. Know what I mean?"

I didn't bother to respond.

She peered out the screen door. "At least he's behaving. You should see Heifer, though. She's glaring him down like a pit bull. Never did like my taste in men. I should tell her that darling Reenie's new hubby was making the moves on me last night. Left his cell phone number on a napkin for me. Wouldn't that just tie her panties in a knot? God, all I heard growing up was Reenie this, Reenie that. She was always just the perfect example of a good Christian woman. I almost fucked him just to bring her down a notch."

I looked up from my endeavor. "Are you talking about Roy Peterson?"

"Is that his name? The Christian guys never want to tell you their names. It's the second time I've seen him, though. He meets with some guy there, looks like business."

"How'd you know it was him?"

"When he was shelling out for a drink, I saw her picture in his wallet. 'Course he'd taken off his wedding band, like I was too dumb to notice the lack of tan around his finger."

"Are you sure it was him?"

"What's it to you?"

I considered telling her about the large amount of money her sisters were about to hand over to this guy, but wasn't sure I trusted her. She was too interested in seeing Reenie humiliated. But a biker bar sure is a strange place for a good Baptist to be holding a business meeting—without his wedding ring. Then again, it might not have been Roy. "You think he'll be back?"

She pulled at the seat of her skin-tight jeans so the top of her thong would show. "How should I know? I kept his number, though. I have a drawer full of 'em at home. Keeps me from feeling lonely."

I licked the adhesive edge of the rolling paper, rolled a thin joint, twisted the ends, but held out on handing it over. "Here's the deal. I don't want any cash for this. I just want you to call me if he comes back."

"Why are you so interested?"

"If it turns out to be him, I'll tell you." Then I remembered I didn't have a working phone. On impulse, I gave her Cadence's number. It would give me an excuse to drop by. I could tell her about Roy.

CHAPTER TWENTY-FIVE

When I pulled into Cadence's rutted driveway, her VW wasn't there. I knocked on her door anyway, then sat down in one of her rockers and waited. It was hot, of course, ninety plus, but the shade from the porch made it almost tolerable, if one didn't have to do anything but rock. It was the time of day when the land itself seemed to be in siesta. White sheets hung on her laundry line, limp in the nonexistent breeze. I pushed all the way back in the rocker and noticed there was a ceiling fan above me. *Was that there the other day?* Of course it had to have been; I was just surprised I hadn't noticed it. It was something I'd never seen before, a ceiling fan on an outdoor porch. For the hell of it, I pulled the chain, and sure enough the thing began whirring. It felt great. I made a mental note that if I ever found myself living somewhere that was this hot, and was lucky enough to have a porch, I'd put in one of these babies too.

I also noticed several little stacks of rocks artistically arranged here and there, another thing I hadn't noticed the other day. *I must have been too busy gazing at her.* A string of small round stones lined the rail, a pyramid of bigger ones were stacked by the step. The area around the house was raked and tidy. *What is she doing in Rauston? And who, or what, is she looking for?* I took a rock from the rail. It had a shell fossil embedded in it. I began rubbing it with my thumb like a worry stone.

A half an hour came and went. Then forty-five minutes. I remembered her saying how she liked to shop the thrift stores in Amarillo. *Or maybe she's at Minnie Bell's.* Either way, I was tired of waiting. I retrieved a scrap of paper and a pen from the truck and wrote:

> *Sorry I missed you. Kilt was a hit. You might get a call from Sweet Ginger. If you do, call me. I'll explain later. I've been having some trouble with my phone service. So if you can't get through, leave me a message at Jameson's.*
>
> *Your pal,*
>
> *Eadie*

Cryptic, but to the point. I figured it was unlikely that Sweet Ginger would call tonight. Roy wouldn't be bar hopping; he'd be at church. And by tomorrow, I planned to have my phone back. If I had to, I'd drive to Amarillo to pay my bill.

I flicked off the fan and took off.

The road was devoid of cars, but I kept hoping I'd see Cadence's VW. Just outside of town, I spotted a young good-old-boy walking along the berm. When he heard my truck, he stuck out his thumb, eliciting in me my usual defensive reaction when I see what I assume is a potential rapist. *Yeah, right, buddy. In your dreams.* Then I saw it was Crash. I pulled over. "What's up, stranger?"

He climbed into the truck. "Hey, Eadie. Am I glad to see you."

"I'll bet. It's a long walk to your place."

"Yeah. I done it before, though."

As I pulled onto the road, he told me his big brother had dropped him by the Teen Center. "Said he'd pick me up in an hour, but the jerk never showed up."

"What was going on at the Teen Center?"

He shrugged. "Nothing. Just the usual, games and shit."

I thought about growing up in Rauston and how little there was to do for kids, especially teenagers. It was amazing they weren't all crack addicts. "Heifer said you were looking for me earlier."

He put his feet on the dashboard. "Oh yeah. Wanted to tell you not to worry about my dad no more."

"How come?"

"My aunt's going to give him the money to do the Jubilee thing. We're going to be rich."

I should have felt relief; Silas was going to be off my back. Instead, I felt myself growing concerned. If it really was Roy Peterson coming on to Sweet Ginger at the Crowbar, he wasn't the guy he wanted us all to believe he was. Not that being a low-down cheater necessarily made him untrustworthy in the financial arena. But it might. I needed to find out more about this Jubilee Trust Fund. And about Roy. *Silas may be an asshole, but he doesn't deserve to...* What? What did I think was going to happen? That Roy Peterson and Pastor Williams were going to abscond with his money? With Piggin and Heifer's money? How could they? Surely Reenie wouldn't let them. She grew up with these people. Still...

I pressed down on the accelerator and glanced over at Crash. He was thwapping his thumb against his knee as if he were doing a drum solo. *I'm probably just being paranoid.*

I made an attempt to sound casual. "Is your dad going to wait for the revival to invest in the Jubilee thing?"

He shrugged. "Probably not. Knowing Dad, he'll do it as soon as he gets my aunt's check."

I'm going to talk to Cadence; see what she thinks.

Chapter Twenty-six

Monday morning, I drove to Amarillo and used some of my dwindling cash reserve to pay my delinquent phone bill. They promised me service by the end of the day. I hadn't calculated in the late fees—meaning when it came time to pay Old Luke, I was going to come up shorter than ever, even with the Helping Hands money.

When Jameson offered me more work later that day, I couldn't believe my good fortune. He wanted the storage closet cleaned out, a water-damaged wall in the bathroom fixed and painted, and a couple of other smaller-ticket items. "I'll pay you direct this time," he said. It was music to my ears. Once Buddy Bud and I were done with the bookshelves, I wouldn't be a Helping Hands recipient anymore. I'd be self-employed. I wondered why Jameson was going to all this trouble, knowing that World Mart would probably be putting him out of business, but thought better of asking. Why talk him out of hiring me? To show my gratitude, I lightly penciled Jameson's Market Will Live On And Prosper! underneath the final coat of paint on the bookshelf. Buddy Bud, seeing my secret message, wanted to do one too. Our Store Is A-1! he scrawled, pressing down so hard on his pencil that it showed through the paint.

"That's okay," I told him. "We can touch it up tomorrow."

"I don't get why it has to be a secret? It *is* A-1."

"It makes the spell stronger if we keep it a secret."

"Can I tell Marty?" he asked, Marty being the name of the ailing bird Cadence had brought him.

"Only if you tell *him* not to tell."

He tromped over to the box and whispered his secret to Marty, then beamed, "Marty says he won't tell."

On the way home, I checked out my phone and was stoked to hear a dial tone. I immediately dialed Cadence's number. She picked up saying, "I never thought about your real name being Edith."

Freakin' caller ID! "Think Piaf, not Bunker."

She laughed. "Whatever you say."

I told her about my conversation with Sweet Ginger.

"Sounds pretty convoluted."

"I don't know. I'm getting this bad feeling about Roy."

"Why didn't you give her your phone number?"

"Like I wrote in my note, I've been having some problems with my phone service."

After an annoyingly long pause, she said, "Right," which I decided to ignore. I wasn't lying. I *was* having trouble with my service.

"So are you in?"

"Let me get this straight. When Sweet Ginger calls me, you want me to call you, so we can dash off for a little midnight sleuthing."

"Something like that."

Another pause, then, "I have the perfect trench coat."

"It's a biker bar."

"Oh." I heard light tapping noise and realized she was working on her computer. *Great. She's multitasking me.* "How about I zip into Amarillo to see if I can find us a couple of leather jackets?" she said finally.

At least she's not saying no. "Look, we'll talk outfits later. For the time being, just promise you'll call me." Which is why, later that night when Wild Thing blared its signature ring, I assumed it was her.

I was lying in my bed in that delicious state of almost-sleep, my body sinking into the mattress, my mind starting to slip into surrealism. It had been a good day. I was getting my shit together. Jameson wanted me to work more, Wild Thing was turned back on, my dealings with Piggin and Heifer seemed to be mellowing out, and the parts for Pebbles were on the parts truck and headed this way. If all went well, in a week and a half I'd be sitting in a foldout chair at the Music Festival with a bunch of topless lesbians. *I need to get a foldout chair...that would be good...* Then again, if for some reason I didn't make it, there was always Cadence. *Maybe she'd want to come with me... We could do the festival together... I could get two chairs...* And just as I was visualizing her in the circle of topless lesbians, Wild Thing, next to my pillow for easy access, started up. I fumbled for it, answering groggily.

"Cadence..."

There was a pause on the other end of the line. "Who's Cadence?"

I shot off my warm pillow, whacking my head against my reading light. "Ruby!"

"You sound guilty." Her voice had that weird mix of slurred and wired that I'd come to know so well.

"Uh, no. I was sleeping. What time is it?"

She began to cry. "You don't love me anymore." The blackness of the night gave her voice a disembodied quality.

"Ruby..."

"You don't. I can tell..."

"Of course I love you."

"Then come home."

This was even more surreal than my quasi dream state. "We don't have a home anymore, Ruby."

"You know what I mean!"

"What are you on, Ruby?"

"Why don't you love me anymore?"

"Are you at Peter and Kevin's?"

"Peter's a prick! An ugly purple prick!"

"Where are you?"

"Bette's. But she doesn't know it yet. She's at work."

Great. Call one ex from the house of another. "How'd you get in?"

"I have a key." She began giggling, like a child who's just divulged a secret stash of cookies. As I listened to her, I realized I wasn't jealous. All those times that Ruby had gone running to Bette's weren't because Ruby still loved her. It was because Ruby needed Bette's love. She fed off it. Just like she wanted to feed off my love now. The only problem was my love for her was all used up.

"I'm in the bathtub," she said, seductively.

"I gotta go, Rube."

"Naked..."

"Don't do anything stupid."

"Eadie!"

I snapped the phone shut, my heart pounding in my ears. *Way to go, Eadie. You did good. She has other people she can call.* I flicked on the light. My diary was open on the cabinet. A half cup of tea sat by it with the last of the snickerdoodles that Piggin had brought by earlier. Part of me felt guilty for hanging up, and part of me knew better. *Is that why Bette always takes her back? Is it the guilt?* For the first time ever I felt sorry for Bette. She was going to come home to a fucked-up Ruby and I knew what that was like. You couldn't give enough, couldn't love enough, couldn't comfort enough to fill that hole. I thought about Old Luke's words. *Them that don't know they got a hole in their soul, it can make 'em dangerous, mean...*

I got out of bed and poured what was left of my tea back into the saucepan to heat up. *No way am I going to be like Bette, her pitiful on-call ex. It's over. I'm done.* Wild Thing started up again, just as I knew it would, but this time I checked the number. I didn't answer. A gust of wind whistled around the trailer, rocking it slightly.

Back in my cozy bed with my reheated tea and snickerdoodle, I toasted my new life. "To Eadie T. Pratt," I said. "Sucker to no one!"

Chapter Twenty-seven

I started out the next day by checking my voicemail. I wanted to see if Ruby'd left a message. She had, all right. And not your basic drunken whine either. No, her message included, among other things, a frighteningly lucid dissection of my personality. I was immature, she said, and promised things I couldn't deliver. She even used the ugly words "emotional retarded" and "wimpy." My mind, good little defense lawyer that it was, began shouting, *Objection! Objection! I did the best I could. Consider Ruby's self-destructive habits, her unwillingness to help with our dire financial straits, the unconditional love I never got as a child.* The prosecution shot back, *Oh come on! Every girlfriend you've ever had has needed more than you could give.*

I waited for the defense's rebuttal. It never came.

What a lousy time to take a nap. Who hired you anyway?

For the rest of the day I couldn't shake the fear that I wasn't built for relationships. I was too dysfunctional. Too fucked up.

At work, Buddy Bud and I pulled everything out of a storage closet that had suffered a plumbing leak some years back. We tossed what was damaged, packed into labeled boxes what wasn't. I sorted through years of unclaimed lost and found items, mostly moldy. As I held up a particularly cute hooded sweatshirt, one I thought might fit, the memory of packing up my apartment in San Francisco wormed its way in, how I'd promised myself no more relationships until I got my shit together. I tossed the sweatshirt into the trash bag.

Later, as Buddy Bud and I were painting over his Our Store Is A-1!, I gave myself one of my pathetic attempts at a pep talk. *If Cadence is gay and she does fall for me, it'll be different this time. She's not the type to suck a person dry. She gives as much as she takes. More, even.* About the time Our Store Is A-1! began seeping back through the paint, my pep talk morphed on me. *Sure, Eadie. You're always so positive at the beginning of relationships. Face it, you're too screwed up for someone as together as Cadence. Once she sees who you really are, she'll bail. That, or she'll stay, but you won't be able to stand the brokenhearted sighs, the sad eyes that follow you from room to room, and you'll be the one who winds up leaving.* By the end of the day, when Jameson came in to check up on us, he was pleased with what we'd accomplished, saying he'd been dreading cleaning the closet since the leak occurred.

Walking out to the parking lot, I couldn't help but ponder the age-old question: *Why is it so much easier to deal with other people's problems than your own?*

Once home, I went directly to bed and slept for three solid hours. Then I cranked up some vintage Melissa Etheridge and began cleaning my own place. Fine red dust was embedded in the carpet, the creases in the accordion blinds, and in between the cushions. Fortunately, the friends who'd sold me the Burro had thrown in a complimentary DustBuster. It was the perfect tool for the job, and I went at it with a gusto.

By nine o'clock, I was onto the last phase of my cleaning therapy: vacuuming the screen on the screen door. The sun had just set and the stars were starting to punch through. *Do women fall for me because they can sense I'm a pushover? Or do I pick the wrong women?* I flicked off the DustBuster. Wild Thing was ringing. Cadence's number flashed on the readout. *Great, call me when I'm feeling like caca...* I turned down the music and flicked on my phone. "Hey."

"You ready to sleuth?"

"She called?"

"Said he just got there."

"Well, you want to do it?"

She must have heard the resistance in my voice because she said, "Don't you?"

❖

Twenty minutes later, I was pulling up to Cadence's. Her porch glowed bug-bulb amber. I got out of the truck and knocked. "Hang on!" she yelled. A few seconds later she flung the door open. "Ta-dah!" She wore a cropped leather jacket, had replaced her pigtailed look with a black bandana, big hoop earrings, tight ratty jeans, and an overdose of makeup. She looked cute as hell—in a biker chick kind of way.

"Won't you be hot?" I asked. Then, realizing the double entendre, corrected, "I mean temperature-wise…" *Good one, Eadie. Real smooth.*

She smiled. "Hey, I take this job seriously."

I willed myself away from the attraction. "I see that."

She produced another leather coat, seventies model, that looked like it came from an episode of *Get Smart*. "I got one for you too. I discovered this great used clothing store."

"The point is *not* to be seen."

"I know, but if we are, we should be ready. My alias is Trina Joy."

"Trina Joy?"

"Yup." She held the jacket up. "So you want it or not?"

"Not."

What a snot you're being, Eadie. I began furiously backpedaling. "Well, only because I brought my own. In the truck. I just thought I'd wait to put in on so I wouldn't be hot." *Please be in the truck. Please be in the truck. Please be in the truck.* My Levi's jacket. I could flip up the collar a la James Dean.

She tossed the jacket on a chair. "It's your operation."

Emotional retard.

"I think we should take the pickup. It'll blend in better," I said, hoping to sound a little more fun loving.

Not much talking happened on the ride over. I was too afraid of screwing things up, and she, well, who knows why she wasn't talking? Probably because she was regretting getting mixed up with a loser like me. I did try to get into the spirit of things by suggesting my alias be Emma.

"Emma?"

"You know, Emma Peel, from *The Avengers*."

"It doesn't sound very Texan," she said, skeptically. "Maybe we should add a second part like Emma Sue, or, Emma Lee…"

"Um…Okay…I guess…"

She scooted around in the seat to face me, her caked-on powder-blue eye shadow luminous from the light of the console. "Are you mad at me? Did I do something?"

How could I tell her I was trying not to have a crush on her? I'd have to begin by telling her that I *did* have a crush… "It's been a weird day."

❖

The parking lot of the Crowbar was strewn with pickups and Harleys. I spotted Sweet Ginger's Dodge Neon immediately. It was in the same place it had been when I dropped her off the week prior. I could feel Cadence's impatience to get on with our caper.

"Shouldn't we get out of the truck?" she finally asked.

"I'm scoping it out," I said. Truth is, I was starting to have second thoughts. What did I think we'd find? And why had I dragged Cadence into this? *Now she's really going to think I don't have a life. I'm stalking a guy I barely know. And for what? Because he's having a business meeting in a bar? Plenty of people have business meetings in bars.*

A group of bikers was hanging out by the side door passing a joint. Roy wasn't one of them. A couple was making out by a pickup truck. The gentleman, if you could call him that, had his lady friend pressed into the cab. Her hands gripped the back of his belt as she pulled his pelvis into hers. He wasn't Roy either.

"Maybe we should synchronize our watches." Cadence said.

"Neither of us is wearing one."

She smiled and punched my arm. "Good point. No wonder you're in charge."

I focused on the parking lot, tears creeping up my throat. *How brain-dead can you get, Eadie? She was joking!* I spotted Reenie's car parked in the most remote corner of the lot. I opened the truck door. "Shall we?"

"Let's," she said.

I slipped on my Levi's jacket. *Just get over yourself and do what you came for.*

Cadence pointed to a wooden sign next to the bar door.

FRIDAY HAPPY HOUR GOES 'TIL 8PM

LADIES' NIGHT: TUESDAYS

"We're in luck. Cheap drinks."

"Cool." I reached for the door, then stopped. "Do you know Roy? I mean, have you actually been introduced to him?"

"Nope. I've only seen him around with Reenie."

"Then you should go first. Let me know if the coast is clear."

Cadence drummed her steepled fingers, eyes flashing mischief, and spoke in a Russian accent. "If I'm not back in five minutes, come after me."

I made myself smile, then watched her disappear behind the door. To my great relief, it was only a few seconds before she stuck her head back out and said, "All clear."

I slipped in behind her. The place was much more upscale than I expected. The décor consisted of a combination of dark wood, classy etched glass, pressed tin ceiling, silk plants, and animal heads—something for everyone. It definitely beat the dives I'd frequented in the city. Sweet Ginger, who was taking orders from a table of spirited cowboys, looked up and gestured for us to sit at an empty booth by the door.

"Do you see him?" Cadence asked, once we were sitting.

A mixed group hung at the bar celebrating somebody's birthday. Two of the three pool tables had games going on, and a couple was slow-dancing on the dance floor to a jukebox—Lionel Richie crooning a very apropos song about being clueless when it came to winning a woman's heart.

But no Roy.

Sweet Ginger sashayed up to our table wearing her usual low-cut blouse, tight jeans, and stilettos. "Nice jacket," she said to Cadence.

Cadence glanced over at me, clearly pleased with herself, and tugged at the jacket's lapels. "You like it? I got it at this hole-in-the-wall thrift store in Amarillo."

"You've got to tell me where," Sweet Ginger said.

As I sat there listening to the two of them gab, uneasiness wormed its way in. *We're here for a reason, you two. Not to talk shopping.* "So is Roy even here?" I asked.

Annoyed by the interruption, Sweet Ginger shifted her attention from Cadence to me. "Of course he is. Think I'd send you on a wild goose chase?" She gestured with a nod. "Over there."

I leaned to my left to see past what looked to me like a couple of Brokeback boys playing pool. Sure enough, there was Roy Peterson in a heated conversation with a grizzly bald guy in a blue work shirt with the sleeves cut off—definitely not church material.

"That's why I told you to sit here. It'll give you your best vantage and still keep you covered." She adjusted a ruffle on the lowest point of her plunging neckline. "So you going to introduce me to your girlfriend or what?"

I shot Cadence an apologetic look. "She's not my girlfriend. Just a friend."

Sweet Ginger sighed. "Sweetheart, in my world, two women who enjoy each other's company are girlfriends. I didn't mean to imply you were engaged in the nasty."

On a better day I would have been able to come up with a zippy retort, but today wasn't one of those days. "Sweet Ginger, this is—"

"Trina Joy," Cadence said with a twang.

"Trina Joy, meet Sweet Ginger."

Cadence leaned in and whispered to Sweet Ginger, "My name's actually Cadence, but I'm using Trina Joy as my alias."

Sweet Ginger, clearly taken with Cadence, winked and whispered back, "You can count on me, sweetheart."

From the table of cowboys came a whistle, followed by, "Sweet Ginger, when are we gonna get that round of drinks?"

Without even turning around, Sweet Ginger spat, "I put the order in, Red. But you're not the only one here, so hold your damn horses."

The men at the table laughed. "You tell 'em, Sweet Ginger!" one of them yelled.

"I love your place," Cadence said.

"Thanks, sweetheart. It's not much, but it's home." She looked at me. "'Course, according to my sisters, it's a den of iniquity. Isn't that right?"

I nodded.

She pulled out her order pad. "So what can I get you two?"

I ordered a Corona and Cadence ordered Jack Daniel's on the rocks, eliciting a look of approval from Sweet Ginger.

"When I get back, I want to hear why you two are so interested in Reenie's man."

It hadn't occurred to me until Cadence and I were waiting for our drinks that this seemed kind of like a date. "So, uh, you're a Jack Daniel's drinker."

"Are you kidding? I've never even tasted Jack Daniel's," she said, flashing me her disarming smile. "It just seemed to go with the outfit." She began fiddling with the red egg-shaped tealight holder. Her nails were clipped short and polished a hot pink. She blended in with the place perfectly.

She's a chameleon.

I glanced over to see if our drinks were coming. Sweet Ginger was back yakking with the cowboys.

"What's he doing now?" Cadence asked. I could tell she was asking this to pull me out of my obvious funk. Which was sweet, really, but wound up making me feel even more like a loser.

She lifted her eyebrows as if to say, Well?

I tuned my antennae to Roy. His demeanor was completely different from the one he donned at the church. He was nervous, edgy, like the guy he was talking to had something on him. "Talking. The two of them are just talking."

A young buck in a tight blue western shirt and cowboy hat approached our booth. "Seems a shame to leave you two pretty ladies sittin' here all by yourselves."

Cadence jumped at the chance to try out her alias. "My name's Trina Joy."

He tipped his hat. "Well, howdy, Miss Trina Joy." Then turned to me. "And who might you be?"

"This is my friend Emma Lee," Cadence said.

I tried to smile, but my lips wouldn't obey. Flirting with cowboys went against my code of ethics, even if it was just acting.

Mercifully, Sweet Ginger approached the table with our drinks. "Oogy, leave these two ladies alone. They're friends of mine and don't need no dinky-dick playboy-wannabe putting the make on 'em."

"Oh come on, Sweet Ginger, I was just being polite."

"Like hell you were. Now scram!"

Oogy tipped his hat, said, "Ladies," and strode off.

"Shoulda' told him you were a man-hating lesbian. That woulda spun his head around backward a time or two."

I glanced over at Cadence, hoping she wasn't buying this portrayal of me as a man hater, but her eyes were on Sweet Ginger, who was pulling a chair up to our table. "Okay, you two, out with it," she said. "Why are you interested in Reenie's man?"

Reluctantly, I spilled out the story about the Jubilee Trust Fund and my suspicions about Roy Peterson and Pastor Williams. It sounded so stupid now. "It's probably nothing. Probably just me being paranoid. That's why I wanted to check this out. I pictured him in some clandestine meeting with a sleazy guy in a biker bar. This place is nice, though. People probably have business meetings here all the time."

Sweet Ginger glanced around to make sure all her customers were happy. "Well, I don't know about that, but we do get all kinds in here. We back up to two dry counties. Only place you can get a drink for miles." She looked over in the direction of Roy and his buddy. "No place for a good Baptist, though. And like I said, he was here last week with that same guy. They sat at that same table in the corner too, like they don't want to be seen."

Cadence twisted around in her seat, clearly frustrated that her back was to the action.

"And it's not like he's here for the women. I mean, sure, he put the make on me last week, but all the boys do that, think they can get some quick parking-lot action—like I don't have a job to do."

Cadence sighed. "It seems stupid to just sit here."

I took a sip of my beer. "We can't exactly go up and ask him why he's here."

A devilish look came over her face. "But we could do some recon." With that, she grabbed her drink and slipped out of the booth.

I was stunned. "What's she doing?"

Sweet Ginger laughed. "Don't worry. Cute girl like her can get away with murder in a place like this." She leveled me with her eyes. "You really got the hots for her, don't you?"

I leaned back in the booth. "I don't even know if she's gay."

Sweet Ginger raised an eyebrow. "By the way she's been looking at you, I'd say she's interested."

I took another swig of my beer. *What does she know? She sleeps with Neanderthals.*

She stood. "I gotta get back to work. But if she finds out anything, I want to know."

"Fine."

I craned my head to see past the pool players. Cadence was standing with her back to Roy's table pretending to watch the Brokeback boys' pool game, but it couldn't have been more obvious that she was trying to eavesdrop on Roy's conversation. My body temperature rose. *She's going to get us caught. He's going to recognize her.* Then one of the Brokeback boys stepped back and knocked into her, sending her drink catapulting to the floor. *Great. Now Roy's going to see her for sure.* A queasiness moved into my gut as I watched her and the Brokeback boy bend down out of sight. I scooted up in my seat to get a better view. Cadence and Brokeback were picking up glass while Roy and the bald guy, too engaged in their conversation, remained clueless. Which brought me back to Cadence and Brokeback, who was seeming less and less Brokeback by the second. *He better not be coming on to her.* I was just about to get up and walk over to intervene when Cadence started making her way back, stopping by the bar to deposit the glass. Men followed her with their gazes, but she seemed too preoccupied to notice. Was it the excitement from what she'd heard? Or that damn Brokeback?

She slid into the table. "Wait 'til you hear!"

"What?"

Like a boomerang, Sweet Ginger returned to the table. "What's the scoop?"

Cadence gestured us into a huddle, then whispered, "I think the guy's his boss. It sounded like he was giving a report. And they were definitely talking about money, something about a revival."

"The revival's this Sunday," I said. "When most people are going to make their gifts."

"The guy was worried about the revival thing. 'Too much exposure,' he said."

The three of us digested this for a moment. "I wonder what Pastor Williams's role is?" I asked.

Cadence glanced over her shoulder, then whispered, "What are we going to do? We can't let all those people invest money if it's some kind of scam. My landlord Minnie Bell is going to invest. She's planning on it funding her business. And I know Jameson is considering it too."

Sweet Ginger made as if she was going to get up. "I tell you what I'm going to do, I'm going to go over there right now and tell those two cocksuckers they better keep their filthy hands off my sisters' money."

I grabbed her arm. "Don't. They'll run."

"And never get caught," Cadence added. "But we should warn Piggin and Heifer."

"What if we're wrong? We'll cause a scandal for nothing. Besides, I like Reenie."

Sweet Ginger exhaled loudly and said in a syrupy voice, "Everybody likes Reenie."

"But if these guys are doing what we think they're doing…" Cadence continued.

"Which is exactly what?" I asked. "You told me that people have been getting returns. Maybe it's legit."

Cadence bit her lower lips, thinking, then said, "Have you ever heard of a Ponzi scheme?"

Sweet Ginger crossed her arms and leaned back in her chair. "Pay off the first few with the money from next few and sooner or later, somebody gets burned."

"Or a lot of people," Cadence said.

It seemed possible. If they timed it right they could leave right after the revival, right at the top of the pyramid.

Sweet Ginger chuckled cynically. "I can see it now, Perfect Little Reenie being shown up as the money-grubbing whore she really is."

"We need more information," Cadence said. "We need to get into Roy's records."

The illegal implications of this statement stopped us all dead.

"What are you suggesting?" I asked.

"I'm not sure," she said. "But whatever it is, we've got to do it soon."

Right then the bartender yelled, "Order up!"

"Shit!" Sweet Ginger said, standing. Before walking away, she added, "Keep me in the loop."

CHAPTER TWENTY-EIGHT

Having spent the better half of the drive home from the Crowbar hashing over every imaginable angle of the Roy Peterson sighting, Cadence and I now rode in silence. The night was warm, so both windows were rolled down. The air streamed across us. Cadence seemed in her own world as she gazed out the window. I flicked on the radio and flipped through stations wishing like hell I could find some jazz, but it was all religious, country western, or pop. I flicked it off. The sweet smell of a distant skunk floated through. If I hadn't been so resigned to not falling in love, tonight would have been the perfect night.

"Tomorrow is Wednesday," Cadence said breaking the silence. "Reenie and Roy will be at church in the evening."

I glanced over at her. *So?*

She continued. "You said he works out of his house, right?"

It took me a second to catch her drift. "You're not suggesting…"

"I don't know what I'm suggesting." She ran her fingers along the rusted rim of the truck window. "Only, if we're thinking of searching his office for incriminating evidence, it would be a perfect time to do it."

My throat went dry. "Were we thinking that?"

"We've got to do something."

We do? The whole situation with Rauston Baptist was getting awfully complicated. "Breaking and entering is a little extreme, don't you think?"

Cadence sat quietly for a few moments. A Lexus convertible doing about eighty miles per hour flashed its lights and passed us.

"How about this?" she said. "How about we drive out to their place on the pretense that we're looking for one of them—Reenie, we'll be looking for Reenie—then, when we discover she's not there, we'll try one of the doors in that friendly-Texas kind of way. You know, 'Yoo-hoo! Anybody home?' And we'll peek around a little."

When I didn't immediately respond, she said, "We won't touch anything."

"And if it's locked?" I swerved to avoid hitting the dead skunk.

She drummed her fingers on her knee, then asked, "Are you scared?"

"No. I just think..." *You think what? Go ahead, Eadie, tell her how you don't like to get involved. How you like to play it safe.* "What would be our reason for wanting to see Reenie on a Wednesday night? Just in case something backfires."

"Like what?"

"Anything could happen. A neighbor could drop by. They might have a gardener..." *Right, Eadie, a gardener who comes at night.*

Despite my lame protests, she took my concern seriously, resting her head on the back of the seat, thinking.

She sat up abruptly. "The crystal vase!"

"Huh?"

"My landlord, Minnie Bell, has a crystal vase belonging to Reenie's mom. She was just saying the other day that Reenie'd probably like to have it back. I'll offer to return it for her."

I pulled into her driveway.

"What do you think?"

I turned off the engine and pushed on the emergency brake. "I guess..."

"Eadie, we can't let Minnie Bell, Piggin and Heifer, and all the other members of the church be bamboozled."

Her use of the word "bamboozled" was so damn cute. "I know. I know. I just think there's an easier way."

"Which is?"

Uhhhhh...

She continued. "Look, between now and tomorrow night, or tonight I should say, I'll do some Internet recon. If the Jubilee Trust Fund is totally legit, I'll be able to find something about it."

Why am I resisting this? The word "wimp" came to mind, followed by several other of Ruby's cutting accusations. "Okay," I said. "I'll pick you up at seven."

But Cadence didn't get out of the truck; she just sat there.

In the moonlight, her get-up made her look like an unruly teenager: the bandana around the forehead, the big hoop earrings, excessive makeup.

What she's waiting for?

She began biting her lower lip.

Is it possible she wants me to kiss her?

I watched, dismayed, as my stalwart resolutions about not pursuing her began disintegrating into a sticky pool of excuses. *It's just a kiss, Eadie, not a relationship. And she wants you to. Look at her!* I began to adjust in the seat. *Even friends kiss.* Leaned forward. *Three, two... Prepare for blastoff... One...*

Just as I began to make my move, she turned to face me. "Okay, I'll tell you."

I hung there in space, like a figurehead on the front of an anchored ship. "Uh…tell me what?"

"I thought you wanted to know what brought me to Rauston?"

"Oh yeah, I did." I settled back in the seat as if I'd simply been adjusting myself for comfort reasons; the hand I'd been planning to run through her hair, I rested casually on the back of the seat. "I mean, I do."

An amused expression passed across her face, then softened. "We have to trust each other, right?"

"Right. Yes. For sure we do. Definitely."

"So I think we should each tell a secret. Or something incredibly private." She folded her hands in her lap. "I'll start."

How could I object? It was the most vulnerable I'd ever seen her, sitting there gazing somberly at her clasped hands. She inhaled and when she finally allowed the exhale, these words floated on the current. "I'm looking for my parents."

Using my best faithful-friend voice, I asked cautiously, "Don't they live in Bakersfield?"

"Those are my adoptive parents."

Now, I'd heard about adopted children searching out their birth parents, but I'd always associated it with soap operas and cheesy tabloids. MOTHER AND DAUGHTER ENJOY TEARY REUNION AFTER FIFTY YEARS!

I tried to wipe any skepticism from my face. “You think they’re in Rauston?”

“I’m pretty sure, at least about my mom.” She pulled a knee toward her and wrapped her arms around it. “You want the whole story?”

What I wanted was a kiss, but that didn’t seem to be in the stars. “Sure.”

She focused on the dashboard as she spoke. “Of course I’ve been curious for a long time…”

“Of course.”

“But I never really actively looked because Mom and Dad were so down on it.”

“That’s understandable.”

“Is it?”

“Well…I mean…you’re wanting to protect them and all…”

“But it isn’t about them, it’s about me.”

“Well, yeah. I just meant…”

“Just because they’re my parents…”

Truthfully, at this point, I had no idea which set of parents she was even talking about, the birth ones or the ones that did all the work, but I kept my mouth shut and took refuge in encouraging facial expressions.

“Anyway, this year, for my birthday, I decided to try and find them. Kind of a present to myself. It hasn’t been easy, though, so I’ve had to get creative.”

Why does this not surprise me? Everything about her is creative.

“My records are all sealed. That’s because I was born in New Mexico. New Mexico’s adoption laws are archaic.”

My curiosity got the better of me. “If you were born in New Mexico, what are you doing here?”

“What I know so far is that there was a Baptist unwed mothers’ house in Tucumcari, New Mexico—about two hundred miles from here—where my mother must have been sent. I know this because I talked to this ancient nurse at the hospital where I was born. She’d worked in maternity for centuries. She’s been my one stroke of luck in this whole journey. She remembered my being born.”

“How could she possibly remember you? If she worked there that long she must have helped deliver hundreds of babies.” I hated to sound so negative, but it sounded so far-fetched.

"Like I said, she was my one stroke of luck. The day I was born was the same day her brother was killed."

A look of disbelief must have crossed my face, because she lifted her hand and said, "Stay with me. He was a tornado victim. He was driving his rig through Rauston when it hit."

I adjusted the handle for the truck window so it wasn't digging into my back. I could tell we were going to be here awhile. "And?"

"And Eileen remembered a teenage girl from Rauston on the ward having to give birth all alone because no one from her family could get out of Rauston to be with her. She remembered feeling sorry for this girl having to go through labor while, at the same time, worrying for her own brother's safety. But the point of all this is that that's why she remembered me, because I was the baby born the day her brother died."

I tried to keep the skepticism out of my voice. "So you think that teenager girl was your mom."

"She had to be. It was the right hospital, the right date, and the only baby born that day."

"If you trust Eileen…"

"A tornado definitely hit Rauston on my birthday. I checked."

The thread she was hanging her hopes on was so thin it was heartbreaking. "So now what?"

"That's the thing. I've kind of stalled out."

"Have you asked around?"

"It's touchier than you'd think. As Minnie Bell, my landlord, keeps reminding me, most people don't want their past to come waltzing back into their lives. I mean, think about it, we're in the Bible Belt. A child born out of wedlock is a pretty shameful thing. What if my mom married, which is pretty likely, what if she never told her husband about me? What if he thinks he was her first?"

"What if she moved?"

Cadence looked out onto the night. "I've thought of that…" An owl hooted. "But what if she didn't?"

"Then you just have to—"

"What? Pray someone will recognize me on the street? Tack signs onto trees like I'm a lost kitten?"

"It's got to be confusing," I said, proving to myself, once again, just how inarticulate I can be. To be honest, I was still a little bummed that the evening hadn't evolved into a romantic one. To be more brutally honest, I was wondering if it still might.

She fiddled with her hoop earring. "What if I'm Kitty's illegitimate sister?"

I laughed. "That's a frightening thought."

She paused, then spoke, her tone now reflective. "It's funny. If my mom hadn't given me up, I'd have been brought up here, in Rauston. I'd be shopping at Jameson's."

Would she have turned out like Kitty? I banished the thought from my mind. "That is pretty weird."

She took off her glasses, rubbed her eyes, and returned her glasses to her face. "The thing is, I can't stay here forever. The gal subletting my apartment in Santa Cruz is going to be moving out in a few weeks."

I readjusted myself on the seat, stretching out my legs and rotating my ankles to keep them from going to sleep. "So what's been your strategy?"

"Get to know Rauston. I mean, you've seen how this place operates. The history is in the people, their stories." She fixed her gaze on me as if she were about to expound upon this theory, but what she said was: "So what's your secret?"

My secret? I'd forgotten all about that part of the deal.

I scanned my brain for an appropriate bit of saucy info, something that would, in fact, make me seem more interesting, maybe even alluring.

"I dropped out of art school."

She waited, sensing there was more.

"I had a full scholarship."

Still, she said nothing.

"It's something I'd worked really hard for."

She cocked her beautiful head.

"I did it so I could be with this girl. We wound up breaking up two months later." *Shit! What did I tell her that part for?* I pressed my lips together to keep any other incriminating information from slipping out.

"Ruby?" she asked.

My lips parted and, with the help of my traitor tongue and traitor vocal cords, began formulating words. "No. A few girlfriends before Ruby."

Cadence lifted an eyebrow. "How many girlfriends have you had?"

Sadly, I didn't have to count. I knew immediately. "Sixteen." She didn't respond, so of course old motor-mouth just kept on going. "And that's only counting the women I was completely crazy in love with… and the women who were into me. I left out the unrequited loves. There are a lot of those too."

She started playing with one of her big hoop earrings. "Wow," she said. "You're quite the Casanova."

"I guess."

"What are you looking for in a woman?"

You, I wanted to say, but I started rambling nonsense instead. "You know, the usual. The one who'll see through all my bullshit to who I really am." My chest began hurting.

"Don't you have to find that for yourself?"

Just read my beads, why don't you? I began tugging at a frayed piece of leather on the steering wheel cover. "You didn't say we were going to therapize each other."

"Do you regret giving up that scholarship?"

I attempted a light laugh, but it came out sounding bitter. "Only when I think about it."

"I'm sorry," she said.

"No reason for you to be sorry. I did it to myself." The tightness in my chest began to intensify, like my heart was going to implode on itself. *I will not cry. I will not cry.* "So, hey, it's getting late. What do you say we resume this fascinating conversation tomorrow?"

She leaned over to hug me. "I'm so glad you told me."

And while I'm all for hugging, especially gorgeous women, this was one hug I was anxious to get out of. It was too intimate. Too full of compassion. Too about-to-make-me-cry. Or fall in love. Despite my anxiety, I couldn't help but notice what a perfect fit our bodies were, like they were made for each other.

Yeah right, Eadie. That's what you always think at first.

When she finally released me, I had to will my pounding heart to settle down.

I started the ignition. "So I'll call you tomorrow, okay?" It was that or I was going to try to make myself feel better by kissing her.

She slid out of the truck, closed the door, and leaned on the chassis to speak through the open window. "I can't tell you what it means to have someone to talk to."

"Yeah, well, me too."

"Sleep tight."

"I'll try." *Don't let her go.* "Uh, Cadence?"

"Yeah?"

"You have a good night's sleep too."

By the time I pulled onto the highway, my body was screaming with a strange brew of desire and self-loathing. *Good one, Casanova. Way to admit to a woman you're falling in love with that you're some kind of sick love addict.* The sad thing was, I was still harboring hopes that we might hook up. It took me a good ten minutes of driving and a rank burning smell to realize my emergency brake was still on.

CHAPTER TWENTY-NINE

Everything about Wednesday went wrong.

I overslept, meaning I had to swallow Kitty's look of disdain when I pushed through the doors to Jameson's half an hour late. Buddy Bud, amped on doughnuts and gummy bears—which Kitty had been feeding him in my absence—kept running around the store instead of helping me, and I wound up having to lecture him, making him, and me, feel like crap, and ended with me leaning against a wall I'd just painted so now my whole upper arm and some of my hair was covered in Navajo semi-gloss. Sweet Ginger, no matter how many times I tried to call her, wouldn't answer her damn phone. And when I dropped by Old Luke's, I found out that something called my input shaft was cracked, which, of course was another part that was impossible to find. Old Luke had assured me he could weld it back together, and he'd said something about taking it to his pal the blacksmith's to heat treat, but all in all it was gonna cost me another hundred fifty, two hundred bucks.

By the time I pulled into the driveway of my new home in a town I'd never planned to live in, I was in such a foul mood all I wanted to do was smoke a big fat joint, paste a DO NOT DISTURB sticker on my trailer door, slam it shut, and hope I baked to death.

But Cadence's bug was parked in my place.

I spotted her sitting out by my mandala. *Shit. My trailer's a mess.*

I realize the word "mess" is a relative term, and what I consider a mess is not even close to what many people endure on a daily basis. Still, it was her first time at my place.

She waved and began walking toward me.

"Hey, what's up?" I said, hopping out of my truck. *There must be a way I can sneak in, wash my breakfast dishes, and make my bed before inviting her in.*

"What happened to you?" she said laughing.

I glanced down at my paint-covered arm. "Had kind of an oops."

"Want some help getting it out of your hair?"

"It'll come out in the shower."

"There's a shower in that tiny thing? This I gotta see."

There was no way around it; she was coming in. Fortunately, the Squirts I'd picked up at Jameson's were still relatively cold. "It's kind of a mess. If I'd known you were coming…"

"You'd have baked a cake. But see this way I'll get to see the real you."

This isn't the real me. The real me wouldn't have left dishes in the sink.

Although it would have been gentlewomanly of me to allow her to enter first while I graciously held open the door, I bolted past her.

"This is so cute," she said, following me in.

I tossed my books off the pint-sized sofa and flipped the sheet up over the bed, shoving my sleeping tee under the pillow. "Have a seat," I said indicating the sofa. I'd take the bed. That way we could face each other.

But she was too busy snooping. She peeked into the bathroom, tried out the kitchen sink to make sure it came equipped with real water, ran her hands down the seventies-style curtains.

"The three-second tour," I said nervously.

At this point, we were in extremely close proximity to one another. Just by leaning in I could have nibbled her earlobe.

"It's like living in a clubhouse."

I held the sodas between us. "Squirt?"

She nodded and sat. "Oh, I added something to your sculpture out there. I hope you don't mind. My earring broke and it seemed like the perfect place for it."

"That's cool. Evolving is what pieces like that are all about."

She leaned forward to look at the pencil drawing I'd taped to the wall the night before. I'd drawn it shortly after dropping out of the art institute: a skeleton standing by an open window. The only color in the picture was outside the window.

"Is this one of yours?"

"Yeah. An early one." I handed her the soda and stuffed the other four in my fridge. "I hope you don't mind drinking from the can. I got up late so I didn't get a chance to do my dishes."

"It's so detailed. So sad. What were you thinking when you drew it?"

"It's a self-portrait."

Having her in my world was like those dreams where you suddenly realize you're in your underwear and nobody else is. I sat on the bed and began picking at the paint on my arm. "So, I gather you found something out about Jubilee."

I heard feet crunching across the dirt toward the trailer. "Youhooo!" Piggin yelled. "Anybody home?"

"In here!" I yelled back, flashing a look of apology to Cadence. "And I've got company!"

Cadence reached up and tenderly touched the edge of the paper, then withdrew her attention preparing herself for Piggin's arrival.

Piggin peered in through the screen door. "I was wondering whose car that was."

"How you doing, Piggin?" Cadence asked. Her ease with Piggin surprised me.

"Besides being hotter'n if I was you know where, I'm doin' just fine." She mopped her forehead with a hanky. "Surely y'all'd rather come over to my place where there's some air-conditioning."

Cadence thanked her, but said that I'd invited her to dinner.

Dinner? I hope she likes bean dip.

The two of them chatted through the screen door for a while about some person I didn't know and his newly inserted pacemaker. By the time I tuned back in Piggin was saying, "Like my mama always said, we got our plans and God's got his. And most of the time they got nothing to do with each other." Then she invited us to her place one more time, this time adding dinner into the invitation. I got the feeling she was trying to save Cadence from my culinary ineptitude. "Nothing special. I still gotta get ready for church, but if you'd like some leftover fried chicken and mashed potatoes, that's what I'm fixing to heat up."

I glanced over at Cadence, giving her the chance to bail on the bean dip. She subtly shook her head. "Thanks anyway," I said, sending Piggin crunching her way back home.

"I've always liked these two," Cadence said.

I got up to wash my dishes. If I was expected to produce dinner, I'd need them. "So what were you about to tell me?"

She kicked off her sandals and crossed her long legs underneath her. "Just that I can't find anything about this Jubilee Trust Fund on the Internet. Doesn't that seem strange?"

I shrugged. "I don't know much about the world of investment."

"You knew that investment brokers don't usually hold their meetings in bars."

I turned to face her. "Yeah, but…"

"We've got to go scope it out. We owe it to Piggin and Heifer. And to Minnie Bell."

"What if we get caught?"

She drew a crystal bud vase out of her bag. "Our alibi."

❖

I pulled out all the stops for dinner. Not only did I unfold the table, I artistically circled the can of bean dip with chips, carrots, and almonds. Then, after a modest dessert of sliced apples and a Snickers bar cut up into bite-sized chunks, I excused myself to take a shower. I was hoping she'd have the courtesy to step outside and enjoy the view, but she picked up my copy of Natalie Angier's *Woman: An Intimate Geography* and began flipping through it.

As I peeled off my sweaty, paint-covered clothes, all I could think about was the pimple that had recently sprouted on my butt. I was going to have to back into the shower. "That's a really good book," I said.

She was clearly making a point to keep her eyes on the book. "I've read her in the *New York Times*. She's great."

None of this changed the fact that I was naked and she wasn't.

Once in the shower, I had a little more privacy, but once out, there we were again. She clothed. Me naked. And this time she looked. "This is a great book," she said. "I'm going to have to get a copy."

Goose bumps sprouted on my body like porcupine spines. I pulled on my underwear—"You can borrow mine"—and my tee.

Her eyes swept over my partially clothed body. "You missed a few spots of paint. Want me to get them?"

We spent the next few minutes with her grooming me like a monkey. Not exactly bolstering for the old self-confidence, but not entirely unpleasant either. In fact, I couldn't help but feel a bit aroused. When she began massaging my shoulders, saying they were tense, I almost laughed. *Uh, yeah they're tense. I'm having to command my whole body to behave.*

Piggin's car taking off for church was a bittersweet reprieve.

"We better get going," Cadence said, grabbing the vase.

❖

Until we pulled up to her driveway, I'd forgotten Reenie had inherited her family's property. An arch made from wrought iron and brick boasted a sign that read:

THE WHEELOCKS

The driveway was flanked by cottonwoods. At the end sat a stately old brick house in need of loving care. The wooden wraparound porch was suffering from an acute case of dry rot and a shutter was missing from an upstairs window—a classic case of people growing too old to take care of what was once their pride and joy. It was evident from the hanging pots of flowers and colorful curtains that Reenie was in the process of sprucing it up. Her car was parked in the carport to the right of the house.

We parked farther back by one of the trees. My heart began to quicken. "Do you think she's home?"

She shook her head. "They probably took Roy's."

"Get out the vase just in case."

The doorbell was one of those old-fashioned twisting deals that sits right in the middle of the door and produces a sound similar to a wind-up toy. Cadence twisted it and we waited. She seemed certain that no one was going to be home. Me, I wasn't so sure. "Try it again," I said. She did, but again, there was no response. She tested the door; it wasn't locked.

"Hello!" she yelled, peeking her head in. "Anybody home?"

I stepped in behind her, whispering, "I don't feel good about this."

"It'll be fine," she whispered back.

The floorboards above us creaked indicating someone was indeed home and creeping around upstairs. We backed out the door, Cadence nearly stepping on my toes. "Now what?" I whispered.

She put her fingers to her lips and listened through the cracked-open door, then yelled, "Anybody home?" again.

The whole mission was starting to feel wrong. Who did we think we were prancing into these people's lives? Their home? Then I heard someone creaking down the old stairs.

"We should go," I whispered.

"That would *really* look suspicious."

So we waited until the mystery creaker came to the door.

It turned out to be Reenie. She peeked out the door, her poofed hair flat on one side, her eyes swollen and red. I might have thought we'd gotten her out of her sickbed except that she was dressed nicely. "Eadie, Cadence, what a surprise," she said, trying to smile. Her lipstick was smeared on one side. "I was in bed. I'm not… I wasn't…" but her words turned into sobs. "Oh for heavens sakes!" she said through gasps. "I'm just being so silly!" She crumpled into herself, shoulders shaking.

"Are you all right?" Cadence asked.

"No, I'm not. No, I certainly am not!" she said through more sobbing.

Whatever we expected to find, this wasn't it. "We can come back," I offered. "If this is a bad time…"

Cadence elbowed me, indicating either that I was giving up too easily or that I was being uncaring. I have no idea which.

Reenie opened the door fully. "No, please. Come in. It's so hot outside."

Cadence shot me a satisfied glance.

Once inside, Reenie said, "Now what can I do for you ladies?"

Cadence held up the vase and told her the story of it winding up with Minnie Bell. "She thought it might be something you'd want back."

Reenie gingerly took the vase from her. "Grandma's sweet pea vase. I haven't seen this in years. Every spring she had it brimming with her sweet peas." She hugged the vase to her chest. "All I ever wanted was the kind of love my mama and daddy had. They loved each other so much. Just understood one another. But I just seem to mess it up."

"Did something happen?" Cadence asked. Unlike me, she was good at this delicate stuff, seemed to have a real sense about when to push and how far.

"Y'all drink coffee?" Reenie asked.

"I'd love a cup," Cadence said, although she'd told me over dinner she didn't like coffee.

I followed her lead. "Me too."

We tagged along behind Reenie into the kitchen and pulled chairs up to the old farm table. Reenie began making the coffee, scooping the grounds from a ceramic canister, filling the pot with water, taking down mugs from the cabinet. The ritual seemed to relax her a bit. "I tell you, I can be so ungrateful! Here I finally find myself a good man, one who loves me just the way I am, and I can't help harping at him." She pulled a tissue from a box in an embroidered cover and blew her nose, then leaned back against the kitchen counter, wrapping her arms around her waist, the tissue still clutched in her hand.

"What happened?" Cadence said tenderly.

"I just flipped my wig, is all," she said laughing through watery eyes. "Roy told me when we got together that his job involved travel, but I guess I didn't want to hear it. I pictured us fixing up this place and making ourselves a home. We talked about it. We had plans. And now he goes and breaks it to me that he's got to take off for a while, that he needs to meet with some of his investors in another state or something." Her voice quivered. "I don't know. He said I'd get in the way if I came with him." Another batch of tears poured out. "In the way!" She grabbed for her box of tissues.

Cadence and I exchanged looks. *Roy is taking off? When? For how long?*

After blowing her nose, Reenie poured us some coffee and slumped into a chair. "I feel so bad not being at church. I just couldn't go, not like this. People around here already feel sorry enough for me with all I went through trying to have a baby." She dumped a full pink pack of sweetener into her coffee. "I'm being silly, I know. Roy has so many people that count on him. Just look at what he's doing for Rauston Baptist!"

Casually filling her coffee cup to the brim with milk, Cadence asked, "How's that going to work with that whole Jubilee thingy?"

I examined Reenie's face for any indication that she thought this question was out of line. I saw none.

"Oh, he's got it all figured out with Pastor Williams. I mean, he explained it to me; I just could barely listen I was so upset. I understand, part of his job is 'socializing and making connections'"—she indicated quote marks around these last few words to let us know they were his—"and 'socializing and making connections' involves travel. It just seems so soon. We haven't been married a year."

We sipped our coffee, listening to Reenie beat herself up for not being more understanding, but didn't learn much more of interest, although not for lack of trying. Cadence was a master at making her interrogation sound like sympathetic prattle. Reenie never had a clue. Then again, she didn't have a clue about much, not about Roy's work, his travel. He was her man and that was enough for her. As we got up to leave, Cadence said, "This is such a beautiful old house. You wouldn't want to give us a tour?"

This girl doesn't give up!

Reenie brightened at this idea. "I'd love to show you around."

So we got the nickel tour, wandering from one room to the next. The whole place was a study in country décor. I'm talking quilts, wallpaper, and gazillions of adorable little porcelain figurines. On our way out, we passed a closed door.

"What's in here?" Cadence asked.

"Roy's office," Reenie said. "But I can't show it to you because he keeps it locked. It's a shame too; it's a real cute room. Has a sweet little built-in bookshelf that my daddy made."

"That's funny that he keeps it locked," Cadence said.

"Oh, you don't know Roy. The man is paranoid about his stuff. He's sure I'll move some of his precious pieces of paper. Or worse, throw them out. I can't imagine the mess in there. He never takes the trash out. It's probably full of Dr Pepper cans and half-eaten sandwiches." She shook her head. "Men!"

Cadence and I both shook our heads too, as if we shared her sentiments, but I knew we were thinking the same thing. *We have to get into that office.*

Before saying our good-byes, Reenie asked if we wouldn't keep her little "boo-hoo" as she put it, private. We agreed, hugged her, and left.

Once we were back in the car and pulling onto the road, Cadence blurted, "That jerk! We've got to nail his ass!" I felt the same way. Whatever reservations I'd had were gone. Not only was he taking advantage of the people at Rauston Baptist, he was also taking advantage of a good, trusting wife. The more we talked, the more revved we got.

The revival started Friday night, giving us only one day to find the evidence we needed—and to act on it.

"She did say she was going to a funeral in Amarillo tomorrow evening," Cadence said. "If only we could find a way to get rid of Roy."

"Let's swing by the Crowbar, see if we can put Sweet Ginger's skills to work," I said as we neared the highway.

Not only was Sweet Ginger willing, she was totally into it.

"Brandie owes me some time. I'll take the night off. How late you want me to keep our lover boy occupied?"

I consulted Cadence, but she was as clueless as I was. "Surely we'll be done by nine," I said.

"I'll keep him out 'til ten then, just for good measure," Sweet Ginger said with a saucy wink. "I'll call you sometime tomorrow to confirm I've made contact."

On the drive back, Cadence drummed her fingers on the truck windowsill. "Did you notice whether Roy's office had a window? Because if it didn't, I don't know how we're going to get in." But I was one step ahead of her; I knew just the guy who could help us out.

CHAPTER THIRTY

I took the afternoon off from Jameson's to round up Crash. I started with the Teen Center, a place he'd told me he hung out most afternoons. Entering the brightly lit, cheerily decorated lounge gave me a major case of the heebie-jeebies. Posters of hair-gelled teens hanging out at parks, playing electric music, gossiping in front of lockers, sported slogans like: DRUGS ARE NOBODY'S FRIEND, and DRUGS ARE FOR LOSERS. On one wall was a teen photography exhibit: artistic close-ups of faucets, spiderwebs, rusty gutters, cow hooves, along with the usual blazing sunsets and artsy portraits.

A few kids scattered on the worn couches read magazines and listened to each other's iPods waiting for what sounded like a two-step dance class to let out. I was just about to ask one of them if Crash was around when I spotted him in the corner playing pinball by himself. I got the feeling the only reason he was there was because it wasn't home.

He brightened considerably when he saw me, glancing around to make sure the other kids saw that the chick with the eyebrow ring was there for him. I asked him if there was somewhere we could talk in private. He gave me a look that said he understood, that nothing worth doing could be done around this bunch of wieners, and ushered me toward a back door. The kids followed us with their eyes. If nothing else, it was clear I'd endowed Crash with a bit of intrigue.

The back door led to a weed-infested area lined with trash cans.

"You here for more pot?" he asked.

I glanced over my shoulder. "No." *What kind of a pothead does he think I am?* "You got plans for tonight?"

"Not really," he said, a confused look on his face, and I realized he thought I was hitting on him.

"Wanna pick a lock for me?" I almost spat out.

This time it was him who glanced over his shoulder. "You in trouble?"

"No, but you and your whole family might be if you say no."

He looked at me skeptically. "Did my dad do something stupid again?"

I suggested we take a drive so I could fill him in.

"Just take me home," he said. "This place sucks."

By the time I pulled up to his mailbox, I'd given him all the details I thought he needed and he was on board.

"This girl Cadence, she'll know what to look for if I can get us in?"

"I'm hoping so."

"My dad's gonna be bummed. He's been bragging all week about how we're gonna be rich." His expression left little doubt that his dad wasn't the only one who was bummed. Who knew what his teenage mind had already spent the money on?

"He didn't write the check yet, did he?"

"No. He was supposed to get a money order from my aunt yesterday, but it didn't come. Boy, did he blow a gasket! Like the stupid U.S. mail was me and my brother's fault."

His inability to look at me as he said this made me wonder if his dad physically abused him. I wanted to ask but couldn't find a tactful way to phrase the question.

He shrugged. "It'll probably come today. I'll watch for the mail so I can hide it. My aunt will kill him if he loses that money. She already thinks he's a good-for-nothing loser."

He was a good kid, Crash, willing to face his dad's temper to protect the family.

"You can't tell him, though," I said. "We don't want these boys to get wind of our suspicions and run."

"I ain't tellin' nobody." He opened the truck door. "What time you gonna pick me up?"

We decided I'd meet him on the highway at seven thirty. "And bring all your tools, or whatever."

He rolled his eyes, "No duh," and jumped out of the truck, slamming the door behind him.

As I pulled back onto the highway, I dug my cell phone from my satchel and gave Cadence a call.

"We're all set to go. I'm picking Crash up at seven thirty."

"I'll be at your place by seven," she said.

The adrenaline as I flew down the highway, hot wind screaming through the open windows, was insane. My mind wouldn't settle down. *This is crazy! We're going to break into a guy's office! His computer! What if Sweet Ginger can't keep him occupied and he winds up coming home early? Will he get violent?* I reminded myself I'd have my cell phone. *Sweet Ginger can call if something goes wrong.*

But am I putting her in danger?

It occurred to me that without my knowing it I'd become the leader of this little escapade. How had it happened? Wasn't Cadence the one who suggested we break into Roy's place? Cadence who'd said things like "We owe it to Piggin and Heifer," and "We can't let him get away with it"? So why was I suddenly the one calling the shots? Setting up the rendezvous points?

Piggin's and Heifer's cars were both in the driveway when I pulled up. I checked my watch. *Five thirty. An hour and a half until Cadence shows up.* All I had to do now was figure out how to occupy myself until then. Showering and eating would take all of twenty minutes. *Then what?* I remembered Heifer asking me to help her move a table when I got the chance. Now being as good a time as any, I knocked on her door.

"It's unlocked! Come on in!"

I stepped inside and was surprised to see that her curtains were actually open. It was amazing how much brighter and airier the place felt. As usual, the air-conditioning was a welcome relief. I took a moment to let my skin suck it up.

"Back here," she yelled from down the hallway.

I found her in the bathroom cutting her hair with a pair of nail scissors. A newspaper was spread out in the sink to catch the clippings, and both vanity mirrors were flipped open so she could see the back of her head. I knew the technique well.

"I guess this is a bad time to help with that table."

"Did it already," she said snipping a lock of hair. "Couldn't stand not having it done once I seen it in my mind."

I peered down the hallway and noted that she had indeed moved her kitchen table next to the window. "Looks good," I said.

"Still needs something, though."

"Maybe a tablecloth?"

"Yeah. That'd be good. Nothing frilly, though."

Why this sudden interest in how her place looks? The open curtains, the rearranging of the kitchen... Of course! Piggin invited Lilah to lunch on Saturday. I suppressed a smile. "Want me to do the back? I'm pretty good."

She eyed me in the mirror. "You're not going to do anything fancy. Nothing Californian?"

I laughed. "What, like giving you a Mohawk?"

She grunted.

"Just give me the scissors. I'll take a little off the back. That's what you want, right?"

She handed them over reluctantly. "Don't want it to look like I got it cut. That's why I don't go to K'Lynn any more. After I get back from a trip to K'Lynn's, always looks like I just got it cut. And she flips it up with that dryer of hers too. I hate that."

"I know what I'm doing, Heifer. I used to cut my friends' hair all the time."

"That's what I'm afraid of."

As I worked on the back of her hair, occasionally glancing at her in the mirror to offer reassurance, something began gnawing at the back of my consciousness. It took a while to figure out, since I was mostly focused on her hair, but when I finally did, I had to keep my hands steady. *She and Cadence have the same nose!*

"It's funny," I said, casually, "but in some ways you and Piggin don't look that much alike...I mean, for sisters."

"That's because I take after our mama and she takes after our daddy. She's the only one of us five didn't get the Wilbourne nose. Used to drive him nuts. He'd accuse Mama of all kinds of whatnot."

I quit cutting for a moment. *The family resemblance is unmistakable.* The more I thought about it, Cadence kind of looked like Sweet Ginger too. *Especially her nose. All three of them have that dimple on the tip.*

I wondered if I should say something to Heifer. *But how can I when I'm not supposed to know about Piggin's baby? I could always wait until I have a chance to talk to Sweet Ginger...*

But I had to go for the gold. It was the least I could do for Cadence.

"Um…Heifer, could I talk to you about something?"

"So long as it doesn't have to do with messing up my hair."

"Actually, it has to do with Piggin…and that meltdown she had the other night…when she burned her eye…"

The muscles in Heifer's shoulders stiffened. "What about it?"

I told her what Sweet Ginger had told me about Piggin putting her child up for adoption. Heifer seemed only mildly surprised by this.

"That Sweet Ginger sure does have a mouth on her," she said.

She even seemed relieved in a way, like she was happy to finally be able to talk about the events of this painful incident in their past. And talk she did. She told me that everyone in town thought Piggin had gone off to a summer camp for girls, and how, as far as she knew, nobody in town knew anything about the baby. "Mama always said it was real convenient it was a summer baby. They didn't have to make up some excuse for pulling her out of school."

Once her talking had petered out, I mentioned that Cadence had come to Rauston in search of her birth mother. "I mean, I'm not saying anything besides…"

Heifer, who was now brushing up loose hairs from the sink—she used an old shaving brush apparently kept for this purpose—grumbled, "You talking 'bout that girl out at Minnie Bell's place?"

"That's the one." I waited for her to say something more, but she just kept brushing up those clumps of hair. "You want me to get the broom?"

She stopped, and from her reflection I could see she was staring at the sink. "The girl I seen at Jameson's helping him out with stuff?"

"Yeah. Her name is Cadence."

A little clicking noise slipped out of the side of her mouth. "Don't that beat all."

"I mean, nothing's for certain."

She resumed her cleanup. "Next time I see her I'll take a closer look."

I went for the broom. By the time I got back, she'd cleaned up the sink and was heading toward the kitchen with her wad of newspaper. The hall, being fairly narrow, forced us to squeeze past one another.

"What do you think we should do? Or should we do anything?" I asked.

Heifer apparently felt no need to respond, so I swept up the hair, tossed it, and trotted back to the kitchen where I found her sitting at the table she'd recently moved by the window. She was gazing out, her focus diffused. I had the feeling that the information I'd just presented her with was descending into the quicksand of unspeakable Wilbourne secrets. I couldn't let that happen.

"Cadence says people who've given up a child for adoption can sign some kind of paper that opens up their file. Then we could find out for sure." I put the broom and dustpan up.

Her chubby fingers unconsciously traced a scar in the oak tabletop. "Thing is, we don't want to get Piggin's hopes up, then have it not be…"

I waited for her to finish her sentence, but she changed the subject instead.

"Don't know why it took me so long to think of putting the table here."

"Maybe if we—you—can talk to her about signing that paper. Then, even if Cadence isn't her kid, at least it opens up the doors for her real kid to find her."

"So you think a tablecloth would brighten it up in here?"

Why had I thought this was a good time to bring this up? I checked the clock. *Forty-five minutes 'til Cadence arrives*. I still had to shower and eat. "Look, I gotta go."

She lifted an eyebrow. "What you got going on?"

"Actually, Cadence is coming over and we're, um, thinking about driving into Amarillo for a movie or something." I could tell by her look that she thought I was lying, probably thought I was covering up some kind of lesbian business.

"You like this Cadence?" she asked.

"She's all right," I said. "We're both from California."

She shook her head almost imperceptibly. "Well, go on, then."

I turned to leave, unsure where we stood on the whole Piggin/Cadence thing.

"Thanks for the cut," she said to my back. "You did real good."

❖

Once inside my trailer, I slammed back a glass of milk and a peanut butter sandwich and hopped in the shower. *Living in Rauston is surreal. On the one level, everything is so nice and polite, but just beneath that tidy surface, storms are howling, ripping apart families, tearing at people's hearts.*

In a strange way, this comforted me.

I was doing the final touches on my hair, which basically amounted to me trying to get a comb through my stubborn mop of black curls, when Cadence knocked. "Come on in!" I yelled.

The first thing she said was, "You're not wearing black."

"Why would I be?"

"So we can blend into the shadows."

"It doesn't even get dark until nine."

She thought about this for a moment. "Okay. So you have a point."

I laughed. "You are a nut."

She shrugged. "Shall we?"

I never answered. I was too busy thinking about that dimple on her nose.

We decided on her car since it was quieter, but I stopped by the truck to pick up a few pairs of latex paint gloves. "For fingerprints," I said, holding them up.

Heifer stepped out her door with a bag of trash, nowhere near ready to dump. In fact, it looked like it had about two things in it. I slipped the gloves in my pocket. "Hey, Heifer!" She waved. I knew what she was doing. "Have you two met?" I asked.

"'Course we have," Heifer said, taking advantage of my entrée and walking toward us. "You're out at Minnie Bell's."

As the two of them chatted about Minnie Bell's health and whatnot, I couldn't get it out of my mind: *Cadence could be talking to her aunt.* My eyes flicked from one to the other.

"Eadie!"

Heifer had said something I missed. "Huh?"

"I said, could I have a quick word with you? In private?"

I checked my watch. *We're running late.* "Uh, sure. A quick one."

We stepped away from the car. Heifer was shook up. "She's got the Wilbourne nose," she whispered. "Just like J.D.'s."

"So what do we do?" I whispered back.

"I'll talk to Piggin about signing those papers." She squeezed my hand. "Now, don't you go telling her anything," she said, indicating Cadence. "We need to be sure."

"I won't," I said. But it sure was tempting.

❖

"What was that all about?" Cadence asked when we were on the road.

"We're planning a surprise for Piggin."

"Is it her birthday or something?"

"Or something," I said. "I'll tell you more later, when we're not in the middle of an illegal caper."

"We haven't done anything illegal yet," she said, but I could tell she too was nervous.

When we got to Crash's, he was sitting on a rock by the mailbox eating sunflower seeds. His cap was flipped backward, making him look even younger than he was.

Am I crazy? I thought as we pulled up next to him. *He's a minor, for Christ's sake!* I glanced over at Cadence. She looked worried.

I pulled my seat forward and Crash climbed into the tiny backseat. "You're late," he said, trying to fold his long legs up in a way that would allow me to click my seat back.

"Cadence, this is Crash. Crash, Cadence."

"Nice to meet you," he said, reaching his knuckled hand over the seat.

"Likewise," Cadence said, twisting around to shake it.

All three of us were edgy. No doubt about it.

CHAPTER THIRTY-ONE

I sat sideways in the car so I could see both Crash in the backseat and Cadence in the driver's. "So here's the plan. Once we reach Wells Road, we're going to pull over somewhere and wait for Sweet Ginger's call confirming that she's with Roy. I don't want any surprises tonight."

Crash, his cheek full of sunflower seeds, spat an empty hull out the open window. "If you don't mind me saying, there's nothing on that stretch. Us, pulled over in a VW, is gonna to look kinda unusual."

I scratched an annoying bug bite on my ankle. *Why didn't I think to scope it out earlier?* "I don't know what to do about that. I told Sweet Ginger…"

"Go to Hunter's Creek," he said. "It's just a couple miles off the road. We won't stick out there."

"I'm not sure we should deviate—"

"He's got a point, Eadie," Cadence said, forging an alliance with him via the rearview mirror. "We don't want anyone asking if we're having car troubles." She directed her next words to Crash. "Where's Hunter's Creek?"

"Next left."

She flicked on her blinker. "Better safe than sorry."

Hunter's Creek turned out to be the local teenage make-out spot. We were one of six vehicles parked by a dry creek bed spotted with trees. We parked as far to one end as we dared in a non-four-wheel drive. Although it was close to eight o'clock, the summer sun had yet to set, but it cast convenient shadows, which the teenagers took full advantage of. *Crash was right. Anyone spotting us here will think we're up to nothing more than harmless, titillating hanky-panky.*

Crash gave us the teenage lowdown punctuated by the spitting of sunflower seeds. "That's Jud Vicker's pick-up. He's probably, um... with Sharla Lee right now. They say they want to get married, but her daddy don't like Jud." Spit. "And over there is Betty Dawson's new Rav-4. Got it for her sixteenth birthday." Spit. "Wonder who she's got with her?" Spit. "And over there..."

"Come here often?" Cadence asked.

"I been here a time or two."

I slumped down in the seat. This is excruciating! Here I am, sitting at lovers' point with a woman I'm extremely attracted to—and there's a friggin' teenage boy in the back! I pulled my ball cap down over my eyes and tried not to think about all the heavy petting going on. *Come on, Sweet Ginger. Call.* From underneath the brim of my hat, I watched Cadence wipe down the console with a Kleenex while trying to block out the soundtrack of Crash munching and spitting seeds.

Fifteen agonizing minutes later, Crash said, "I gotta take a leak."

We watched him disappear behind an outcropping of mesquite.

"Somehow I didn't realize he was going to be so young," Cadence said.

"I told you he was sixteen."

"I guess I thought sixteen was older."

Neither of us said what had to be going through both of our heads. Should we back out now while we still could?

Wild Thing rang. I flicked it open. "Yeah?"

"He's just walked into the Crowbar. Wish me luck!" Sweet Ginger said, then hung up.

"We're on," I said to Cadence.

She started the engine.

"Where the hell is Crash? It's been over five minutes."

"Relax," she said. "All three of us are wound up."

I focused on my breathing. *In. Out. In. Out.* Then couldn't contain myself any longer. "What all did he have to do? Zip down his pants, take a whiz, shake a little, and zip back up."

"Maybe he ran into trouble."

"Like what? Getting his wee-wee stuck in the zipper? I'm going after him."

Before I had a chance to follow up on my threat, he bolted out of the bushes, his face and one forearm scratched up. And he was laughing. Climbing past me into the backseat, he said, "Oh my God! That was so funny!"

Right then a clean-cut teenager shot out of the bushes, fist raised. "Milsap! You asshole!"

Cadence threw it into reverse and peeled out.

I couldn't keep the annoyance from my voice. "What happened?"

"I peed on Ashley Renée and Dirk Junior! I swear to God I didn't see 'em! They were kinda under this ledge and there was all this mesquite. I didn't think nothing about it. Just whipped out my pecker and started doing my thing. Then I hear this scream! So I finish peeing fast as I can and go to help. I thought someone was hurt or dying or something. Turns out it was just Ashley Renée giving a blow job to Dirk Junior in the creek bed."

"So how'd you get so scraped up?"

His mood changed. "Tried to apologize. Fucking Dirk, man. Fuck him and the whole fucking football team! They're such jerks!"

"So much for being inconspicuous," I moaned.

"Ashley Renée won't let him tell. She'd die if anyone knew she was out there."

"What about the other cars?'

"Don't worry about them. They'll just think…" He didn't finish his sentence, but we all knew what he was going to say: that he was out there smooching with the only person in town who had a vintage VW bug.

Cadence laughed. "You're giving me a bad reputation, Crash."

"I'm sorry. I didn't mean—"

"We need to focus, you guys. We're going to be there in no time." The whole situation was starting to give me a serious stomachache.

Ten minutes later we pulled up to Roy and Reenie's. This time neither of their cars were in the carport, but Cadence bypassed the carport anyway, pulling around the back behind the old barn. The implicit dishonesty of the act made me nauseous. "Is everybody still feeling good about this?" I asked, vaguely hoping one or both of them would want to back out.

"I am," Crash said.

"Me too," Cadence said.

Resigned, I handed out latex gloves. "Okay. If anybody at any time does get a bad feeling, just say the word and we abort."

They pulled on their gloves, nodding.

Like before, the front door was unlocked. Cadence did the requisite "Yoo-hoos" and "Anybody homes?" just in case. How we would have explained the three of us standing there in latex gloves, I had no idea. Fortunately, this time the house really was empty. We tiptoed anyway, straight to Roy's office.

"There it is," I whispered to Crash. "Think you can handle it?"

He chuckled. "God, you guys. You made it sound like this was going to be hard."

"It's not?"

He knelt and pulled out what looked like a tobacco pouch full of filed-off Allen wrenches, safety pins, unbent paper clips, and other handmade lock picks.

"This is just like my first lock at Nanna's."

He chose one of the larger Allen wrenches. "We used to live there." He wiggled the wrench around in the lock. "It's how I learned there was no Santa. See, my mom didn't want me thinking that Santa had forgotten me, so she explained that my dad was struggling with the devil and he'd hocked all my presents…" He leaned in to listen as he wiggled the wrench, then picked up one of the paper clips and did the same thing, all the while prattling on about his childhood. It was driving me nuts.

Cadence put her hand on my arm. That helped a little.

"Next year, I decided I wanted to at least see my presents before he hocked 'em, so I broke into the closet where my mom had 'em locked up." More wiggling and listening. "He didn't hock 'em that year, though. So Christmas I didn't get any surprises. It kinda sucked." The door clicked open.

Cadence and I looked at one another with a mix of astonishment and dismay. The kid was good, too good.

"I told you it would be easy," he said.

Roy's office was a pigsty. There were Dr Pepper cans and sports pages from the local newspaper scattered everywhere. A plate with a half-eaten sandwich sat on the floor, one full of pizza crusts on the wide windowsill. A desk that housed his computer, a filing cabinet, and an ancient copier were stationed around the office with no regard whatsoever for esthetics. A light blinked on the copier indicating a paper jam.

Cadence went straight for the computer. I went for the filing cabinet, tugged at the handle. *Locked.* "Crash, see what you can do with this."

Cadence clicked on the computer. "It would have to be a PC," she grumbled. "I'm much more comfortable with Macs."

"This lock's going to be a little trickier," Crash said.

I walked back down the hall and peered out the front window. It wasn't so much that I wanted to scope things out—I was pretty certain we were all covered on that front—but I needed to move. When I returned to the office, Crash was still fiddling with the lock on the filing cabinet.

The computer chimed, signaling it was booted up and ready to go. "Oh good," Cadence said. "He's lazy. He's got it set so it bypasses the login." She wiggled the mouse around. "Wow. His desktop is a mess."

"How you coming?" I asked Crash.

"Not so good," he said. "But I'll get it."

"Well, the guy loves computer games," Cadence said, jockeying the mouse around. "I can't find any documents labeled Jubilee or Trust Fund, though. I'm going to have to run a search on their contents."

Right then, the front door clicked open. "Anybody home?"

We all froze. *Pastor Williams!*

I put my finger to my lips, not that I needed to. The two of them had stopped mid-breath and now appeared like one of those life-size dioramas you see in natural history museums. I tiptoed to where I could—slowly—swing the office door closed. Mercifully, it didn't squeak. It was too risky to shut it completely. The click of the door would give us away.

"Roy? Reenie?" he yelled.

I tiptoed backward toward the wall so if Pastor Williams entered the house and for some reason opened the office door I'd be right behind it. I don't know what I thought I'd do. Jump out and attack Rambo style?

We listened soberly as he entered the house.

Shit! What does he want?

He closed the door behind him and began his way down the hall humming what sounded like a hymn. As the humming got louder, I almost pissed my pants. *What will we do if he notices the open door? Or does he have a key? Maybe this is his office too. Maybe he'll...*

He passed the door and headed for the kitchen.

All three of us, I believe, took our first breath since we'd heard him.

He continued to hum.

I peered out the crack in the door and saw him writing a note at the kitchen counter.

Crash crept over to the window, tried to open it, but it was painted shut. He looked at us apologetically. We listened to Pastor Williams open the refrigerator, rummage around in it, and finally pop a soda.

Is he planning on staying?

He picked up the kitchen phone and dialed a number. It sounded like he was retrieving his messages.

Cadence sat, very slowly, back in the chair, making sure it didn't squeak. Crash squatted by the window, but his elbow caught the sunflower seed bag in his pocket and they went scattering across the wood floor.

Cadence and I glared at him. He mimed shooting himself in the head, but other than that, none of us moved. *Could Pastor Williams have possibly heard?*

An interminable amount of time passed before he continued with his phone business. *The dude is returning calls.* Most of them had to do with the revival in one way or another: yes, there'd be time for the kids to do an extra song; no, he didn't think Charlene Wandra would be staying both nights.

Why doesn't he do his business at his own place? Why does he have to do it here?

Cadence tried once to access a file in the computer, but the clicking of the keyboard just about gave us all a coronary. There was no choice but to wait him out.

When Pastor Williams finally strode past the office and out through the front door, the three of us let out a collective sigh. We waited for the sound of his car starting before getting back to work.

"How much time do we have left?" Cadence whispered, touching a key to wake the computer back up.

"I told Sweet Ginger we'd be done by nine."

Crash bent down and began sweeping up his spilled sunflower seeds.

Cadence gazed at the computer screen. "This guy is totally unorganized. I don't think he understands the concept of folders!"

By now, the blinking light on the lousy Xerox machine was driving me totally nuts. I'd been staring at it the whole twenty minutes. *Once a Copy Specialist, always a Copy Specialist,* I thought, and walked over, flipped open the panel where the jams are usually located. Sure enough, the master was caught between the rollers. Following a hunch, I gingerly pulled it out. *Just as I thought. Glue stick!*

I peeled back what he'd tried to stick on. "This is interesting…"

"What's that?" Cadence said, not looking up from the computer.

"It's some kind of legal document, but he's got the Jubilee Trust Fund letterhead stuck over another letterhead."

"What's the other letterhead?"

I peeled it back further. "Faith Promises International."

Cadence looked up from the computer. "Faith Promises International?"

"Yeah."

"They're, like, major bad guys. When I was searching the Internet the other day, I kept coming across their name. They were busted last year for fraud—"

Wild Thing started blaring. All three of us jumped. Sweet Ginger's number came up on the readout.

"Hey kiddies, I had to let the bird fly. He was starting to get a little too fresh. You come up with anything?"

"Yeah, I think so. I'll call you in a few."

Cadence, now that she knew what to look for, wanted to spend more time searching on the computer. "It should be easy now."

Crash and I, however, were of a different sentiment: *Time to get the hell out of here*. "We've got what we came for," I said, making a copy of the mangled letterhead.

"Yeah," Crash said. "None of this will be admissible in court anyway."

Cadence and I looked at him taken aback. "How do you know that?" I asked.

He shrugged. "TV. They always gotta have a search warrant on TV."

I sent the master back through, adding a little extra glue stick for good measure. Sure enough, it jammed again. *Good old Xerox. You can always count on them for a jam*

Cadence flicked off the computer. We all three watched the screen to make sure it turned off, then locked ourselves out of the office. Before leaving, I snuck into the kitchen to see what Pastor Williams's had written to Roy and Reenie. His note was on the bottom of a program for the weekend's revival with Roy's parts circled in red. His first presentation would be Friday night. What he'd scrawled was:

> *Roy, I stole one of your Dr Pepper's from the fridge! I owe ya, Bud!*
>
> *Also, Sylvia wants to know if you guys would like to do dinner sometime soon?*

Back in the car, Cadence was furious, not because of Roy's affiliation with a group of hardened criminals that took advantage of good churchgoing folks, but because she'd been unable to come up with the evidence by searching his computer. "The guy's an idiot! I was looking under Jubilee Trust Fund! All the records were probably Faith Promises International." She adjusted her rearview mirror. "People like him shouldn't be allowed to have a computer."

I called Sweet Ginger to see how it had gone on her end. "Smooth as malt whiskey," she said. "I got him to buy me dinner and a few drinks. Then, when it looked like he was starting to expect dessert, Buzzard came over and acted like my jealous ex. Worked like a charm."

I told her about the letterhead.

"That son of a bitch! I swear, it's always the clean-cut ones you gotta watch out for." She took a hit off a smoke, then said, "Talk to Heifer. She and the sheriff go way back. They used to shoot bottles together on the weekends."

CHAPTER THIRTY-TWO

Cadence dropped off Crash first although it meant doing fifteen minutes of backtracking on her part. There were plenty of reasons she might have done this. She might have felt awkward being alone in the car with him. Or she could have thought since he was a kid, he needed to be home early. Or maybe she wanted to talk to me about what to do next about Roy Peterson.

Then again, maybe she liked me.

I adjusted my seat back to stretch out my legs. "I've got a beer we could split back at my place. You know, to celebrate the success of our mission."

She shifted into fourth gear. "I think we should talk to Heifer tonight—if she's still awake."

My fantasy of sweet kisses in a candlelit trailer withered into a curl of diminishing smoke. "Well, sure, if she's still awake." I looked out the window into the moonlit night. *I'm such a jerk. Here we are, sitting on a scam that could radically screw over tons of people, and what have I got on my mind? Romance.*

We pulled into the driveway. The lit curtains of Heifer's trailer indicated that she was indeed still awake. "I guess we're on," I said, getting out of the car. If we were going to do this, I wanted to do it and get Cadence safely back to her place and me back to mine. No more teasing myself with thoughts of us being any more than friends.

The vastness of the night made our small compound of trailers seem so vulnerable, like a band of covered wagons stopping over for a night on the long westward journey. Or at least that's how they always made them look in the movies—right before the obligatory Indian attack. Although there was plenty of moonlight, Cadence tried to squeeze on one of those LED keychain lights, but it was dead. "Shoot!" she said, shaking it. "I have rotten night vision."

"Mine's pretty good," I said, holding out my arm.

The feeling of her warm hand lightly gripping my upper arm set my body tingling. *False alarm! False alarm!* my intellect screamed, but it was useless. My dim-witted body thought it was in love. I sighed, led her down the path to Heifer's, and knocked. *Bunch of stupid nerve endings.*

Cadence removed her hand from my arm. My reaction to this was an odd mix of sadness and relief. While I loved the feeling of her being on my arm, that last thing I needed was for Heifer to think I, this veteran lesbian and sinner extraordinaire, was corrupting her sweet, innocent, newfound niece. It's a known fact that people who act all groovy with you being a lesbian show a whole new face when you show an interest in their daughter…or their niece.

Heifer came to the door wearing her favorite Dallas Cowboys T-shirt, sweatpants, and some jellylike goop on her face. The expression she wore was one I bet Jehovah's Witnesses get all the time. "You got back from Amarillo awful quick." A TV babbled in the background. I decided not to ask about the goop.

"Actually, we didn't go."

The single lifting of an eyebrow clued me in that she thought our ill-timed arrival had something to do with Cadence's search for her mother. I racked my brain for a way to set her mind at ease without cluing Cadence in. I came up blank. "Can we come in? This is important."

My words only seemed to add to her distress. Leaving the door open, her only indication that we were welcome, she headed toward a box of Kleenex on her kitchen counter and began wiping the goop off her face.

I glanced at Cadence, my expression asking: "Do we really want to do this now?"

She nodded.

I closed the door behind us. An ironing board with blue and white checkered fabric across it was set up facing the TV in the living room. On the TV screen a bunch of women in mini-skirts stood on platforms, holding suitcases. The audience was cheering wildly, "No deal! No deal!" We headed for the kitchen.

“Is that a new tablecloth on the ironing board?” I asked, hoping to alleviate the tension.

“Yeaup. Had ’em at the hardware store.” She popped open the trash can with her foot and tossed in the goopy Kleenexes. “Once I pulled it out of the pack, though, it was full of creases.”

Cadence looked back into the living room. “It’s really cheerful. It’ll look great in here.” She waited for Heifer to respond, but Heifer was too busy staring at her, a mix of heartbreak and accusation on her face. There was still a little goop in the crease of Heifer’s nostrils, but I wasn’t going to be the one to tell her. “How about some Cokes?” she said finally.

“That would be great,” I said, pulling up a chair.

Cadence, obviously confused by Heifer’s odd behavior, followed suit. “Me too.” She began fiddling with a silver chain around her neck, then glanced at me as if to say, Should I start? Or are you going to? Which was all well and good, except I couldn’t figure out how. I’d already dropped one bombshell on Heifer today and wasn’t sure she was in the mood for a second. Heifer stood at the refrigerator, her back to us in such a way that it exaggerated the pockets of sagging fat above her elbows.

Here goes... “So we didn’t go to the movies tonight because there was something we needed to check out.”

“7up, Orange Crush, or Dr Pepper?”

“7up,” I said.

“Dr Pepper,” Cadence said.

The game show audience, chanted: “Low! Low! Low!”

Heifer placed a soda in front of each of us. There would be no glasses or ice tonight. We were doing them straight up, from the can.

It was that exact moment of can touching table that I understood the underlying presumption of Heifer’s discomfort: She thought we were going to confront her for being part of a family that would give up a newborn baby. What’s more, she was working herself up to confront the situation. My mind whizzed through possible statements she might make. “Eadie had no right to bring you here,” “I’m sorry my sister gave you up, but you have to understand, she didn’t have a choice,” “There’s no proof you’re family.” I couldn’t let this happen; it would be awful for Cadence to find out this way.

“It has to do with the Jubilee Trust Fund,” I blurted.

The TV audience cheered wildly.

Heifer, who was about to lower herself into her chair, an action involving some commitment on her part due to arthritic knees, stopped mid-descent. "Jubilee?"

"Uh-huh."

She took this in, then continued her way down to the chair using her hands on the table for support. Once sitting comfortably, she said, "You come knocking on my door at quarter to ten to talk church business?" She pulled the tab on her Dr Pepper can.

While I was glad we'd made it over the first hurdle, the second one still loomed.

I opted for the show-and-tell method of presentation, pulling the folded photocopy from my pocket and spreading it on the table. My hope was it would be clear, just by her looking at it, that someone had tried to paste Jubilee Trust Fund over Faith Promises International.

She gestured for me to hand her a pair of reading glasses that were sitting behind me in a catchall bowl by the phone.

I did.

She put them on and returned her attention to the paper, first turning it over to see if something was on the back, then turning it right side up. "You gonna explain this?"

I was vaguely hoping Cadence would speak up, but she didn't. And who could blame her? Heifer was doing everything possible to pretend she wasn't there. "The original was stuck in Roy Peterson's copy machine," I finally said. "Still is, actually."

Heifer peered over the top of her glasses at me. "How'd you happen to come across it?"

Cadence and I glanced at one another. She hadn't even opened her soda.

"Um..." I said.

"Well..." she said.

"See, the thing is," I said. "Faith Promises International, they're—"

"Crooks," Cadence said, finishing my sentence. "They were busted last year for fraud."

At first Heifer didn't move, and I wondered if she'd heard what Cadence had said. Then I noticed her grip on the paper was causing it to buckle. She pushed her glasses onto her head, involuntarily sweeping up a lock of hair, which pointed straight up like a lone antenna. She directed this next question to me. "So you're not going to tell me."

"We could," I said. "But it's probably better if you don't know."

"Better for you," she said eyeing me with an intensity that threatened to melt the skin off my already flushed face.

"Well, yeah…" It seemed as good time as any to take a swig of soda, so I did. Swallowing, however, turned out to be impossible. That is, until she took her eyes off me and returned her attention to the paper.

She cleared her throat and asked me. "So, if I get you right, you're suggesting Reenie's husband is taking us for a ride."

I turned toward Cadence, hoping like hell she'd take this one, but could see she was taken aback by Heifer's blatant ignoring of her.

I steepled my fingers, then, deciding it appeared too arrogant, unsteepled them. "There are a few other things that made us suspicious."

"Like?"

"The day Sweet Ginger came over to"—*buy a joint*—"look for her wallet"—*Come on, Eadie, you can do better than this*—"she told me that Roy had been"—*making the moves on her*—"acting inappropriately with her…"

And so the story came out, haltingly. I said that Cadence and I had been "invited" by Sweet Ginger to see where she worked, and that Cadence had "accidentally" overheard Roy's conversation with a guy who appeared to be his boss. I also reused the vase alibi when explaining how we'd shown up at Reenie's and found her in tears, and how Reenie had told us that Roy was planning an unexpected, indefinite, trip the day after the revival. Heifer listened carefully, never once picking up her soda or waving away the nocturnal fly that had begun circling the table.

"So you still didn't tell me how you got this," she said gesturing to the photocopy.

The last thing I wanted to do was confess to breaking and entering, or Crash's involvement. "We just did," I said.

She leveled me with her eyes. "If this turns out to be true, which I hope it isn't, you're gonna have to tell somebody how you wound up with that little piece of evidence."

"Can we just deal with it then?" I pleaded.

She shrugged. "Okay by me. I'm not the law."

I glanced over at Cadence for the umpteenth time. *Help me out here, would you?*

"So what's y'all's theory on Pastor Williams?" Heifer asked.

"From what I've read," Cadence began cautiously, "these con guys gain the trust of a congregation by getting influential people in the church to invest first. Then, when they get paid off, people feel like it's a sure thing."

"Pastor Williams might be their patsy," I added, relieved that Cadence and I were working as a team again.

"Chances are, they're working more than one church," she said.

Heifer stood, once again using the table to assist her, and directed her words to me. "Always thought Jubilee was too good to be true. Told Piggin that too, but of course she didn't listen. Never does, not when she's got some man in a fancy suit telling her what's what." She headed down the hallway to the back of her trailer. "This is gonna break Reenie's heart. Gonna break a lot of people's hearts. Jubilee's been a real miracle around here." She stopped just short of the bathroom. "It'll slow down the building of the new church too." Then she disappeared inside.

Cadence and I, unsure how much Heifer would be able to hear from inside the bathroom, listened to the TV burbling commercials for a while. I tried to reassure myself that we'd done the right thing. If we hadn't uncovered the Jubilee scam, many innocent people would, over the next few days, be scraping up money they barely had and turning it over to a couple of assholes who were preying on their goodness.

I don't know what Cadence was thinking, or didn't until she whispered, "Does Heifer have any reason to be mad at me?"

What could I say to explain Heifer's apparent rudeness? "I think she's just tired," I said. "And upset about this whole Jubilee thing."

The bathroom door clicked open and Heifer made her way back to the kitchen. "Well, I guess I should thank you. Whether or not this turns out to be true, least you're doing what you think is right. Let's just hope it isn't."

Cadence and I both stood.

"What are you going to do?" I asked.

"Call Gotch. Put him on the scent."

"Gotch?"

"The sheriff." Heifer picked the soda cans up off the table. "He don't much care for Roy as it is." She tossed them into the trash. "Gotch and Reenie were sweet on each other back in high school, but his family wasn't good enough for her daddy. Never quit carrying a torch for her, though. Never could find anyone could live up to his precious little Reenie."

Cadence wrote her phone number on a slip of paper. "I'd be happy to show him what I found on the Internet about Faith Promises International."

Heifer took the phone number. "I'll pass it on." The next words she spoke came out bluntly and were aimed directly at Cadence. "Sometimes people just do things, see? And you don't always get to know why."

I was aware of Cadence's stance stiffening, and it broke my heart. She had no idea that Heifer wasn't talking about Roy and the Jubilee stuff. She thought that Heifer was reprimanding her.

The lack of air-conditioning that hit us as we made our way out the door came as a relief. I needed real. Real air, real stars, real crickets. The moon, low in the sky, cast long eerie shadows across the Wilbourne property. You could feel the night creatures watching.

"That was weird," Cadence said accompanied by a little shiver.

"Heifer can be that way sometimes. Just ignore her."

She took my arm. "You still feel like sharing that beer?"

I threw a towel over the brick hearth of the old house. The lights in Heifer's trailer blinked out. One, then the next, then the next. Soon, it was just us and the night.

Cadence drank from a glass and me from the bottle. The mandala, reflecting the light from the moon, looked magical and made me think about the power of symbols and our need to find something in this life to believe in. I spotted Cadence's earring near the center, a beaded number with crystals, and it occurred to me Cadence might be sitting on the foundation of the house where a teenage Piggin had bravely, secretively, carried her. How terrified Piggin must have been. How long had she carried the baby before telling someone? Or had someone noticed her swelling belly, her bouts of nausea?

Without even thinking about it, I put my arm around Cadence. It was a protective move on my part. One I hoped she'd perceive as friendly, caring. To my surprise, though, she leaned into me and laid her head on my shoulder.

My heart quickened. *Is this a friendly lean? Or is she…*

"Sometimes I wonder what I'm doing here," she said.

Does she mean with me? Or does she mean in Rauston? "I know what you mean," I said testing the waters by laying my head on hers and breathing in the light fragrance of her hair.

She played with the frayed edge of my shorts. "It's like, you get delivered to earth without an instruction manual, you know? All of us just get dropped off with a 'good luck' and a 'see you on the other side,' if there even is another side."

I was having difficulty following her words. The feeling of her hand occasionally brushing against my thigh, the smell of her hair, the curve of her body into mine… I brushed my lips against her cheek.

She stopped fiddling with my shorts and I was afraid I'd gone too far, that I'd pushed past what was acceptable. Then she turned to meet my lips, and it wasn't me kissing her; it was her kissing me. Our tongues searched each other's out, twirling around one another, exploring. Lips locked, we twisted our bodies around so we could face one another. My bottle of beer knocked to the ground but didn't break. At least it didn't sound like it did. And as we kissed, I noticed that something was missing. Something I'd always felt before wasn't there. It was that bit of disappointment when you think, her lips are too tight, or too slack, or her mouth feels dry. Cadence was what my mouth had been looking for. She was my perfect kiss. My mouth's soul mate. I reached behind her to pull her closer, closer.

We kissed for what seemed like hours. At one time I remember hearing an owl hooting in the distance. I also remember seeing one of Heifer's lights go on, then out again. Part of me ached for more, wanted to invite Cadence into my trailer, wanted to undress her, kiss by kiss, but a stronger part of me said, *Don't rush. Go slow.*

A band of coyotes began yelping and howling very close by. We pulled apart to listen.

"Don't you love them?" she whispered.

"Yeah," I said, trying to catch my breath.

We were lying side by side on the brick hearth and one of her legs was draped over mine. "Have you ever done this before?" I asked.

There was a slight pause before she said, "Yup."

I turned to look at her. "With women?"

"Yup." A Cheshire grin spread across her face.

You little minx! "How come you didn't tell me before?"

She propped herself up on her elbow. "I'd decided to quit women."

"Why?"

She ran her fingers through my black mop, got caught on a tangle, and then just stayed there. "They're so much more complicated than men."

Before I could stop it, an incredulous chortle erupted from my mouth. "And you're not, Miss Chameleon Princess?"

Delighted surprise flashed across her face. Then she tipped her head back, laughing. "My point exactly. We all are. And I just think it would be so much easier if…well…"

"I could try to be simple."

She shook her head. "No way. The second I saw your artwork, I knew you weren't going to be simple."

"You've been thinking about me since then?"

She nodded.

Warm rays spread from my chest through my entire body. "So what do we do?"

She thought for a moment. "Try to stay in the present? Just keep ourselves right in the moment, whatever moment that is."

I pushed myself up to sitting. "Works for me. This is one of the best moments I've had in a long time." I cradled her face between my hands. "You are One. Damn. Good. Kisser."

In the moonlight I could see her collarbone rise, then fall. "I've never been *this* good before," she whispered her lips so close to mine they were almost touching.

I smiled, knowing exactly what she meant, and dove in for more.

Later, when she was lying in my arms and we were just listening to each other breathe, she said, "I should probably go."

"Why?"

"I just should." She lightly kissed me one more time, then stood.

We walked to her car, hand in hand, and there was another kiss, not as passionate as on the hearth, but just a sweet.

"I must be crazy," she whispered into my ear.

"I don't think so," I whispered back, my arms circled around her waist.

Then somehow she was in her car and we were kissing through the open window.

"Call me tomorrow," she said.

"You know I will," I said.

And she drove off.

I watched until it was just me in the dark, then walked back to my trailer. My eyes were wet. *That's weird,* I thought. I'd never cried out of happiness. Before me, the moon cast a squatty version of myself on the ground. I imagined it was giving me a glimpse of the hole in my soul. I spread out my arms and became a thunderbird.

CHAPTER THIRTY-THREE

Washing Jameson's windows turned out to be harder than I'd expected. Every time Buddy Bud and I thought one was finished, the light shifted slightly and streaks mysteriously emerged. "Uh-oooh," Buddy Bud would sing while pointing excitedly. "There they are again!"

The final touches almost done, I leaned back against the Duraflame logs and scanned. I was having a difficult time getting into Buddy Bud's game. Probably because each time we did discover a streak, Kitty, working her register, graced us with one of her disapproving looks, as if to say, "I knew Jameson was wrong to hire you!"

I bit back all kinds of snotty retorts such as, "What financial scam have you saved the church from today?" and "Just wait and see who Rauston is thanking after this weekend!"

I'd be vindicated soon enough.

Of course, each new streak also meant that much longer until I got to see Cadence. That is, if she wanted to see me. I hadn't had the nerve to call her yet. It was now well past two; I'd been holding back from calling since I'd tumbled out of bed at nine. The last thing I wanted was to come across all needy like one of those people who, after the first kiss, start planning the color scheme for our shared bedroom. *Stay in the moment.* I had a good excuse to call, though, one that had nothing to do with my aching need to see her again or with my growing insecurities. Heifer had suggested Cadence and I come to the kickoff of the revival. "Seeing as for some reason, God chose you two to come to our aid."

"Hey look, Eadie!" Buddy Bud said pointing out the newly cleaned window. "There's Old Luke!"

Sure enough, Old Luke was making his way across the parking lot. Sparkplug, in the bed of the pickup, looked on in that stately manner that dogs often adopt when their owners abandon them. "I'd go with him," Sparkplug seemed to say, "but he needs me here to guard the truck."

Old Luke looked mildly uncomfortable when the doors of the store automatically swung open, as if he wasn't sure whom to thank.

Buddy Bud ran over to meet him, his bottle of Windex and crumpled newspaper left behind. "Hey, Old Luke! Me 'n Eadie are washing windows!"

Old Luke nodded his head. "They look real nice, Buddy Bud."

"'Cept we keep getting streaks! Don't we, Eadie?"

"I think we've got most of them taken care of now," I said, using a pair of needlenose pliers to pull a useless staple from the wooden trim.

Buddy Bud returned to his window washing as if to show Old Luke what a good window washer he was, squirting Windex smack in the middle of a window we'd already finished.

"Buddy! We already did that one!"

A smile tickled the corner of Old Luke's slit of a mouth. "You got yourself a real good helper there, Miss Eadie."

Buddy Bud turned his circular wiping onto high speed.

"Be careful you don't wear a hole in it," I said, trying not to show my frustration.

Old Luke picked up a grocery handbasket. "I expect your car will be ready tomorrow," he said so quietly I barely heard him.

"Really? I mean, ready ready?"

He nodded. "It's been quite a project, Miss Eadie. Otis Ray and I had quite a time with that input shaft."

"Otis Ray?"

"Blacksmith. He did the forging with a bunch of horseshoes. Didn't charge you nothing neither. Just threw it in for free."

"You'll have to thank him for me," I said, confused by my conflicted feelings.

A week ago I would have been thrilled to hear my car was ready. Now, I wasn't so sure. Would Piggin and Heifer expect me to leave immediately? Our deal was that I could stay until my car got fixed. Then again, if I left by Sunday, I'd still be able to make it to the women's festival. But where would that leave me with Cadence? I could invite her to join me, but if Piggin was her mom…

"Does that mean you'll be leaving?" Kitty asked.

I spun around. She was right behind me getting a box of foot-long matches for one of her customers. "Well, soon…I guess…" I sputtered.

Buddy Bud flew into a panic. "Where you going, Eadie?"

Before I had a chance to answer, Kitty said, "She doesn't really live here, Buddy Bud. She's just a visitor, a guest. Didn't she tell you?"

I stepped toward Buddy Bud, to reassure him, but it was too late. He threw his bottle of Windex to the floor and tore out of the store.

I glared at Kitty, then took off after him, yelling my sincere thanks to Old Luke over my shoulder.

I found Buddy Bud squatting by the Dumpsters, making little whimpering sounds like a puppy. He was rocking back and forth, back and forth, and refused to look at me.

"Hey, Buddy," I said in what I hoped was a soothing voice. "We need to talk. What do you say we clean up and go for an ice cream?"

It took me a while to convince him, but I did, finally.

❖

The ice cream place was in actuality the drugstore, or a corner of it. A small freezer filled with three-gallon buckets of your basic flavors of ice cream, and a rack of cones and Styrofoam dishes, sat next to a couple of white plastic outdoor tables with chairs to match. We sat down and waited for the teenage cashier to finish ringing up a pharmacy customer so she could serve us. She pulled on clear plastic gloves before handling the scoop. We both ordered sundaes.

Buddy Bud ate his quietly, avoiding my eyes.

"These are pretty good, huh?"

He nodded.

"Do you always get the same thing?"

He nodded again, but couldn't keep from adding, "When Dad lets me. Sometimes I'm only 'lowd to get a cone."

I asked him a few questions about this and that, just to keep him talking, then segued into the fact of my ultimate departure. He listened carefully, squinting in that way that kids do to show their anger. I told him that Piggin and Heifer's wasn't *my* home, that it was *their* home and they were just letting me stay there until my car got fixed.

"Where's your home?" he asked.

"I'm looking for it," I told him.

"Why can't it be here?"

This simple question was surprisingly difficult to answer. How do you explain homophobia to a kid who only understands love? I didn't even try. I just made up some stuff about "things I had to do" before I could "find my home." He accepted this like any kid faced with adult hedging: He turned inside to find his own answers. I could see it in his furrowed brow.

"You're a really great friend and a really great helper."

He shrugged. "Could I have a dollar?"

"What for?"

"I want to buy my dad a present."

How could I refuse?

He took the dollar and headed into the novelty section of the store. I pulled my cell phone from my pocket and dialed Cadence. I got her voicemail and thought about hanging up, which, after I'd left my message, I wished I had.

"Hey. It's me. Um…that was really nice last nice…night…and um…well, I just wanted to call. Oh yeah, and Heifer thinks we should be at church tonight…so if you want to go, we could meet there…or go together, if you want. Then again, maybe you don't want to go… Maybe you've had enough Baptist services for a lifetime…ha ha. Anyway, bye. Call me if you want…"

I hung up—*Way to go, Casanova*—then tried Sweet Ginger. She didn't answer either, so I had to talk to her machine too. I filled her in on Cadence's and my talk with Heifer and invited her to come down to the revival, quoting Heifer on the God thing. It was a bummer she didn't answer. I could have used some of her acerbic wisdom.

By the time I got off the phone, Buddy Bud was returning with his purchase. A red and black plastic snake.

"It was the prettiest one," he said, holding it up.

"Your dad's going to love it."

"It's not for my dad," he said. "I told you a lie. Dad says it's okay to tell a lie when you have a good secret."

"If it's not for your dad, who's it for?"

"You." He held it up for me to take.

The back of my throat went dry. "Me?"

He threw his arms around me. "I love you!"

I wrapped by arms around his awkward frame. *Why did he have to go and say that?*

CHAPTER THIRTY-FOUR

I spent the rest of the afternoon waiting for Cadence to return my call. I did all kinds of things to distract myself—straightening up The Egg, calling the information line at the Womyn's Music Festival to see what kind of weather to expect, clipping my nails—but basically I was waiting. Every minute that clicked by was torture. *She's wishing she hadn't kissed me. I shouldn't have called.*

I was in the shower getting ready for church, my head covered in suds, when my phone finally rang. I withstood the first two rings on principle. *I'm not that desperate.* On the third ring, I bolted from the shower, slipping on my towel bathmat and cracking my knee into the toilet. Naked, wet, and soap in my eye, I flicked open the phone. It was her all right, but the voicemail had already nabbed it. I made the executive decision to rinse off before calling in for her message.

"Hey, Eadie. Got your call. Sorry I didn't call back sooner. I've been over at Minnie Bell's helping her sort through the donations for the kids clothing swap. Anyway, if Heifer thinks we should go, I'll meet you there. No need to call back." She paused, then spoke in a softer voice. "I keep thinking about last night…" She didn't finish her sentence, but she didn't hang up either, not for a good four seconds. What was I supposed to make of that? I played the message back and this time was sure she'd meant it to be seductive.

But I've been known to misinterpret women's intentions before.

I was just about to replay the message one more time when the phone rang again. This time it was Piggin. She and Heifer were already at church setting up the potluck. "You haven't left yet, have you?" she asked.

"Nope. I'm just about to," I said, pulling on a pair of drawstring pants I was hoping to dress up with a gauzy button-down shirt.

"Could you stop by my kitchen and pick up a bag of serving spoons? I left them on the table."

"Sure."

"Hang on just a sec," she said, then spoke to someone there with her. "Desserts are going over by the window." She came back on the line and whispered, "That was Reenie. She baked the prettiest pie for tonight." Then to someone else, "The table with the red tablecloth!" Then back to me: "Nobody's told her yet. It's heartbreaking."

That's odd, I thought as we said our good-byes, my stomach twisting into a knot. *Why haven't they charged Roy?* Here I'd thought we were going to be the big heroes of the night, that people would be pumping our hands in gratitude. Now my mind was manufacturing another scenario. Women in huddles, glancing slyly and whispering, "She rolled into town, leeched off the church, then showed her thanks by accusing, of all people, Roy Peterson, of fraud. Can you believe? Roy Peterson!"

I trotted over to Piggin's for the spoons, tempted to continue past her trailer and on to the Texas border.

Twenty-five minutes later, I pulled into the church parking lot, my stomach now completely knotted. The lot was packed. I spotted Cadence's VW between two SUVs. I snagged a spot in a dirt area and headed for Fellowship Hall, my excitement about seeing Cadence dampened by anxiety.

Piggin was waiting for me at the door. "Thank goodness you're here," she said, relieving me of the serving spoons. "Folks were going to have to use their own forks to serve themselves."

Before I had a chance to grill her about what was going on, she disappeared into the crowd. I scoped out the room. The potluck, it seemed, was just getting underway. People were gathering into a line, Chinet plates in their hands. They laughed and talked the way people do after a long workweek. There was no indication of scandal, and no one seemed to give a good goddamn that I was there—with the unfortunate exception of Silas Milsap. He spotted me immediately and began making his way across the room.

"Well, howdy, Eadie. Nice to see you." He looked like a new man, all scrubbed up and in a suit. He was even smiling.

His congenial demeanor made me uneasy. "Hi, Silas."

"How's the truck working out?"

"Uh"—I glanced around the room, wishing someone would wave me over—"fine. I shouldn't need it much longer. Old Luke's just about finished up with my car."

"That mean you'll be leaving us?"

"Looks that way."

He slipped his thumbs into the waistband of his thrift store pants and shook his head. "Well, sorry to hear it, Eadie," he said.

"Thanks, Silas."

After a bit more small talk, I excused myself, even more confused than I was before, and made my way into the crowded room.

Crash sidled up next to me. "What did he say?"

"Your dad?"

"Anything about me?"

"No. Why?"

He pulled me over by the water fountain, away from the crowd. "Mom found the check," he whispered.

"What?"

"She found my aunt's check!"

"Where?"

"In my drawer!" He looked truly panicked. "Did it seem like he was mad at me?"

"Not really. Like I said—"

"Maybe Mom didn't tell him," he said more to himself than to me. "Maybe she told him it came in the mail today."

I realized he was trying to gauge how much trouble he was in. And with a dad like Silas, I had a feeling the high end of the punishment spectrum could be pretty severe.

"It'll be okay," I said, the tone of my voice betraying my uncertainty. "The sheriff knows…"

"Then why did Pastor Williams ask my dad to be the first one to make his blessing?"

"He what?"

"When my dad called Pastor Williams to say he'd finally gotten the money, Pastor Williams asked him if he'd start off the gifting tonight. Right after Roy Peterson says his stuff, my dad's supposed to stand with his check in the air." He wrapped his arms around his waist and looked down at his boots as if he was sick. "My dad's been pumped up all afternoon, like he's famous or something."

His words literally hurt my heart. After all the lousy parenting Crash had been subjected to, he still didn't want to see his dad make a fool out of himself. What could I say to ease his mind? "I don't have an answer for you, Crash, but there's nothing either one of us can do about it now," is what I came up with.

He looked up at me. Without his cap, I got a good look at his eyes, and those long-lashed brown peepers were swimming in vulnerability.

"You want to get something to eat?" I asked.

"I guess."

We made our way to the potluck table, our moods in stark contrast to the upbeat bantering around us. I grabbed a plate and swung around, nearly smacking into Cadence. She had a full plate of food in each hand and was beelining to a table.

"Hey," I said, my face suddenly flushed.

"Hey," she said.

And for the split second that our eyes met, the chaos swirling around inside me subsided and everything seemed as it should be. I didn't give a shit about Roy, or Silas, or the scary painted Jesus on the wall. All I cared about was Cadence, that she was smiling—just a hint of a smile, but one that I knew was meant just for me.

Then Crash cleared his throat, bringing us both back to the reality of our situation.

I was relieved that Cadence had the wherewithal to speak, because I did not. "How's it going, Crash?" she said, clearly trying to sound as if nothing more were going on than a potluck on a beautiful day.

He shrugged and said, "All right, I guess," but his voice bristled with tension.

I glanced around. We were surrounded by but parishioners. There was no way we could talk about what was on all our minds. Our eyes darted from one to the other, as we tried to act as if everything were normal, as if the night before we hadn't broken into the office of a prominent member of the church.

"You hungry or what?" I asked, indicating her two plates of food.

She laughed a little too loudly. "One's for Minnie Bell. You can come sit with us if you want. With me and Minnie Bell."

I glanced over at Crash.

"Fine by me," he said.

We spent the rest of the potluck listening to Minnie Bell talk food. If I hadn't had so much on my mind, I probably would have found her entertaining. Minnie Bell was a spry old bird and excellent storyteller. Each potluck item elicited a witty tale about the person who'd cooked it, or her mother, or husband, or kid. She was one of those people who enjoyed talking so much she didn't notice that no one was listening.

Crash wolfed down his chicken-fried chicken and potato salad, glancing every few seconds at the table his father occupied. I picked at my food, my mind whizzing with questions. *Why are they going on with the Jubilee thing? Were we wrong?*

And Cadence, who knew what she was thinking? I prayed it had nothing to do with me being too complicated.

❖

As Cadence, Crash, Minnie Bell, and I walked down the cement path from the annex to the church, Minnie Bell ran into some friends and was swept into their conversation, leaving the three of us, temporarily, alone.

Cadence peeked over her shoulder to make sure no one was in earshot, then whispered, "So what have you heard?"

"Nothing," I whispered back. "When I talked to Heifer, she said she'd left it in the sheriff's hands. He told her not to talk to anyone else about our suspicions."

She frowned. "That's weird. I spent the morning showing him the stuff I'd found on the Internet about Faith Promises International. He seemed really interested."

"But what did he say?"

"That he'd look into it."

Crash groaned. "That's it? They're not going to arrest him?"

"We don't know," I said. "They probably had to do some fact checking."

"How's that going to help my dad?"

I put my hand on his shoulder intending to console him, but Crash, spotting his mom at the church entrance, yelled, "Mom, can I sit with these guys?"

She nodded and smiled.

We sat in the back row. Me on the aisle, then Cadence, then Crash. I so wanted to talk to Cadence about what was happening between us, to assure her that we could take it slow if she needed. But her focus was on the stream of people entering the church. I willed my pinky to stay in place. It was making a compelling case for sneaking across the chasm between her thigh and mine.

"Crash, you're not sitting with your family."

I looked up. It was Piggin. She was standing in the aisle, her face tense with worry.

"No, ma'am. I asked my ma, and she said I didn't have to."

Piggin nodded, her fingers gripping the arm of the pew in front of ours. "Well…guess I'll go take my seat, then." She stood there a moment before walking off and I couldn't get it out of my head that she was Cadence's mom.

Am I bad that I haven't told Cadence?

Piggin headed toward her seat, her plump hand brushing the worn pews along the way. Once she reached her own, she squeezed by Heifer, who was already seated.

The organist began to play.

The revival was like the church service—only on steroids. Join! Join! Join! was the motto of the evening. Pastor Williams, the emcee for the various events, talked a lot about "the abounding love of God" and "gathering in His name," always with the subtext that Christ would more readily wash you with His love if you dedicated, or rededicated, your pitiful, sinful, sorry-excuse-for-a-life to Him. Pastor Williams, eliciting amens from the crowd like an auctioneer would bids, was definitely in his element. "My friends," he said earnestly, "if this next group of young men and women doesn't inspire you"—he paused for emphasis—"if they don't make you reach deep down and ask yourself, 'Am I doing right by Him?' 'Am I giving enough of myself to Him?'" Another pause. "Well, then I feel sorry for you. In fact, you ought to just go on home now." He looked over the crowded room, daring someone to stand. "You heard me right. Go on! Get out!" He pointed toward the door. "Because when I see the kind of time and dedication this group of our youth have put into picking out and arranging and rehearsing these songs, even I have to ask myself, me, a man who's given up his life to

Christ, 'What more can I give? What little part have I held back that I could offer up to Jesus?'"

As Pastor Williams heaped on the accolades, the Praise Chorus, a group of about twelve gangly teenagers—one on electric guitar, one on electric bass, one on a small trap drum set, and the rest singers—stood by, unsure what to do with themselves: some listened solemnly as if the pastor were talking about some other group of teenagers; some picked at their clothing self-consciously; while still others spaced-out in that I'm-going-to-pretend-this-isn't-happening kind of way. Only one girl in the front seemed comfortable with all the attention. She stood, chin up, as if she were Miss America about to receive her crown.

Once Pastor Williams gave them the go-ahead, the Praise Chorus broke into an oddly arranged pop version of a popular hymn. Then another. Everyone seemed impressed. That is, except Crash. He was slunk so low his knees pressed into the pew in front of him. "Friends of yours?" I whispered.

He rolled his eyes, leaned over Cadence, and whispered, "That snooty girl in the front is who I peed on last night."

I smiled, but all I could think was, *Why are we here? This is just an ordinary revival.* I tried to get a look at Piggin and Heifer, but could only see the back of their heads. Frustrated, I returned my attention to Pastor Williams. He was returning to the podium.

"And now, I'd like to bring your attention to something very exciting going on here at Rauston Baptist." He put up his hand as if to hold off a response. "I mean, *besides* the Praise Chorus."

Several people chuckled politely.

"And no, my friends, I'm not talking about our excellent youth program, which offers opportunities to the youth of our church; or the Helping Hands program, which has supported many a church member in their time of need…" He took a breath, then launched into his next sentence. "And I'm not talking about our Ladies' Bible Club, who have been so instrumental in organizing the events of this weekend; or those folks donating their time to the Church Wagon to pray and bring communion to the homes of those too sick to come into church." Another breath, accompanied by a teasing grin. "Nor am I talking about the fact that tomorrow evening, in this very church, one Charlene Wandra is going to be singing!"

Lots of excited murmuring.

He unclipped the microphone from the stand and slowly walked around the podium, cord in one hand, mic in the other. "I'm talking about the fact that we're going to get ourselves a new church!"

Amens shot up from the crowd like popcorn.

"I'm talking about a congregation so dedicated to bringing people to Christ, that they've outgrown their little church!" He swept his hand across the congregation. "Look around, we're busting out the seams!"

Lots of craning of necks.

"Yes, my friends, an amazing opportunity has come to us through one of our own members to help us make this dream a re-al-i-ty! That's what *I'm* talking about." The next words came out almost affectionately. "Roy Peterson, would you come up here, please?"

A zing went through my spine, jolting me up in my seat. Crash and Cadence also straightened up in theirs. Again, I tried to get a look at Piggin and Heifer. Again, all I could see was the back of their heads.

Roy, his usual dashing self, stepped up to Pastor Williams and mock-punched him in the shoulder. Pastor Williams laughed and handed over the mic.

At first, Roy didn't speak. He stood with the microphone poised in his hand looking out over us. Finally, he raised the mic to his mouth. "Ladies and gentlemen," he said, his voice earnest, soft. "I gotta admit, when my beautiful wife Reenie Wheelock, as I believe y'all still call her, told me we needed to move to a little town in the middle of nowhere where she grew up, I'll admit, I was skeptical."

A round of chuckling rolled through the crowd.

"In fact, I won't even tell you the methods she used to get me to agree." His implication flew just beneath the wire of propriety, adding to his naughty charisma. "But I got to say, I can't thank her enough."

People who knew Reenie smiled at her knowingly. She returned their smiles and shook her head, feigning embarrassment, but you could tell she was proud.

He gestured toward the congregation. "But it's you people, that's right, *you*, that welcomed this city boy into your lives like I was one of your own. That's why this new church means so much to me…"

Why isn't someone doing something?

"Now, most of y'all already know about the Jubilee Trust Fund. But for those of you who don't, our guests, or those of you haven't been coming to church like you should," he wagged his finger as he said this, "you're gonna be hearing a lot about it this weekend, because Jubilee Trust Fund is gonna help us get that new church we're dreaming of. And I'm not just talking your low-budget model either. I'm talking about a church that shows Him what He means to us. A church twice this size with a steeple so high you can see it in the next county! A church with an organ that can be heard by wayfaring strangers for miles around! A monument, my friends, my fellow lovers of Jesus Christ, that is a testament of our love for Him! A testament of our devotion."

This is insane. The guy is a crook.

He looked down at the floor, spent, and stayed this way for a few seconds before slowly returning his gaze to us. "After services, I'll be at a table out in the entry to tell those of you who want to know more what this is all about. But in a nutshell, let's just say, I have come upon a glorious investment opportunity for good Christian people like yourselves that will not only help us raise the funds we need for our new church, but will help you in your own hour of need as well. Because that's how God works. He doesn't pick and choose. He wants to take care of all of his flock. All of his children."

A young father sitting in front of me put his arm around his adolescent son. I peeked over at Crash. He was riveted on Roy Peterson.

"Now at this time," Roy said, "I'd like to ask if there's anyone in the congregation tonight that would like to offer a blessing to the Jubilee Trust Fund."

Silas Milsap shot to his feet, waving his check in the air. "You can count on me, Pastor!" He was the picture of a man ready to start his new life. No longer the church's number-one Helping Hands recipient. No, the man who strutted down that aisle was Silas Milsap, investor and philanthropist.

Crash slouched back in the pew, dropping his head to his chest and covering his eyes with his hand as if staving off a waking nightmare.

I leaned into Cadence. "Someone's got to stop this."

Without taking her eyes off Silas, she asked the simple question, "Who?"

Silas reached the podium and indicated to Roy that he'd like to say a few words to the congregation. Roy glanced over at Pastor Williams, who nodded reluctantly. Roy handed the microphone to Silas.

"Don't worry, fellas, I'm not fixin' to talk too long," Silas said, eliciting an uneasy chuckle from the congregation. "Alls I want to say is how proud I am to be a part of this church. Seems to me one of the big problems of the world is folks don't look out for each other how they should. But here we take care of each other."

A man yelled, "Amen, Silas!"

Silas looked down at the floor, trying to disguise his delight at being the center of attention, and for a moment, I thought he was going to say more. I think he thought so too; he just didn't know what.

He handed the microphone back to Roy.

Then he handed over his check.

The moment the check was in Roy's hand, a man sitting on an outside aisle toward the front of the church stood. "Roy Peterson," he bellowed, "I'm placing you under arrest."

Immediately, three other men dressed in plain clothes also stood.

There was a gasp from up front.

Crash pulled his hand off his eyes and sat up straight.

"That's Gotch," Cadence whispered. "The sheriff."

A look of desperation flashed across Roy's face as the sheriff and the other three men began walking toward the podium. He glanced over at Pastor Williams who, although clearly dumbfounded, managed to utter, "Now, hang on, Gotch. What's this about?"

Gotch hauled out a set of handcuffs from his back pocket and ordered, "Everybody please stay in your seats."

Silas, unsure if he was implicated as well, stood next to Roy, frozen, and watched the four law officers approaching, two from one side and two from the other.

Crash stood.

Reenie stood. "Gotch, whatever are you doing?"

Gotch, hearing the voice of his high school sweetheart, turned his head.

Seeing an opening, Roy tossed the microphone and bolted for the center aisle. Gotch and the three law officers clambered to follow, but had to get by the communion table on one side and Pastor Williams on the other.

I jumped to my feet. I'm not sure what I thought I was going to do. Throw my body in front of him? Wrestle him to the floor? I never got a chance to do either.

Halfway down the aisle, a foot wearing immaculate white lace-up Keds stuck out, tripped Roy, and sent him falling to the floor, face down.

In seconds, the officers had him pinned. We all sat, or stood, watching Gotch and his men handcuff Roy and bring him to his feet. The ceiling fans whirred, benches creaked. A baby cried. But other than that, it was ghostly silent. Then an eerie sound rose out of the church, reverberating off the rafters and stained glass windows. It was gruff, gravelly. I searched for the source of the sound, my eyes scanning the ceiling, the back of the church, then finally landing on Silas. He had the microphone gripped in his two hands and pressed to his lips and he was singing in the most heartfelt voice I'd ever heard. I've no idea the exact hymn, but it had something to do with surrender, and Jesus of course. After a few lines, Pastor Williams joined in, his beautiful tenor voice floating above Silas's odd rumbling.

One by one, frazzled congregation members began to sing. But my eyes were on Reenie, standing third pew from the front facing the back of the church, watching Gotch and his men lead a handcuffed Roy out the door. She clasped trembling hands in front of her mouth, her eyes filled with tears. It almost looked like she was praying.

CHAPTER THIRTY-FIVE

I was frolicking with a school of long-haired, velvety mermaids. While not a mermaid myself, I was having no trouble breathing underwater and swam at lightning speed around colorful coral mountains and dense seaweed forests. Just as I burst through a school of sleek silver fish, sending them splaying around me like millions of shooting stars, Wild Thing began pounding its way into my consciousness. *Yeah! I'm a wild thing all right. Watch this!* I shot up out of the water, intending to dolphin-twist in the air, but shot right out of my dream instead.

The phone. What time is it?

Panicked, I rolled out of bed in search of my now-silent phone, consciousness clawing its way through my cottony brain. I picked up my satchel. *Not there. So where the hell is it?* I started pawing through a pile of laundry on the couch.

It had been a late night. Everyone was upset about Roy Peterson's arrest. They wanted answers, and I was one of the few people who had any. The answers I didn't have were presumably going to be provided this morning before the revival proceedings kicked in. Sheriff Gotch was facilitating an early morning Q & A over doughnuts and coffee.

Wild Thing began an encore.

Pants pocket. They were on the kitchen counter. When I reached for them, Wild Thing dropped to the floor. I swiped it up. "Hello?" My voice sounded as if I'd swallowed a frog.

"You ready?" It was Heifer and she sounded tense.

"Uh, yeah. I'll meet you out at the car. Just give me five minutes," I said, picking up my drawstring pants from the floor.

"Make it two," she said and hung up.

Once dressed in drawstring pants and blouse, my church uniform, I bolted out the door. Heifer was already in the passenger seat of the car, waiting. "Where's Piggin?" I asked through the open window.

"Beats me."

I was too tired for her bullshit. "I'll go get her."

I found Piggin in her kitchen furiously yanking things from the freezer.

"That nincompoop of a sister of mine forgot to remind me that Lilah is coming for lunch this afternoon. I swear she's wound up tighter than an eight-day clock! Been ticking to high heaven all morning. 'Course I don't blame her. This Roy Peterson business has gotten way outta hand. My phone's been ringing off the hook all morning. Even got a call from Toopie Johnson wanting an inside scoop for The Weekly. Can you imagine? Glory be, I feel for Reenie."

"Can I help you with anything?"

"Think I just about it got it—Oh! Almost forgot the steaks!—I should tell you Minnie Bell and Cadence are coming for lunch too. Spoke to Minnie Bell this morning."

Even in my brain-dead state, I couldn't help but trip out at the way Piggin and Cadence were circling into one another's lives, drawn together by some kind of weird force of fate; but the thought, too complex for my pre-caffeinated brain, fizzled into the present. "Uh, Piggin, the freezer door didn't close all the way."

"Lord, give me strength to make it through this day!" Piggin said, turning to close it, then grabbed her purse. "Shall we?"

❖

On the ride over to the church, Piggin recounted the various phone calls she'd received that morning. "And I got one from Doxie Frank too; she doesn't even go to our church!"

Wild Thing began to chime.

"What on earth?" Piggin said.

"It's just my phone," I said clicking it open. It was Cadence.

"I just wanted to warn you," she said, "it's crazy here at the church."

There was so much background noise on her end it was hard to make out what she'd said. "What?"

"It's crazy!"

"How so?"

"There's two camera trucks out front, one's from Amarillo and I don't know about the other one…"

"Could you speak up?"

"Two camera trucks! And the place is beyond packed! Half of Rauston is here."

I relayed this to Piggin and Heifer.

Piggin pressed down on the accelerator. "Sweet Jesus!"

"And get ready to walk," Cadence said as we barreled down the highway, "because there's no parking. But we'll save you some seats."

Once off the phone, I passed this on too. We decided that they'd get out and secure our seats while I parked the car. The thought of the two of them huffing and puffing down the highway was more than I could bear.

"You'll have to park at K'Lynn's," Piggin said.

"Fine."

After that, we rode in silence.

Sure enough, the parking lot was packed, so I let them out at the door and pulled back onto the highway. K'Lynn's lot was full too, but I moved a few trash cans to make a spot. Then I began hoofing it back to the church.

Cars were parked all along the berm and others circled around still searching. There were plenty of people walking too. Whether they were walking from cars or from home I had no idea. I just hoped there'd be some coffee left when I got there.

As I approached the church, I saw a guy point me out to a young woman standing by one of the two news vans. She scuttled toward me, a cameraman right behind.

"Excuse me," she said thrusting out a microphone. "I understand that you're one of the women responsible for exposing these criminals." She wore gaudy gold clip-on earrings and a blue power suit. Her hair was so hairsprayed it looked like a football helmet.

I tugged at my loose-fitting blouse, hoping to smooth out the wrinkles. "It was really pretty much the sheriff." *Did I brush my teeth?*

"That's not what the word around here is. And if I'm correct, you're not even a member of the church…"

I smiled at the camera without revealing any teeth. "That's all I have to say right now. I don't want to be late for this meeting."

Fellowship Hall was a beehive of activity. All the folding chairs facing the podium on the stage were either taken or reserved. Pods of inquisitive onlookers clustered around the standing-room-only areas. I spotted Cadence up front with Minnie Bell. Piggin and Heifer sat directly behind them, an empty chair between them.

First, coffee.

I pushed through the crowd and nabbed one of the last Styrofoam cups, filled it to the brim with watery coffee, and headed for the artificial coffee whitener at the other end of the table. I was aware of people pointing me out and murmuring who knew what, but was too overwhelmed and under-caffeinated to let it bother me. I set my cup down on the table and reached for the whitener, then heard a familiar voice.

"That's right. I was handing over my check. Almost did too, but that was the signal for the Sheriff and his men. They couldn't make the bust 'til I handed over that check." Silas, puffed up like a rooster at the county fair, stood in the center of a group of captivated townsfolk. "And you know the strange thing of it is, right when I was about to hand him the check, I seen evil in his eyes. Pure evil! Like I was staring down the devil himself. That's exactly what I told them reporters too. They interviewed me, you know. Had me talk right to the camera…"

I dumped whitener in my coffee and pushed through the crowd to my seat.

"Here she is," Piggin said. "I was starting to think you mighta gotten lost."

"This is crazy," I said, sitting down.

"Can you believe?" Piggin said. "Most of these folks don't even come to church."

"Can't make it to the revival," Heifer muttered, "but give them some kind of scandal, and they swarm in like flies on you-know-what."

I leaned forward to speak to Cadence. "Hey."

She twisted around in her seat. She was wearing her hair in pigtails like the day we'd met. "You made it."

"My body did. I'm not quite sure about my brain. I could barely sleep."

She nodded. "I was pretty wired myself. I almost called you at three a.m."

"You could've."

Over her shoulder, I spotted Crash. He was standing by the Jesus mural surrounded by a bunch of teenagers who were riveted on something he was saying.

"Tell me he's not stupid enough to blab about his involvement."

She looked over her shoulder to see what I was talking about. "I hope not."

I raised my hand to get his attention. He glanced up and, seeing me, lifted his chin, the physical equivalent of saying "Yo." I gestured for him to zip up his mouth. He gave me a dismissive look and went back to his audience, clearly of the mind that I was acting like a stupid adult.

"Doesn't he realize how much trouble he could get into?"

"He's a teenager, Eadie." Then Minnie Bell said something to her, so she turned back around.

I took a swig of tepid coffee, and, for the first time ever, tried praying. *God, if you do exist, look after that boy. He's a good kid. And while you're at it, tell him to keep his mouth shut.* That finished, I glanced around the room. "Any sign of Reenie?" I asked Piggin.

She shook her head. "From what I understand, there's police at her place right now."

"Jameson went out to be with her," Heifer said.

"My heart's just breakin' for her," Piggin said. "She came back to town so proud to have a man that loved her the way he did."

Sheriff Gotch stepped up to the podium, followed by Pastor Williams.

"Could I please have your attention?" the sheriff said, tapping on the mic. "Can you hear me?"

The room quieted. "Morning, everybody. If you don't already know me, which most of y'all do, I'm the sheriff. And this here is Pastor Williams."

Pastor Williams raised a hand, then promptly crossed his arms. From up close where we were sitting, you could see his jaw muscles pulsing.

"I'm sorry the occasion of our little get-together isn't a happier one," the sheriff continued, "but we'll try and be as expedient as possible." He glanced at one of the news cameras and adjusted his tie. He was a big man with a ruddy complexion, strong arms, and a thick neck. He rested his hands on the lip of the podium. "How we're going to work this is, I'll talk first, then we'll open up for questions—Oh, and Pastor Williams has asked me to tell you're welcome to stay on afterward and attend the revival."

I took another swig of crappy coffee. It was going to be a long morning.

Much of what the sheriff said, I already knew, like the fact that the Jubilee Trust Fund was an offshoot of Faith Promises International, a group that had been busted the previous year. But what I didn't know was that Faith Promises International was a tri-state operation, and that during its heyday, it had bilked millions of dollars from trusting Christians of three targeted faiths: Baptists, Assembly of God, and Church of God. He also told us that his officers had conducted a preliminary search of Roy's office and, if Roy was involved, he was allegedly pretty low on the chain of command, which meant that the bulk of the operation was still out there somewhere.

Then he opened up for questions, asking people to raise their hands.

The first up was a middle-aged woman with a large birthmark on her face.

"This is so wrong! Roy and Reenie Peterson are good Christians! And we owe it to them—"

Sheriff Gotch put up his hand to silence her. "As I said earlier, we have no evidence of Reenie being involved in any way…"

Piggin whispered, "This must be breaking Gotch's heart. He's had soft spot for Reenie since high school."

The woman continued. "Well…Roy, then. I just think the way y'all are treating him today"—she shot a look in Cadence's and my direction—"the way y'all are taking the word of outsiders and forgetting the good he's done—"

"Good?" A man jumped up, clearly grandstanding for the cameras. "Good? He still owes me my money! How do you explain that, Delora?"

"Can't the sheriff tell the press to leave?" I whispered to Heifer

"Are you kidding? Gotch is in hog heaven."

A sun-weathered rancher raised a gnarled hand.

"Yes, Zeb?"

"What happens to those of us already made our gifts? And don't tell me we're just plumb out of luck."

Pastor Williams indicated to Gotch that he'd like to take this one. Gotch reluctantly handed him the mic.

"Hey, Zeb, that's a real good question. After the revival, the deacons and I are going to get together with the sheriff and see if we can't—"

"*After* the revival?" A plump young woman with a baby under her arm shot to her feet and yelled. "That's easy for you to say! You got your money!"

"That's right!" a guy with lamb-chop sideburns yelled. "How do we know you weren't in on it from the start?"

The birthmark woman yelled, "We shouldn't be taking this out on the pastor! Wasn't him who did it!"

"But I trusted him!"

"So did I!"

"People! People! Try to calm down!" Sheriff Gotch yelled, reaching for the mic. "We're all doing the best we can!"

Pastor Williams, however, wasn't ready to let the mic go. "Just to let y'all know, my wife and I have decided to return our blessing, every penny of it."

"Is she even here?" I whispered to Piggin. "I thought you said she never came."

Piggin pointed out a gorgeous, if overly made up, woman in the front row. She was brandishing her perfectly formed teeth in a smile for one of the cameras. She seemed impervious to the heat in the room.

"You can be sure it wasn't her idea to return the money," Heifer grumbled.

Just seeing Mrs. Williams gave me a whole new perspective on the pastor. He was married to the Snow Queen.

He continued, "As soon as we can get an accurate record of who gave Roy money—"

"Don't you know?" a guy with a crew cut asked. "Doesn't the church have records?"

"This wasn't a church program," Pastor Williams said quietly, a bead of sweat cutting down his already glistening forehead. "All we did was endorse it."

"That's all? That's *all*?"

The birthmark woman stood back up; by now all pretense of hand-raising was gone. "I'd just like to say, that it's times like these that we're tested as Christians. I think we need to ask ourselves what Jesus would be doing in our situation—"

"I agree with Delora Nell!" Kitty from Jameson's said. "What I don't get is why these people—who don't even belong to our church—are here to begin with?" She pointed out Cadence and me. "This is none of your business! Go home!"

A number of people started clapping.

I focused on my coffee cup. *Just remember, Kitty. Revenge is a mother.*

Piggin rested her hand on my leg. "Don't you pay them any mind. You are welcome here, you hear me?"

I swear if it weren't for her, and Heifer, I would have split. I would have taken Cadence by the hand in front of all of those hypocrites and marched us both out of there. Instead, I just slunk down in my seat and tried to project an I-couldn't-care-less demeanor. It was pathetic the way people were attacking those who tried to help them. I watched Pastor Williams squirm under their cross-examination. Couldn't they see he was a victim too? He'd believed Roy was his friend.

I glanced over at his wife, the arctic beauty. She'd pulled a compact from her purse and was applying a bit of powder to her nose. *Way more interested in camera angles than she is in her husband's predicament.* Apparently Pastor Williams had the same problem with Sylvia as I'd had with Ruby. He'd been unable to distinguish inner and outer beauty. He'd mistaken need for love, charisma for authenticity.

Comparing his and my neuroses was not a comfortable line of thought, so I tuned in to what he was saying.

"It took great courage on the part of these two young women to step into the circle of our church and present us with this unfortunate news, and I, for one"—he gestured toward us—"want to thank them. I truly do. And I hope you will find it in your hearts to do the same."

I gnawed on the edge of my Styrofoam cup. *Why doesn't he just shut up already? He's not going to make any friends saying what he's saying.* Then I thought about his hero, the man himself, the Big J. He wasn't in it for the friends either.

I removed my coffee cup from between my teeth. It was time to quit hating Pastor Williams. The guy was sticking his neck out for me.

❖

I wasn't wild about going to the revival, but seeing as I'd ridden with Piggin and Heifer, I had no choice. As we headed toward the church—me, Piggin, Heifer, Minnie Bell, and Cadence—we had to pass by the cameras again. Fortunately, Pastor William's wife had them captivated. "I just can't tell you," she said, wringing a hanky between shaking fingers, "what it's like to have your trust broken in this way. And we're such a little church, so vulnerable!"

We walked on, Cadence and I letting ourselves fall behind—quite a feat considering how slow the other three walked.

"This whole thing has been so weird," she whispered.

"Makes you wonder if we shouldn't have just let them get reamed by Golden Boy."

"Yeah, but I could never have forgiven myself." Then she told me she had to go to the bathroom, leaving me standing there all by myself in the church lobby. Once again, I resorted to the brochures, choosing one about the Teen Center.

It beat having to face the gawking onlookers.

I'll admit I was feeling pretty sorry for myself. Here I'd helped these people from getting screwed by Roy and his buddies and they were acting like I was somehow the criminal. It was during this pity-fest that a coltish young cowboy and his very pregnant wife approached me.

"Excuse me," he said. "I hate to interrupt your reading."

I looked up from the brochure. "No problem. I just was just waiting, really, for my friend."

"Well, me and Avalene, we want to thank you."

"You do?"

"We were gonna make our gift today," he said, looking at his hands. "I don't know what we woulda done if we'd a lost that money."

Avalene kneaded her lower back. "We woulda been sunk is what we woulda been. Already the doctor's costing more than we thought."

"She's a week overdue," he said, putting his arm around her.

I put the brochure back on the table. "It was no big deal…I mean…I think anybody would have done what I did—we did—if they…well… you know…"

"Well, God bless you and your friend," he said.

He then went on to tell me he had a brother in California, and after a minute or two of trying to figure out if I might know his brother, which of course I didn't, I said, "Thanks for saying thanks. And, uh, good luck with your, you know, family and all. I'll see you in church."

Cadence returned. "Sorry for the wait. It's a one-holer."

"No problem."

"Who was that?" she asked indicating the cowboy and his wife.

"They just came up to thank me."

"Good for them," she said, giving my hand a blatant squeeze. Given the nature of our surroundings, the boldness of this gesture filled my heart.

We were some of the last to be seated, but Piggin, Heifer, and Minnie Bell had saved us spots. The church was fuller than it had been for the rest of the revival, but nothing compared to the Q & A. The press, thankfully, was not present. I don't know whether this was an ethical move on their part or if they'd been asked not to come, but I suspected the latter.

Pastor Williams ascended to the podium looking shaken, tired. "I know that many of you, like myself, are deeply troubled by what has gone on in our church…"

His voice cracked.

He cleared his throat and continued. "And I know too, that sometimes it feels as if God has forsaken us." He paused and looked down at his folded hands resting on the podium. "I don't think He has. In fact, I know He hasn't. He has too much love for you…for me… even for Roy Peterson." His top thumb worried back and forth over his clasped hands. "And last night as I lay in bed, unable to sleep, I tried to think about what I was going to say to y'all this morning. What would ease your hearts…and I just couldn't find the words." He chuckled to himself. "Can you believe it? Me, unable to find the words."

Piggin reached in her purse for a tissue. Her eyes were filled with tears.

Pastor Williams continued. “And I prayed for our dear Lord to help me out. Told Him I had nothing to say, that I’d misled my flock… that there were no words deep enough to express my shame. Well, I kneeled there for quite some time…even let the phone ring through once or twice.” A hint of a smile crossed his face. “Sorry if it was any of y’all trying to reach me…

“And right about the time I was ready to give up, that I thought God had forsaken me for the pitiful, flawed man that I am, I realized what the problem was. There was a song stuck in my head that just wouldn’t let go. ’Course I had to laugh then. There I was, so low, thinking He’d forsaken me, and the whole time He’s trying to give me this song. I was just so busy feeling sorry for myself I never listened. I didn’t hear Him. But He didn’t give up. No, He didn’t. He just kept on and kept on with that song, like a fly buzzing around on a hot summer day, until I heard it. That’s love, my friends. That is love.

“He didn’t forget me. And won’t forget you. He can’t. His love is that true. He cherishes you that much.

“And it’s for that reason I’d like to start out today a bit different. Before we get into the planned revival proceedings, I’d like to start out with a song. His song. The one he gave me last night. And if you’ll bear with me here, I think I’d like to lead you through it myself. Please stand and join with me as we sing the hymn ‘Just As I Am.’”

He turned toward the organist. “Ida Sue didn’t get a chance to rehearse this one, so give her a break if she misses a note or two.” Then he gave us the hymn number and we all flipped open our hymnals.

I stood along with everyone else. It wasn’t a difficult tune, and by the third verse, I was surprised to hear myself joining in. I’m not much of a singer, but in a crowd this big it didn’t matter. There was something really apropos about accepting each of us for who we are—blind, wretched, gay… Okay, the song didn’t say gay, but I knew in my heart as I sang, that if there was a God, she didn’t give a shit about my sexuality. She loved all of us just how we were.

Once it was over, I was a bit embarrassed by the fervor with which I’d sung and glanced at Cadence. She was putting the hymnal back in the shelf, an amused twinkle in her eye. “The singing was always my favorite part too,” she whispered.

I could have kissed her. Wanted to, actually.

Needless to say, my fervor didn't carry over to the rest of the revival proceedings. As usual, the Him He His stuff kept getting in the way. Even in the singing. It was all "Praise Him this" and "King of Kings that." Nothing I could relate to. But I held on to that "Just as I am" lyric, even as I let my mind wander.

If we left the next day, Sunday, we'd still have time to get to the Womyn's Music Festival. I pictured Cadence and me basking in an incredibly romantic week, listening to music (her in my arms), making love in my trailer (me in her arms). We'd take our time coming back—see some country along the way, check out some national parks. Then we'd swing back through Rauston so Cadence could pick up her stuff. When we returned we'd find out that Heifer had talked Piggin into signing the papers that opened up the adoption file and Cadence and she would be reunited. Once Cadence realized how instrumental I'd been in hooking the two of them up, she'd marvel at how much restraint I'd shown and fall even more in love with me than ever. Piggin and Cadence would then spend a few weeks bonding before Cadence and I moved to Santa Cruz to start our new life. I'd get a job as an artist illustrating something really cool, like CD covers or children's books, and she'd keep on with her Web pages. Of course we'd have to come back once a year to visit, but by then Piggin and Heifer would have come to accept us as lesbians. And the rest of Rauston would realize how we saved them from Roy Peterson and Faith Promises International and they'd consider us heroes.

So it was a long shot. But it beat listening to all the He Him His stuff. Besides, I reminded myself, *Just as I am!*

I tuned back in to hear Pastor Williams reminding everyone to come back that night for Charlene Wandra.

❖

Walking back to K'lynn's to retrieve the car, I pulled my phone from my satchel. I figured it was as good a time as any to catch Sweet Ginger up on the whole Roy scandal. After all, she was part of the team that had brought him down.

She answered on the fourth ring, her voice groggy.

"Whoever this is, it better be important."

"Late night?" I asked.

She laughed. "You could call it that."

"I thought you'd want to hear what came down last night."

"You sound out of breath."

"It's a long story," I told her, "and I don't have time for all of it right now."

She spoke to someone presumably in bed with her. "Baby, wake up and get me some coffee." Her someone grumbled something. "Baby, you have one of those every morning," she said to him. He grumbled some more. "Well, you shoulda thought about that last night when you drank so much you couldn't get it up. Now go get me my coffee."

I listened as she lit up and sucked in a lungful of smoke. "Okay, so tell me."

I gave her a rough sketch of the previous day's events to the present, and her only disappointment was that Reenie hadn't gone down with Roy.

"I swear to God that bitch is resilient. She could spend the night in a bucket of shit and still come up smelling like a damn rose."

"You should have seen her. She was devastated."

She took a drag on her smoke. "Yeah, well."

As I drove the car back down the highway to pick up Piggin and Heifer, I went on to tell her about Lilah coming for lunch and how Piggin had said Heifer was "ticking to high heaven" all morning. My motives for telling her were less than exemplary. It was gossip, plain and simple.

"This I gotta see," she said. "My old maid dyke sister face-to-face with her one and only lezzie love."

I immediately felt like a heel and began backpedaling. "It's just a few people getting together. It's no big deal, really."

"I'll be there," she said. "I wouldn't miss this for the world."

As I hung up the phone, I couldn't help thinking I'd betrayed Heifer.

Chapter Thirty-six

Lilah was the first to arrive. She wore a light blue dress and pearls, her white hair swept into a French twist. Classy. "I hope I'm not too early," she said. "I was fixin' to attend the revival, but ever since Sissy's been on oxygen, she's gotten so nervous about being left alone. She wouldn't let me leave until my nephew from Dallas showed up." She closed the door behind her. "I hope the revival's going well. I hear the new pastor's pretty good. I sure liked him when I heard him."

Piggin, Heifer, and I exchanged glances. Obviously, she hadn't heard about the scandal.

"It's certainly been interesting," Piggin said cautiously. She was wrapped in a sunflower print apron, her hands covered in flour. She'd just begun the messy process of tossing steaks in an egg mixture, then covering them in flour.

Heifer, sitting in her favorite chair by the air conditioner, had a most unnatural smile frozen on her face. I wasn't the only one who noticed this either. Piggin studied her for a moment, then said, "Eadie, would you pour Lilah up a glass of sweet tea? We got to fill her in on all that's going on."

I grabbed some glasses from the cabinet. "Got it."

"Interesting?" Lilah said absentmindedly. "That doesn't sound good." Doing a three-sixty, she took in the trailer "Rose, you have done so much with this place."

Piggin tossed another egged steak in her pie pan of flour. "I should hope so. Last time you were here, there were seven of us squeezed into this place. Can you imagine?"

I handed Lilah her iced tea. She sat catty-corner to Heifer. "Grace, it must be so nice for you to have a place of your own."

Heifer pulled at a thread from the edging of the checkered oilcloth. It started to unravel. Unsure whether to keep pulling or tie it off, she let it drop, leaving the thread dangling. "It's real good."

"'Course, she spends all her time here," Piggin said.

I could hear Heifer's heart from across the table.

Tick…Tick…Tick…

Lilah was oblivious. "I think it'd be wonderful to have a place to escape to. Honestly, between the kids and Rude…well, when he was still around…and now Sissy…I don't believe I've had a moment to myself in years."

Tick…Tick…Tick…

Piggin glanced again at her sister, then, trying to mask her concern, said brightly, "I'd have thought your kids would have moved out by now, Lilah."

Lilah's hand flew to her heart. "They never move out." She laughed. "But just move back in! My son moved back earlier this year, and my oldest daughter *never* left. Thirty-two and she's still living at home. Can you imagine?"

Could Lilah be more brain-dead? Of course they can imagine! They never moved away from home either! They couldn't. They had to bring up their brothers and sisters, make house payments, put food on the table. But Lilah, clueless to the foot she'd just shoved down her throat, kept rambling on. "I'm not complaining. She's a godsend when it comes to stuff around the house. She loves to cook. Honestly, I don't think I've even had to boil a pot of water in years."

Piggin put away a ceramic flour canister that had to have been her mother's.

Heifer went back to her thread.

Tick…Tick…Tick…

"That must be nice," I said, "to have someone do *all* that work for you."

Right then, Minnie Bell pushed through the kitchen door, followed by Cadence.

"Lordy Lordy!" Minnie Bell said. "What a couple a days this has been!"

"Amen!" Piggin said, clearly relieved by the change in topic.

I took the bowl of chow-chow that Cadence was holding. My hand brushed against hers, sending a shock wave down to my winkie. "Sweet tea?" I asked.

She looked straight into my eyes. "Love some."

"Me too. It is hot out there!" Minnie Bell said, plopping herself down across from Lilah. "Lord, that air-conditioning feels good."

I walked over to the counter to pour the tea, an unfamiliar feeling of domestic contentment invading my body. There, in Piggin's wonderfully cluttered kitchen, I was experiencing what it was *supposed* to feel like when you brought your girlfriend home to meet the family. Of course Cadence wasn't technically my girlfriend, and Piggin and Heifer weren't really family, but still…

"So what's the big revival news you were going to tell me?" Lilah asked, breaking into the comfortable quiet of everyone soaking up air-conditioning.

Minnie Bell, thrilled to discover a virgin audience, sat straight up in her chair. "Shall we tell her or make her wait for this evening's news?"

But of course they told her. Who could resist? It was a story meant for telling, one full of greed, deception, heartbreak, and heroics. Especially the way Minnie Bell and Piggin told it. They were naturals, interrupting one another like a rehearsed routine. Occasionally even Heifer would forget herself and add some detail or opinion. Then again, she was one of the champions of the story.

Minnie Bell clapped her hands together. "Heifer, every time I think about that foot of yours sliding into the aisle and tripping that crook I can't keep from bustin' up."

"I didn't even realize she'd done it!" Piggin said. "All's I could think was: He's running right for us! What if he takes one of us hostage? What if he has a gun?"

"Wait," Lilah said. "What's this about Grace?"

Minnie Bell sat back in her chair, attempting to quell her laughter. "You shoulda seen it, Lilah! It was the best part of the whole thing. She did her special kung fu on him."

"Really?"

Heifer grunted something modest, but it was obvious as Minnie Bell dove into a colorful—and by now much-practiced—account of Roy Peterson's escape attempt, that she was pleased.

"Why, Grace," Lilah said over our hoots of laughter, "you're a regular hero!"

Heifer put up her hands kung-fu style and emitted a low growl.

"What the hell's so funny?" Sweet Ginger asked, pushing through the door. "We could hear y'all laughing from the car."

Piggin transferred a steak from the bubbling grease to a platter covered in paper towels. "Just in time. Eadie told me you might be joining us, so I had her put the extra leaf in the table."

Sweet Ginger gestured to someone outside the door. "Hurry up, wouldja?"

Buzzard the Neanderthal loped in behind her. To his credit, he'd cleaned himself up. But there was no getting around it, the guy was a biker dude: long hair, rolled bandana, and burly arms covered in tattoos featuring bleeding hearts and swords.

Heifer bristled, undoubtedly on the verge of defending her territory, but Piggin beat her to the punch. "Well, aren't we the lucky ones. We're going to have a man at the table. Welcome."

I got up to get the newcomers a glass of sweet tea. I actually felt sorry for Buzzard; he looked so out of place, so self-conscious, like he was certain he was going to break something or speak inappropriately. "Nice to meet you," he mumbled with each new introduction.

"Why don't you sit you at the head of the table?" Piggin said. "In Daddy's old spot."

Heifer rolled her eyes, but to her credit, kept her mouth shut.

Sweet Ginger took the place next to her man. It was a tight fit, elbow room definitely not one of the amenities. "Do you even remember me?" Sweet Ginger asked Lilah.

"'Course I do," Lilah responded warmly. "You taught me to play that card game, Old Maid, remember?"

I braced myself for one of Sweet Ginger's caustic remarks, could even see it forming in her mouth, but the ever-oblivious Lilah continued on without interruption.

"When my girls were young we played Old Maid all the time, and each time I thought of this house and that afternoon I babysat you."

Sweet Ginger shot me an incredulous look, which I took to mean, Can you believe this woman? then asked, "What's for lunch? I'm starved." Whatever her reasons for reining it back, I was glad. I wanted

Heifer to look good today. Petty as it sounds, I wanted Lilah to wish she'd never left Heifer. I wanted her chewing on regret.

Piggin placed several platters on the table and joined us. "Buzzard, would you like to lead us in prayer?"

Sweet tea nearly shot out my nose. *The Neanderthal?*

Buzzard's face got so red I thought it might pop. He began to stammer. "Er…ah…"

"Go ahead," Sweet Ginger coaxed, her hand on his arm. "I know your mama taught you."

Sweat sprouted from his brow as he commenced to fold his giant callused hands and drop his scruffy head. He took a big breath, then mumbled, "Dear God. Thank you for this meal. We're very thankful. Yes, we are. All of us. Very very thankful. Very. Amen."

"Amen," we replied.

Cadence, sitting across from me, tapped my foot with hers. It was all I could do to keep from laughing.

Next, we began filling our plates, disintegrating the conversation into "Could you pass the…" and "Hand me the…" After that it was just a lot of eating and hashing over the Roy Peterson scandal.

That is, until dessert.

❖

Popcorn balls and peach ice cream were the dessert menu.

Cadence was serving the ice cream, which Piggin was scooping into humongous portions. Our conversation, slowed into a post-digestion pace, was further hindered by toothpicks that had been passed out to dislodge corn bits from our teeth. We were all digging away and smacking our lips when Lilah asked casually, "What brought you to Rauston, Cadence?"

I wondered how Cadence would answer.

Heifer put her toothpick down. She too seemed curious.

Cadence placed a bowl of ice cream in front of Heifer, then folded her arms. "I guess I can tell you."

Minnie Bell cleared her throat, meaningfully.

A tired patience swept across Cadence's face. "I know you think I shouldn't, but these are my friends."

Minnie Bell broke her toothpick in half. "Like my mama used to say, don't go digging if you don't like skeletons."

"You're assuming that people don't change. That what was once buried wants to stay buried."

Piggin laughed. "Now you *have* to tell us. This is too good!"

Heifer picked her toothpick back up and began massaging it between her fingers like a worry stone.

"I'm with Piggin. Now you have to tell." Sweet Ginger chased her statement with a swig of iced tea, then gave her glass a contemptuous look and set it down.

Piggin handed Cadence a bowl of ice cream for Minnie Bell.

"All right, I'll tell you. I came here looking for my birth mother."

"Birth mother?" Lilah asked.

"I was adopted."

Piggin continued dishing ice cream. "What makes you think your mother was from Rauston?" Her tone of voice remained even, as if she was just making conversation, but there was no air underneath her statement.

"They told me at the hospital up in Farmington. New Mexico, that's where I was born."

"You need some help with that ice cream, little sister?" Heifer asked gently.

"I'm fine," Piggin replied. "Just fine."

Minnie Bell picked up her spoon, then realizing everyone hadn't been served yet, put it back down. "That don't make it true, Cadence. Coulda been that nurse and her story of the tornado was full of flooey."

"She had no reason to lie to me."

I picked up a popcorn ball and began peeling off bits and nervously sticking them in my mouth.

Piggin, having stopped all pretense of scooping ice cream, spoke with her back to us. "What tornado?"

I glanced at Heifer. Sweet Ginger caught me. She knew what we were thinking.

Before Cadence had a chance to answer, Minnie Bell said. "Some nurse up in Farmington filled her head with a cockamamie story about a poor little girl whose mama couldn't get out of Rauston because of some tornado. Said she remembered it because the poor thing had to give birth all alone, no family, no nothing. I tell you it sounds like a bunch of flooey to me. And even if it isn't, who wants their past to come knocking like that? I sure don't! That little girl's all grown up by now. Probably has a family, a husband—everything."

The room grew silent. Cadence looked like she'd been slapped. I tried to think of something to say.

Buzzard, still at the head of the table, began self-consciously patting out a rhythm on his thighs.

Sweet Ginger pushed her chair out and walked over to Piggin. She took the scoop from her trembling hands. "I remember that tornado. Don't you, Heifer?"

Heifer nodded her head once. "Certainly do."

Lilah squinted her eyes as if trying to remember.

Sweet Ginger wrapped her arm protectively around Piggin's rounded shoulders. "Those winds were howling and Mama was *still* trying to get into that car. I don't know what she thought she was going to do once she got in it. There were highway patrolmen keeping everyone off the roads."

"She woulda found a way past those patrol cars," Heifer said.

"J.D. wouldn't let her," Sweet Ginger said, tightening her hold. "He yanked Mama from the car. You know how he could get. All that wind, and him screaming at her, telling her she was crazy. That you deserved just what you were getting." Piggin's shoulders began to shake. She brought her hand to her mouth and pulled away from Sweet Ginger as if Sweet Ginger had tried to interlope on what was hers alone. But Heifer wouldn't let her block the harsh truth.

"He wanted you to give birth in shame. Wanted you to know what you did was wrong."

"But you weren't wrong, Piggin." Sweet Ginger added, "You were in love. What you had with Shoe Boy was love. Nothing more. Nothing less. Just love."

Piggin buried her face in her hands. The next words she spoke came out so high they were almost a squeak. "They wouldn't even let me touch her..."

Cadence's eyes locked on mine. She wasn't breathing. She was just standing there with that frozen bowl of ice cream in her hands, afraid to move, as if she thought she might ignite. I held her with eye contact.

"It wasn't your fault," Heifer said. "J.D. couldn't stand the idea of you being with anybody…"

I felt the unspoken words *…but him* hovering in the air like a ghost.

Cadence blinked. Then blinked again. *Stay with me, Cadence. Everything's going to be all right.*

From the corner of my eye, I was aware of Sweet Ginger walking over to Piggin, taking her by the arm, and leading her to Cadence.

Cadence, finally finding the courage to break our gaze, turned to Piggin, her eyes filled with tears.

"I'm so sorry," Piggin said. "I wanted to keep you more than anything. You were mine…"

Cadence nodded her head to indicate she understood Piggin's words, but her own quivering lips stayed pinched shut. I could tell that her emotions and questions were too scrambled for thought, for language. But she had to do something. There was Piggin standing before her shaking with guilt. Cadence handed the ice cream bowl to Sweet Ginger, then reached out to take Piggin's hands. Once she had them, she pressed them to her heart, and the two of them stood this way, gazing into one another's tear-streaked faces, for what seemed like an eternity.

Then Buzzard said, "I know this is emotional and all, but anybody mind if I step out for a smoke?"

Chapter Thirty-seven

I sat in the church wedged between Buddy Bud and Sweet Ginger, listening to an ancient, rhinestone-studded, Lee-press-on-nail-wearing Charlene Wandra warble hymns. It was Saturday evening. I hadn't planned on going back to church. I'd picked up Pebbles earlier in the day—she was running like a dream—and now, I had packing to do. But everybody told me, "You can't miss Charlene Wandra! She's who put Rauston, Texas, on the map."

A few seats away, Piggin and Cadence sat hand in hand, glowing—and I do mean glowing. The setting sun penetrating the stain glass window shone directly on them, making Cadence's hair blaze red while Piggin's radiated a soft gold. It was the magical wish-come-true most people only dream about. And I was happy for them. I was.

I was also happy I hadn't bought Cadence a lawn chair yet.

I settled back into my pew, amused how quickly I'd become incidental to my own story, then closed my eyes and tuned in to Charlene's reedy voice. While not as powerful as I'm sure it once was, her voice had a seductive devotion that beckoned. She was singing about being in some garden—alone.

There it was again. *Alone.*

Just as I am. But if I were going to ask God, or Cadence, or anybody to take me just as I was, just me, alone, didn't I first have to take myself that way? Without all the baggage? Without the need to predict the future or replay the past?

I tipped back my head and let the current from the ceiling fan have its way with my face. *What would it be like to believe?*

I thought about my friends in Tucson, the ones who'd sold me the trailer. They were all into Wicca and the Goddess, always thanking her for this or that. Were they happier for it? Or were they simply filling in that hole in the soul that Old Luke had talked about? *Maybe that's what my love addiction is about too. I'm just trying to fill up that hole.*

I looked around the rapt congregation and imagined all of us, these hollow beings, each desperate to find a way to quit feeling so empty, so scared. For the first time since I'd sat in that church, I didn't feel quite so removed, quite so superior. We were all Old Luke smoking his cigarette listening to his meadowlark sing, Piggin going back for that second round of food, Silas wheeling and dealing in used tires and other people's money, Buddy Bud protecting spiders and injured birds. Even Ruby was doing the best she could, snorting more and more coke, hoping to eventually fill up that hole.

But why had Cadence come into my life now? Was I really supposed to just walk away until I had my shit together? How could I be sure she'd still be there when I was ready? What if I lost her?

❖

After the concert, which in my opinion ran a few songs too long, our little group was standing around the doorway to the church putting off leaving. It was as if Piggin and Cadence were afraid they might lose one another again. And the rest of us, well, we had our own reasons for sticking around: Heifer and Lilah were finally having what looked like a normal conversation; Crash was showing Buddy Bud how to whistle through a blade of grass; Sweet Ginger was introducing Buzzard to several of the Bible Club Ladies. And me? I wanted a moment alone with Cadence.

I got my chance when Pastor Williams approached Piggin with a question about the next day's potluck. I sidled up next to Cadence. "Could I talk to you for a minute?"

"Sure," she said, squeezing Piggin's hand to let her know she'd be right back.

We strolled quietly down to the edge of the cement path stopping right before it turned into a dirt parking lot. I'd made a big decision while listening to Charlene Wandra. I was going to skip the music festival. Sure I'd be out the money, the experience, but so what? Cadence needed me. She was so vulnerable, so open.

I pictured the two of us listening to Piggin and Heifer tell us about her father, her family; the two of us taking a stroll out to the spring together so she could process what she'd learned; the two of us wound around one another having a midnight hear-to-heart in my candlelit trailer; the two of us— My fantasy was interrupted by a totally un-Eadie thought: If we were meant to be, couldn't it wait? Couldn't I?

Before I had a chance to process this thought, she said, "I don't want to be the one you drop out of art school for."

"Huh?"

"You know what I mean," she said softly.

And of course I did. This trip was important to me, and she knew it.

A small stone sat next to my left Teva. I picked it up and lobbed it across the highway, making a small exploding sound when it hit the asphalt. "If I leave now I might still get a prime spot." Even as I spoke these words, my mind was whining, *Please beg me to stay.*

She let this information soak in for a few seconds, her face taut with emotion. "I think that's good. 'Cuz things just got a little crazy in my life and I don't know if I could really start a new…"

"I know," I said. "The timing's kind of—"

"Bizarre," she said, then glanced back at the church toward her newfound mom.

Piggin waved.

"You've got a lot on your plate," I said, sounding more secure than I felt.

"So do you," she said.

I picked up another stone, and just about hurled it, then noticed her eyes glistening with tears. I took her by the shoulders and assured her with my gaze. "Hey. Don't cry. Just because I'm going to the festival doesn't mean we won't see each other again." I wanted to kiss her so bad it hurt, but the last thing either of us needed was to draw more attention to ourselves. "I tell you what," I said. "We can hook up after the festival."

"We can talk before that, though, right?"

"Of course."

"I'd like that," she said, slipping her hands under her glasses to wipe back the tears.

We held each other briefly, the way two friends might. Then

released. After that, there wasn't much more to say; we were just going to have to see how it worked out—if it worked out. Trust the moment. And just as that thought passed through my mind, my eyes rested on the sign we were standing next to. GO WITH GO ! I nearly laughed. My answer had been there all along.

I glanced at the church entrance. Heifer was animatedly recounting some story to Lilah, who stood with her dainty hands covering her mouth and wide eyes. A few feet to her left, Piggin conversed with Pastor Williams. She shot a worried look in our direction, then, when she saw Cadence, relaxed and held up two chubby fingers to indicate she'd be just two minutes longer.

Cadence, catching this, smiled and waved, then sat on the brick base of the sign, removed her lime green cat-eye glasses and cleaned them on the hem of her pink and black fifties style dress. "I still can't believe it," she said. "Piggin is my mom."

I joined her on the brick pedestal. "It's perfect."

She blinked a few times and returned her glasses to her face. "Think about how easily I could have missed her."

I remembered back to the Sunday before last when I'd first laid eyes on Piggin and Heifer waddling their way down the cement path, one in teal and one in yellow, Tweedledee and Tweedledum. The words "unclaimed blessings" skipped through my mind. At first I couldn't remember where I'd heard them, then remembered Pastor William's sermon about the acres of heavenly warehouses, each stacked to the brim with thousands of boxes crammed full of unclaimed blessings. And it surprised me to be thinking of Pastor Williams at such an emotionally charged moment in my life. But why not? It's his job to supply comfort in times of need. And if ever I was in a time of need, this was it; I was literally having to bite back the words, "Don't worry, I won't go. I'll stay here with you." But if we were going to have a future together, it needed to be built on a strong foundation—one without holes.

It was time for me to learn to live with myself.

Time to start claiming blessings.

About the Author

Clifford Henderson lives and plays in Santa Cruz, California. She runs The Fun Institute, a school of improv and solo performance, with her partner of seventeen years. In their classes and workshops, people of all genders and sexual orientations learn to access and express the myriad of characters itching to get out. When she's not teaching or performing, she's writing, gardening, and twisting herself into weird yoga poses.

It's been said her work is "…reminiscent of the bawdy sensibility of writer Fanny Flagg's *Fried Green Tomatoes*" (*Santa Cruz Sentinel*) and that she has a "… wry imagination and refreshing insightfulness" (*Santa Cruz Sentinel*).

Clifford's work has appeared in *Romantic Interludes 1: Discovery*, *Porter Gulch Review*, and *The Bear Deluxe*.

Visit Clifford online at www.cliffordhenderson.net.

Books Available From Bold Strokes Books

The Middle of Somewhere by Clifford Henderson. Eadie T. Pratt sets out on a road trip in search of a new life and ends up in the middle of somewhere she never expected. (978-1-60282-047-0)

Paybacks by Gabrielle Goldsby. Cameron Howard wants to avoid her old nemesis Mackenzie Brandt, but their high school reunion brings up more than just memories. (978-1-60282-046-3)

Uncross My Heart by Andrews & Austin. When a radio talk show diva sets out to interview a female priest, the two women end up at odds and neither heaven nor earth is safe from their feelings. (978-1-60282-045-6)

Fireside by Cate Culpepper. Mac, a therapist, and Abby, a nurse, fall in love against the backdrop of friendship, healing, and defending one's own within the Fireside shelter. (978-1-60282-044-9)

Green Eyed Monster by Gill McKnight. Mickey Rapowski believes her former boss has cheated her out of a small fortune, so she kidnaps the girlfriend and demands compensation—just a straightforward abduction that goes so wrong when Mickey falls for her captive. (978-1-60282-042-5)

Blind Faith by Diane and Jacob Anderson-Minshall. When private investigator Yoshi Yakamota and the Blind Eye Detective Agency are hired to find a woman's missing sister, the assignment seems fairly mundane—but in the detective business, the ordinary can quickly become deadly. (978-1-60282-041-8)

A Pirate's Heart by Catherine Friend. When rare book librarian Emma Boyd searches for a long-lost treasure map, she learns the hard way that pirates still exist in today's world—some modern pirates steal maps, others steal hearts. (978-1-60282-040-1)

Trails Merge by Rachel Spangler. Parker Riley escapes the high-powered world of politics to Campbell Carson's ski resort—and their mutual attraction produces anything but smooth running. (978-1-60282-039-5)

Dreams of Bali by C.J. Harte. Madison Barnes worships work, power, and success, and she's never allowed anyone to interfere—that is, until she runs into Karlie Henderson Stockard. Eclipse EBook (978-1-60282-070-8)

The Limits of Justice by John Morgan Wilson. Benjamin Justice and reporter Alexandra Templeton search for a killer in a mysterious compound in the remote California desert. (978-1-60282-060-9)

Designed for Love by Erin Dutton. Jillian Sealy and Wil Johnson don't much like each other, but they do have to work together—and what they desire most is not what either of them had planned. (978-1-60282-038-8)

Calling the Dead by Ali Vali. Six months after Hurricane Katrina, NOLA Detective Sept Savoie is a cop who thinks making a relationship work is harder than catching a serial killer—but her current case may prove her wrong. (978-1-60282-037-1)

Dark Garden by Jennifer Fulton. Vienna Blake and Mason Cavender are sworn enemies—who can't resist each other. Something has to give. (978-1-60282-036-4)

Shots Fired by MJ Williamz. Kyla and Echo seem to have the perfect relationship and the perfect life until someone shoots at Kyla—and Echo is the most likely suspect. (978-1-60282-035-7)

truelesbianlove.com by Carsen Taite. Mackenzie Lewis and Dr. Jordan Wagner have very different ideas about love, but they discover that truelesbianlove is closer than a click away. Eclipse EBook (978-1-60282-069-2)

Justice at Risk by John Morgan Wilson. Benjamin Justice's blind date leads to a rare opportunity for legitimate work, but a reckless risk changes his life forever. (978-1-60282-059-3)

Run to Me by Lisa Girolami. Burned by the four-letter word called love, the only thing Beth Standish wants to do is run for—or maybe from—her life. (978-1-60282-034-0)

Split the Aces by Jove Belle. In the neon glare of Sin City, two women ride a wave of passion that threatens to consume them in a world of fast money and fast times. (978-1-60282-033-3)

Uncharted Passage by Julie Cannon. Two women on a vacation that turns deadly face down one of nature's most ruthless killers—and find themselves falling in love. (978-1-60282-032-6)

Night Call by Radclyffe. All medevac helicopter pilot Jett McNally wants to do is fly and forget about the horror and heartbreak she left behind in the Middle East, but anesthesiologist Tristan Holmes has other plans. (978-1-60282-031-9)

I Dare You by Larkin Rose. Stripper by night, corporate raider by day, Kelsey's only looking for sex and power, until she meets a woman who stirs her heart and her body. (978-1-60282-030-2)

Truth Behind the Mask by Lesley Davis. Erith Baylor is drawn to Sentinel Pagan Osborne's quiet strength, but the secrets between them strain duty and family ties. (978-1-60282-029-6)

Lake Effect Snow by C.P. Rowlands. News correspondent Annie T. Booker and FBI Agent Sarah Moore struggle to stay one step ahead of disaster as Annie's life becomes the war zone she once reported on. Eclipse EBook (978-1-60282-068-5)

Revision of Justice by John Morgan Wilson. Murder shifts into high gear, propelling Benjamin Justice into a raging fire that consumes the Hollywood Hills, burning steadily toward the famous Hollywood Sign—and the identity of a cold-blooded killer. (978-1-60282-058-6)

Cooper's Deale by KI Thompson. Two would-be lovers and a decidedly inopportune murder spell trouble for Addy Cooper, no matter which way the cards fall. (978-1-60282-028-9)

Romantic Interludes 1: Discovery ed. by Radclyffe and Stacia Seaman. An anthology of sensual, erotic contemporary love stories from the best-selling Bold Strokes authors. (978-1-60282-027-2)

A Guarded Heart by Jennifer Fulton. The last place FBI Special Agent Pat Roussel expects to find herself is assigned to an illicit private security gig baby-sitting a celebrity. (Ebook) (978-1-60282-067-8)

Saving Grace by Jennifer Fulton. Champion swimmer Dawn Beaumont, injured in a car crash she caused, flees to Moon Island, where scientist Grace Ramsay welcomes her. (Ebook) (978-1-60282-066-1)

The Sacred Shore by Jennifer Fulton. Successful tech industry survivor Merris Randall does not believe in love at first sight until she meets Olivia Pearce. (Ebook) (978-1-60282-065-4)

Passion Bay by Jennifer Fulton. Two women from different ends of the earth meet in paradise. Author's expanded edition. (Ebook) (978-1-60282-064-7)

Never Wake by Gabrielle Goldsby. After a brutal attack, Emma Webster becomes a self-sentenced prisoner inside her condo—until the world outside her window goes silent. (Ebook) (978-1-60282-063-0)

Remember Tomorrow by Gabrielle Goldsby. Cees Bannigan and Arieanna Simon find that a successful relationship rests in remembering the mistakes of the past. (978-1-60282-026-5)

The Caretaker's Daughter by Gabrielle Goldsby. Against the backdrop of a nineteenth-century English country estate, two women struggle to find love. (Ebook) (978-1-60282-062-3)

Simple Justice by John Morgan Wilson. When a pretty-boy cokehead is murdered, former LA reporter Benjamin Justice and his reluctant new partner, Alexandra Templeton, must unveil the real killer. (978-1-60282-057-9)

Remember Tomorrow by Gabrielle Goldsby. Cees Bannigan and Arieanna Simon find that a successful relationship rests in remembering the mistakes of the past. (978-1-60282-026-5)

Put Away Wet by Susan Smith. Jocelyn "Joey" Fellows has just been savagely dumped—when she posts an online personal ad, she discovers more than just the great sex she expected. (978-1-60282-025-8)

Homecoming by Nell Stark. Sarah Storm loses everything that matters—family, future dreams, and love—will her new "straight" roommate cause Sarah to take a chance at happiness? (978-1-60282-024-1)

The Three by Meghan O'Brien. A daring, provocative exploration of love and sexuality. Two lovers, Elin and Kael, struggle to survive in a postapocalyptic world. (Ebook) (978-1-60282-056-2)

Falling Star by Gill McKnight. Solley Rayner hopes a few weeks with her family will help heal her shattered dreams, but she hasn't counted on meeting a woman who stirs her heart. (978-1-60282-023-4)

Lethal Affairs by Kim Baldwin and Xenia Alexiou. Elite operative Domino is no stranger to peril, but her investigation of journalist Hayley Ward will test more than her skills. (978-1-60282-022-7)

A Place to Rest by Erin Dutton. Sawyer Drake doesn't know what she wants from life until she meets Jori Diamantina—only trouble is, Jori doesn't seem to share her desire. (978-1-60282-021-0)

Warrior's Valor by Gun Brooke. Dwyn Izsontro and Emeron D'Artansis must put aside personal animosity and unwelcome attraction to defeat an enemy of the Protector of the Realm. (978-1-60282-020-3)

Finding Home by Georgia Beers. Take two polar-opposite women with an attraction for one another they're trying desperately to ignore, throw in a far-too-observant dog, and then sit back and enjoy the romance. (978-1-60282-019-7)

Word of Honor by Radclyffe. All Secret Service Agent Cameron Roberts and First Daughter Blair Powell want is a small intimate wedding, but the paparazzi and a domestic terrorist have other plans. (978-1-60282-018-0)

Hotel Liaison by JLee Meyer. Two women searching through a secret past discover that their brief hotel liaison is only the beginning. Will they risk their careers—and their hearts—to follow through on their desires? (978-1-60282-017-3)

Love on Location by Lisa Girolami. Hollywood film producer Kate Nyland and artist Dawn Brock discover that love doesn't always follow the script. (978-1-60282-016-6)

Bold Strokes
BOOKS
WEBSTORE
PRINT AND EBOOKS
Romance
Mystery
Intrigue
MATINEE BOOKS
LIBERTY
EDITION
BOLD
STROKES
BOOKS
Adventure
victory
EDITIONS
ECLIPSE
Erotica
Fantasy
Sci-Fi
http://www.boldstrokesbooks.com